THE LORD'S WOR
Carole was on a one-
"them" from sucking
America. . . .

DRACUSON'S DRIVER *by Richard Laymon*—
She was blonde, and beautiful, and driving a
hearse, and he never suspected whose funeral
she was going to. . . .

NIGHT CRIES *by Daniel Ransom*—He knew
she was in trouble the minute she got into his
cab. But what he'd never anticipated was that
helping her might prove the death of him. . . .

THE CURE *by W. R. Philbrick*—By ones and
twos they came, those sick in body or spirit,
seeking the "cure" that only the Count could
grant. . . .

These are just four of the blood-chilling tales
that await you in—

DRACULA:
PRINCE OF DARKNESS

DRACULA:
PRINCE OF DARKNESS

EDITED BY
MARTIN H. GREENBERG

DAW BOOKS, INC.
DONALD A. WOLLHEIM, FOUNDER
375 Hudson Street, New York, NY 10014

ELIZABETH R. WOLLHEIM
SHEILA E. GILBERT
PUBLISHERS

DAW Book Collectors No. 889.

First Printing, September 1992

1 2 3 4 5 6 7 8 9

CONTENTS

INTRODUCTION
by
Stefan Dziemianowicz

We live in the age of the vampire. Its familiar countenance leers out at us regularly from book racks, movie screens, even breakfast cereal shelves at the grocery store. It walks through the landscape of our popular culture masquerading under a variety of familiar guises, including the monster, hero, anti-hero, heroine, aristocrat, lover, and buffoon. Its image is so pervasive in the late twentieth century that it has become an instantly recognizable symbol of evil: for example, no explanation was needed in 1990 when deposed Romanian president Nicolae Ceausescu was depicted in cartoons and news broadcasts as a predatory monster who had bled his country dry.

Though the myth of the vampire has been with us for many centuries, evolving out of the superstitions of countless civilizations, its current popularity in Western culture can be traced back to a specific moment: 1897, and the publication of Bram Stoker's Victorian thriller *Dracula*. *Dracula* was by no means the first work of fiction to employ the vampire, having been preceded into print by John Polidori's *The Vampyre* (1819), the bloated Victorian "penny dreadful" *Varney the Vampire* (1847), Joseph Sheridan Le Fanu's influential novella "Carmilla" (1872), and a host of less distinguished works that have since been forgotten. But it was the first vampire story derived from the exploits of a historical figure, rather than a generic folktale, and therein lies part of the secret of Count Dracula's literary immortality.

The historical Dracula bears very little resemblance to his fictional counterpart. The ruler of Wallachia (one of the feudal states that would eventually be incorporated into Romania) between 1456 and 1462, Dracula—whose name has been interpreted to mean "son of the devil"—was a highly regarded leader credited with saving his country from annexation by the Turks. His infamy rests on his preferred means of disciplinary action: impalement. Ruthlessly protecting his country against invasion from without and dissension from within, Dracula is reported to have killed thousands of enemies and deterred many more by means of this grisly torture, a reputation that earned him the nickname "Vlad Tepes," or "Vlad the Impaler."

If the foundation of all superstition is fear, then it is not surprising that a ruler who governed by fear as Dracula did should become the source for so many legends. In the years after Dracula's reign, storytellers translated his bloodthirsty tactics into a literal appetite for blood. Other embellishments with vampire lore followed naturally over the centuries until they overwhelmed the truth. It was no doubt these crude appraisals of Dracula as an incarnation of supernatural evil that Stoker came across while researching his novel.

Had Stoker opted for historical fidelity in his delineation of Dracula, the state of horror fiction in general and the vampire tale in particular might be considerably different today. Fortunately, he erred heavily on the side of imagination. Realizing that in the figure of Dracula he had grist for a morality tale that would reinforce the values of the Victorian age, he set about updating and fleshing out the Dracula legend. It is not clear how much Stoker embellished existing legends of Dracula with vampire lore from other sources, or to what extent the capabilities of the fictional Dracula are cut from the cloth of Stoker's own fancy. What *is* clear almost one hundred years later, though, is that in his efforts to adapt a medieval legend as a horror story with resonance for his era, Stoker defined an archetype, a monster that transcended time and place. His depiction of Dracula as an embodiment of primitive instinct erupting through the civilized veneer of late-nineteenth century England no doubt represented the worst horror imaginable during that straitlaced time. Indeed, Stoker wisely portrayed Dracula as a violator of taboos crucial to the integrity of his society: his vampire is a cannibal, a violator of women and children, and a clear threat to sexuality sanctioned by the marriage vow.

The success of *Dracula* can be measured by how faithfully the vampires of most stories written in its wake are modeled on Stoker's Transylvanian Count. They look like normal people except for their pointed canine teeth and agelessness. They are sophisticated and worldly beings who have cultivated an urbanity that deflects suspicion from them. They sleep by day in a coffin filled with the soil of their native land. By night, they drink the blood of the innocent to sustain their immortality. Those for whom their bite is fatal eventually rise from the grave as vampires themselves. Among their uncanny powers are superhuman strength, the ability to transform into wolves and bats, and control over armies of vermin. They cast no shadow or reflection in a mirror, are powerless to cross a threshold without invitation or a stream of running water, and can be repelled by garlic, holy water, and the image of the cross. The only way to kill them is with a wooden stake through the heart, followed by decapitation.

It is ironic that *Dracula* should be looked to as having established these as the traits of the traditional vampire, for if Stoker's novel proved anything it is that the vampire's durability lies not in a rigidly defined set of characteristics but in its ability to adapt for survival to the demands of each new era. At the heart of *Dracula* is the same fear that gave rise to superstitions surrounding the historical Dracula over four centuries before: the fear of victimization. It was a stroke of genius on Stoker's part to recognize that the predator-prey relationship between the vampire and its victim occurs in many different forms within a society, and that because each time and place creates its own victims, the spirit represented by Dracula can never really die.

The stories that follow are a testimony to the durability of that spirit. Though some are more traditional than others, each elaborates an aspect of the Dracula legend that continues to fascinate readers and writers today. All extend the legacy of Dracula, Prince of Darkness, by another century and in so doing lay the foundation for his adventures in centuries to come.

THE LORD'S WORK
by
F. Paul Wilson

<And what are you doing, Carole? What are you DO-ING? You'll be after killing yourself, Carole. You'll be blowing yourself to pieces and then you'll be going straight to hell. HELL, Carole!>

"But I won't be going alone," Sister Carole Flannery muttered.

She had to turn her head away from the kitchen sink now. The fumes stung her nose and made her eyes water, but she kept on stirring the pool chlorinator into the hot water until it was completely dissolved. She wasn't through yet. She took the beaker of No Salt she'd measured out before starting the process and added it to the mix in the big Pyrex bowl. Then she stirred some more. Finally, when she was satisfied that she was not going to see any further dissolution at this temperature, she put the bowl on the stove and turned up the flame.

A propane stove. She'd seen the big white tank out back last week when she was looking for a new home; that was why she'd chosen this old house. With New Jersey Natural Gas in ruins, and JCP&L no longer sending electricity through the wires, propane and wood stoves were the only ways left to cook.

I really shouldn't call it cooking, she thought as she fled the acrid fumes and headed for the living room. Nothing more than a simple dissociation reaction—heating a mixture of calcium hypochlorate and potassium chloride. Simple, basic chemistry. The very subject she'd taught bored freshmen and sophomores for five years at St. Anthony's High School over in Lakewood.

"And you all thought chemistry was such a useless subject!" she shouted to the walls.

She clapped a hand over her mouth. There she was, talking out loud again. She had to be careful. Not so much because someone might hear her, but because she was worried she might be losing her mind.

She'd begun talking to herself in her head—just for company of sorts—to ease her through the long empty hours. But the voice had taken on a life of its own. It was still her own voice, but it had acquired a thick Irish brogue, very similar to her dear, sweet, dead mother's.

Maybe she'd already lost her mind. Maybe all this was merely a delusion. Maybe vampires hadn't taken over the entire civilized world. Maybe they hadn't defiled her church and convent, slaughtered her sister nuns. Maybe it was all in her mind.

<Sure, and you'd be wishing it was all in your mind, Carole. Of course you would. Then you wouldn't be sinning!>

Yes, she truly did wish she were imagining all this. At least then she'd be the only one suffering, and all the rest would still be alive and well, just as they'd been before she went off the deep end. Like the people who'd once lived in this house. The Bennetts—Kevin, Marie, and their twin girls. She hadn't known them before, but Sister Carole felt she knew them now. She'd seen their family photos, seen the twins' bedroom. They were dead now, she was sure. Or maybe worse. But either way, they were gone.

But if this was a delusion it was certainly an elaborate, consistent delusion. Every time she woke up—she never allowed herself to sleep too many hours at once, only catnaps—it was the same; quiet skies, vacant houses, empty streets, furtive, scurrying survivors who trusted no one, and—

What's that?

Sister Carole froze as her ears picked up a sound outside, a hum, like a car engine. She hurried in a crouch to the front door and peered through the sidelight. It *was* a car. A convertible. Someone was out driving in—

She ducked down when she saw who was in it. Scruffy and unwashed, lean and wolfish, bare chested or in cutoff sweatshirts, the driver wearing a big Texas hat, all of them guzzling beer. She didn't know their names or their faces, and she didn't have to see their earrings to know who—what—they were.

Collaborators. Predators. They liked to call themselves cowboys. Sister Carole called them scum of the earth.

They were headed east. Good. They'd find a little surprise waiting for them down the road.

As it did every so often, the horror of what her life had become caught up to Sister Carole then, and she slumped to the floor of the Bennett house and began to sob.

Why? Why had God allowed this to happen to her, to His Church, to His world?

Better question: Why had she allowed these awful events to change her so? She had been a Sister of Mercy.

<Mercy! Do you hear that, Carole? A Sister of MERCY!>

She had taken vows of poverty, chastity, and obedience, had vowed to devote her life to teaching and doing the Lord's work. But now there was no money, no one worth losing her virginity to, no Church to be obedient to, and no students left to teach.

All she had left was the Lord's work.

<Believe me you, Carole, I'd hardly be calling the making of plastic explosives and the other horrible

*things you've been doing the Lord's work. It's killing!
It's a SIN!>*

Maybe the voice was right. Maybe she would go to
hell for what she was doing. But somebody had to
make those rotten cowboys pay.

* * *

King of the world.

Al Hulett leaned back in the passenger seat of the
Mercedes convertible they'd just driven out of somebody's garage, burning rubber all the way, and let the
cool breeze caress his sweaty head. Stan was driving,
Artie and Kenny were in the back seat, everybody had
a Heineken in his fist, and they were tooling along
Route 88 toward the beach, catching some early summer rays on the way. He casually tossed his empty
backward, letting it arc over the trunk, and heard it
smash on the asphalt behind them. Then he closed his
eyes and grooved.

The pack. Buddies. The four of them had been together since grammar school in Camden. How many
years was that now? Ten? Twelve? Couldn't be more
than a dozen. No way. Whatever, the four of them had
stuck together through it all, never breaking up, even
when Stan pulled that short jolt in Yardville on a B&E,
even when the whole world went to hell.

They'd come through it all like gold. They'd hired
out to the winners. They were the best hunting pack
around. And Al was one of them.

King of the fucking world.

Well, not king, really. But at least a prince . . . when
the sun was up.

Night was a whole different story.

But why think about the night when you had this
glorious summer day all to—

"Shit! Goddamn shit!"

Stan's raging voice and the sudden braking of the

car yanked Al from his reverie. He opened his eyes and looked at Stan.

"Hey, motherfu—"

Then he saw him. Or, rather, it. Dead ahead. *Dead* ahead. A corpse, hanging by its feet from a utility pole.

"Oh, shit," Kenny said from behind him. "Another one. Who is it?"

"I dunno," Stan said, then he looked at Al from under the wide brim of his cowboy hat. "Whyn't you go see."

Al swallowed. He'd always been the best climber, so he'd wound up the second-story man of the team. But he didn't want to make this climb.

"What's the use?" Al said. "Whoever he is, he's dead."

"See if he's one of us," Stan said.

"Ain't it *always* one of us?"

"Then see *which* one of us it is, okay?"

Stan had this pale, cratered skin. Even though he was in his twenties he still got pimples. He looked like the man in the moon now, but in the old days he'd been a pizza face. Once he almost killed a guy who'd called him that. And he had this crazy blond hair that stuck out in all directions when he didn't cut it, but even when he cut it Mohican style like now, all shaved off on the sides and all, it looked crazier than ever. Made Stan look crazier than ever. And Stan was pretty crazy as it was. And mean. He'd been thinking he was hot shit ever since he got out of Yardville. His big head had got even bigger when the bloodsuckers made him pack leader. He'd been pissing Al off lately, but this time he was right: Somebody had to go see who'd got unlucky last night.

Al hopped over the door and headed for the pole. What a pain in the ass. The rope around the dead guy's feet was looped over the first climbing spike. He shimmied up to it and got creosote all over him in the process. The stuff was a bitch to get off. And besides, it made his skin itch. On the way up he'd kept the pole between himself and the body. Now it was time to look. He swallowed. He'd seen one of these strung-up guys up close before and—

He spotted the earring, a blood-splattered silvery crescent moon dangling on a fine chain from the brown-crusted earlobe, an exact replica of the one dangling from his own left ear, and from Stan's and Artie's and Kenny's. Only this one was dangling the wrong way.

"Yep," he said, loud so's the guys on the ground could hear it. "It's one of us."

"Damn!" Stan's voice. "Anyone we know?"

Al squinted at the face, but with the gag stuck in its mouth, and the head so encrusted with clotted blood and crawling with buzzing, feeding flies darting in and out of the gaping wound in the throat, he couldn't make out the features.

"I can't tell."

"Well, cut him down."

This was the part Al hated most of all. It seemed almost sacrilegious. Not that he'd ever been religious or anything, but someday, if he didn't watch his ass, this could be him.

He pulled his Special Forces knife from his belt and sawed at the rope above the knot on the climbing spike. It frayed, jerked a couple of times, then parted. He closed his eyes as the body tumbled downward. He hummed Metallica's "Sandman" to blot out the sound it made when it hit the pavement. He especially hated the sick, wet sound the head made if it landed first. Which this one did.

"Looks like Benny Gonzales," Artie said.

"Yep," Kenny said. "No doubt about it. That's Benny. Poor guy."

They dragged his body over to the curb and drove on, but the party mood was gone.

"I'd love to catch the bastards who're doing this shit," Stan said as he drove. "They've gotta be close by around here somewhere."

"They could be anywhere," Al said. "They found Benny back there, killed him there—you saw that puddle of blood under him—and left him there. Then they cut out."

"They're huntin' us like we're huntin' them," Kenny said.

"But I wanna be the one to catch 'em," Stan said.

"Yeah?" said Artie from the back. "And what would you do if you did?"

Stan said nothing, and Al knew that was the answer. Nothing. He'd bring them in and turn them over. The bloodsuckers didn't like you screwing with their cattle.

Kings of the world . . . princes of the day. . . .

If you could get used to the creeps you were working for, it wasn't too bad a setup. Could have been worse, Al knew—a *lot* worse.

They all could have wound up being cattle.

Al didn't know when the vampires had started taking over. People said it began in Eastern Europe, some time after the Communists got kicked out. The vampires had been building up their numbers, waiting for their chance, and when everything was in turmoil, they struck. All of a sudden it was the only thing on the news. Dracula wasn't a storybook character, he was real, and he was suddenly the new Stalin in charge of Eastern Europe.

From there the vampires spread east and west, into Russia and the rest of Europe. They were smart, those bloodsuckers. They hit the government and military bigwigs first, made them their own kind, then threw everything into chaos. Not too long after that they crossed the ocean. America thought it was ready for them but it wasn't. They hit high, they hit low, and before you knew it, they were in charge.

Well, almost in charge. They did whatever they damn well pleased at night, but they'd never be in charge around the clock because they couldn't be up and about in the daylight. They needed somebody to hold the fort for them between sunrise and sunset.

That was where Al and the guys came in. The bloodsuckers had found them hiding in the basement of Leon's pool hall one night and made them an offer they couldn't refuse.

They could be cattle, or they could be cowboys and drive the cattle.

Not much of a choice as far as Al could see.

You see, the bloodsuckers had two ways of killing folks. They had the usual way of ripping into your neck and sucking out your blood. If they got you that way, you became one of them come the next sundown. That was the method they used when they were taking over a place. They got themselves a bunch of instant converts that way. But once they had the upper hand, they changed their feeding style. Smart, those bloodsuckers. If they got too many of their kind wandering around, they'd soon have nobody to feed on—a world full of chefs with nothing to cook. So after they were in control, they'd string their victims up by their feet, slit their throats, and drink the blood as it gushed out of them. When you died that way, you stayed dead. Something they called true death.

But they'd offered Al and Stan and the guys *un*death. Be their cowboys, be their muscle during the day, herd the cattle and take care of business between sunrise and sunset, do a good job for twenty years, and they'd see to it that you got done in the old-fashioned way, the way that left you like them. Undead. Immortal. One of the ruling class.

Twenty years and out. Like the army. They gave you these crescent-moon earrings to wear, so they'd know you were on their side when they ran into you at night, and they let you do pretty much what you wanted during the days.

But the nights were theirs.

Being a cowboy wasn't so bad, really. You had to keep an eye on their nests, make sure no save-the-world types—Stan liked to call them rustlers—got in there and started splashing holy water around and driving stakes into their cold little hearts. And if you wanted brownie points, you went out each day and hunted up a victim or two to have ready for them after sundown.

Those brownie points were nothing to sneer at either. Earn enough of them and you got to spend some stud time on one of their cattle ranches—where all the cows were human. And young.

Neither Al nor Stan nor any of their pack had been to one of the farms yet, but they'd all heard it was incredible. You came back *sore*.

Al didn't particularly like working for the vampires. But he couldn't remember ever liking anybody he'd worked for. The bloodsuckers gave him the creeps, but what was he supposed to do? If you can't beat 'em, join 'em. Plenty of guys felt the same way.

But not all. Some folks took it real personal, called Al and Stan and the boys traitors and collaborators and worse. And lately it looked like some of them had gone beyond the name-calling stage and were into throat-slitting.

Benny Gonzales was the fifth one in the last four weeks.

Apparently the guys who were behind this wanted to make it look like the vampires themselves were doing the killings, but it didn't wash. Too messy. These bodies had blood all over them, and a puddle beneath them. When the bloodsuckers slit somebody's throat, they didn't let a drop of it go to waste. They licked the platter clean, so to speak.

"We gotta start being real careful," Stan was saying. "Gotta keep our eyes open."

"And look for what?" Kenny said.

"For a bunch of guys who hang out together—a bunch of guys who ain't cowboys."

Artie started singing that Willie Nelson song, "Mama, Don't Let Your Babies Grow up to be Cowboys" and it set Stan off.

"Knock it off, god damn it! This ain't funny! One of us could be next! Now keep your fucking eyes open!"

Al studied the houses drifting by as they cruised into Point Pleasant Beach. Cars sat quietly along the curbs of the empty streets and the houses appeared deserted, their empty blind windows staring back at him. But every so often they'd pass a yard that looked cared for, and those houses would be defiantly studded with crosses and festooned with garlands of garlic. And every so often you could swear you saw somebody peeking out from behind a window or through a screen door.

"You know, Stan," Al said. "I'll bet those cowboy killers are hiding in one of them houses with all the garlic and crosses."

"Maybe," Stan said. "But I kinda doubt it. Those folks tend to stay in after sundown. Whoever's behind this is working at night."

That made sense to Al. The folks in those houses hardly ever came out. They were loners. Dangerous loners. *Armed* loners. The vampires couldn't get in because of all the garlic and crosses, and the cowboys who'd tried to get in—or even take off some of the crosses—usually got shot up. The vampires had said to leave them be for now. Sooner or later they'd run out of food and have to come out. *Then* they'd get them.

Smart, those bloodsuckers. Al guessed they figured they had plenty of time to outwait the loners. All the time in the world.

They were cruising Ocean Avenue by the boardwalk area now, barely a block from the Atlantic. What a difference a year made. Last year at this time the place was packed with the summer crowds, the day-trippers and the weekly renters. Now it was deserted. The sun was high and hot, but it seemed like winter had never ended.

They were gliding past the empty, frozen rides when Al caught a flash of color moving between a couple of the boardwalk stands.

"Pull over," he said, putting a hand on Stan's arm. "I think I saw something."

The tires screeched as Stan made a sharp turn into Jenkinson's parking lot.

'What kind of something?''

"Something blonde."

Kenny and Artie let out cowboy whoops and jumped out of the back seat. They tossed their Heineken empties high and let them smash in glittery green explosions.

"Shut the fuck up!" Stan said. "You tryin' to queer this little roundup or what? Now you two head down to the street back there and work your way back up on the boards. Me and Al'll go up here and work our way down. Get going."

As Artie and Kenny trotted back to the Risden's beach bathhouses, Stan squared his ten-gallon hat on his head and pointed toward the miniature golf course at the other end of the parking lot. Al took the lead and Stan followed. Arnold Avenue ended here in a turretlike police station, still boarded up for the winter. Its big warning sign informed anyone who passed that alcoholic beverages and dogs and motorbikes and various other goodies were prohibited in the beach and boardwalk area by order of the mayor and city council of Point Pleasant Beach. Al smiled. The beach and the boardwalk and the sign were still here, but the mayor and the city council were long gone.

Pretty damn depressing up on the boards. The big glass windows in Jenkinson's arcade were smashed and

it was dark inside. The lifeless video games stared back
with dead eyes. All the concession stands were boarded
up, the paralyzed rides were rusting and peeling, and
it was *quiet*. No barkers shouting, no kids laughing, no
squealing babes in bikinis running in and out of the
surf. Just the monotonous pounding of the waves against
the deserted beach.

And the birds. The seagulls were doing what they'd
always done. Probably the only thing they missed was
the garbage the crowds used to leave behind.

Al and Stan headed south, scouring the boardwalk as
they moved. The only other humans they saw were
Kenny and Artie coming up the other way from the
South Beach Arcade.

"Any luck?" Stan called.

"Nada," Kenny said.

"Yo, Alphonse!" Artie said. "How many Heinies
you have anyway? You seein' things now? What was
it—a blonde bird?"

But Al knew he'd seen something moving up here, and
it hadn't been no goddamn seagull. But where . . . ?

"Let's get back to the car and keep moving," Stan
said. "Don't look like we're gonna make us no
brownie points up here."

They'd all turned and were heading back up the
boards when Al took one last look back . . . and saw
something moving. Something small and red, rolling
across the boards toward the beach from between one
of the concession stands.

A ball.

He tapped Stan on the shoulder, put a finger to his
lips, and pointed. Stan's eyes widened and together
they alerted Artie and Kenny. The four of them crept
toward the spot the ball had rolled from.

As they got closer, Al realized why they'd missed
this spot on the first pass. It was really two concession
stands—a frozen yogurt place and a salt water taffy

shop—with boards nailed up over the space between to make them look like a single building.

Stan tapped Al on the shoulder and pointed to the roof of the nearer concession stand. Al nodded. He knew what he wanted: the second-story man had to do his thing again.

Al got to the top of the chain link fence running behind the concession stands and from there it was easy to lever himself up to the roof. His sneakers barely made a sound as he crept across the tar of the canted roof to the far side.

The girl must have heard him coming, because she was already looking up when he peeked over the edge. Al felt a surge of satisfaction when he saw her blonde ponytail and long thick bangs.

He felt something else when he saw the tears streaming down her cheeks from her pleading eyes, and her hands raised, palms together, as if praying to him. She wanted him to see nothing—she was *begging* Al to see nothing.

For an instant he was tempted. The plea in those frightened blue eyes reached deep inside and touched something there, disturbed a part of him so long unused he'd forgotten it belonged to him.

And then he saw that she had a little boy with her, maybe seven years old, dark-haired but with eyes as blue as hers. She was pleading for him as much as for herself. Maybe more than for herself. And with good reason. The vampires *loved* little kids. Al didn't understand it. Kids were smaller, had less blood than adults. Maybe their blood was purer, sweeter. Someday, when he was undead himself, he'd know.

But even with the kid there, Al might have done something stupid, might have called down to Stan and the boys that there was nothing here but some old tomcat who'd probably taken a swat at that ball and rolled it out. But when he saw that she was pregnant—*very* pregnant—he knew he had to turn her in.

As much as the bloodsuckers loved kids, they went *crazy* for babies. Infants were the primo delicacy among the vampires. Al once had seen a couple of them fighting over a newborn.

That had been a sight.

He sighed and said, "Too bad, honey, but you're packing too many points." He turned and called down toward the boardwalk. "Bingo, guys. We struck it rich."

She screamed out a bunch of hysterical "No's," and the little boy began to cry.

Al shook his head regretfully. It wasn't always a pleasant job, but a cowboy had to do what a cowboy had to do.

And besides, all these brownie points were going to bring him that much closer to some stud time at the nearest cattle farm.

* * *

Sister Carole checked the Pyrex bowl on the stove. A chalky layer of potassium chloride had formed in the bottom. She turned off the heat and immediately decanted off the boiling upper fluid, pouring it through a Mr. Coffee filter into a Pyrex brownie pan. She threw out the scum in the filter and put the pan of filtrate on the windowsill to cool.

She heard the sound of a car again and rushed to a window. It was the same car, with the same occupants—

No, wait. There had been only four before. Two in front and two in back. Now there were three squeezed into the back and they seemed to be fighting. And did that third head in front, sitting with the red-haired cowboy in the passenger seat, belong to a child? Oh, my Lord, yes. A child! And in the back a woman, probably his mother. Jesus, Mary, and Joseph, the poor thing was pregnant!

Sister Carole suddenly felt as if something were tearing apart within her chest. Was there no justice, was there no mercy anywhere?

She dropped to her knees and began to pray for them, but in the back of her mind she wondered why she bothered. None of her prayers had been answered so far.

< Sacrilege, Carole! That's SACRILEGE! Now tell me why you'd be thinking the Lord would answer the prayers of such a SINNER? God doesn't answer the prayers of a SINNER!>

Maybe not, Carole thought. But if He'd answered *somebody's* prayers somewhere along the line, maybe she wouldn't have been forced to turn the Bennetts' kitchen into an anarchist's laboratory.

The Lord helped those who helped themselves, didn't He? Especially when they were doing the Lord's work.

* * *

Artie and Kenny had been fighting over the blonde since they'd all left Point. She'd put up a fight at first, but she'd been nothing but a blubbering basket case for the last few miles. By the time the Mercedes hit Lakewood, Artie and Kenny were ready to start swinging at each other.

The blonde's little boy—Joey, she called him—looked up with his baby blues from where he was sitting on Al's lap and said, "Are they gonna hurt my mommy?"

Stan must have overheard. He said, "They better not if they know what's good for 'em." He looked at Al and jerked his head toward the back seat. "Straighten them out, will ya?"

Al turned in his seat and grabbed Artie since he was closest.

"You ain't gonna do shit to her, Artie!"

Artie slammed his hand away. "Yeah? And what are we gonna do? Save her for you? Bull*shit!*"

Artie could be a real asshole at times.

"We're not saving her for me," Al said. "For Gregor. You remember Gregor, don't you, Artie?"

Some of Artie's bluster faded. Gregor was the big shot bloodsucker in charge of the Jersey Shore. One mean son of an undead bitch. You didn't mess with Gregor. Al knew Artie was probably thinking of Gregor's smile, how most times it looked painted on, how with all those sharp teeth of his he managed to look both happy and very, very hungry at the same time. Gregor was a big guy, with broad shoulders, dark hair, and a pale face. All the vampires looked pale. But that wasn't what made Al's skin crawl every time he got near one. It was something else, something you couldn't see or smell, something you *felt.* But they had to meet with Gregor every night and tell him how things had gone while he was cutting his Z's or whatever it was the bloodsuckers did when the sun was up. It was part of the job.

"Course," Artie said. "Course I know Gregor. But I don't wanna suck her blood, man," he said, jamming his hand down between the blonde's legs. "I got other things in mind. It's been a long time, man—a *long* time—and I gotta—"

"What if you screw up the baby?" Al said. "What if she starts having the baby and it's born dead? All because of you? What're you gonna tell Gregor then, Artie? How you gonna explain that to him?"

"Who says he has to know?"

"You think he won't find out?" Al said. "I tell you what, Artie. And you, too, Kenny. You guys want to get your jollies with this broad, fine. Go ahead. But if that's what you're gonna do, Stan and me are stopping the car here—right here—and walking away. Am I right, Stan?"

Stan nodded. "Fuckin' ay."

"And then you two clowns can explain any problems to Gregor yourselves tonight when we meet. Okay?"

Artie pulled his hand away from the blonde and sat on it.

"Jesus, Al. I'm hurtin' bad."

"We're all hurtin', Artie. But some of us just ain't ready yet to get killed for a little pregnant poontang, know what I mean?"

Stan seemed to think that was real funny. He laughed the rest of the way down County Line Road.

* * *

Sister Carole finished her prayers at sundown and went to check on the cooled filtrate. The bottom of the pan was layered with potassium chlorate crystals. Potent stuff. The Germans had used it in their grenades and land mines during World War One.

She got a clean Mr. Coffee filter and poured the contents of the pan through it, but this time she saved the residue in the filter and let the liquid go down the drain.

<Lookit after what you're doing now, Carole! You're a sick woman! SICK! You've got to be stopping this and praying to God for guidance! Pray, Carole! PRAY!>

Sister Carole ignored the voice and spread out the potassium chlorate crystals in the now empty pan. She set the oven on LOW and placed the pan on the middle rack. She had to get all the moisture out of the potassium chlorate before it would be of any use to her.

So much trouble, and so dangerous. If only her searches had yielded some dynamite, even a few sticks, everything would have been so much easier. She'd searched everywhere—hunting shops, gun stores, construction sites. She found lots of other useful items, but no dynamite. Only some blasting caps. She'd had no choice but to improvise.

This was her third batch. She'd been lucky so far.

She hoped she survived long enough to get a chance to use it.

* * *

"You've outdone yourselves this time, boys."

Gregor stared at the four cowboys. Ordinarily he found it doubly difficult to be near them. Not simply because the crimson thirst made a perpetual test of being near a living font of hot, pulsing sustenance when he'd yet to feed, urging him to let loose and tear into their throats; but also because these four were so common, such low lifes.

Gregor was royalty. He'd come over from the Old Country with the Master and had helped conquer America's East Coast. Now he was in charge of this region and was in line to expand his responsibilities. When he was moved up, he would no longer be forced to deal directly with flotsam such as these. Living collaborators were a necessary evil, but that didn't mean he had to like them.

Tonight, however, he could almost truly say that he enjoyed their presence. He was ecstatic over the prizes they had brought with them.

Gregor had shown up shortly after sundown at the customary meeting place outside St. Anthony's church. Of course, it didn't look much like a church now, what with all the crosses broken off. He'd found the scurvy quartet waiting for him as usual, but with them they had a small boy and—dare he believe his eyes—a pregnant woman. His knees had gone weak at the double throb of life within her.

"I'm extremely proud of all of you."

"We thought you'd appreciate it," said the one in the cowboy hat. What was his name? Stanley. That was it. Stan.

Gregor felt his grin grow even wider.

"Oh, I do. Not just for the succulence of the prizes

you've delivered, but because you've vindicated my faith in you. I knew the minute I saw you that you'd make good cowboys.''

An outright lie. He'd chosen them because he guessed they were low enough to betray their own kind, and he had been right. But it cost him nothing to heap the praise on them, and perhaps it would spur them to do as well next time. Maybe better. Although what could be better than this?

''Anything for the cause,'' Stan said.

The redheaded one next to him—Al, Gregor remembered—gave his partner a poisonous look, as if he wanted to kick him for being such a bootlick.

''And your timing could not be better,'' Gregor told them. ''Why? Because the Master himself is coming for a visit.''

Al's mouth worked as if it had suddenly gone dry. ''Dracula?''

Gregor nodded. ''Himself. And I will present this gravid cow to him as a gift. He will be enormously pleased. This will be good for me. And trust me, what is good for me will eventually prove to be good for you.''

Partly true. The little boy would go to the local nest leader—he'd been pastor of St. Anthony's during his life and he had a taste for young boys—and the pregnant female would indeed go to the Master. But the rest was a laugh. As soon as Gregor was moved out of here, he'd never give these four walking heaps of human garbage another thought.

But he smiled as he turned away. ''As always, may your night be bountiful.''

*   *   *

A little after sundown, Sister Carole removed the potassium chlorate crystals from the oven. She poured them into a bowl and then gently, carefully, began to grind

them down to a fine powder. This was the touchiest part
of the process. A little too much friction, a sudden
shock, and the bowl would blow up in her face.

< *You'd like that, wouldn't you, Carole. Sure, and
you'll be thinking that would solve all your problems.
Well, it won't, Carole. It will merely start your REAL
problems! It will send you straight to HELL!*>

Sister Carole made no reply as she continued the grind-
ing. When the powder was sifted through a 400 mesh, she
spread it onto the bottom of the pan again and placed it
back in the oven to remove the last trace of moisture.
While that was heating, she began melting equal parts of
wax and Vaseline, mixing them in a small Pyrex bowl.

When the wax and Vaseline had reached a uniform
consistency she dissolved the mix into some camp
stove gasoline. Then she removed the potassium chlorate powder from the oven and stirred in three percent
aluminum powder to enhance the flash effect. Then
she poured the Vaseline-wax-gasoline solution over the
powder. She slipped on rubber gloves and began stirring and kneading everything together until she had a
uniform, gooey mess. This went on the windowsill to
cool and to speed the evaporation of the gasoline.

Then she went to the bedroom. Soon it would be
time to go out and she had to dress appropriately. She
stripped to her underwear and laid out the tight black
skirt and red blouse she'd lifted from the shattered
show window of that deserted shop down on Clifton
Avenue. Then she began squeezing into a fresh pair of
black pantyhose.

< *You're getting into THOSE clothes again, are you?
You look cheap, Carole! You look like a WHORE!*>

That's the whole idea, she thought.

*   *   *

Al walked home. He could have driven, but he liked
to keep a low profile. He didn't care to have too many

survivors knowing he was a cowboy. Not that there were all that many people left running around free, but until they caught up with the guys who were behind the cowboy killings, he'd play it safe. Which was why he'd removed his earring tonight, and why he lived alone.

Well, one of the reasons he lived alone.

Stan, Artie, and Kenny lived together in one of the big mansions off Hope Road. They liked to brag that one of the Mets used to live there. Big deal. Al spent all day with those guys. He couldn't see spending all night too. They were okay, but enough was enough already. He'd taken over a modest little ranch that gave him everything he needed.

Except maybe some electricity. The other three were always yapping about the generator in their place. Maybe Al would get one. Candles and kerosene lamps were a drag.

He looked up. At least there was a moon out tonight. Almost full. Amazing how dark a residential street could be when there was no traffic, no streetlights. At least he had his flashlight, but he held that in reserve. Batteries were like gold.

He'd just turned onto his block when he heard the voice. A woman's voice.

"Hey, mister."

He jammed his hand in his pocket and found his earring, ready to flash it if the owner of the voice turned out to be one of the bloodsuckers, and ready to keep it hidden if it belonged to somebody looking for a new cowboy to kill.

He clicked on his flashlight and beamed it toward the voice.

A woman standing in the bushes. Not undead. Maybe thirty, and not bad looking. He played the light up and down her. Short dark hair, lots of eye makeup, a red sweater tight over decent-sized boobs, a short black skirt very tight over black stockings.

Despite the warning bells going off in his brain, Al felt a stirring in his groin.

"Who're you?"

She smiled. No, not bad looking at all.

"My name's Carole," she said. "You got any food?"

"I got a little. Not much."

Actually, he had a *lot* of food, but he didn't want her to know that. Food was scarce, worth more than batteries, and the vampires made sure their cowboys always had plenty of it.

"Can you spare any?"

"I might be able to help you out some. Depends on how many mouths we're talking about."

"Just me and my kid."

The words jumped out before he could stop them: "You've got a kid?"

"Don't worry," she said. "She's only four. She don't eat much."

A four-year-old. Two kids in one day. Almost too good to be true. The whole scenario started playing out in his mind. She could move in with him. If she treated him right, they could play house for a while. If she gave him any trouble, she and her brat would become gifts to Gregor. That was where they were going to wind up anyway, but no reason Al couldn't get some use out of her before she became some bloodsucker's meal.

And maybe he'd get *real* lucky. Maybe she'd get pregnant before he turned her in.

"Well . . . all right," he said, trying to sound reluctant. "Bring her out where I can see her."

"She's home asleep."

"Alone?" Al felt a surge of anger. He already considered that kid his property. He didn't want any bloodsucker sneaking in and robbing him of what was rightfully his. "What if—"

"Don't worry. I've got her surrounded by crosses."

"Still, you never know. We'd better take her along to my place where she'll be safe."

Did that sound sufficiently concerned?

"You must be a good man," she said softly.

"Oh, I'm the best," he said. *And I've got this friend behind my fly who's just dying to meet you.*

He followed her back to the corner and around to the middle of the next block to an old two-story colonial set back among some tall oaks on an overgrown lot. He nodded with growing excitement when he saw a child's red wagon parked against the front steps.

"You live here? Hell, I must've passed this place a couple of times already today."

"Really?" she said. "I usually stay hidden in the basement."

"Good thinking."

He followed her up the steps and through the front door. Inside there were candles burning all over the place, but the heavy drapes hid them from outside.

"Lynn's sleeping upstairs," she said. "I'll just run up and bring her down."

Al watched her black-stockinged legs hungrily as she bounded up the bare wooden stairway, taking the steps two at a time. He couldn't wait to get her home.

And then it hit him: Why wait till they got to his place? She had to have a bed up there. What was he doing standing around here when he could be upstairs getting himself a preview of what was to come?

"Yoo-hoo," he said softly as he put his foot on the first step. "Here comes Daddy."

But the first step wasn't wood. Wasn't even a step. His foot went right through it, as if it was made of cardboard. As Al looked down in shock he saw that it *was* made of cardboard—painted cardboard. His brain was just forming the question "Why," when a sudden blast of pain like he'd never known in his life shot up his leg from just above his ankle.

Screaming, he lunged back, away from the false

step, but the movement tripled his agony. He clung to
the newel post like a drunk, weeping and moaning for
God knew how long, until the pain eased for a second.
Then slowly, gingerly, accompanied by the metallic
clanking of uncoiling chain links, he lifted his leg out
of the false tread.

Al let loose a stream of curses through his pain-
clenched teeth when he saw the bear trap attached to
his leg. Its sharp, massive steel teeth had embedded
themselves in the flesh of his lower leg.

But fear began to worm through the all-enveloping
haze of his agony.

The bitch set me up!

Stan had wanted to find the guys who were killing
the cowboys. Now Al had, and he was scared shitless.
What a dumbass he was. Baited by a broad—the oldest
trick in the book.

Gotta get outta here!

He lunged for the door but the chain caught and
brought him up short with a blinding blaze of agony
so intense that the scream it elicited damn near shred-
ded his vocal cords. He toppled to the floor and lay
there moaning and whimpering until the pain became
bearable again.

Where were they? Where were the rest of the cowboy killers? Upstairs, laughing as they listened to him
howl like a scared kitten? Waiting until he'd exhausted
himself so he'd be easy pickings?

He'd show them.

Al pulled himself to a sitting position and reached
for the trap. He tried to spread its jaws, but they were
locked tight on his leg. He wrapped his hand around
the chain and tried to yank it free from where it was
fastened below, but it wouldn't budge.

Panic began to grip him now. Its icy fingers were
tightening on his throat when he heard a sound on the
stairs. He looked up and saw her.

A nun.

He blinked and looked again

Still a nun. He squinted and saw that it was the broad who'd led him in here. She was wearing a bulky sweater and loose slacks, and all the makeup had been scrubbed off her face, but he knew she was a nun by the wimple she wore—a white band around her head with a black veil trailing behind.

And suddenly, amid the pain and panic, Al was back in grammar school, back in Our Lady of Sorrows in Camden, before he got expelled, and Sister Margaret was coming at him with her ruler, only this nun was a lot younger than Sister Margaret, and that was no ruler she was carrying, that was a baseball bat—an *aluminum* baseball bat.

He looked around. Nobody else, just him and the nun.

"Where's the rest of you?"

"Rest?" she said.

"Yeah. The others in your gang? Where are they?"

"There's only me."

She was lying. She had to be. One crazy nun killing all those cowboys? No way! But still he had to get out of here. He tried to crawl across the floor but the chain wouldn't let him.

"You're makin' a mistake!" he cried. "I ain't one o' them!"

"Oh, yes you are," she said, coming down the stairs.

"No. Really. See?" He touched his right earlobe. "No earring."

"Maybe not now, but you had one earlier." She stepped over the gaping opening where the phony tread had been and moved to his left.

"When? *When?*"

"When you drove by earlier today. You told me so yourself."

"I lied!"

"No you didn't. But I lied. I wasn't in the basement.

I was watching through the window. I saw you and your three friends in that car." Her voice suddenly became cold and brittle and sharp as a straight razor. "I saw that poor woman and child you had with you. Where are they now? What did you do with them?"

She was talking through her teeth now, and the look in her eyes, the strained pallor of her face frightened the hell out of Al. He wrapped his arms around his head as she stepped closer with the bat.

"Please!" he wailed.

"What did you do with them?"

"Nothing!"

"Liar!"

She swung the bat, but not at his head. Instead she slammed it with a heavy metallic clank against the jaws of the trap. As he screamed with the renewed agony and as his hands automatically reached for his injured leg, Al realized that she must have done this sort of thing before. Because now his head was completely unprotected and she was already into a second swing. And this one was aimed much higher.

* * *

<*You've done it again, Carole! AGAIN! I know they're a bad lot, but look what you've DONE!*>

Sister Carole looked down at the unconscious man with the bleeding head and trapped, lacerated leg and she sobbed.

"I know," she said aloud.

She was so tired. She'd have liked nothing better now than to sit down and cry herself to sleep. But she couldn't spare the time. Every moment counted now.

She tucked her feelings—her mercy, her compassion—into the deepest, darkest pocket of her being where she couldn't see or hear them, and got to work.

The first thing she did was tie the cowboy's hands good and tight behind his back. Then she got a washcloth from the downstairs bathroom, stuffed it in his mouth, and secured it with a tie of rope around his head. That done, she grabbed the crowbar and the short length of two by four from where she kept them on the floor of the hall closet; she used the bar to pry open the jaws of the bear trap and wedged the two by four between them to keep them open. Then she worked the cowboy's leg free. He groaned a couple of times during the process, but he never came to.

She bound his legs tightly together, then grabbed the throw rug he lay upon and dragged him and the rug out to the front porch and down the steps to the red wagon she'd left there. She rolled him off the bottom step into the wagon bed and tied him in place. Then she slipped her arms into her knapsack loaded with all her necessary equipment and she was ready to go. She grabbed the wagon's handle and pulled it down the walk, down the driveway apron and onto the asphalt. From there on it was smooth rolling.

Sister Carole knew just where she was going. She had the spot all picked out.

She was going to try something a little different tonight.

* * *

Al screamed and sobbed against the gag. If he could just talk to her, he knew he could change her mind. But he couldn't get a word past the cloth jammed against his tongue.

And he didn't have long. She had him upside down, strung up by his feet, swaying in the breeze from one of the climbing spikes on a utility pole, and he knew what was coming next. So he pleaded with his eyes, with his soul. He tried mental telepathy.

Sister, sister, sister, don't do this! I'm a Catholic! My mother prayed for me every day and it didn't help, but I'll change now, I promise! I swear on a stack of fucking Bibles I'll be a good boy from now on if you'll just let me go this time.

Then he saw her face in the moonlight and realized with a final icy shock that he truly was a goner. Even if he could make her hear him, nothing he could say was going to change this lady's mind. The eyes were empty. No one was home. The bitch was on autopilot.

When he saw the glimmer of the straight razor as it glided above his throat, there was nothing left to do but wet himself.

*   *   *

When Sister Carole finished vomiting, she sat on the curb and allowed herself a brief cry.

< *Go ahead, Carole. Cry your crocodile tears. A fat lot of good it'll do you when Judgment Day comes. No good at all. What'll you say then, Carole? How will you explain THIS?*>

She dragged herself to her feet. She had two more things to do. One of them involved touching the fresh corpse. The second was simpler: starting a fire to attract the other cowboys and their masters.

*   *   *

Gregor watched as Cowboy Stan ran in circles around his dead friend's swaying, upended corpse.

"It's Al! The bastards got Al! I'll kill them all! I'll tear them to pieces!"

Gregor wished somebody would do just that. He'd heard about these deaths, but this was the first he'd seen—an obscene parody of the bloodletting rituals his nightbrothers performed on the cattle. This was acutely embarrassing, especially with the Master newly arrived from New York.

"Show yourselves!" Stan screamed into the darkness. "Come out and fight like men!"

"Someone cut him down," Gregor said.

One of the other two from Cowboy Stan's pack finished stamping out the brush fire at the base of the utility pole and began to climb.

"Let him down easy, Kenny!" Stan yelled.

"The only thing I can do is cut the rope," the one on the pole called back.

"Dammit, Al was one of *us!* Cut it slow and I'll ease him done. C'mere, Artie, and help me."

The one called Artie came over and together they caught their friend's body as it slumped earthward and—

The flash was noonday bright, the blast deafening as the shock wave knocked Gregor to the ground. His first instinct was to leap to his feet again, but he realized he couldn't see. The bright flash had fogged his night vision with a purple, amoebic afterimage. He lay quiet until he could see again, then rose to a standing position.

He heard a wailing sound. The cowboy who had been on the pole lay somewhere in the bushes, screaming about his back, but the other three—the two living ones and the murdered one—were nowhere to be seen. Gregor began to brush off his clothes as he stepped forward, then froze. He was wet, covered with blood and torn flesh. The entire street was wet and littered with bits of bone, muscle, skin, and fingernail-size pieces of internal organs. There was no telling what had belonged to whom.

Gregor shuddered at the prospect of explaining this to the Master.

Tonight's murder of Al had been embarrassing enough by itself. But this . . . this was humiliating.

*   *   *

Sister Carole saw the flash and heard the explosion through the window over the sink in the darkened kitchen of the Bennett house. No joy, no elation. This wasn't fun. But she did find a certain grim satisfaction in learning that her potassium chlorite plastique worked.

The gasoline had evaporated from the latest batch and she was working with that now. The moon provided sufficient illumination for the final stage. Once she had the right amount measured out, she didn't need much light to pack the plastique into soup cans. All she had to do was make sure she maintained a loading density of 1.3 G./c.c. Then she stuck a #3 blasting cap in the end of each cylinder and dipped it into the pot of melted wax she had on the stove. And that did it. She now had waterproof block charges with a detonation velocity of about 3300 M/second, comparable to 40 percent ammonia dynamite.

"All right," she said aloud to the night through her kitchen window. "You've made my life a living hell. Now it's your time to be afraid."

* * *

The Master's eyes glowed redly in the Stygian gloom of the mausoleum. Even among the Old Line of the undead, Dracula was fearsome looking with his leonine mane, his thick mustache, jutting nose, and aggressive chin. But his eyes seemed to burn with an inner fire when he was angry.

His voice was barely a whisper as he pierced Gregor with his stare.

"You've disappointed me, Gregor. Earlier this evening you petitioned me for greater responsibility, but you've yet to demonstrate that you can handle what you have now."

"Master, it is a temporary situation."

"So you keep saying, but it has lasted far too long already. Besides our strength and our special powers, we have two weapons: fear and hopelessness. We cannot control the cattle by love and loyalty, so if we are to maintain our rule, it must be through the terror we inspire in them and the seeming impossibility of ever defeating us. What have the cattle witnessed in your territory, Gregor?''

Gregor feared where this was headed. "Master—"

"I'll tell you what they've witnessed, Gregor," he said, his voice rising. "They've witnessed your inability to protect the serfs we've induced to herd the cattle and guard the daylight hours for us. And trust me, Gregor, the success of one vigilante group will give rise to a second, and then a third, and before long it will be open season on our serfs. And then you'll have real trouble. Because the cattle herders are cowardly swine, Gregor. The lowest of the low. They work for us only because they see us as the victors and they want to be on the winning side at any cost. But if we can't protect them, if they get a sense that we might be vulnerable and that our continued dominance might *not* be guaranteed, they'll turn on you in a flash, Gregor.''

"I know that, Master, and I'm—"

"Fix it, Gregor." The voice had sunk to a whisper again. "I will be in this territory for three days. Remedy this situation before I leave or I shall place someone else in charge. Is that clear?''

Gregor could scarcely believe what he was hearing. Removed? And to think he'd just made the Master a gift of the pregnant cow. The ungrateful—

He swallowed his anger, his hurt.

"Very clear, Master.''

"Good. It is only a few hours until dawn—too late for any action now—but I expect you to have a plan ready to execute tomorrow night.''

"I will, Master.''

"Leave me now.''

As Gregor turned and hurried up the steps he heard

an infant begin to cry in the depths of the mausoleum.
The sound made him hungry.

*   *   *

Sister Carole spent most of the next day working
around the house. She knew it was only a matter of
time before she was caught and she wanted to be ready
when they came for her.

<*I wish they'd come for you NOW, Carole. Then
this shame, this monstrous sinfulness would be over
and you'd get what you DESERVE!*>

"That makes two of us," Sister Carole said.

She didn't want to go out again tonight but knew
she had to.

Her only solace was knowing that sooner or later it
was going to end—for her.

*   *   *

Gregor smiled as one of his assistants smeared
makeup on his face. He would have preferred to have
kept his plan to himself, but he couldn't use a mirror
and he wanted this to look right. Scruffy clothes, a
cowboy hat, a crescent-on-a-chain earring, and a ruddy
complexion.

He was going to decoy these vigilante cattle into
picking on him as their next cowboy victim. And then
they'd be in for quite a surprise.

He could have sent someone else, could have sent
out a number of decoys, but he wanted this kill for
himself. After all, the Master was here, and his presence mandated bold and extraordinary measures.

He checked the map one last time. He had marked
all six places where the dead cowboys had been found.
The marks formed a rough circle. Gregor set out alone
to wander the streets within that circle.

Hours later, Gregor was becoming discouraged.

He'd walked for hours, seeing no one, living or undead. He was wondering if he should call it quits for tonight and return tomorrow when he heard a woman's voice.

"Hey, mister. Got any food?"

* * *

As Sister Carole led the cowboy back to the house, she had a feeling something was wrong. She couldn't put her finger on it, but she sensed something strange about this one. He wore the earring, he'd reacted just the way all the others had, but he'd been standoffish, keeping his distance, as if he was afraid to get too close to her. That bothered her.

Oh, well, she thought. God willing, in a few moments it would be over.

She rushed into the candlelit foyer but when she turned she found him poised on the threshold. Still standoffish. Could there be such a thing as a shy collaborator?

"Come in," she said. "Have a seat while I fetch Lynn."

As he stepped inside, she dashed upstairs, being sure to take the steps two at a time so it wouldn't look strange hopping over the first. She went straight to the bedroom and began rubbing off her makeup, all the while listening for the clank of the bear trap when it was tripped.

Finally it came and she winced as she always did, anticipating the shrill, awful cries of pain. But none came. She rushed to the landing and looked down. There she saw the cowboy ripping the restraining chain free from its nail, then reaching down and opening the jaws of the trap with his bare hands.

With her heart pounding a sudden mad tattoo in her chest, Sister Carole realized then that she'd made a terrible mistake. She'd expected to be caught some day, but not like this. She wasn't prepared for one of *them.*

<*Now you've done it, Carole! Now you've really DONE IT!*>

Shaking, panting with fear, she dashed back to the bedroom and followed the emergency route she'd prepared.

*   *   *

Gregor inspected the dried blood on the teeth of the trap. Obviously it had been used before.

So this was how they did it. Clever. And nasty.

He rubbed the already healing wound on his lower leg. The trap had hurt, startled him more than anything else, but no real harm had been done. He straightened, kicked the trap into the opening beneath the faux step, and looked around.

Where were the rest of the petty revolutionaries? There had to be more than this lone woman. Or was there? The house had an empty feel.

This was almost too easy. Gregor had had a bad moment there on the threshold. He couldn't cross it unless invited across. He'd still be out there on the front porch if the silly cow hadn't invited him in.

But one woman doing all this damage? The Master would never believe it.

He headed upstairs, gliding this time, without touching the steps. Another trap would slow him up. He spotted the rope ladder dangling over the windowsill as soon as he entered the bedroom. He darted to the window and leapt through the opening. He landed lightly on the overgrown lawn and sniffed the air. She wasn't far—

He heard running footsteps, a sudden loud rustle, and saw a leafy branch flashing toward him. Gregor felt something hit his chest, pierce it, and knock him back. He grunted with the pain, staggered a few steps, then looked down. Three metal tines protruded from his sternum.

The cow had tied back a sapling, fixed the end of a pitchfork to it, and cut it free when he'd descended from the window. Crude but deadly—if he'd been human. He yanked the tines free and tossed them aside. Around the rear of the house he heard a door slam.

She'd gone back inside. Obviously she wanted him to follow. But Gregor decided to enter his own way. He rose into the air, then hurled himself through the dining room window.

The shattered glass settled. Dark. Quiet. She was here inside. Where? Only a matter of time—a very short time—before he found her. He was making his move toward the rear rooms of the house when the silence was shattered by a bell, startling him.

He stared incredulously at the source of the noise. The telephone? But how? The first things his night-brothers had destroyed were the communication networks. Without thinking, he reached out to it. It was an automatic gesture.

The phone exploded as soon as he lifted the receiver.

The blast knocked him against the far wall, smashing him into the beveled glass of the china cabinet. Again, just as with last night's explosion, he was blinded by the flash. But this time he was hurt. His hand . . . agony . . . he couldn't remember ever feeling pain like this. And he was helpless. If she had accomplices, he was at their mercy now.

But no one attacked him, and soon he could see again.

"My hand!" he screamed when he saw the ragged stump of his right wrist.

Already the bleeding had stopped and the pain was fading, but his hand was gone. It would regenerate in time but—

He had to get out of here and get help before she

did something else to him. He didn't care if it made
him look like a fool, this woman was dangerous!

Gregor staggered to his feet and started for the door.
Once he was outside in the night air he'd feel better,
he'd regain some of his strength.

*   *   *

In the basement, Sister Carole huddled under the
mattress and stretched her arm upward. Her fingers
found a string that ran the length of the basement to a
hole in one of the floorboards above, ran through that
hole and into the pantry in the main hall where it was
tied to the handle of an empty teacup that sat on the
edge of the bottom shelf. She tugged on the string and
the teacup fell. Sister Carole heard it shatter and snug-
gled deeper under her mattress.

*   *   *

What?

Gregor spun at the noise. There. Behind that door.
She was hiding in that closet. She'd knocked something off a shelf in there. He'd heard her. He had her
now.

Gregor knew he was hurt—*maimed*—but even with
one hand he could easily handle a dozen cattle like
her. He didn't want to wait, didn't want to go back
without *something* to show for the night. And she was
so close now. Right behind that door.

He reached out with his good hand and yanked it
open.

Gregor saw everything with crystal clarity then, and
understood everything as it happened.

He saw the string attached to the inside of the door,
saw it tighten and pull the little wedge of wood from
between the jaws of the clothespin that was tacked to
the third shelf. He saw the two wires—one wrapped

around the upper jaw of the clothespin and leading back to a dry cell battery, the other wrapped around the lower jaw and leading to a row of wax-coated cylinders standing on that third shelf like a collection of lumpy, squat candles with firecracker-thick wicks. As the wired jaws of the clothespin snapped closed, he saw a tiny spark leap the narrowing gap.

Gregor's universe exploded.

* * *

I'm awake! Gregor thought. I survived!

He didn't know how long it had been since the blast. A few minutes? A few hours? It couldn't have been too long—it was still night. He could see the moonlight through the hole that had been ripped in the wall.

He tried to move but could not. In fact, he couldn't feel anything. *Anything.* But he could hear. And he heard someone picking through the rubble toward him. He tried to turn his head but could not. Who was there? One of his own kind—*please* let it be one of his own kind.

When he saw the flashlight beam, he knew it was one of the living. He began to despair. He was utterly helpless here. What had that explosion done to him?

As the light came closer, he saw that it was the woman, the she-devil. She appeared to be unscathed. . . .

And she wore the headpiece of a nun.

She shone the beam in his face and he blinked.

"Dear sweet Jesus!" she said. Her voice was hushed with awe. "You're not dead yet? Even in this condition?"

He opened his mouth to tell her what she no doubt already knew very well: That there were only certain ways the undead could succumb to true death, and a concussive blast from an explosion was not one of them. But his jaw wasn't working right, and he had no voice.

"So what are we going to do with you, Mr. Vampire?" she said. "I can't risk leaving you here for the sun to finish you—your friends might show up first and find a way to fix you up. Not that I can see how that'd be possible, but I wouldn't put anything past you vipers."

What was she saying? What did she mean? What had happened to him?

"If I had a good supply of holy water I could pour it over you, but I want to conserve what I've got."

She was quiet a moment, then she turned and walked off. Had she decided to leave him here? He hoped so. At least that way he had a chance.

But if she wanted to kill him, why hadn't she said anything about driving a stake through his heart?

Gregor heard her coming back. She had yellow rubber gloves on her hands and a black plastic bag under her arm. She rested the flashlight on a broken timber, snapped the bag open, and reached for his face. He tried to cringe away but again felt no response from his body. She grabbed him by his hair and . . . lifted him. Vertigo spun him around as she looked him in the face.

"You can still see, can't you? Maybe you'd better take a look at yourself."

Vertigo again as she twisted his head around, and then he saw the hallway, or what was left of it. Mass destruction—shattered timbers, the stairs blown away, and . . .

Pieces of his body—his arms and legs torn and scattered, his torso twisted and eviscerated, his intestines stretched and torn. Gregor tried to shout out his shock, his horror, his disbelief, but he no longer had lungs.

Vertigo again, worse than before, as she dropped his head into the black plastic bag.

"What I'm going to do, Mr. Vampire, is clean up as much of you as I can, and then I'm going to put you in a safe place, cool, dark, far away from the sun. Just the sort of place your kind likes."

His remaining hand was tossed into the bag and landed on his face. Then a foot, then an indescribably mutilated, unidentifiable organ, then more, and more, until what little light there was left was shut out and he was completely covered.

What was she doing? What had she meant by "just the sort of place your kind likes"?

And then the whole bag was moving, dragging across the floor, ripping as it caught on the debris.

"Here you are, Mr. Vampire," she said. "Your new home."

And suddenly the bag was falling, rolling, tumbling down a set of stairs, tearing open as it went, disgorging its contents in the rough descent. More vertigo, the worst yet, as Gregor's head tumbled free and bounced down the last three steps, rolled and then lay still with his left cheek against the cellar floor.

The madwoman's voice echoed down the stairwell. "Your kind is always bragging about how you're immortal. Let's see how you like your immortality now, Mr. Vampire. I've got to find another house, so I won't be around to see you anymore, but truly I wish you a long, long immortality."

Gregor wished his lungs were attached so he could scream. Just once.

*   *   *

Sister Carole trudged through the inky blackness along the center of the road, towing her red wagon behind her. She'd loaded it with her Bible, her rosary, her holy water, the blasting caps, and other essentials.

< *You're looking for ANOTHER place? And I suppose you'll be starting up this same awful sinfulness*

CULT
by
Warner Lee

My name is Edward Long, and I am in a business that does not advertise. Clients hear of me through a friend or on the grapevine. Some have spent weeks trying to find me, not really sure that I truly existed.

I have no office, for being at a known location would put me in jeopardy. I have many enemies, you see, people who would delight in seeing me dead. What I do is illegal and dangerous, so I am very expensive. Thus I only have to work occasionally to earn a comfortable living.

I retrieve people.

Who do not wish to be retrieved.

Usually this means snatching someone from a cult and delivering him or her to the deprogrammers. On one occasion, though, it was much more than that. *Much* more. As you can imagine, a person in my line of work would have some wild stories to tell. But the one I am going to relate to you now is the most bizarre and frightening one in my collection. I have never told it before, because no one would believe it. I am revealing it now because . . . well, because it's a simmering, volatile thing, and maybe letting it out will enable me to put it to rest.

It began in October two years ago. I had received word from Tom, the bartender at the Buena Vista Lounge, that a man was looking for me. As with my other contacts, Tom had no idea where to find me. I called him periodically from a phone booth, and if anyone had been looking for me, he passed on the information. For this service I slipped him a hundred dollar bill every Christmas, and Tom seemed happy with the arrangement.

The potential client was a middle-aged man. I'd told Tom to let him know that I'd be in the Oasis at eight Tuesday evening. He should wear a fedora, so I could recognize him. Yes, I know it sounds corny, but as I've said, there are a lot of people out there who would like to kill me, and most of them have fanatical organizations behind them.

The Oasis is a place where young people with money can get together and try to experience what it must have been like for people in Humphrey Bogart's era. On the weekends a live dance band plays from an eclectic repertoire that includes Tommy Dorsey's greatest hits and rearranged Beatles' tunes. This being midweek, there was no band. I sat at a corner table, drinking a beer and keeping an eye on the other patrons.

I first saw him as a reflection in the mirror that ran the length of the bar. A tall, dark-haired man in a gray double-breasted suit. I almost missed the fedora because he was carrying it rather than wearing it. Either he didn't like anything on his head, or he believed in the custom of a gentleman's removing his hat whenever he stepped indoors.

Approaching a vacant table near the bar, he carried himself with an air of superiority, his movements smooth, graceful, elegant. He ordered a Scotch and soda, then unobtrusively surveyed the premises, his eyes passing over me as if he didn't even see me, although I knew he had assessed everyone in the place. When his drink arrived, he left it untouched on the table while he waited.

I called over the waitress. She was new, a buxom young woman with curly blonde hair whose name tag identified her as Kimberly. ''Would you ask the gentleman at that table to join me, please,'' I said. ''The one with the hat on the chair beside him.''

Kimberly did my bidding, and a moment later the man with the gray fedora was sitting at my table. ''Allow me to introduce myself,'' he said. ''I am Miguel La Durca.''

His speech contained the hint of an accent, barely discernible, but there. European, I thought. He was extremely fair complected, which seemed to rule out the Indian blood carried by most Latin Americans.

''Are you from Spain?'' I asked.

''Yes. Barcelona. I represent a firm that makes computer chips. We are trying to wean your manufacturers away from the Japanese chips in favor of ours.''

''Are you having any luck?''

''Some.'' He studied me with eyes so deep and dark that looking into them was like peering into bottomless blackness. ''I have need of your specialty,'' he said.

''You have someone you want rescued.''

''Yes, rescued. A good choice of terms.''

''I can be expensive—especially when it involves things that are illegal.''

''This, I think, will be illegal.''

''A son or daughter?''

''No. My wife.''

''And where is your wife at this moment?''

''In the hands of a group called the Church of Seven. Have you heard of it?''

''No. What is it?''

''I think the name refers to Lucifer, which contains seven letters.''

''Devil worshipers?''

''Yes. Or something similar. They live in a compound near Foley Lake. They sleep all day, and at night they hold their disgusting rituals. I've heard they sacrifice animals, dance naked.''

"How did your wife get involved with people like this?"

"My wife is English, not Spanish. Since she isn't Catholic, she doesn't have the teachings of the church to fall back on. She . . ." He frowned, letting his words trail off. "I am not being totally honest with you. My wife requires psychiatric help. She ran into some of these people a couple of months after she checked herself out of a private mental hospital—over the doctor's objections, I'm afraid. It was a time when she was quite vulnerable. They prey on people like her, these cultists, people who are confused, weak, receptive—and who have money to give them."

"How much have they taken from her?"

"Before I could get her access to the accounts cut off, it had passed a hundred thousand dollars."

"I won't cost you nearly that much," I said.

"How much will you cost me?"

"It depends on the situation. Tell me about this compound of theirs."

"It covers several acres in a valley. The buildings themselves are surrounded by a high stone wall. I've noticed surveillance cameras on the wall, and there are also guards."

"Armed?"

"They don't display any weapons, but I wouldn't be surprised if they have them."

"Getting someone out of a place like that could be very expensive."

"I can afford whatever you charge, Mr. . . ."

"Long."

"Long, yes. No one seemed to know what you were called. In any case, I have money, Mr. Long. You get Sarah back, and I will pay whatever you ask."

"You understand that I may have to force her to come with me."

"She would not accompany you willingly. I only ask that you do not harm her when you kidnap her."

Reaching inside his jacket, he produced a photo, which he handed to me. It was a picture of a truly beautiful woman. She had shiny dark hair, which hung below her shoulders. Her face might have been just a little too long, but her features were flawless. She had an aristocratic mouth, a knowing smile, eyes that seemed simultaneously sly and innocent, high cheekbones, a nose that curved gracefully to its slightly upraised tip. Everything in balance, nothing too large or too small, too thick or too thin. Although it was the face of a northern European, there was something vaguely exotic in her appearance, something that hinted of warm nights along the Nile or Gypsy caravans. I could certainly see why he wanted her back. She was one of the most stunning women I had ever seen.

"There is one other thing," La Durca said. "You must take her in the daylight."

"Why?"

"They sleep then. At night they are all awake."

"Even so, the darkness could be helpful."

He shook his head. "They would kill her before they'd let her go. I can't take that chance. It has to be done while they're sleeping."

I sighed. I didn't like it when clients started making rules. "Have you been inside the place?"

"No, they wouldn't let me in. I hired a private detective, who told me the place is run by a man called Vladimir. He's the high priest. That's his title. I'll give you the detective's report. It may save time."

He produced an envelope, which he slid across the table to me. Kimberly asked if we wanted to order more drinks. La Durca, who hadn't touched his Scotch, said no. I had another beer.

"I'll need a thousand-dollar nonrefundable retainer," I said. "And all that commits me to do is look over the job. If I can do it, there will be a more substantial fee."

Reaching into his inner pocket, the Spaniard said, "I understood those were your terms."

* * *

The Church of Seven was an hour-and-a-half drive from the city. I shaved fifteen minutes off that by leaving early enough to beat the morning rush.

It was a pretty day, the sun shining warmly in a cloudless sky, creating the illusion that this year winter might not come. The countryside was New England-like, with small farms nestled among trees whose leaves were turning red and amber and gold. From time to time I passed hand-painted signs that said things like "HOMEMADE CIDER" and "FRESH EGGS."

At first glance, the Church of Seven was just another farm. But on closer inspection, it became clear that nothing had been grown there for years. The fields were covered with weeds and grass; in places bushes and saplings had taken root. A barn and some smaller structures whose use had presumably been agricultural had fallen into disrepair. But then La Durca had said the residents slept all day, so they would not be involved in farming.

The part of the place that was in use was surrounded by a tall stone wall. I spotted the surveillance cameras. The gate was unmarked except for a single sign. In red letters on a white background, it said:

PRIVATE PROPERTY
ADMISSION BY APPOINTMENT ONLY

The gate was made of thick steel bars. It was closed. A wooden guardhouse stood beside it, with a khaki-uniformed security man inside. Through the gate I could see an asphalt drive leading to a two-story farmhouse with a red roof. Though larger than most, it was as unpretentious as any other farmhouse, and the massive gate, the guards, and the security cameras seemed incongruous.

I pulled up to the gate as if I had business there. I was driving my ten-year-old Ford Escort. I have newer, fancier cars, but when I'm looking over a job I prefer something modest and inconspicuous. The guard emerged from his wooden dwelling. Behind him I could see a bank of TV monitors. As he approached my side of the car, I rolled down the window.

"You have an appointment?" the guard asked, his tone making it clear that he knew I didn't. He wasn't wearing a hat, and his blond hair was cut in a flattop. He had a large, boxy face, a square jaw. He looked like a onetime athlete who, no longer the star of his high school, had lapsed into inactivity, losing the muscles but not the weight. On his shoulder was a patch that said "Grigson Security."

"No, I just wanted to ask if the outfit you work for might be hiring."

"Grigson?"

"Yeah. I used to work for a security company in Albuquerque, and I thought maybe my experience would help."

The guard shrugged. "Don't know. I don't have anything to do with that. You'd have to talk to Mr. Grigson."

"Where do I find him?"

"In town. At the company's office."

I noticed that two other guards had shown up. They stood inside the gate, watching with bored expressions on their faces. I couldn't see any weapons, but they wore Ike style uniform jackets, unbuttoned, which could conceal shoulder holsters.

"Do new guys have to start on the graveyard shift, or would my experience count?"

"If you're interested in working here, you won't have to worry about that. The church does its own guarding at night. We're just here during the day."

"I never heard of that before. Usually it's the other way around."

"They're all members of some oddball religion in there," the guard said, inclining his head toward the gate. "As I understand it, they stay up all night and sleep all day. Apparently it's part of their religion that they can't be out while the sun's shining."

"Well, I'll be damned," I said.

"It's easy work though. No one ever comes in or goes out. Food's delivered once a week—while they're all asleep. Taylor's Grocery brings it out and puts everything away for them. Other than that nothing ever happens. Some days I spend the whole shift reading a fishing magazine or listening to the radio, and the only people I see are the ones who drive by on the highway."

"I'll talk to Mr. Grigson."

"Office is on 53rd, just north of Stottard. You can't miss it."

"Thanks," I said, and backed away from the gate.

The nearest town was a place called Ridgecrest. It had three traffic lights, two churches, and one grocery store—Taylor's. I bought a few things and struck up a conversation with the checker on my way out.

She said, "They call that place a church, but I don't believe it for a minute. It's one of those groups of weirdos—like the Moonies."

"Some people would say that's a church," I said.

"Well, I certainly wouldn't. A church is an institution that recognizes Jesus as our Lord and Savior."

"Of course," I said. "Do they come into town very often?"

"That's one good thing. We never see them."

"Not even to buy groceries?"

"We deliver to them. Every Wednesday morning."

Next I located a road leading to a hill overlooking the compound and spent the rest of the day watching the place. There were four guards. One in the gatehouse, and three who roved the grounds. No one arrived. No one left.

Shortly after nightfall, the lights came on in the former farmhouse, and the guards left. A light stayed on in the gatehouse, and through the window I could see shadows move, indicating that the post was still manned—presumably by a resident of the compound. For some reason, I had not seen the replacement guard arrive, even though I was watching through special nightvision binoculars.

I stayed there for about three hours after the sun went down, never so much as glimpsing a member of the Church of Seven. Just before I left, I thought I saw something slip over the wall and move into the surrounding woods, but I couldn't be sure.

On the way back to town, I considered the private detective's report La Durca had given me. Practically nothing was known about the Church of Seven. It had bought the property from a farmer's estate three years ago and moved in. The PI had spent a day researching the church, finding nothing. He said it appeared to be a publicity shy local organization with a only handful of members, although he could not be sure of the exact number.

The high priest, Vladimir, had authored no books, consented to no interviews, and no photos of him seemed to exist. Unknowns included where he came from, what he'd done before becoming the leader of the church, and whether Vladimir was his real name.

As far as the PI could tell, no one had ever complained to the authorities about the Church of Seven. No one had sued it. No one from its ranks had been arrested.

Strange, I thought.

The word hung there, an invisible passenger that accompanied me all the way back to the city.

The next day I drove to the apartment of Paul Flanders. Paul is a sort of junior partner of mine. We met while working as mercenaries in a Third World country whose name really doesn't matter. We're alike, Paul and I, Vietnam vets who'd been programmed for action by the U.S. Government and never deprogrammed. Unable or unwilling to adapt to the workaday world, we'd become soldiers of fortune, and when we'd grown too old for that life, Paul had tried being a policeman and failed, while I had fared only slightly better in a variety of occupations ranging from bounty hunter to bodyguard.

But now we had found our niche. And we were quite good at it. Probably the best in the world.

I said, "The problem will be what happens once we get inside. We don't know where Sarah might be, which means we'll have to go from room to room until we find her. If we accidentally wake someone up, and he sounds the alarm, we could be in trouble. I don't know how many of them we might be up against."

"You get the plans?" Paul asked.

I handed him the copies I'd obtained at the county courthouse. "They were filed twenty-two years ago," I said. "Who knows what changes might have been made since then?"

"Two stories with a basement," Paul noted, studying the documents. He looked like the aging warrior he was, a big, ruddy-skinned man who appeared at home in a uniform, regardless of whether its origins were Latin American or African or Middle Eastern. His broad shoulders seemed naked without the strap of an Uzi or an AK47.

Running his fingers through the remaining strands of light brown hair, Paul said, "How do we get in?"

I told him the plan, and when I was finished Paul said, "Piece of cake as long as you don't mind committing about half a dozen felonies. How much you going to charge him?''

''A lot,'' I said.

* * *

I met La Durca that evening at the Oasis. He ordered the same drinks, Scotch for him, beer for me.

''I can do it,'' I said.

''When?''

''Day after tomorrow.''

''How much will it cost me?''

''Twenty-five. Half in advance, the rest when I deliver.''

''And if something goes wrong? Say Sarah has been moved somewhere else.''

''You get your money back, except for the thousand dollar retainer.''

''You'd like cash, I presume.''

I nodded.

''All right, Mr. Long, we have a deal.''

We shook hands. His flesh was cool, and his grip was unusually firm.

''I'll have the money for you tomorrow night,'' he said.

After he left, I remained at the table, finished my beer, and ordered another.

''Huh,'' Kimberly said when she brought me the fresh beer.

''Huh what?'' I asked.

''Your friend.''

''What about him?''

''He always orders Scotch, then never drinks any of it.'' She picked up La Durca's still full glass.

''Maybe he's a teetotaler,'' I said, ''but he doesn't want to make an issue of it.''

''Yeah,'' Kimberly said, ''maybe.''

I didn't consider the matter further. If the man

wanted to buy Scotch he didn't drink it was okay with me.

* * *

I met him again the next evening, and the Spaniard presented me with an envelope containing $12,500.

"There's a picnic area on state highway 384, just north of Paddington. I'll meet you there."

"Have you arranged for deprogrammers?" I asked.

"They'll be with me."

He again bought Scotch he didn't drink.

* * *

The next morning Paul and I were waiting at a bend in the two lane highway leading from Ridgecrest to the Church of Seven. We were using a BMW with fake plates. It was pulled to the side of the road with its hood up. I chose the Boomer because anyone driving anything that expensive would be unlikely to be viewed as a potential lowlife robber-murder-rapist. We also wore suits and ties; we were the image of respectability. When I stepped into the path of the van from Taylor's Grocery, frantically waving my arms, the driver pulled over immediately.

"Car break down?" he asked. He was about eighteen, a skinny kid with pimples. When I stuck the Ingram in his face, he blanched, his eyes widening in fear.

"Scoot over," I said. "I'll drive."

The kid obeyed. To the right was a narrow dirt road leading into the woods. I followed it until we were out of sight from the highway. Paul and I changed into our working clothes—British issue camouflage uniforms. Our gear included tear gas, gas masks, smoke, grenades, and automatic weapons. The guns were primarily for show, to obtain compliance. But they were loaded. We would use them if our lives depended on them.

But then such circumstances seemed quite unlikely. The guards from Grigson Security were not in our league.

We hid in the back of the van while the terrified teenager drove to the Church of Seven. The guard I'd spoken to yesterday was on the gate again.

"Morning, Billy," he said to the teenager. "Andy will ride up with you."

Another guard climbed in with the driver, never even glancing into the cargo area. He was about thirty, a thin man whose dark hair had been trimmed in an uneven home-done barbering job. As the truck started forward, Paul pressed the barrel of his MAC11 against the guard's neck.

"Surprise," Paul whispered.

"Shit," the guard said.

The teenager drove to the rear of the house and stopped. They were out of sight from the gate.

"Do what you'd normally do," I said. "And remember, these Ingrams can fire twelve hundred rounds a minute. You can't run from that—not and get very far. Do you understand?"

The guard and driver said they understood completely.

Two guards were patrolling along the stone wall. I waited until they were out of sight before letting our hostages out of the truck. The guard unlocked the door, and the teenager began carrying cardboard boxes full of groceries into the kitchen.

It was a normal family kitchen, the range and refrigerator from Sears, the wooden table large enough to seat six comfortably, eight in a tight squeeze. I wondered how many people could live here if this was it for cooking facilities. While Paul kept an eye on the teenager, I bound and gagged the guard.

I looked into the boxes the boy was brining in. They

contained mainly canned goods. Beans, peas, corn, soup, beef stew, chili with beans. Perishables were limited to small quantities of milk, cheese, eggs, and two heads of lettuce, which the teenager put in the refrigerator.

"They put the canned stuff away themselves," he said.

I checked the refrigerator's top freezer section. It was empty except for ice cubes.

"Who decides what goes into the order?" I asked.

"It's standard," the teenager replied. "It never changes."

I looked into the cabinets. There were a handful of plates, K-Mart quality stuff. In the cabinets beneath the counter I found a couple of frying pans, a few pots, cookware intended for home use, not the sort of thing that would be used to feed a large number of people.

"Something's screwy here," I said to Paul.

"Maybe they don't eat much. It's part of their religion."

I looked at the kid, and he looked back blankly. He had no explanations to offer.

"I'm going to tie you up," I told him. "We'll untie you when we leave. As long as you cooperate, no harm will come to you."

"I . . . I'll cooperate," he said.

I bound and gagged the teenager and locked the door we'd entered through. Then I tried the only door leading from the kitchen into the rest of the house. It was locked. With a good quality dead bolt. It took Paul about a minute to pick it. The hostages, gagged and with their hands tied behind them, sat with their backs against the wall, their eyes taking in everything we did.

The rest of the house was absolutely silent and pitch black. We switched on our flashlights. We were in a living room that looked as if it were never used. There were no newspapers or magazines around. The couch, two upholstered chairs, and a reading lamp were arranged haphazardly. A fine layer of dust covered everything.

There was no TV set.

No stereo.

No telephone.

"What the hell have we got here?" I whispered to Paul.

"Some very strange people," he replied.

The windows had been covered from the inside with layers of a heavy black material. Absolutely no light came in; the darkness was as absolute as a photographic darkroom's.

Ahead was a hallway. We entered it, moving silently. I gently opened a door on the right, finding an empty room. Paul tried the one on the left; it, too, was empty. As were all the rooms on the ground floor.

We went upstairs. It was as dark here as it had been downstairs. And all the rooms were dusty and empty. Paul and I exchanged looks. The only thing left was the basement.

The entrance to the cellar was sealed with a dead bolt lock, which Paul picked. The door opened onto a set of wooden stairs that extended downward into a blackness so thick and menacing it almost seemed palpable. Paul and I exchanged glances, but we were both soldiers, men of action, unwilling to admit that this whole business was beginning to unnerve us.

As we descended the stairs, the beams of our flashlights poked into the darkness, revealing cobwebs, dust, concrete walls, a cement floor. Odors, dank and musty, assailed my nostrils. And another scent, less well defined. It was reminiscent of the musky animal smell of a menagerie, and at the same time it reminded me of the sour aroma that came from a refrigerator when something inside was starting to go bad.

Some primitive something deep within me was starting to writhe. It wanted out of that place. Desperately.

Paul tapped my arm, pointed. A mountain of canned goods was piled in the corner. All the deliveries from Taylor's Grocery. Never touched. What became of the milk and cheese and vegetables? Were the perishables simply thrown away?

What did the people here eat?

The answer seemed obvious. There *were* no people here. This was some sort of giant deception. The guards, the groceries delivered each week, it was all a hoax. But why? What was the point?

And then I saw something that shot that explanation totally to hell. At the far end of the cellar, people were sleeping. About two dozen of them. Some were on small mattresses. Some were on the hard floor. All of them were dressed in street clothes.

Paul and I stared at each other, neither of us comprehending what we were seeing.

I pulled out the photo of Sarah La Durca and began moving among the sleeping forms. They came in all age groups. I saw a silver-haired man wearing a suit and tie, a lovely blonde woman in an evening gown, a teenage boy in blue jeans, a girl of about ten in a red dress, a man with big, rough-looking hands in worker's overalls. They seemed more drugged than asleep, I realized, for there was no heavy breathing, no snoring, no moans, no rustling of clothing as slumbering bodies shifted position.

They were totally silent.

As still as the subjects of a photograph.

I spotted Sarah lying on a dirty, tattered mattress. She was as beautiful as her picture. She lay with her eyes closed, her white face pointing upward, framed by the lustrous black hair. She wore a blue and red dress, cut in a V in front to reveal the beginning of her cleavage. She was every bit as lovely as in her photo. I picked her up.

She wasn't heavy, but she was a dead weight, as inanimate as a basket of laundry. As I started up the stairs with her, it occurred to me that I might have stumbled on some bizarre mass suicide. Sarah La Durca felt cold, lifeless. Had the cult members come down here to drink poison like their fellow nut cases had done in Guyana?

In the kitchen I found the teenager and the guard where we'd left them, watching us with wide, fear-filled eyes. In the light coming in through the windows, I studied the woman in my arms. She seemed so limp, so—

She wasn't cold anymore, I realized suddenly. I could feel warmth now. She might be drugged, but she wasn't dead.

Paul untied the teenager. After checking to make sure the coast was clear, we slipped out of the building, leaving the bound guard where he was. The sunshine felt good after the dark and eerie cellar. It warmed my flesh, chasing away the basement's cool dankness.

"What the hell kind of a place is this?" Paul asked. His voice had an edge to it I had never heard before.

"I don't know," I said. "Let's just get out of here."

Paul opened the side door of the van, and I found myself staring into the barrel of a shotgun. It was held by one of the guards. One of the others appeared from around the corner of the building, aiming a pistol at us.

"Everybody stay exactly where you are," the guard with the shotgun said, climbing out of the van.

"Should I call the cops?" his partner asked.

"No, not yet. I think we should interrogate these scumbags ourselves first. We can learn things the cops can't." I'd seen the type before. Wanted to show how tough he was. A big man with size twelve shoes and mean little eyes.

I did the one thing he wouldn't have expected me to do. I handed him Sarah La Durca. It confused him for a split second, and that was all I needed. Although I am skilled in several forms of the martial arts, there was nothing sophisticated about what I did. I kicked him in the balls. When he doubled over, I kicked him in the face, and that was the end of the fight.

Glancing over my shoulder, I saw that Paul had dispatched the other guard. We took them inside and tied them up. That left only the guard at the gate, and we would have to see that he joined the others. I put Sarah La Durca in the van. The grocery delivery boy was just standing there, afraid to get involved, lest he pick the losing side.

We made him drive us to the gate. The guard was apparently unaware that his colleagues had discovered intruders—a very sloppy way to do things, but then these guys probably earned just slightly better than the minimum wage. Paul and I got out with our Ingrams and politely invited the guard to accompany us to the house. Looking at me, he said, "I guess you didn't ask Mr. Grigson for a job."

"No," I said.

We tied him up along with the teenager and locked them in the house with the other guards. Then we drove to the spot where we'd left the BMW. As Paul was transferring Sarah to the back seat of the car, he said, "Man, she sure is hot."

"Fever?"

"I don't know. I mean she's *really* hot, like a furnace. Maybe it's the effects of the drugs—if she was drugged."

I tried not to think of all the ifs as I drove toward Paddington.

"That was the damnedest place I've ever seen," Paul said.

"Yeah," I said, and then we fell silent because we didn't have any answers, which made asking the questions seem pointless.

In the rearview mirror the road behind me appeared

misty, although the day was clear and sunny. "Look behind us," I said.

Paul turned around. "Jesus Christ."

"What is it?"

"Her."

I jammed on the brakes.

Sarah La Durca lay in the back seat, steaming. Or maybe she was smoking. Her cheek seemed to shrivel as I watched. All of a sudden she looked middle aged, and in very poor health. She was still recognizable as the beauty I'd carried from the cellar, but only barely.

"What the hell are we going to do?" Paul asked. The car was filling with . . . something. It looked like smoke, but it was odorless.

"Get her to a hospital," I said. "La Durca wants his wife alive."

"What about Paddington?"

"That's at least forty-five minutes away. There's a town just ahead. There's a small hospital. I noticed it the other day."

By the time we slid to a stop outside the emergency entrance of Bolton Community Hospital, Sarah La Durca's flesh had begun to undulate and quiver. We ran inside and grabbed the first two people we saw who had white coats and name tags. As they loaded Sarah on a gurney, a deep crack spread across the flesh of her right hand. Steam erupted from it.

Sarah's eyes flew open, and her mouth formed into the shape of a primal scream, but all that came out was a stream of smoky mist and a muffled croak.

The white-coated figures rolled her inside and disappeared through a large swinging door, telling us to wait there. The emergency room entrance was filled with a grayish-white haze.

Ten minutes later, a doctor came through the swinging door. His eyes were wide, his face drained of color. I asked how Sarah was, but the doctor just stared straight ahead, as if he hadn't heard me.

Finally he said, "She . . . she . . . oh, God."

"She what?" I demanded. "What the hell happened?"

"She . . . she . . . spontaneous combustion."

"She burst into flames?" Paul said.

The doctor nodded.

"You mean . . . *poof?*"

"Yes," the doctor said. "Poof. She set the whole bed on fire. We . . . we had to use a fire extinguisher to get it out." He shook his head. "I've got to sit down."

We got out of there.

* * *

Miguel La Durca never showed up at Paddington, and it was two days later before he left a message with Tom the bartender saying he wanted to meet me. I left word that I'd see him at the Oasis the following evening. I didn't think he'd ask for his money back. For one thing, I was pretty sure I'd figured out who he was.

"Mr. Long," he said, sitting down at my table.

"Would you like a Scotch and soda?" I asked.

He shook his head. "It is not what I drink."

"No," I said.

He studied me with his bottomless dark eyes. "You did not deliver Sarah to me as agreed."

"You didn't expect me to. You didn't even show up at Paddington."

"Still," he said, "I would be within my rights in asking for a refund."

"The woman, Sarah, what was she?"

His eyes mocked me. "What do you think she was?"

"I think she was a vampire."

"A vampire? Mr. Long, you can't be serious."

"A week ago I would have thought such a notion

preposterous. Now I think the Church of Seven was a group of vampires.''

''I hope you don't plan to embarrass yourself by saying this in public. I mean, really, Mr. Long. Vampires?''

Ignoring his sarcasm, I said, ''Who was she, the woman you had me murder?''

''Murder? If, as you claim, she was a vampire, then she was already dead. How could you have murdered her?''

''Legally it's a gray area. Still, you used me to dispose of her. Who was she? Why did you go to all that trouble to get rid of her?''

He smiled. ''All right, Mr. Long. I believe I owe you an explanation. Sarah was my . . . companion, shall we say. We don't exactly get married in the way you do, as I'm sure you understand. She had been my companion for over two hundred years. She was a very domineering woman. She wanted to possess me totally, to control every aspect of my existence.''

I noticed that he didn't say ''life.''

He sighed. ''Two centuries of that is enough. I tried to get her to go away, but she refused. She saw the relationship as eternal, I think. Think of it, Mr. Long, eternity with a shrew.'' He shook his head. ''Who could be expected to bear such a thing?''

''Why didn't you simply dispatch her yourself?''

''Dispatch her? Mr. Long, Sarah was immortal. How does one dispatch a being who is immortal?''

''She couldn't be stabbed or shot or suffocated?''

''Of course not. She was a vampire.''

''I was able to kill her—even if I didn't know that's what I was doing.''

''Ah, but what you did could only be accomplished in the daylight, and I must sleep in total darkness while the sun shines. It's the only thing that works, exposure to sunlight. The other things you hear about—silver, wooden stakes through the heart, crucifixes—it's all nonsense. The sun kills us. Nothing else. All the rest is pure fiction.''

"How about garlic?"

"Garlic does not affect me. I have a reflection in the mirror just like anyone else.'' He shrugged. ''It's all nonsense. Except for the sunlight part.''

"Do you live on human blood?''

"Of course.'' He raised his upper lip, displaying a pair of sharply pointed fangs. ''I am many times stronger than you are. And I can cloud your mind. If I decided to have you, there would be nothing you could do about it.''

It was not a comforting thought. ''Is that what happened to the teenager and the guards I left tied up out there?''

"No. Fortunately for them, they managed to free themselves before dark. By the time the police arrived, night had fallen and we had gone. We are through with that place, by the way. We will not use it again.'' His eyes explored mine.

Did he think I'd planned to go out there and drag all the sleeping vampires into the sunshine? It hadn't occurred to me. Maybe it would have; I don't know.

"Why did you have the food delivered?'' I asked, not wanting to dwell on the likelihood of my being a threat.

"If we didn't ever buy food, someone would notice, start to wonder. Even reclusive cultists have to eat.''

"Who are you?'' I asked.

"Vladimir, the high priest of the Church of Seven.''

"There are seven letters in Lucifer, you said.''

"Yes.''

"There are also seven letters in vampire.''

"Indeed.'' He smiled—without showing the fangs, thank goodness. ''There are seven letters in other things as well. And I think you know what they are.''

I didn't reply to that.

He said, ''Although I could technically ask for a

refund, the fact is you have accomplished what I wished you to accomplish. Therefore it seems only fair that I pay you the remainder of the agreed upon sum.'' He tossed an envelope on the table. ''And that, Mr. Long, concludes our business.''

He rose, nodded once curtly, turned . . . and vanished. I tell myself he simply walked into the shadows in the dimly lit bar. Maybe that's so, but the truth is that one second he was there and the next he was not.

Remaining at the table, I took out a pen and wrote *vampire* on the small paper napkin. Seven letters. Then I wrote another seven letter word: *La Durca*. I rearranged the letters, making another name:

Dracula

Then I tore up the napkin and left the bar, glancing over my shoulder as I walked through the shadow-filled parking lot to my car.

THE BLACK WOLF

by
Wendi Lee and Terry Beatty

The St. Louis train, bound for San Francisco, had just pulled in to the town of Lacey, and passengers were milling around the platform, eager to board. The stationmaster was helping ladies get off the train, and porters were unloading and loading luggage. Marshal Ed Walker leaned against a wooden post and took it all in.

"Slow day, eh, Marshal?" land agent Sylvester Mayfair hailed in his booming voice.

Walker grinned and shrugged. "I like it this way."

"You may be in for a little excitement soon," Mayfair replied, a gleam in his eyes. He looked around in a secretive manner, then withdrew a wrinkled telegram from his pocket. "This came yesterday from the Caulfields."

"They wired you from Europe?" Walker was impressed. The Caulfields were an older couple who owned a large house that overlooked all of Lacey. When the enormous place had been completed, Mrs. Caulfield insisted on naming it Caulfield Manor. Everyone in town just called it The Mansion.

"It seems they met this fella in London," Mayfair said, consulting the wire as he talked. "They've agreed to rent their house to him until they return."

"So we're going to have a little new blood in town," the marshal replied.

"Not only that," Mayfair looked up and grinned, "but he's royalty, too."

"Royalty?"

Mayfair waved the telegram. "It says here that he's a Count. Those are his boxes over there." Mayfair pointed to several large wooden crates that had already been loaded onto a wagon.

"Was the Count on this train?"

"Nope. I just got instructions to take these crates up to the Caulfield place. He's supposed to be arriving later. Don't know if he's comin' by train or stagecoach or what all." Mayfair stared at the crumpled telegram and scratched his head.

A woman let out a scream at the other end of the platform. Walker turned to see what the commotion was, when a thin, wild-eyed Shoshone burst through a huddle of passengers.

He kept shouting something in his language. Although it was a warm day, he was shivering. When the Indian caught sight of the marshal, he lunged toward him, continuing to gibber. Mayfair backed away as if the Indian were a leper. Walker couldn't blame him. While contact with the nearby Shoshone tribe had been friendly in the past, this man was clearly not quite right.

"The black wolf," the Indian managed to say in English before reverting back to Shoshone. He grabbed the marshal's sleeve, tears running freely down his face as he continued to babble.

Just as quickly as he had appeared, the frantic Indian ran off, scattering the astonished crowd and leaving Walker too stunned and confused to chase after him.

"What in the Sam Hell was that about, Marshal?" Mayfair asked, his eyebrows raised and his forehead wrinkled in disbelief.

Living so near the Shoshone village, Walker had found it necessary to learn their language. "He said," Walker paused and rubbed his hand across his chin, "they're all dead. Everyone in his village. The black wolf. It was the black wolf with eyes like fire. He came in the night and now they're all dead.''

''What did he mean, the black wolf?'' Mayfair asked. He was now standing beside Walker, his eyes wide.

The marshal shook his head. ''Your guess is as good as mine.''

Back at his office, Walker's deputy was playing mumblety-peg, trying to throw his jackknife as close to the edge of the wall as possible. Walker took off his hat.

''I heard there was some ruckus at the depot,'' Chase, the deputy, said casually.

''You heard right. And I'm sending you out to look for the cause of it.'' He described the Shoshone Indian to Chase as best he could, giving him a brief account of what had occurred.

''What are you going to do while I'm looking for him?'' Chase asked. It was obvious that there were times when the deputy resented being doled out the smaller tasks. Walker had the feeling that Chase sometimes thought all Walker did was pass the work onto him.

''I'm rounding up a posse and riding out to the Shoshone village. That Indian came from somewhere, and that's as good a place to start as any.'' Walker jammed his hat back on his head and started for the door.

''What should I do with the Indian when I catch him?''

''Put him in a cell. We'll decide what to do with him when I get back. There's a good chance that our friend just had a little too much firewater, but on the other hand, there might be something to that crazy story he told.''

Walker found three reliable men, deputized them, and headed out of town. The Shoshone village was familiar to the townsfolk of Lacey, some of whom would visit the Indians just before winter set in to trade for furs. The Shoshone were a pleasant people, well-known for their hospitality. The Shoshone village that the marshal knew was a bustling, happy, comfortable place. But the village that the posse came upon was silent, with the kind of eerie silence that made a man anxious.

"You hear something, Marshal?" Brady Tucker asked, hunching his shoulders and looking around.

"Not much to hear, Brady," Walker replied. "Place is awful quiet." Just then, a strong wind whipped through the site. He could have sworn he heard moaning, low and hollow. Walker spotted a figure in the distance, a young Shoshone woman wearing a red necklace. She was sitting against a large rock, sunning herself while tending the communal cookpot. "There's someone," he addressed his men and spurred his horse onward.

The scene looked normal until he was within ten feet of her. It was then that he realized she hadn't moved since their approach. There was no fire under the cookpot. Her neck was situated at an unnatural angle and she wasn't wearing a red necklace—her throat had been slashed, leaving a look of terror frozen on her features.

Walker's stomach surged. He closed his eyes and took a couple of deep breaths to calm himself. The posse joined him. When Brady Tucker saw the unfortunate girl, he let out a yelp that sent their horses into a skittish dance. Denton, the youngest and least experienced of the posse, leaned out from his saddle and vomited into some nearby bushes. Eldon, the oldest, was white-faced, but otherwise seemed calm enough as he took in the scene.

"Looks like you got yourself a problem, Marshal," Eldon volunteered, spitting out tobacco juice.

Walker gritted his teeth and got off his horse. "Let's see if anyone's left alive to tell us what happened." The rest of the village contained similar scenes of carnage: mothers with their babies, young braves, grand-mothers and grandfathers, all slaughtered, their throats savagely torn. Some of the victims looked as if they had tried to fight back, but whatever had killed them had been too strong.

With a dark, ugly feeling in the pit of his stomach, the marshal muttered to himself. "How could one wolf do all this? Had to have been a pack. Even then . . ."

Eldon heard him and answered, "Take a look at these tracks, Marshal."

They were animal tracks all right, but they were huge, more like the size of bear tracks.

"Could a bear have done this?" Walker asked no one in particular.

Eldon chewed a wad of tobacco thoughtfully. "I never seen no bear or wolf or pack of wolves that could do this. I'm not sayin' it couldn't happen, but I just never seen it before."

"Whatever it was, we'd better track it down and kill it before anything like this happens again," Walker said.

Brady Tucker, a few yards away, and bent over look-ing at the ground, called out, "Marshal, we'd have a mighty hard time tracking whatever it was that did this."

"What do you mean, Brady?" Walker asked.

"The tracks—they just stop." Brady had a look on his face like he'd just been hit in the head with a log. "Right here on this sandy patch they just stop—like whatever it was up and flew away."

Walker and the posse made no attempt to clean up the carnage of the Shoshone village. There was simply too much to deal with, and the sight of that much death had left all of them feeling sick and over-whelmed. Later, Walker told himself, he would gather a group of volunteers to go back and bury the bodies. For now, he needed to get to the bottom of this thing, and he began to wonder if, just maybe, a lone, crazy

Shoshone could have dressed in an animal skin and slaughtered his entire village.

Night had fallen by the time the men returned to Lacey and went their separate ways. Walker stopped by the jail.

Chase looked up at Walker and grimaced. "No sign of him yet, Marshal. To tell you the truth, I'm not sure we'll ever see him again. If I were him, I'd be worried that I scared a lot of white folks and would get out of Lacey real fast."

Walker shook his head. "Maybe. I don't know." He stretched, feeling the aching and weariness from riding most of the day catching up with him. He yawned and adjusted his hat. "It's late, and I'm headin' home to get some sleep. We'll start looking for that Indian in the morning."

" 'Night, Marshal," said Chase.

" 'Night, Chase," Walker replied as he started to leave.

"By the way, Marshal," Walker stopped, the weariness overcoming his limbs, and waited for Chase to continue. "I think that foreign count has moved into the Mansion. I saw lights up there earlier tonight."

Almost everyone in town knew about the incident at the depot this morning, and the posse members would spread the word about the massacre at the Shoshone village. Walker wouldn't have to warn the townsfolk about the situation. But this newcomer might not know. Walker sighed heavily. "I'll stop up there on my way home. The Count ought to be warned to keep his doors and windows locked."

The Caulfield house was a giant silhouette against the starry night sky. Walker hitched his horse to the post in front and walked up to the door. He heard the knocker's echo reverberate inside the empty hall. Listening for footsteps but hearing none, Walker was startled when the door opened.

"Evening, sir. I'm Marshal Ed Walker. I'd like to

have a word with you if I may.'' He removed his hat and nervously worried the brim. He wasn't quite sure how he was supposed to address royalty.

In the doorway stood a tall, pale man with iron gray hair, thick mustache, and an aquiline nose. Dressed in fancy evening clothes of a European cut, there was no doubt that he was an aristocrat. The fierce, proud eyes seemed to burn clean through the marshal from beneath bushy eyebrows.

With a sweeping gesture of his hand, the Count spoke. ''Welcome to my house. Enter freely and of your own will.'' The strong accent was not one that Walker could place.

The marshal stepped inside and offered his hand to the Count. He assumed even royalty shook hands. The Count's grip was strong, and his hands as cold as ice.

''I wanted to welcome you on behalf of the townspeople. I have to tell you, you're the first royalty I've ever met, er . . . ?''

The foreigner gave him a cold smile. ''Count Dracula. I was born of Romanian nobility.''

Walker stared, mesmerized. ''Romanian. I see.'' He had never heard of such a country, but if this strange Count Dracula said it existed, then it probably existed. Shaking himself out of his trance, he asked, ''And how are Mr. and Mrs. Caulfield? I understand you met them in London.''

''Ah, yes. They were a bit,'' the Count paused for a moment, ''drained from their trip by the time I took my leave, but I believe they were journeying on to enjoy the Adriatic Sea.''

Walker nodded. He would have to look up the Adriatic Sea and Romania on a map of Europe tomorrow.

Meanwhile, the Count's gaze was fixated on Walker's shirt; he moved closer, his hand reaching out to touch the fabric. ''Blood,'' he said in a silky voice. His eyes grew bright and a small smile softened his severe features.

Walker involuntarily stepped back and looked down at the large spot of dried blood on his shirt. It must have gotten there when he bent over the body of the young Indian girl.

The count tore his gaze away from the sight and asked curtly, ''Was there anything else, Marshal? The hour is late and I grow weary.''

''I wanted to warn you that there is a mad Indian on the loose. Maybe someone told you about the ruckus at the train depot today.''

Dracula shook his head. ''I have no knowledge of this incident. Do stay and tell me of it. Perhaps I could offer you a brandy? As for myself, I do not partake of spirits, but it would please me to make you welcome.''

Walker caught a glimpse of the library, a cozy fire burning in the hearth. It was tempting, but he shook his head. ''Thank you, but no. I'm on my way home.'' He briefly recounted the incident and the subsequent visit to the Indian village.

Dracula listened raptly and, when Walker had finished his account, smiled. ''There are many wolves in the Carpathian mountains of my beloved homeland. They too have been known to travel in packs and to kill. I suspect witnessing such an event would drive a man to madness.''

Walker put his hat back on and again extended his hand. The Count's grip was as cold as the corpses of the Shoshone.

* * *

The next morning, Chase burst into the office in a breathless panic. ''Marshal, you got to come quick. There's been a killing.''

Walker jumped up from his chair and grabbed his gun and his hat. ''Who?''

''Old Mrs. Holder.''

''Who found her?''

"Agatha Grimes, the woman who cooks and cleans for her," Chase replied. "Mrs. Grimes told me that when she got to the house, the front door was wide open."

As they hurried toward the Holder house a few hundred yards down the boardwalk, Walker asked, "Any idea who might have done such a thing?"

Chase hesitated, finally saying, "I'm not so sure it's a who, Marshal. More of a what."

When they got to the house, Walker instructed Chase to get the doctor. Meanwhile, Walker went into the kitchen to talk to Agatha Grimes. Ben Grimes had his arm around his trembling, white-faced wife. In a shaking voice, Agatha Grimes told Walker the same story Chase had related to him.

When she was finished, Walker said, "You can take her home now, Ben. I'll have the doctor stop over at your place to give her something for her nerves."

Walker prepared himself for the bloody sight that met his eyes in the parlor. Mrs. Holder was sprawled on the floor. Her throat had been torn open, as if by an animal bite. Walker cleared away the spectators who had gathered inside the house just as Chase and the doctor arrived. When the doctor laid eyes on the victim, he turned pale. "Sweet Jesus . . ." he muttered. It took him a moment to compose himself before he bent over the corpse.

Walker asked, "You got a notion of what might have done this, Doc?"

The doctor laughed nervously, but soon began coughing to cover up his impropriety. "Marshal, it's pretty clear this was done by some kind of animal."

A frustrated Walker helped carry the body out to the waiting undertaker's wagon. He turned to Chase, who, due to his weak stomach, had been controlling the crowd outside. "We have to find that Indian."

They spent all day searching for a sign of the crazy Shoshone, with no luck. The next morning, they discovered there had been another killing; this time, the victim was a saloon girl who worked at an unsavory gambling and drinking parlor near the tracks. Walker organized a group of men to go searching for the animal—if it was an animal—that might have done this.

As the marshal sent the men off on their search, the blacksmith came running toward Walker's office. "Marshal, you're not gonna believe this, but I think I've found your Indian."

He was curled up, sound asleep in the loft above the smithy's forge. Walker shook the fugitive's shoulder. The blacksmith stood at the ready with a pair of manacles. The Shoshone sat up, his wide eyes filled with terror, and screamed as if he were having a nightmare. "The black wolf," the Indian sobbed, saying it over and over again.

The prisoner went quietly, almost appearing relieved at having been caught. Chase was confident that they had caught the killer. "Lacey ought to be safe now. No more killings. We gonna string him up tonight, Marshal?"

Walker shook his head. "He gets a fair trial, Chase. Besides, I'm not completely convinced he's the killer. Let's just wait and see."

There were no murders that night. The next day, Walker reluctantly came to the conclusion that the Indian had indeed done the killings. He knew that the circuit judge would be coming around to Lacey at the end of the month, and the Indian's guilt or innocence would be proven then. The search party had turned up no sign of a wild bear or pack of wolves, and Walker was confident that the town could now get back to the business of everyday life.

The following day, Walker had just brought food to his prisoner when Chase came in, a blank expression on his face. "Marshal," he said in a weary voice, "you better come. There's been another."

Walker passed his hand over his face in disbelief. "Who is it this time?"

It was Helen Powers, wife of the general store owner. She was lying in an alley between her home and the store. Jim Powers was cradling her body in his arms, his glassy eyes staring out at nothing. When the doctor arrived, Marshal Walker gently pulled Jim to his feet and led him away from the scene.

"I was working late last night," Jim explained, "counting my store stock. Helen was supposed to bring my dinner to me. I didn't notice what time it was until the sun came up. I was worried, so I went home."

"You didn't notice her in the alley then?" Walker asked.

Powers shook his head. "I took a different way home. The children were up already and were worried that neither of us was home. I became frightened for her and walked back to the store, this time using the same path Helen always took." His voice broke. Jim Powers buried his face in his hands. "That's when I saw her."

When the body had been carted off to the undertaker's, the marshal walked Jim Powers home, then went back to the office. His deputy and the posse were crowded into the small room when he walked in.

Chase looked up. "Marshal, I think you'd better talk to these men. They want to lynch that Indian right now."

Walker sighed. "Gentlemen, he's been in jail for two nights. He definitely didn't kill Helen Powers, and I don't think I can hold him for the murders of the other two. I'm beginning to think it *is* some sort of animal we're looking for." He sat behind his desk, the men moving over to him.

"Marshal, something has to be done about these killings," Eldon said. "If this continues, we ain't gonna have no womenfolk left."

Brady Tucker spoke up. "The mayor's callin' a town meeting tonight."

Since there was no town hall in Lacey, Walker knew the meeting would take place at a saloon. "Where are you holding this meeting?"

Eldon replied, "The Red Bucket. After dinner."

The men left the marshal's office, considerably more calm than when they'd come in.

With a sigh, Walker headed back to the cells. The Indian was crouched in a corner of his cell, rocking back and forth and muttering to himself. He looked up sharply at Walker.

Unlocking the cell door, Walker addressed the Indian. "I'm letting you go now. Another woman was killed last night and unless you can be in two places at once, there's no reason to hold you."

The Indian didn't move. His unblinking stare unnerved Walker, who moved inside and took the prisoner's arm. "Did you hear me? I said you can go now."

The Indian whimpered and backed against the wall. Walker grabbed both of his arms and hauled him out of the cell. "You're free," he shouted in exasperation, dragging the uncomprehending Shoshone toward the door. "Here, you can go." Walker lightly shoved the Indian into the street. He watched the former prisoner stand there dazed, blinking in the sunlight, a terrified look on his face. Walker reluctantly closed the door, wondering what would become of him, this forlorn man who had lost his entire tribe.

That evening, The Red Bucket had more business than it could handle. Although it was the largest saloon in town, people were filling up every nook and cranny in the place. A large, bar-length mirror was a recent addition to The Red Bucket and never failed to attract ladies into the saloon for a chance to preen at their reflection and, perhaps while they were there, to order a lemonade on a hot day.

The mayor stood on a wooden crate in the front corner of the room, talking to the uneasy crowd.

"I can assure you that Marshal Walker is doing all he can on this matter," Mayor Mosley was saying. "I have a meeting with him tomorrow morning to discuss what can be done to halt these killings."

This was news to Walker, but then it was typical for Mosley to stick his head in the sand until things got bad. Then he talked about meetings and began pointing fingers at everyone else. Walker couldn't see who spoke up next. "What good is a meeting between you and the marshal when our womenfolk are gettin' killed right and left?"

Murmurs of assent and dissatisfaction traveled through the restless crowd. Walker could see the panic in Mayor Mosley's expression until he suddenly locked his gaze on Walker. "There's Marshal Walker right now. Why don't we ask him how the investigation is going?"

Hands pushed and shoved Walker toward the soapbox. He suddenly found himself facing the worried and angry expressions of the townsfolk of Lacey.

"When will these killings stop?" One voice shouted above the rest.

"When will the streets be safe for our womenfolk to walk at night?" said another anonymous voice.

Walker raised his arms to quiet the crowd. "My deputy and I are doing the best we can, but there are no clues to follow. The only advice I can give is to stay in your homes at night, menfolk too. If you must go out, make sure there are several people with you."

"But Mrs. Holder was killed in her home," someone pointed out. Walker frowned, not sure how to answer.

He scanned the crowd. His thoughts drifted to the Count, who apparently hadn't been told of the meeting.

A woman screamed. There was silence and confusion for a moment, then Walker realized that it came from outside. He leapt off his makeshift podium and headed toward the door, the crowd miraculously parting for him. As he crossed the saloon threshold and stepped onto the boardwalk, his eyes had to adjust to the dark. A shadowy black shape was hunched over in the street near The Red Bucket. The figure held the unconscious body of a young woman, no more than nineteen or twenty, her throat torn and bloody.

Walker boldly stepped closer, peering at the shape. For a moment, he could have sworn it was a wolf, a huge black wolf with eyes like glowing coals. But as the figure rose, he realized that it was Dracula.

"What are you doing?" Walker shouted. Count Dracula turned and glared at the marshal, his only answer a guttural snarl. The night was dark, but the Count's face glowed white in the moonlight. His mouth was smeared with blood. He began to move toward the marshal. Walker hesitated, a cold chill running through him. He knew he should go to the girl, but he had the feeling that he wouldn't get the chance to find out if she was still alive. "Don't come any closer," he said, knowing full well the warning would do no good. Dracula advanced as Walker drew his gun.

The marshal fired three shots directly into Dracula's chest. At least he thought he did. At this distance, he couldn't have missed, but the creature kept coming toward him. He felt himself shiver as he backed up into the saloon.

Most of the people in the saloon had fallen silent, but a few voices in the back were heard to ask, "What's happening? Who screamed? What was that shootin' about?"

Gus, the town drunk, stood directly in front of Marshal Walker. "You look like you just seen a ghost! Have a drink."

He handed Walker a shot glass full of whiskey. Ed reached out to take it and saw that his hands were shaking. He threw back the shot even as he heard the crowd gasp. Turning around, he saw the demonic face of Count Dracula peering over the bat-wing doors of the saloon. The room went deathly quiet, and then Gus spoke.

"Well, what are you waitin' for," the drunk hiccuped, "an engraved invitation?" Walker shuddered as Gus said to the Count, "Come the hell on in."

Count Dracula needed no more prodding. He walked through the doors as if they weren't even there—as if he had no more substance than fog. The crowd, as one, stepped back in fear.

"Look in the mirror!" someone shouted.

Marshal Walker, his gun in hand, took his eyes off the apparition before him for just a moment and looked to the mirror. He could see himself and the saloon doors, but Dracula's image was not where it should have been."

"You have no reflection," Walker muttered.

Gus overheard him and leaned over. "You seein' what I'm seein'? I thought it was the drink."

Dracula smiled a terrible smile on his thin, pale lips. He looked younger, his hair darker, than when Walker first saw him.

"The charade has ended," Count Dracula announced. He swept his cloak across his face, then smiled fully, revealing fangs as large and deadly as a wolf's.

Unexpectedly, a young tough, Mike Grady, threw himself at Count Dracula.

Dracula hissed and caught Grady easily, snapping his back as if the boy were a dry twig. He tossed Grady against the opposite wall.

Pandemonium erupted, townspeople running toward the exits like stampeding cattle, some throwing themselves out the windows. Walker's head was reeling. The place was now empty, except for Walker, Dracula, and a young woman who now struggled in the creature's grip. Walker recognized her as the new schoolteacher.

"Let her go, whatever you are," Walker said. His voice was shaky, but his gun was trained on the Count. "Let her go or I'll shoot."

The Count only laughed and stepped forward. "Here. Let me make it easier for you."

Walker fired once, twice, three times—the bullets penetrating the monster's fine linen shirt. But there was no blood. Count Dracula's laughter echoed in the nearly empty saloon. A terrible truth dawned on Ed Walker and he felt his gun dropping to the floor as he said in a hoarse whisper, "You're the black wolf, the one who killed an entire Shoshone village. What kind of devil are you?"

"I am the Prince of Darkness. I am the Lord of the Undead. Nosferatu. King of the Vampires. Vlad Dracul. Vlad the Impaler. The Dragon. Count Dracula. My name is legion."

Walker felt frozen, paralyzed, as the Count turned his attention to the schoolteacher, her eyes wide with terror. A whimper escaped her lips as she tried to free herself.

"No, no," she cried, "please no."

The Count was beginning to pull her high collar away from her neck when a gold necklace came untangled and fell free. A small cross hung on the chain. Dracula hissed sharply and pushed her away. She fell to the floor, then scrambled to her feet and ran toward the back door.

Now Dracula turned his attention toward the marshal. Walker faced Count Dracula, certain that he was about to die.

Dracula growled and grabbed Walker's shirtfront, lifting the marshal off his feet. Dangling in midair, Walker tried to twist out of the monster's grip, but found that he could not look away from Dracula's eyes, which were now as red as his victims' blood. Walker's will to escape slowly drained away, leaving him limp and unable to struggle. Dracula bared his deadly yellow fangs. Walker shuddered and said a silent prayer as he waited helplessly to die.

But instead of feeling the vampire's bite, Walker felt the monster lurch, his grip suddenly weakening. The marshal fell with a thud to the dusty saloon floor. He watched as Dracula clutched at his chest with clawlike hands. The monster, blood spewing from his mouth, let out an unearthly scream, then spun around, trying to get at the slim wooden arrow embedded in the center of his back. He clawed at it frantically, ineffectually, as he seemed to age by decades each second. His hair turned white, his skin wrinkled, and he crumbled to dust before his screams stopped echoing in the cleared out saloon.

Walker reached out to touch the arrow that lay in the midst of the pile of dust and rags that had once been Count Dracula. A Shoshone arrow. The marshal stood and turned to see the lone survivor of Dracula's attack on the Shoshone village. The Indian stood just inside the back door, his face painted, a bow gripped tightly in his hand. He looked directly, calmly, into Walker's eyes.

"The black wolf," he said, and turned and walked back out into the night.

BLOOD DRIVE

by
Rex Miller

Night in the besieged city: a coven of thirsty river gul-lymen, lips bloodied in crimson sludge fresh and tacky as 10W40 times glue, sat idling under a Vaseline Alley arc, its pale light bathing the street below in weird lavender.

Aletha, her Barbie waist bound in silver chain, posed on the hood of the lead burner.

"Come **on**," she whined, her full lips orchid in the arc light.

From an unseen speaker, Fogbound Dogpound rocked "Clumsy Stumblin Barefoot Rattler Round-Up Blues" out of high-end audio.

They were stalkers. They could almost smell their target across Barlow inside Fastfood, and every time J'Velle caught a glimpse of her shapely brown legs in white sandals, or her edible bulge of calf and curva-ceous thigh, he made a low growl in his throat. Tasting it. The luminous clock on the dash of his command burner moved its minute hand to 10:02. Across the blacktop he could see they were shutting down for the night.

There were thirteen of them driving four stripped-down dune jobs. A full mill, four-barrel Fisher 660 on a tubular steel chassis with frame seats, tank, racing slicks, roll bars, and a jolly roger on the whip. Flat black burners meant to do only one thing.

You saw a quad convoy of black buggies roaring through the night you had no question who it was:

river gullymen. The dune buggies were their logo.
They owned the Northeast and some of the Southeast
section of the city. The river gullymen ran everything
from River Avenue to the North all the way to Southtown. There was a bit of contested turf down around
the stock pens that the other side claimed. But most
of the Eastern half was r.g. turf.

The ravenites, which were two gangs in one, the old
West K-Town mob and the Midnight Drovers com-
bined, ran everything West of Vaseline Alley. The strip
of North Street that bisected the old part of downtown
was nicknamed Vaseline Alley for the things that rou-
tinely took place there. It was where the decadent
cults, the vampire gangs, the dopers, the gangsta
pervs, and the occult practitioners plied their sordid
trades.

This was a coven of thirteen Southtown blasters,
river gullymen trolling for blood and meat. They were
in the parking lot of an abandoned storefront on Barlow, across from Fastfood, a burger joint. They'd eye-
balled a little vulnerable mama and they were waiting
to cut her out of the pack, both figuratively and literally.

At a few minutes past ten she came out in her Fastfood costume and they silently jumped into the dune
jobs. Robbie, amorphous sixteen-year-old, behind the
wheel. All the Pseudohermaphrodites—as opposed to
merely androgynous gullymen—packed the lead
buggy. Robbie was the ultimate wheelman, with lightning reflexes and a physical inability to accept second
place. Two of them were adreno-genital types, with
endocrine vampirism. That was black, ziggurat-headed
Neff and the young girl Lady. But the other two, Zee-
dee, the tall zipperheaded tattoo boy in pearls and basic black, and Robbie, were 46 double-X and 46 XYs
respectively; XX ovarians with ovotesticular XYs.
Vampire mosaics.

Boigerlz from Boise was driver of the car that rode

the point man's slack, and packed in with him were tiny Prew, beautiful Aletha, Texas—their sniper hunter-killer, and handsome, long-haired Clean—whose complexion and skin sores could scarcely be viewed. They were all homosexual, transexual, or transvestite X-linked recessives with vampiric karyotypes.

Deadest, the mustachioed pirate, wearing six gold earrings in each ear, drove the third car with Tanker sprawled in the special seat. Tanker weighed 870 pounds, give or take an eighth of a ton. Both of these gullymen were X chromosome anomalies.

Superspiked Bad Bob drove the tail car with their leader in the back, controlling a 93 kg vehicle-mounted STRYK missile. It had a 4000 meter range, 900 mm ap capability, and fired a 6 kg warhead. J'Velle, the head boy of the thirteen gullymen, could ice a prowl team at three miles. His eyes constantly swept the scene for the distinctive scalloped-edge bat-tails of the enemy. The ravenites drove heavily-armored but slow moving low riders; powerful behemoths with windows like mail slots; lowered, chopped, channeled vans and specials; always in black, burnt orange, and sienna. "Fagmobiles" as J'Velle called them. Both spiky Bad Bob and the honcho were vampiric intersexers, although Bob had ambiguous external genitalia.

All thirteen of them were deadboys—taints to the man—the lot of them carrying the curse, as it was called. Ghettoblood. Call it what you will—the end result was the same. They were doomed vampires—one and all.

The young girl started the engine of her parents' moss green Lumina sedan, pulled out of the Fastfood lot, and headed west down Barlow.

"4 to car 1. Read?" The driver of the first car, Robbie, answered.

"Loud and clear."

"Let the livestock mosey." J'Velle said over the two-way.

"Affirmative." Robbie tapped the brake a couple of times and the quad convoy sat patiently on line as the girl put distance between herself and them. When she was nothing but red taillights, Robbie wheeled it on out and kicked ass.

They sped through Belfast Gully, the girl in her Lumina rocking along about 60, well ahead of them. Belfast Gully, a ghetto infamous for being the site of a terrible ravenites/river gullymen war, was a stinking maze of alleys faced in crumbling concrete, flattened soda cans, corrugated tin doors, and rusting signs for roofs.

They shot by houses advertising McCann's Ice Cream, Lime Kiln, Waverly Milk, Old Dutch Cleanser, Conoco, Trojans, Drummond's Restaurant, and Tallymon Malt Liquor, as part of their embattled facades.

On the other edge of Belfast Gully the girl hung a left and entered a darkened and silent residential section. There was an absence of traffic.

"4 to car 1. Kill the lights."

"Yo." The convoy was running on black. The Lumina went up a winding driveway and parked in front of a rich two-story Colonial.

She was getting out of the vehicle, taking something out of the backseat, when Aletha, Prew, Boigerlz, Clean and Texas hit her in that sequence.

Model-gorgeous blonde-haired Aletha with her exquisite cheekbones and full-lipped smile; heartbreakingly beautiful, full breasted, tiny waisted, high-assed; long-legged figure a blur of motion, came up in the darkness and severed her left leg at the knee just as Prew drove a sharp thing into her back. Boigerlz and Clean each swung at the head and neck, and Clean's blade decapitated her. Tex chopped a hand off and sucked bloodflow from the wrist.

The second crew to reach her, the lead car, and the third car's heavy load, all descended on the body more or less simultaneously. Bad Bob and J'Velle came along and took their hits, and while everybody was orally drinking their leader began fusing the torso.

It was a sloppy way to do it, but some members of the gang were fairly zooted, and drinking it at least got that stuff into the bloodstream, even if it wasn't effective as a straight fuse. It was blood, that was the thing, and it came from an untainted human. When you were chilled down, that was all that mattered. Getting that rich red taste.

It would take ten or fifteen minutes to exsanguinate her fully, and J'Velle and a couple of the others who weren't as zooted out as the rest herded the crews back in their dune jobs. Everybody had a piece of the girl, a hand, a foot and part of a leg—something—so they could feed and take the sting off until they got back home and could fuse a pint properly.

What with bloodspill and other random factors, it would take at least one more straight kill to meet the needs of the thirteen river gullymen for that night.

Deadest looked over at Tanker feeding.

"You're fucking disgusting, you know that?"

He had the head and his face was down in the "trough." Deadest thought he looked and sounded like a huge hog, a fucking sow, with his face dripping, getting his blood all over the vehicle, making a loud slurping noise as he fed.

Tanker only sucked harder in response.

* * *

An attractive woman in her late thirties with streaked, dark blonde hair worn medium length, a pleasant face, and a somewhat stern expression, paced the length of the small conference room. Her name was Ellen DuChamp. Her official title was Senior Councilperson, but that said nothing about the clout she wielded. She was dressed in a dark navy power suit with an expensive silk blouse and very little jewelry.

"We've got to do something." She shook her head rapidly back and forth, chewing the corner of her lower lip.

"I'm aware of that," the man on the sofa said. He was fat in the stomach and through the lower face. Rubbery fat hung from his jowls and belly, but he was not heavy looking in the face, chest, or elsewhere. He had trim, muscular athlete's legs, for some reason, which had never gone to fat. He was proud of his "slam dunk ass," his jocular name for his butt, which was hard as rock, like his legs—which had served him well as a younger man. Nobody seeing City Administrator Al Ghieri for the first time would guess that he'd been a famous basketball star in high school. That was too many filets ago. Too much hollandaise sauce under the asparagus; a river of drawn butter had dripped over the lobster since those days.

He wore clear, square rimmed glasses. He had neat, short dark hair, olive skin, a bulbous nose, and very white teeth which he displayed frequently in a politician's ready smile.

"They've got to go." DuChamp said firmly. "Whatever it takes."

"Right."

"Let's get this Vilicuva. He's behind them. Those are *his* people. I think it's all drugs. That's the key. The common bond that links the gangs and the big players. The violence always boils down to the same two things—drugs and blood."

"Let's hear Dante's report and take it one step at a time."

"I'm just saying if it's calling out the military—if it's getting the governor to declare the city an emergency war zone—whatever it takes, we have to stop the slaughter."

"I hear you. Your constituency is my constituency.

I know what everybody's saying—wipe out the vampire gangs. That's all well and good, but when you're cutting people loose from prison who have the virus, and they go out and get recruited by bleeders—you're creating the very people you want eradicated. There's no end to the circle.''

"The point is to make an example. We've got to show serious force. Do something." She stopped pacing and flopped down in a chair. Ghieri took up nearly half of a sofa with his bulk and he had to fight to get himself on his feet. With a great grunt he managed to stand and shook out the trousers of his suit where they'd been pressed into wrinkles by his corpulent heft.

"You ready?" he asked.

"Yeah." She nodded, and he walked over and opened the conference room door, smiling, and extending his hand to the P.I. who was waiting in the anteroom.

"Come in, Johnny."

The investigator entered the conference room. He was a short, wiry man with very black hair and eyebrows, dark, heavy-lidded eyes, and a fleshy mouth. Johnny Dante, a/k/a John Michael Dantiova, who'd been bounced out of Wackenhut, Pinkerton's, and other big time shops for one thing and another, held a sheaf of papers and a tape recorder.

"Hello." He acknowledged the woman's presence.

"Hi," she said. "What about Vilicuva?" she asked, getting right to it.

"Okay. I'll give you the bottom line first, all right?" he said. Nobody had offered him a seat. Ghieri flopped back down on the sofa, glad to take the load off. He nodded. "He's willing to do a deal. He'll take them out—that is, he said he'll make it possible for us to round them up. He claims he'll set them up for his price."

"What's the price?" she asked.

"You'll be as surprised as I was. It's not drugs or money. He wants blood."

"You're kidding."

"Nope. He wants us to make a citywide blood drive for fresh, untainted blood. A twenty-five-year contract of so many fresh units per week. In other words, run a continuing drive like the Red Cross does, but he gets the blood."

"Jesus! So he is a vampire."

"In a manner of speaking. I got the whole report. You want to hear everything?"

"Of course," Ghieri said. Dante looked at his notes and began.

"Department of Motor Vehicles trace on S. L. Vilicuva's Special Model Checker stretch-type limousine, (vanity tags: "666"), Customized Dodge Security Van, (vanity tags: "ABO-Rh"), and Mack Road Warrior, (vanity tags: "MONSTER"), indicate corporate registration by Roundhouse Industries, Incorporated, whose current incorporation taxes have been paid by Inter-Cities Accounting Ltd., licensed in Belmont County, and listed as official leasor on said vehicles, which are registered in the name of the leasing company, and subleased to "Dealer S. L. Vilicuva." He looked up. "Which—by the way—happens to be an anagram for Evil Dracula Lives."

"Abstract, tax, and property traces: Roundhouse Industries, Inc. is owner of record of the two warehouses on Wildwood to the west of 1 Sunset Drive. The two buildings are Leather Products Manufacturing, Inc. and Warehouse Imports Ltd., both registered to Roundhouse as per the DMV registrations. These two buildings are located between Wildwood and West River Avenue, and south of Shadow Lane. Casablackstone Storage and City Generators Inc. are the two buildings on the opposite side of 1 Sunset Drive. They are between East River and Ash, and to the south of Riverfront Woods. Same owner of record. Our investigation with the utilities people revealed that all of the buildings are interlinked with underground tunnels. This area could be where his disposal system, threat sensors, generators, and underground warehouses are located. It's likely he has other ways of entering Casablackstone besides the Sunset Drive street level vehicle and pedestrian entranceways.

"Now as to the audio surveillance." He held up the recorder.

"On his surveilled numbers 826-7473 and 372-2852, the tapes reveal four alternating variations on the same prerecorded message. The messages were professionally recorded at American Audion, a telemarketing services company licensed and bonded in Belmont County. Its corporation taxes have been paid up, and there are no ties between American Audion and Mr. Vilicuva. The service and equipment was paid for by a front corporation also licensed and bonded in Belmont County, Mid-Continent Health Services, Incorporated, which is in turn owned by an out-of-state holding company, Medco Industries, owned by an anonymous party. A typical prerecorded message ran as follows." Dante hit Play.

"What do you desire in life that you cannot legally obtain? Drugs? Bomb-grade plutonium? Your ex-husband's present address? The combination to your employer's safe? A new identity? Wealth? Sexual liaisons outside of what is considered 'the norm'? A masterpiece that currently hangs in your favorite museum? Everything is available for the right price, and that price is not always money. What do you have for trade? If you can offer a scarce commodity, perform a special service, or produce a rare item that someone else desires, we may be able to match your barter goods or services up with a party who can give you that thing you want above all else. For discreet information about our unique exchange contact Warehouse Imports today. Write or call dealer S. L. Vilicuva for particulars. The address is Casablackstone, 1 Sunset Drive. To leave a recorded message, if you have a touch-tone phone press 1 now. . . . if you wish to leave a recorded message and you have a pulse phone press 2 now.''

Johnny Dante stopped the playback unit.

''On the morning of the twentieth, at approximately 9:30 A.M., this operative parked in the customer parking area on the east side of the office building located at 1 Sunset Drive, and rang the front door buzzer. The following recording, which is cataloged as Covert Recording 5-S, was made at that time.'' He touched Play again.

(Buzzer sound)

Voice on monitor:

''Good morning, may we help you?''

Operative:

''Yes. Good morning. My name is Johnny Dante. I have an appointment to speak with Mr. Vilicuva.''

Voice on monitor:

''Yes, Mr. Dante. Will you come in, please?''

(Electronic sound, sound of door opening.)

''At this point,'' Dante explained, ''I entered the building. I found myself in a brightly-lit room which was furnished with the sort of seating one finds in the lobby or foyer of a typical upscale business office. The area is approximately forty feet wide by fifteen feet deep. A long section of the area was unfurnished. A door opened and an electronic voice could be heard on the speakers around the room. It was a female voice and prerecorded.'' Dante clicked the playback unit back on.

Voice on monitor:

''Mr. Dante, please come in and take a seat.''

(Sound of door closing.)

Voice on monitor:

''Make yourself comfortable, sir. Mr. Vilicuva will be with you very soon.

"Meanwhile, please listen to this brief recording, which is intended to help familiarize you with our services, and answer questions which we have found many persons have; questions about donor requirements, safety, company goals, and trade procedures. We also provide you with a booklet which answers other questions not covered in this introductory session, so please help yourself to one or more of the booklets you see in the tray on the desk.

"As you were informed when you phoned for your appointment, our company charges one pint of blood as an initial consultation fee. The reason we do this is simple: because of the nature of our business many persons would arrange appointments out of curiosity, or for other motives, which would not result in mutual barter agreements. The unusual fee of a pint of the donor's blood, given in advance, precludes many of the curious from taking up Mr. Vilicuva's time. This pint of blood does not in any way indicate that a deal is in effect, either implicit or explicit, between our company and yourself. This fee is immediately forfeitable should Mr. Vilicuva decline to enter into an agreement with you. If you wish to leave please press the large button on the desk marked **EXIT**. If you wish to hear the rest of this message, press the small button on the desk marked **CONTINUE**. . . . Thank you.

"Before we can accept your pint of blood, two things must occur: (1.) we must test your blood to determine that it is acceptable, and (2.) you must sign a contract giving us permission to (a.) test your blood, and (b.) collect one pint of your blood should that test prove satisfactory to us. The contract, which is a simple agreement, is to the left of the plastic tray on the desk. While you're welcome to look at it at any time, we ask you **not** to sign it at this juncture, prior to your complete understanding of our terms. There is a large button on the desk marked **QUESTION**. Later, following this recording, and before you are tested, you will have an opportunity to ask questions. Please do not ask those questions until this recording ends.

"There are general safety guidelines which protect us mutually, and these must be adhered to if you are to act as a blood donor.

"You must weigh at least 110 pounds, whether you are male or female. If you are unsure of your weight, an accurate scale can be found to the left of the desk. Feel free to weigh yourself now. . . .

"If you have ever tested HIV positive, tested positive for AIDS antibodies, or have been exposed to anyone with AIDS, if you have sickle cell anemia, epilepsy, heart disease, or cancer, you may not donate. A minor skin cancer or several minor skin cancers do not count as cancer for our testing purposes.

"If, during the past 36 months, you have had malaria, or been the recipient of suppressive therapy for malaria, had rabies, German measles, yellow fever, oral polio, or mumps, we ask you not to test.

"If you're a female and have had a baby or an abortion, including by C-section or other means, you cannot donate for at least one year. If you have had a RhoGAM injection, you cannot donate for at least one year. If you are pregnant, you cannot donate.

"If you have consumed alcohol during the last twelve hours, please do not test. If you have taken acetaminophen or Tylenol, please do not test for at least twelve hours after taking.

"If you have received blood, plasma, or serum, or had surgery including minor outpatient surgery during the last six months, please do not attempt to test or donate.

"If you have had jaundice or any form of hepatitis, please do not test or donate.

"Now, here are some of the questions we are most often asked:

"*What happens when I am tested?* Our Automatic Infection-protection Donor System uses a sanitary autolet to prick your finger. A drop of blood is obtained in a capillary tube, placed in copper sulfate and an initial test is made. If you are rejected or deferred, you can try again in a week. Your body temperature, pulse rate, blood pressure, red cell ratio, and iron level are also automatically taken at that time.

"Does the test hurt? No."

Again, Dante stopped the playback unit.

"At this point a screen on the desk advised me in English and Spanish that if I wished to leave I could do so and if I wanted to be tested for possible donor purposes I should approach the interior door. I went to the door and was told to press a certain switch, and after doing so, the door opened and closed behind me as I entered the room. It was a very sterile appearing room with only two pieces of furniture, a white metal table and chair. There was an envelope with my name on it on the table. I opened it and found a typed card informing me to remove my recording devices, all microphones, any minicameras I might have, and place them on the desk. I did so, fully expecting the unit or at least the tape to be confiscated or erased. As you heard, it was not.

"Then another voice on the monitor speaker told me to go through the next door and be seated. Looking in, I saw a large device a bit like a dentist's chair, the arms of which had built-in equipment for testing. I went through the blood test, and after a few minutes was allowed to donate a pint of blood. Everything was automatic and extremely efficient. When I'd paid the fee, I was permitted to speak with Vilicuva or a person claiming to be him.

"I remained in the testing chair, and his voice came on the room speaker. He asked me what I wanted and I told him that I represented the city. Explained what you had said to me. He wasn't surprised, by the way. He of course denied at first that he was involved in any way with the gangs, but when I offered to strike a deal with him for a negotiated sum, in exchange for controlling the murders, he made his counteroffer. He was not interested in money or confiscated narcotics, but if we would keep him in fresh blood products he would make it possible for us to wipe out the warring gang factions. That's his phrase—"wipe out." In return for one hundred and forty fresh units of blood per week, every week, fresh **untainted** blood, for a period of twenty-five years, he will do the deal. He—"

"WHAT?" The woman in the room was incredulous. "A hundred and forty units a **week**?"

"Yes, ma'am. That's his price. He said if the city ever decided to double-cross him certain action would be taken that would—" he glanced at his notes again— "in effect destroy the city."

"How can he guarantee that we can wipe them out?" The obese City Administrator asked.

"He said the map would speak for itself." Dante unfolded a map he'd been carrying in his jacket pocket. He showed it to the fat man. It depicted a cutaway view of the Vaseline Alley area of K-Town where the doomed vampire gangs—the "ragers"—the decadent cults, and the dope and perve gangbangers had their turf. Vilicuva's map showed how the underworld of the city was a maze of tunnels, drainage pipes, utility conduits, and pilings. It was marked MEETING CHAMBER at one place far below the city.

"This is an emergency area for citywide gang conferences. It's only been used a couple of times, he claims. If we'll agree to supply him with the blood he wants, he'll arrange with the gang leaders to call an emergency session of all the vampires.

"The chamber is in a huge underground catacomb that was once part of the old slave railway. There literally was an underground railway, he says—and this was where it originated. The tunnels are simple to block. Once the gangs are in place we could dispose of them effectively by several different means, explosive charges, poison gas, or even by flooding the chambers. As part of the deal, he would aid in the logistics of their eradication.''

Ghieri handed the map to Ellen DuChamp with a grunt of effort and she examined it. The details were remarkable: she saw gas and electricity pipes, duct banks, the innards of the city's water supply and sewage system, storm drains, conduits, phone cables, slurry walls, and foundation piers that supported the crumbling city. The chamber was clearly marked down to the detail of a street-level entranceway through an electrical manhole ''chimney.'' It looked like an excellent spot for a subterranean ambush, theoretically easy to seal off and where a series of blasts or a deadly infusion of poisonous gas could be safely contained.

''He guarantees he can get them all down there?'' she asked.

''That's what he says.''

She looked at the fat administrative head.

''I say, let's do the deal.''

''Um.'' The heavy man on the sofa pursed his thick lips for a moment as if in deep thought. ''Okay. Tell him it's a done deal.''

* * *

S. L. Vilicuva, dealer, the king of counterculture barter, was pleased to hear the news.

''You did well, Johnny.''

''Thanks, Mr. V,'' the private eye said.

''Go ahead and enjoy yourself. You've earned it. I'll be upstairs. We'll talk later if you like.''

''Yes, sir,'' he said. He sat back in the chair and prepared for the strike of the snake fang that would begin his total cleansing. It had been so simple to engineer the thing. A basic campaign of terror, Mr. V had called it. He relaxed as the old blood drained from one arm and the fresh, untainted fluid filled his thirsty system.

Upstairs, alone in his elevator, lined in black coffin silk, a small, very frail old man waited for the bump that signaled the arrival at the third floor. He pushed the door button and stepped into his interior security vault, where the auxiliary generator system was barely audible, and then into his spacious fumigation and sleeping vault. The vault had a sun/moon roof which was opened for brief periods daily when he was not in occupancy. His smell had become a serious health hazard.

Although Vilicuva derived a degree of pleasure and comfort from long soaks in scented bubble bath, his steadily deteriorating skin condition imposed a number of problems that could potentially create a threat to his welfare. He was constantly looking for better surveillance and monitoring equipment with which to thwart potential high-flying aircraft that might try salting the atmosphere with crystals of invisible poison to "rain" down on his sleeping chamber. He didn't fully trust the chemical sensors in the same way he'd learned to trust his blood testing devices, which were state of the art.

The notion that vampires were immortal was just one of the bits of lunacy about his people. The myths had started for obvious reasons: for example, because clinical vampirism retarded the aging process one's peers always predeceased a vampire, helping to give rise to the bit about them living forever. To the contrary, they could be destroyed by many means more prosaic than wooden stakes and silver bullets: they could be run over, get cancer, or slash their pathetic wrists and **bleed** to death. The usual death menu applied.

The idea of a V not having a reflected image in a looking glass was nonsense. We reflect, he mused, we just don't enjoy the view. Vilicuva had skin the color and texture of burnt marshmallow. Vampires couldn't tolerate the sun? Vampires couldn't tolerate **stupidity.** Older Vs did find all light uncomfortable, but certainly bearable.

Dealing with the straights was always odious, and he did not look forward to having to help eradicate some unruly children, but it was not as if he might be aiding in the execution of **clinical** vampires—these infected kids had nothing but agony ahead of them.

He felt very tired. Tired blood was no joke. He would fuse soon. If "straights" thought chronic arthritis pain was severe, they should transfuse a couple of times a day at his age. His body was so sore it was all he could do to sit or recline on a pile of pillows.

True vampires such as himself generally tended to suicide before the process of decomposition began. The pain and disorientation would eventually begin to be too great. Even total transfusions would not be enough. Yet human nature forced one to continue to try to survive—in a medicated, intoxicated, drugged parody of extreme old age. It was, he thought, Dracula's legacy, the ultimate curse of the undead. The slow, lonely, frightening atrophy of the night people . . . who decompose without dying.

HARD TIMES

by
Bentley Little

She could not forgive him for the way he died.

He had always been so strong, so tough, so unapologetically macho, and though she'd often chided him for it, that hypermasculinity had appealed to her, had been one of the things about him she had found most attractive.

But when they shot him, when the first bullet entered his gut, he began screaming like a girl, emitting high-pitched cries of terror and pain that she would not have believed his vocal cords capable of making. He fell to the ground, still screaming, his face all red and twisted, tears streaming from his eyes, and his screaming grew worse as the other slugs were pumped into his body. She smelled shit, saw a stain spread across the front of his pants as he pissed himself. The gang members ran, not bothering with her, and she stood there as he cried in his piss shit pants and begged her to hold him.

She was screaming too, so utterly terrified that she could neither move nor think straight, but somewhere deep inside her, in a secret place beneath the pain and horror and panic and grief, she looked upon him with disgust, unable to forgive him for his weakness even as the life bled out of him.

And then *he* was there.

Afterward, she realized that she had not seen where the man in black had come from. Indeed, she had not seen him come from anywhere. He had simply appeared, standing suddenly between her and Rafael's body. He was there for only a moment, bending over Rafael, then lifting him and carrying him off, running but not running, speeding somehow, disappearing into the darkness. She had seen the man's face for the briefest second, a flash of alabaster in the moonlight, but in that second she had noted the hardness of his features, the firmness of his jaw, the coldness of his eyes, and the force of that first impression stayed with her when the police arrived, while the detectives interrogated her, and long after.

They'd found Rafael two hours later, in an alley off Olympic, shriveled and drained of blood.

Drained of blood.

A vampire?

She'd visibly blanched when told of the state of the body, shocked but . . . but somehow not surprised. There'd been something inhuman about the man in black, something superhuman about his strength as he'd picked up Rafael's body and run. She'd known that instantly. He had ignored her completely, though she knew he had seen her, and the sense of menace he'd exuded was far different, far more profound, than the everyday physical threat posed by the gang members and their guns. It frightened her even now to think about him.

But she thought about him anyway.

She found that she liked to think about him.

* * *

His thirst was slaked, his body sated, his physical needs more than met.

Still he remained unsatisfied.

He knew the cause but did not want to acknowledge it. He stared down at the shrunken husk at his feet, an old lady who'd been living out of a shopping cart until she'd had the misfortune to stumble upon him while he was drinking. He touched her once with the toe of his shoe, felt bone, heard the whisper of dried skin. Scowling now, he kicked her. Hard. Her rib cage shattered, and when he kicked her again, harder, her left leg broke off with a muffled crack.

Angry more with himself than anything else, he whirled away from her and was off, becoming one with the darkness, speeding unthinkingly toward home though dawn was still several hours away.

Home.

He called it that, but it was not really home to him. He had no home, could never have a home again. He had only lodgings, places where he slept.

He arrived at his dwelling, a bungalow in Laurel Canyon, emerging from the shadowed darkness into the open moonlight. Deeply shaded by hills and closely growing trees, it was acceptable, the closest he could come to adequate in this sun-drenched, darkness-forsaken land. He glanced disdainfully around at the house as he walked inside. It served his purposes, but it was not what he would have chosen for himself had he had an option. It was, he acknowledged, a huge step down from his European accommodations.

In the old country he had had a castle, in England a mansion.

Why had he ever come to America?

He knew full well why he had come to America, though it pained him to admit it now. The fame. His never-ending search for immortality. He stared into the mirror in the foyer, saw no reflection, only the hat rack on the wall behind him. He had achieved physical immortality long ago by becoming one of the undead, but he had eventually come to realize that it was not enough. He wanted more. He wanted the immortality granted to Grendel and Beowulf, to Odysseus and Oedipus, to Hamlet and Macbeth. He wanted the immortality afforded by art.

And he had found it.

In the nineteenth century, he had been in his glory. Then he had been the stuff of legend. His acts had been transformed by artists into art, by art into myth. His exploits had been inspiration for the finest minds and talents of the age. His seductions had been renowned, his kills even more so. Flaubert had made the cause of Emma Bovary's death self-poisoning, but it had been his exquisite exsanguination that had really brought about her much desired demise, and it was his dark shadow that lurked behind the overly precise descriptions of the book. Tolstoy had seen in him a profound despair, Hardy an anger at the inevitability of fate, and both had had heroines commit sacrificial suicide in his honor, Anna Karenina's death as well as that of Eustacia Vye a genuflection to the unfathomable darkness of his never-ending need.

Even his inspiration of that third-rate hack Stoker had resulted in art, his existence the source of the sole spark of greatness in that otherwise undistinguished literary career. Ironically, it was Stoker's portrayal of him, not those of other greater lights, that had caught the world's fancy and had lasted in the public's eye through succeeding generations, and it was that portrayal he had striven to emulate and embellish upon. He had been absurdly flattered by the attention drawn to him, and he had loved to hear others speaking his name: "Dracula."

He had been at his peak then, his dual strivings toward immortality dovetailing perfectly, and each kill had been a work of genius, a consummate act of artistry in itself.

Rodin had come to him. And Mahler. His status and influence in the European artistic community had been unparalleled.

It was the films he did not like, and it was the films that had eventually led to his downfall. They had taken him too literally, tried to make concrete what was ephemeral. He should have known that from the first.

Max Shreck had been a caricature; Lugosi's portrayal was, by turns, wooden and melodramatic—although he'd gotten the accent right. The succession of talentless actors who had followed had been even worse: Lon Chaney Jr., a dunderheaded clod, Christopher Lee, an arrogant stiff.

Then it had been "Dracula's Daughter" and "Billy the Kid Versus Dracula" and "Blackula" and "Dracula's Dog," and then, the lowest of the low, a cartoon commercial caricature for a children's cereal: Count Chocula.

He had always drawn sustenance as much from the art made from his life as he had from blood itself, the art he'd inspired had in turn inspired him, and this low entertainment, this bastardization of art, this travesty of the twentieth century had led to his precipitous decline. In literature, in painting, in sculpture, even in music, he had served as inspiration for the best, the masters, bringing his profound understanding of darkness and the soul to men who could successfully transform the truths of his being into expressions of universality.

He had had hopes of doing the same in film, had wanted Welles to update his story, Bergman to symbolically illuminate the moral dilemma of his existence, Fellini to capture the empty surrealism of his undead life, but none of those men had had need of him. They had mined their own ideas for their art, and had not required outside inspiration. He'd nurtured a small hope for Warhol, who, despite his penchant for self-promotion, had a legitimately artistic soul, but Warhol had farmed out the film to someone else, lending only his name to the project, and the result had been self-conscious kitsch.

Now, it seemed, artists no longer knew what to do with him. It was as if he had been typecast forever by Stoker and his descendants, trapped in a guise of nineteenth century romanticism.

He walked into the living room, picked up the remote control, turned on the television. A movie was on. A wealthy business-suited man was bludgeoning to death a poor blue-collar laborer, and he was reminded of his public killing of a respected but poverty-stricken weaver in London, the inspiration for Stephen Blackpool's death in Dickens' *Hard Times*.

Hard times.

There was an appropriate phrase.

He pressed a button, changed the channel. On KNBC, an overnight repeat of the earlier eleven o'clock newscast was on, and he saw the alley where he'd discarded the man's body cordoned off and crawling with cops.

Now he was reduced to scavenging road kill, his exploits the stuff of page 22 news stories and twenty second sound bites.

He was no longer art, he was filler.

The camera focused for a few brief seconds on a white body bag on the ground, then pulled back to reveal the microphone wielding reporter giving a professionally dispassionate description of the murder.

He sat down on the couch. He was little more than a parody of his former self, but it didn't have to be that way. He could make an effort. He could take the initiative and choose a woman, seduce her, then kill her. He could hone his technique, keep up his skills, flex his creative muscles before they atrophied.

He could.

He *should*.

But, somehow, he always seemed to be just too damn tired.

* * *

He haunted her dreams, the man in black. His presence was such a pull on her subconscious, such a constant focus of her imaginings, that she quickly began to doubt whether she had seen him at all. She had not been in the most rational of moods at that moment, had been hysterical and possibly in shock, and it was conceivable that her mind had created him because it needed him, required his existence to deal with the horror and tragedy.

No, that wasn't true.

He existed.

Rafael's body had been drained of blood.

When she thought of that night—and she thought of it often—she always found herself thinking of the man in black. Not Rafael. Something about the man—

the vampire

—struck a chord, spoke to her, excited her.

Now she forced herself to think of Rafael. She had never fooled herself into believing that she loved him, but she had been attracted to him and had cared for him—and the sex had been great.

So why didn't she care that he was gone?

She saw in her mind his powerful chest, his pinup good looks, his swaggering walk. He had always been so self-assured, had always acted so self-important, when really his life had been meaningless, inconsequential. She reached over to the nightstand next to her bed and looked again at the short article from the *Los Angeles Times:* ''Producer's Boyfriend Murdered.'' There'd been more information about her in the article than about Rafael—he'd been treated as though he was nothing, a pet—and though she knew she should find that sad, she didn't.

As before, her eyes focused on the single sentence describing his death: ''. . . died from multiple gunshot wounds and massive blood loss.''

Massive blood loss.

It was such an innocuous euphemism for what had happened, a phrase she would not even have noticed had she not been personally involved and known firsthand the facts of the case. Since then, of course, she'd begun carefully reading all reports of gang shootings and street murders.

The phrase "massive blood loss" was like a thematic motif, running through the articles, recurring in the police descriptions.

She found that terrifying and, at the same time, exhilarating.

She thought again of the man in black, recalled his hard face, his powerful build, and her right hand slid down her body and beneath the elastic waistband of her panties. As her fingers moved through her thick thatch of wiry pubic hair, continuing down until they found the wet spot, she thought of the way he had lifted Rafael's bleeding body and carried it into the darkness.

She pressed her middle finger against the opening and gasped, pushing it all the way in.

There was a casting call at six for the part of a serial killer in a TV movie opposite a currently hot sitcom star. The director was merely a hired hand on the project, and already it was clear that the real battles were going to be between the star and herself.

She was at the studio at five thirty, bringing coffee and doughnuts, making friendly small talk with the skeleton technical crew, recruiting future allies should she need them.

They sat through four full hours of auditions, and she'd drawn up a list of three acceptables and ten possibles, when Bill Stevens walked in. There was something about the actor—a certain deadness in the eyes, a sense of physical power in the muscles—that reminded her of the man in black.

The vampire.

"Him," she said before the actor had spoken a single word.

To her surprise, to her pleasant surprise, the star instantly agreed.

The audition itself was a mere formality.

For a few brief seconds, while he read the lines of
the killer, she allowed herself to entertain the fantasy
that this *was* the man in black, that this was the man
who had carried off Rafael's body and drained it of
blood. But, of course, she knew that was impossible.

It was daytime.

And the sun had already been out for four hours.

*   *   *

Night.

He opened the door to the house, stepped into the
lightless shadow of the hill, reveled in the cool darkness. He felt different, better than he had in quite some
time. He breathed in the air, looked into the smoggy,
artificially illuminated night sky. Was someone . . .
thinking about him?

That was how it felt. He experienced a gentle tugging on his mind, a pulling of his attention toward a
. . . a woman. He closed his eyes. It was not the strong
clear signal he would have received from a true artist,
but it was full of life, full of intelligence, and somehow related. The picture that came to him was that of
a tall, dynamic brunette. Her features were closer to
familiar than strange, yet he could not seem to place
her.

What was happening here?

Whatever it was, it felt good, and instead of hitting
his usual haunts and feeding on carrion, he had the
sudden urge to take down live prey.

He followed the shadows of downtown Hollywood,
found himself lurking at the side of a movie theater.
He stood in the darkness. Watched. Waited.

There.

Two teenagers. A couple, a boy and a girl. In the
old days, he would have met them first, worked on
them, seduced them. But it had been a long time and
he was like a frequently denied lover with a hair-trigger

fuse, and he attacked full on. There were witnesses, people were screaming, but he didn't care, and he held the girl with one hand while he ripped open the throat of the boy, drinking in the glorious heat of the blood, tasting the familiar spicy flavor, made suddenly more appetizing by the presence of so much vibrant, fighting life. He felt brave, reckless, and he tossed aside the boy before the veins were empty, pulling the girl to him, tearing off her head and shoving his face directly into the gushing fountain, feeling the spurting hot liquid spray onto his skin, into his mouth, up his nose. There was none of his usual stealthy fastidiousness. He was boldly, brazenly, rashly oblivious to the niceties of social convention, and he grunted like an animal as he burrowed down into her headless neck, the thick sticky blood matting his hair, staining his clothes.

A would-be hero jumped on his back, tried to take him down, but he was strong, flush with blood and power, and he threw the man off and flew into the darkness, crowing with triumph, invigorated, high on accomplishment, anxious to feed again.

* * *

It came to her in a dream.

She was lost, cruising the streets in her Ferrari, when she happened upon a killing. Three gang members standing in a semicircle, taking turns stabbing an old lady who was on her knees in front of them, and then *he* appeared, taking concrete form from the patchwork shadows. The gang members ran away, scattering, screaming, and he bent down over the old lady, picked her up with one hand, pulled her to his lips and bit into her neck, drinking her blood.

And then *she* was the old woman and the vampire was drinking *her* blood, and it felt so good to be crushed and hurt by those powerful arms, to have the life sucked out of her by that cruel cold statue mouth. It felt so good to die.

She awoke aroused and inspired, knowing what she had to do.

She masturbated before taking her shower.

At the studio, she checked in with her secretary to make sure there were no meetings scheduled that morning, then quickly headed over to the trailer of Jim Quinn, a macho actor making the transition from television to features, who had been trying to get in her panties since his first day on the lot.

As she'd hoped, as she'd expected, he jumped at the chance to go out with her, immediately suggesting the name of this month's trendiest eatery. She said no, she had something else in mind, something different, and he instantly said that he'd be willing to take her wherever she wanted.

She walked back to her office feeling at once nervous and excited. If things worked out the way she wanted, Jim Quinn would be dead tomorrow.

And she would be with the man in black.

She didn't know how or why it had happened, but she couldn't deny that he had stirred something within her, awakened some previously dormant sense that she had not known she'd possessed. She walked past one of the soundstages and for some reason she found herself thinking of Henrik Grieg, the director, knowing how much he would love to meet the vampire, wondering if the vampire would be willing to go along with such a meeting. The pairing was instinctive, a natural, the idea born from that ability of hers to match talents: writer to director, director to star.

Why had she thought of that?

This wasn't a business deal she was contemplating. She wasn't lining up talent for a project.

Still, the more she thought about it, the better the idea sounded and the more importance it seemed to have. She had been thinking about the man in black almost nonstop for the past few weeks, knowing that she wanted to see him again, wanted to meet him, but now knowing why. The desire had been strong within her, but the reasons vague. She could not deny that she'd been attracted to the vampire, impressed by the unapologetic coldness of his strength and will after the disgusting softness of Rafael at the end, and she'd half-assumed that her reasons for wanting to meet him were sexual.

But she no longer lent that idea much credence. This seemed better, this seemed right, and the thought that she had been *chosen* for this purpose, picked specifically so she could bring Henrik and the vampire together established itself unshakably in her mind. The Norwegian had originally been signed to direct a sexually charged film noir based on a Jim Thompson novel, but he had quit in a rage after the first month and had been mired in a blue funk ever since. He'd been drifting for the past year, doing nothing, accomplishing nothing, creating nothing.

This would inspire him.

She smiled. Henrik was pale, thin, and defiantly unathletic, not her type at all. But they were friends. They shared an attraction to darkness, an interest in the underside of human nature. That was why she'd convinced Guberman to sign him in the first place. That and the fact that she honestly believed he could inject some much-needed artistic integrity into the commerce mill that was establishment Hollywood. She had been blown away by his first feature, a Foreign Language Oscar nominee about an eighteenth century Norwegian farmer and his darkly murderous feelings toward women who resembled his father.

And she'd liked the fact that the darkness of his work was reflected in his life.

She remembered that first meeting at Henrik's house, seeing him beat his butt boy, a Cambodian youth he kept on for household chores and sexual favors. The director had repeatedly slapped the boy hard across the face, raking the child with his sharp rings until nose and cheeks and lips were bloody, and the boy had done nothing to defend himself, had neither tried to run away nor raised his own hands to ward off the blows.

Something about seeing such total subservience, such complete abasement, had excited her, and she had offered to help Henrik clean the boy up afterward. She had assisted him in wiping the blood off the boy's face, treating the cuts and abrasions, and the three of them had gotten so into it that it had been almost a sexual experience.

She had to get those two together, Henrik and the man in black.

What came out of that meeting could be glorious.

Jim Quinn picked her up at eight at her house. He asked where they were going, but she didn't know so she told him it was a surprise and she would direct him there.

He grinned. "I love surprises," he said.

She smiled back. "Do you?"

She had him get on the 405, heading south, and told him to get off on Martin Luther King Boulevard. She had no idea where they were, but she invented a story about an authentic rib joint, the latest thing, and had him cruise the streets of Compton until she spotted a rundown bar with several gang-jacketed black youths lounging around in front. The thugs were leaning against the wall of the building, sitting on the hood of a parked car.

"Here," she said.

She watched his face and was gratified to see fear. "Are you sure you want to go here?" he asked. "I know a great rib restaurant in Westwood—"

"Turning pussy?"

He looked at her, was about to comment, but said nothing and pulled up in front of the bar.

She got out when he did, opening her own door. The gang members on the sidewalk closed ranks, moving together threateningly, and then one of them recognized Jim and called out the name of the hard-boiled cop he'd played on television. She was scared, but her adrenaline was running. She hoped the youths would try to prove how tough they were, to show how he was just a wimpy actor while they were the real thing, but to her surprise they seemed genuinely excited to meet him, and when he put on his tough guy act and laced his speech with realistic street obscenities that he was not allowed to use on TV, they laughed and high-fived him and treated him as one of their own.

She took his arm, and the two of them had an escort into the bar.

Jim was the hit of the evening, signing autographs, trading his false stories for their real ones, good-naturedly greeting the friends and relatives who arrived en masse after being called by the bar's patrons.

Against her will, she found herself aroused by this macho bonding, and when it became clear that her plans were not going to come to fruition, that nothing was going to happen here, she had Jim drive her back to her house.

Later, in the bedroom, naked, on her hands and knees while Jim knelt behind her, she found herself thinking of the man in black

the vampire

and merely thinking about him made her wetter, brought her excitement to a fever pitch.

She saw his hard white face in her mind, saw his thick powerful build, and she screamed in pleasure and pain as Jim pulled out, readjusted himself, pressed against the higher hole and roughly shoved it in.

* * *

The night was his.

After the months, the years, of hiding, of using shadows and gloom as a protective cover, he was again asserting himself, assuming his rightful place as the undisputed master of darkness.

This time he had actually gone out and met a woman, using legitimate means to attract her, and he had insinuated himself in her desires, playing her, manipulating her in order to use those desires against her.

She had invited him home with her.

It was the influence of the woman again. The *other* woman. The one he felt calling out to him, the one he saw but did not see, whose face was familiar yet not recognizable. He felt her pull on him more strongly now, as though she had been far off but was now much closer, and that thought stimulated him, made him anxiously await their meeting. For he had no doubt that they would meet. That certainty was part and parcel of the growing bond they shared, a feeling he had experienced far too often to be able to misinterpret. Additionally, though it was faint and its precise nature uncertain, there was about her the aura of the artistic. He sensed that she had it in her power to reinstate him to his former prominence, to grant him immortality anew, and that was not something he had expected to experience ever again.

He was about to be reborn.

The woman he had met tonight emerged from the bathroom, still fully clothed, and walked over to where he stood. There was fear in her eyes and in her voice, but she tried to appear dominant and in control because that was what he had made her believe he wanted. She kissed him, felt him, then pushed down on his shoulders until he was on his knees before her. She lifted up her short skirt and pressed her panty-covered pubis outward. "Lick it," she ordered.

He rubbed her gently through the silk, then roughly

yanked down her underwear, bit into her crotch and drank.

Her screams were like music.

* * *

A week passed.

She wanted to try it again.

It was a good plan, a workable plan. She had simply tried to do it with the wrong person.

This time she selected Jorge, the most flamboyantly gay fashion designer at the studio. Jorge was a friend, but this had gone far beyond the triviality of traditional friendship loyalties. This was a full-fledged obsession. She knew it, and she knew it was dangerous, but it was not something she could put a brake on now. The camera was rolling and the scene had to be played out to its end.

She used the same line—the story about the authentic rib joint—and drove into what she had been assured by a contact at the LAPD was the worst gang area in Los Angeles. Jorge was too naive to be nervous, apparently assuming that the protective bubble of unreality that existed in Hollywood would protect him on the streets, and when she roughly and deliberately pushed him into a bulging-biceped black youth in front of a liquor store, he didn't realize how serious it was.

"I'm so sorry," Jorge said, practically lisping the words.

The youth laughed, grabbed, and held him. "Lookee here," he said to his friends. "Lookee what I found."

It went on from there.

She wished she could help, wished she could actively do something to guarantee that Jorge would become the night's newest statistic, but she was out of the loop, her role relegated to that of the terrified audience. She played it to the hilt, though, crying when

Jorge was punched and knocked down, screaming when they started kicking him, and her reactions inspired the gang, ensured that the beating would continue.

They wanted to come after her next—she could sense it—but her screams had attracted attention, heads peeking out of windows, figures stepping into doorways, and they could not chance it.

They did not run, though. They were too cool, too tough for that. They walked.

The leader grabbed his crotch, winking at her as he sauntered away, the others following.

Quickly, she dragged Jorge out of the light, into the shadow of an empty building. He was hurt but alive, and something told her he had to be dead.

"Julie," he moaned.

He watched her remove the knife from her purse.

"Julie!" Fear now.

"Yes," she said. She bent down, stabbed him in the stomach. The knife sank deeply and easily into the flesh. She was surprised. She'd expected it to feel like cutting a frozen chicken, but it was more like filleting a fish. The sensation seemed erotic somehow, sensuous, and she thought again about cleaning the wounds of Henrik's butt boy.

Jorge moaned, feebly tried to sit up, tried to grab the knife, but he was too weak and his head fell back onto the sidewalk, and then he was still.

There was a moment of doubt, several seconds when people in the other buildings were calling out to her and she stood there and waited and the man in black did not come.

Then he was there, emerging from the shadows.

Coldness accompanied him, a chill wave like the blast of an air conditioner, and she suddenly found it hard to breathe. He looked the way he had before, the way he had in her dreams and imaginings, only more so. His powerful body seemed more powerful, the whiteness of his skin more white, the strange aura about him more alien.

She felt terrified and jubilant at the same time. She wanted to pick up Jorge's body and present it to him as a sacrifice, but she only stood there, looked at him, smiled. "I've been waiting for you."

He smiled back, and the smile, like his face, was cold, hard, dead. "I know," he said.

* * *

It was strange seeing her in person. There was something disappointing about it. He had expected more. He'd known ahead of time that she was not an artist, but something had led him to believe that she would be more . . . inspiring. The thought of her had promised more than the reality was able to deliver.

"I am . . . Dracula," he said. He was aware that this was a line made famous by the movies, and he instantly regretted saying it.

a parody of a parody of himself

The look that passed over her face, though, was worth it. She did not know if he was playing with her, lying to her, threatening her, and though she tried to maintain her composure, her terror was evident.

So was her desire.

She looked at him, wanting to turn away but forcing herself to meet his gaze. Her eyes were weak, frightened, but determined. "I know what you need," she said.

He could have taken that to mean many things, but suddenly he knew exactly what she was driving at, why he had sensed the air of the artist about her.

"Who?" he whispered.

"Henrik Grieg."

He had never heard of this man, but that meant nothing. Shelley and Byron, Tolstoy and Lermontov—

they had been nobodies when he had touched their lives and their work.

He took her hand, felt its beat, its pulse. "Take me there," he said.

She nodded toward the body. "Don't you want to—?"

"No," he said.

She nodded. "I can drive—"

"I can fly."

They were in the air then, one with the night, and they no longer needed to talk. Through her, he saw where they were to go, and he took them there, to a mansion in a neighborhood of mansions. They stood for a moment in the shadows next to the door. From inside the house, he felt the invigorating energy of talent, those intense and intensely personal vibrations peculiar to the brilliant and creative.

The door opened a beat before the woman rang the bell, and a man stood in the vestibule, backlit by lamplight, a thin man with a brooding countenance and a will as dark and strong as his body was pale and weak.

He looked at the man and he felt it. The Connection. An almost electric buzz that passed between them and made him feel energized, stimulated. He could make this man great.

This man could make him immortal.

Again.

He walked inside, looked around the room, feeling the need to do something, to demonstrate his power, to show to this man the depth of his darkness. He felt wired, on edge, every fiber of his being crying out for release.

His gaze fell upon the woman.

She was looking at the man, the director. "He's a vampire." Her voice was proud, frightened.

"I know." The director was terrified but curious, wanting to run but willing to stay, needing to see what only he, Dracula, could show him.

There was a moment of silence.

"How do you do it?" the director asked, whispered. "The neck? Like in the movies?"

There was something in his tone, in the frightened jumble of syllables, that reminded him of Goethe.

He nodded. "Usually."

"Could you . . . show me?"

In answer, he grabbed the woman, his fingers crushing the delicate bones of her forearm. She did not scream, did not struggle, but seemed resigned, as if she'd known this was coming, as if she'd not only been expecting it but wanted it. There was pain on her face, but it was only the pain of the body, and underneath it was an understanding acceptance, a knowledge that she was to be part of something big, something important. Her voice was a pained rasp. "Yes," she said.

He smiled. There was no preamble, no savoring of the moment, no shared acknowledgment of her offering and his acceptance. He bit into her neck, feeling the warmth of her life pumping into his mouth, and as he did so he looked up at the director.

The spark was struck, the fire lit. He saw revelation, inspiration, in the director's face. The feeling ricocheted, already coming back to him. It was like a rush of adrenaline to his system, and a series of visions exploded in his brain. He felt invigorated, and the combination of the director's blossoming creativity and the woman's hot blood conspired to make him slightly giddy. He wanted to laugh, he wanted to scream, he wanted to jump up, he wanted to dance. But he held onto the woman, drank her dry, let her withered, empty body fall from his grasp onto the floor.

There would be a movie now. No. Not a movie. A film. And, after that, more films from the same mold, branches off the original root. Already, although nothing had yet been created, he could feel a stirring in the artistic zeitgeist of the film world, a building wave of intensely stimulating sustenance.

They were out there. Others. He could sense them now, the artists who had so long been denied him. He could feel them flickering into existence on the map of his mind, winking on like little bulbs: directors, screenwriters, composers, actors. They would expose him to their lights, and he would expose them to his darkness.

His immortality would be updated and renewed. He would not simply exist. He would *live*.

He said his name aloud: "Dracula." It no longer sounded like a campy moniker from an earlier age. It no longer sounded like the clichéd name of an over-exposed matinee monster. Once again, it was dynamic yet dignified. Once again, it had about it the ring of greatness.

He said it again, drawing it out: "Drac-u-la."

Proudly: "Dracula."

There was a sound behind him. The director. He turned, met the man's gaze, nodded, bowed, then moved away, heading quickly through the door.

"Wait!" the director said.

But he was off, into the dark.

It had been a long time—too long—and he was tired of waiting. There was work to be done, scripts to be typed, scores to be written. He was finished with this director, but there were others—many, many others—to be inspired.

Finally, after all these years, after all this time, the talent of Hollywood was expecting him.

And he was ready.

LOT FIVE, BUILDING SEVEN, DOOR TWENTY-THREE

by
John Shirley

"He's my last hope," said Oliver Dunsmuir. "It's him or despair."

"What's underneath despair, Ollie?" asked Rodney Collins, in his affable, abstracted way.

They were walking through underground hallways that still smelled of new concrete. They passed now under lot five of the Spiritual Freedom Complex, the corridors seemingly endless and empty, the sound of their footsteps echoing against the metal pipes snaking the ceiling.

All the circumlocution to reach the Teacher was a bit of a bore, really, Dunsmuir thought; it smacked of the folderol the Sufis and the Tibetan monks put you through before you could reach their inner sanctums. The point was some psychological state they wanted you in, and not the supposed secrecy of the Teacher.

O Dark Truth, spread your cape for me; O Vlad the Living Gateway, open your white lips and show me the key. . . .

"I mean," Collins was saying, "what are the *borders* of despair?" His long strides were making it difficult for the shorter, stockier Dunsmuir to keep pace with him. His English accent and his English reserve made even a subject like despair seem cool, detached. But glancing at him, Dunsmuir saw the glimmering again, just for a moment, in Collins' dusty blue eyes, and a warmth in the rueful curve of Collins' mouth.

Collins ran a work-reddened hand through his receding, curly brown hair and went on, "You've got to go through in order to come out, what?"

Dunsmuir shrugged. The remark was an esoteric commonplace, and nothing new, nothing new at all.

They'd at last reached the elevator at the end of the hall. Ordinary blue-painted metal doors. Dunsmuir and Collins looked up at the little camera lens over the elevator. A light beside the camera was flashing red. "My name's Rodney Collins," he said. "I know Webb." There was an electronic hesitation. Then the elevator doors opened.

In the elevators, riding up, Dunsmuir mused over the exchange with the security computer. "You said you knew Webb. Is that a code-phrase or . . . ?"

"No. He's head of Security. They buzzed him and he may be willing to see me."

"I thought you said you'd been here before—that you were *in* here!"

"I said nothing of the sort, my dear fellow—ah, here's our floor."

They stepped out into the shiny hallway. The entire wall on their right side, as they moved down the hall, was a tinted window. Beyond it, the towers and elevated tramways of New York. He could make out the brown smudge of what had been Central Park; the plants and trees were uniformly dead now, of course. There was talk of putting a bubble over the park, but they probably wouldn't get the funding. Spiking the horizon, the Earth-to-Orbit access shaft, under construction since 1999, was like some whiskered-alloy Tower of Babel gouging the ceiling of clouds. Looking at it, Dunsmuir had an intuition that, like the Tower of Babel, the ETO would never be finished.

They strode past potted plants, and pleasant, meaningless murals. "You *did* say," Dunsmuir went on, "you were in with Vlad. You knew the Teacher."

Collins chuckled. "No matter how much one learns

about the filters of the mind, it's always astonishing the sort of things that people *think* they hear. No, old chum, I did not say I knew the Teacher. I said I was going to see him—and you could come along.''

"But—you've never—?''

"No. I've never been here before.''

"Well, fuck. Then this is a waste of time.'' Dunsmuir felt frustration and fury simmer up in him. So much had been a waste of time. The Gnostic Christians, the Theosophists, the Buddhists, the practitioners of the Fourth Way; the Children of Crowley; the Temple of Set; the half dozen other esoteric disciplines he'd pursued and the therapeutic scam artists he'd fallen victim to. They were all either complex frauds, like the Scientologists, or they simply posed new ways to ask the questions; they offered no answers.

Dunsmuir knew about wasted time.

"I mean,'' he went on, gritting his teeth to keep his temper, "I've been this far before, right up to the door of Building Seven. With Singh. He used to get in—but they won't even let him in to see the Teacher now. They say the Teacher's sequestered for good.''

"Oh,'' Collins said breezily. "I think we'll see him. It's a matter of timing, you see.''

"I've tried every day of the week and every hour of the day, Collins!''

"I meant time in a broader sense. And in a more holistic sense. In several directions at once.''

Dunsmuir sighed. "More mystical claptrap. I've heard it all, Collins, from Christian Rosenkruz to Steiner to Blavatsky to Franklin Jones to Crowley to Ouspensky. Spare me.''

"I hope to, actually.''

They'd come to a white desk at the end of the rust-colored carpet. Sitting behind the desk was a black man in a security guard's uniform. Dunsmuir knew damn well he was a lot more than a security guard. He was a middle-aged man, in dark glasses, with a silver *V* stapled through his left ear, a symbol worn by most of the Teacher's followers. He looked disdainfully at Dunsmuir, glanced at Collins, turned back to Dunsmuir as if to rebuke him—then did a double take right out of a twentieth century movie, turning back to stare at Collins. He swallowed. "I . . ." He shook his head. "I can't."

"You can," Collins said. He reached out to touch the black man . . . who fell backward out of his chair to dodge that touch; who turned and bolted from his desk. Ran in terror from Collins' mild eyes, the gentle touch of his callused hands.

* * *

"The Center for Spiritual Freedom is not interested in comforting panaceas, in maternalistic therapies, in soaking you for your money in return for false promises. The Teacher who is at the Center for Spiritual Freedom is interested only in—"

"—'radically transforming your life, inner and outer,' " Danitra muttered, finishing it along with the videotape narrator. "Christ. What *is* this. I'm going *backward.*" Danitra Johnson shifted in her chair, watching the big video screen at the other end of the waiting room. She was a long-legged black woman, her hair shaven close to her skull and cut into the symbols of the initiate; she wore the standard black jeans and T-shirt, and the black sandals of the initiate; she had the *V* in her left ear, she had a year of initiatory seminars in her head and now she had a suspicion she was lost in some sort of theocratic bureaucracy.

But she made herself watch the Introductory Video. It could be that this video—the same one she'd seen when she first joined the Center a year before—was here only to test her patience, or perhaps there was something encrypted in it she hadn't seen the first time. . . .

She was, herself, on a video screen in the next room.

* * *

James Webb, the direct descendant of the man Bram Stoker had called "Van Helsing," was frowning as he watched Danitra on the video screen. The black woman, a former model, was a stroke of charcoal and chocolate against the pastels of the waiting room. She fairly quivered with suppressed energy. Oh, yes, *He* would enjoy her, of course, as much as He could enjoy anything, anymore. But Webb was beginning to think that there would never be a "critical mass" with Him; there would never be the hoped-for moment of Divine Satiety. And this exquisite, intelligent creature would simply be wasted. Webb considered cutting her out from the herd for his own uses. It wouldn't be the first time. . . .

He shivered; he felt a chill go through him. Was it His influence, reaching through the walls—or a withdrawal from the specially treated cigarettes Webb smoked? Probably it was the synthetic morphine. Only a mild addiction so far. Not like the other one—the ancestral addiction to *Him*. That, now, was worth fighting. This girl might be a worthwhile test. A test to answer the question: Could *He* really be denied?

Webb glanced at the other monitors. Collins and his friend were presumably gone; sent away by the guard, as per Webb's instructions. He didn't see them on the monitor. So perhaps he was free to dally with the girl.

Webb made his decision. He went through the door into the waiting room. "Ms. Johnson?"

"Yes?" She uncoiled from her yellow plastic chair like a pit viper.

O Divider and Unifier, O Destroyer and Renewer, cauterize from me the irrelevancies of pity and fear, and remake me, remake me utterly. . . .

"I'm Jim Webb."

"I know who you are." She grimaced at her own impatience. "I'm sorry. This video—"

"It seems like old hat? Well. Yes and no." Webb smiled, trying for his charming patrician look—the older man with the disarming smile, the white temples, the dark, confident eyes. He'd always had good luck with that particular image.

"It's just that I feel . . . I *know* . . ."

"That you're ready. I'm sure you are. But as you know—and the general announcement went out—*He* is not seeing anyone at this time."

"But Georgei said, on the telephone—"

"That there are exceptions. Yes." And I hope you won't have to be one, he thought. "But—The Teacher is not ready at this time. *He's* in deep intra-cyclic meditation."

She stared at him. She glanced past him, at Door Twenty, then she glowered at the floor. "Very well. It's back to the Ashram?"

"No. To my meditation temple. We'll prepare ourselves there till He is ready. However long it takes. . . ."

He could imagine her long, muscular limbs against his. The thought of her African-dark thighs cupping his pale, tumescent genitals. He hoped she didn't note the growing bulge in his pants' crotch.

He stepped to the door opposite—moving hastily to hide the telltale evidence of his intentions—and opened the door for her. It swung inward—and she shoved Webb through it. She was *strong;* the story of her being a black belt might well be true.

He turned in time to see her slam the door in his face. Then he heard her wedge a chair against it on the other side.

* * *

Danitra's heart was pounding. Webb had made the mistake of leaving the other door unlocked. She wasn't going to lose the chance. She'd gotten through Door Twenty. From what she knew of Building Seven, that meant there were only two more doors between her and the Teacher.

She was fairly sure—or so she told herself, as she strode down the forbidden hallway—that *He* wanted her to do just this. To break the rules. That sending Webb out to seemingly misdirect her was a test.

My rules are rigid, inflexible, and utterly neces-sary—and also completely expendable. You'll know when that time comes. You will then be One Who Knows. . . .

* * *

Even through the heavy walls of the Center for Spiritual Freedom, Dunsmuir could hear the sirens announcing a Toxic Front. The few people daring the upper streets would be scrambling for the underplex air locks. Another Black Wind was coming, bearing lethal toxins manufactured in the upper atmosphere by evaporated pesticides and manufacturing by-products, pollutants chemically transfigured by the UVs; the heavier UVs, admitted now that the ozone layer was all but gone. The same ultraviolets that slowly toasted the world on the spit of its axis, destroying crops and oceanic plankton, shattering the food chain, initiating the famines: the riots, the hundreds of brush wars over the globe's pockets of resources. The complexes of urban undergrounds and sealed buildings, especially thy hydroponic high rises, had kept the race staggering on. Especially those born into money like Dunsmuir. But sometimes he thought that despite all the electronic and concrete barricades, the walls would fall. . . .

"The siren's a frightening sound, isn't it?" Collins murmured, seeming not at all frightened.

They were walking up a stairway now. The guards had frozen the elevators, but Collins always seemed to know where there was an unlocked door.

"The siren?" Dunsmuir was thinking that he was more frightened of Rodney Collins, now, than of the Black Winds. The way the guard had reacted; the way the doors seemed to come unlocked at his touch.

What did he know about Collins? Precious little. Collins was a self-styled "servant of God," who traveled from community to community—and had done so even before they went underplex—and offered his services as "a builder—of whatever is needed." He built housing of metal and wood and plastic, whatever was around. He seemed to know most of the Masters of the various spiritual disciplines, and to come and go as he liked. He knew a great deal about yoga, and just as much about the Stations of the Cross and the lives of the Saints. He had studied in "certain Schools" as a young man, and that sort of mysteriousness always set Dunsmuir's teeth on edge—but in Collins' case, it scared him. Collins was altogether too casual about it all.

"The sirens have frightened people into looking for God," Collins was saying, "and they have given the powers of entropy great joy, since most people have, in their panic, run the wrong way. But it's been lovely for the televangelists and the Scientologists and the other parasites. All things being relative. Tell me . . . what brought you to the 'Teacher'?"

There was real irony in the way he said "Teacher."

Dunsmuir was puffing with effort at the climb; Collins didn't seem to feel it.

"The miracles, of course," Dunsmuir said, knowing it would sound jejune. He was supposed to be attracted to the Teacher purely for His Spiritual Profundity. "He was tested every which way by every skeptic in the world. All the best stage magicians, electronic techies—no one could explain the levitations, the power over animals, the vanishings . . . the other miracles.''

"Did you ever notice that the miracles were always performed at night?" Collins asked, offhandedly.

"He explained that—the sun's vibratory energy is . . . I can't remember exactly. . . .''

"It never *does* fail to astonish me," Collins said, chuckling.

They reached the top landing. A security camera whirred toward them—and then froze. The camera seemed as spooked as the black security guard had been. "Is this it?" Dunsmuir asked, almost childlike in his sudden eagerness.

"What? Oh no, no," Collins said, putting his hand on the door. *Click-click.* "No, we've got to go *down* now.''

He opened the door and Dunsmuir followed him through—and found to his horror that they were now *outside.* They were standing on a metal outdoor stairway, a sort of emergency escape stairs, in the open air. There was some shelter from a metal roof over the stairway, but it wasn't sealed off. The dirty wind teased their nostrils with hydrocarbons, sulfites, PCBs, and heavy metals.

"We'll choke out here!''

"The toxic front isn't here yet," Collins replied, with maddening unconcern, "I think we'll make it into Building Seven before it gets here.''

"You *think!* We haven't got respirators!''

But Collins was already clattering down the pitted metal stairs. Dunsmuir, palms sweating, turned to the door behind him. He was going back. The hell with Collins.

The door was shut; the knob wouldn't turn. He was locked out. "Oh God, oh fuck!''

He turned and hurried after Collins.

He's insane. I'm going to die out here with a madman.

*   *   *

She might have known it. Door Twenty-three was locked.

But she could feel *Him* in there: a pulsing from beyond the door; a throbbing of sheer presence, unheard, but distinctly felt, in the bone sockets and teeth.

If I can feel Him, she thought, then He can feel me.

She knelt before the door and began to pray.

"That won't get His attention, though he might enjoy the pose if He could see it," Webb said, stepping up behind her.

Danitra got slowly to her feet and turned to face him, expecting him to be accompanied by several burly security guards.

But Webb was alone. "I'm going to give you a chance to save your life," Webb said, "not because I'm any kind of philanthropist—I'm too much of a scientist for that—but because I prize beauty."

"What are you threatening me with?" Danitra asked. She decided she could take him, long before he could pull a gun from his suit jacket.

"Me? Not a thing. I won't do a thing to you myself. You go through that door, though, well. . . ." He shrugged.

"Test me, then," she said. "And I will pass the tests. And I know this is another of them."

He actually laughed in her face. "You're so bright and so childlike at the same time! My dear Danitra, all tests are quite concluded, except those that involve Him. My hypotheses with respect to Him have been disproved, or nearly so. I have studied him long enough. And I know."

"You're . . . *studying* him?"

To her astonishment, Webb lit a cigarette. You didn't see them often anymore. "I'm Studying him, yes. My esteemed ancestor began the practice. Funny old Professor Von Weber. Whom Stoker called Van Helsing—and made look like some sort of scientifically-minded saint. But the real 'Van Helsing' was a pederast, a heroin addict, and had an unwholesome fascination—one I understand all too well—with Vlad Veovod. Known, back home in Wallachia, as The Son of the Dragon. The Impaler. Whom Stoker renamed: Dracula.''

She smiled. *"This* test is rather transparent.''

"Oh, get over it.'' Suddenly Webb seemed much older, much wearier. "We *can't* study him, you know. That's what I've come to believe. . . .'' He leaned against the wall beside her. "You can only serve him or fight him.'' He glanced up and down the hall. "I wonder where all the guards have gone . . . could it have come to that?''

They heard another warning yowl of sirens. The drawn-out note sounded almost like trumpets. Like a clarion call from the sky itself.

"Another damned Toxic alert. He made them—Dracula, the entity you call the Teacher—anyway, He helped make them, with His influence, and then, a grand irony, people like you ask Him to remake the world.'' He offered her the cigarette. "Want a hit of this? A bit of smokable morphine in it. I'm afraid I'm kind of jonesed for it.''

She shook her head. Was he joking? Or testing her again? The smoke *did* smell strange.

Webb's eyes glazed over as he drew on the cigarette, and he went on, his voice slurring slightly, "He was like a spiritual tumor in the social brain, you know. The bloodsuckers . . . all the bloodsuckers he encouraged along . . . I remember Mike Milken—that was before your time—and Charles Keating and the Dow-Corning people and the Chevron people and the Bank of Credit and Commerce people and Union Carbide and the mob and the Vatican bankers . . . all the *bloodsuckers*. How He relished it all, how it fed Him . . . but, of course, drinking on that level was never enough for ol' Vlad. His appetites are very basic, really.''

She shook her head. Webb—the Teacher's High Devotee—was either stoned, crazy, or acting. ''Open the door,'' she said.

Webb looked at her and shook his head firmly. ''Downstairs there's a ride-tube to my plex. High security, high comfort. Lots of everything that makes life in an ant farm still worth living. Come with me.''

She gazed at him and saw real lust, real loneliness, and real fear. *But that shouldn't surprise you*, said something less than a voice in her head. *It is the Judas effect*. The ones closest to Jesus, too, were often the blindest. . . .

She turned and pounded on the door.

To her astonishment—and Webb's dismay—it opened.

The door was opened by an old man with a bald head, a walrus mustache, and striking, sad, black-brown eyes. He wore a vaguely Middle Eastern outfit, baggy trousers and sandals and a rough tunic from some other century—or from a costume shop. And around his neck was a heavy iron collar, rusted with age. It was studded and bolted and it must have been painful, even after an hour or so. She could tell by the marks on his neck it had been there for years.

''You wish come in, Miss?'' the old man said.

She recognized his Russian accent and gravelly voice. Georgei Ivanovitch. She'd only spoken to him on the phone.

''Georgei,'' Webb said dangerously, ''close that door and go away.''

"Can not do, Dr. Van Helsing—"

"That is *not* funny."

Georgei smiled as if to say, it *was* funny, in a sad sort of way. "Sorry. 'Doctor Webb.' Can not close door. The Master, He feel her here. Is too late."

Webb closed his eyes as if enduring cryptic pain. "Where are the guards?" he asked, his eyes still shut, nervously sucking at the stub of his cigarette.

"He take them too. Could not wait. He very afraid now."

"What! He took . . . *all* of them?" Webb opened his eyes and looked sharply at Georgei.

"Yes. So many! But growth does not stop."

Georgei threw Door Twenty-three wide open and stepped back. "Both, please come. Pretty Lady wants, Pretty Lady gets."

Danitra hesitated, feeling as if someone were dripping a thick, cold liquid along her spine. Webb didn't move.

Georgei turned to Webb. He chuckled. "You come to say hello to Teacher too, Von Weber."

"You're in a damned cheerful mood," Webb said, glaring at Georgei. "For a slave."

"I have seen in dream: my atonement ends. It ends today. The Angel Looisil, he speaks to me."

Webb snorted. "Bullshit."

Danitra hesitated on the threshold of the dimly lit, black-curtained room beyond. It smelled of iron and sweat. But then she remembered the Twenty-third Invocation: *At the brink of your salvation, I tremble in fear. Open wide your wings and enfold me.* . . .

She took a deep breath and stepped through. Then she turned to see if Webb was coming. She preferred more company, here.

Behind her, Webb was shaking his head. "I'm going home." He turned away—and then turned unwillingly back toward the door. Moving like a man caught in an unseen current, he staggered through the door, and into the black curtained room beyond.

* * *

Dunsmuir was only a little surprised to find Door Twenty-three unlocked and unguarded. True, it went contrary to everything he knew about the Center. But with Collins along, surprise was at the same time inevitable and inappropriate.

The room beyond the door was a vast one, draped in shadows; it seemed to have been an airplane hangar at one time. Its cavernous interior spaces reached five or six stories up, hundreds of feet across. The concrete floor was dusty but for the path between Door Twenty-three and the huge idol dimly seen at the far end of the room. High overhead, hunched forms crouched on the guano-crusted steel rafters. Black velvet curtains covered the windows near the ceiling; the far walls were stark and murky.

It was cold here; they could see their breath in the faint light that struck in shafts, here and there, where the curtains were not quite snug against the high windows. Dunsmuir and Collins walked on, through the break in the dust.

"What is that?" Dunsmuir asked in a whisper, peering at the idol. "A Buddha?"

Collins laughed softly at that. "Buddha!" And he laughed again.

Nearer the idol was a circle of high black curtains on runners about thirty feet above the floor; the curtains were drawn partly back so Dunsmuir could see only the silhouette of the idol beyond.

As they neared the curtained-off area, Dunsmuir's eyes adjusted—or perhaps there was a kind of black light emanating, almost unseeably, from the bulky figure on the dais. It was cold; but Dunsmuir found he was sweating.

As they reached the curtain, there came a cry that was something less than a wail and more than a moan, a cry of soul-deep disillusionment and betrayal. A woman's voice.

And then they stepped past the partition.

The figure lying on the cushioned dais, propped on an elbow, was big as a two-story house; was not an idol. It was the "Teacher." In the flesh, "living" but not breathing; he had no need to breathe.

Dracula was draped in the same sort of black velvet cloth—hundreds of square yards of it—that hung from the runners and covered the windows. He was a giant. He was bloated, piglike now, though no pig had ever grown this big, the size of a blue whale—and his face was tormented by hunger. The deep-set eyes, the heavy eyebrows, the Slavic cheekbones, the seductive mouth—all of it quivered with a tortured need, as if with each new victim he only grew thirstier. He'd gone bald and his great hands—big as krakens—shook as he reached for the man hanging on a hook beside his head.

It was the black guard who'd run from Collins below. He was stripped nude, and hanging by a hook through the jaw, alive and wriggling but unable to speak, choked with trickling blood. Vlad Veovod, Dracula, the Son of the Dragon, lifted the black man off the hook—the man groaned and twisted in pain— and took him in his two hands, and brought him to his mouth.

Dunsmuir and the others—Webb, the black woman who knelt before Dracula amid the ruins of the drained people, and Rodney Collins—watched in dull amazement as Dracula punctured the black man's chest and belly with his fangs, fangs the size of sabers, so that his victim writhed out gushes of thick red. But rather than drinking it thus, Dracula withdrew his fangs and raised the man over his head and wrung him like a wet rag, squeezed him out into his mouth. . . .

Though choked, the black man managed a single piercing shriek before his spine was twisted apart, and he split open between the two rents in his torso, showering Dracula's upturned lips with blood.

"Behold, the *Teacher*," Collins said dryly.

"It's . . . an illusion . . . a vision. . . ." Dunsmuir stammered.

"My, you *are* in denial, Oliver," Collins commented.

Dracula *roared* in frustration and disappointment, and tossed the gutted, drained corpse disgustedly onto the floor before him. It fell with a sickening slap.

"Not enough yet, Vlad?" Collins asked airily, stepping forward. At Collins' feet, below the dais, were the wreckages of other victims—judging by the uniforms and outfits that had been stripped away like the peels of fruit, they'd been the inner circle of devotees and bodyguards and cult executives; those the "Teacher" had saved till last.

A great moan went up from the rafters—where crouched hundreds, Dunsmuir saw, of Dracula's "initiates." Those not fortunate enough to be simply drained and destroyed.

Someone came from the shadows, toward Collins—with a sword in his hand. It was Georgei.

"Look out, Collins!" Dunsmuir said, staggering back.

Collins turned toward the man wielding the sword—but he only smiled. Georgei had raised the sword over his head . . . ritualistically. He made several passes in the air with it, each one a sigil of some kind, then knelt before Collins, weeping with joy, and handed him the sword. "Oh, Angel, I beg you now release me." He said something more in Russian-Armenian. Collins answered in the same dialect. Then he accepted the sword and struck down with it. The ornate sword struck the collar on Georgei's neck—and split it. The blade shouldn't have been able to break iron, but it did. Georgei cried out and fell on his face, shaking, the life going from him, babbling in joy.

"You have atoned long enough, G. No longer will you have to bring innocents to him. Go to the Between place, and await Word."

In a movement as startling as a house unfolding itself, Dracula stood, draperies flapping with a bullwhip sound, floor shaking under his bare feet. Dunsmuir threw himself down, crawling away from the heat of Dracula's rage, and found himself crouched beside the black girl. He'd seen her at one of the seminars. Danitra.

"Oh no, it's a lie it's a lie it's a lie . . ." she wept.

Dracula bent and snatched up Georgei and started to raise him to his lips—but Collins made a gesture, and Georgei's body vanished, replaced with a cloud of silver butterflies that fluttered up into the air and about Dracula's head like a mockery of a halo. Dracula howled and swiped at them, and they drifted away and up and became a luminous mist that slipped right through the ceiling.

"It's frustrating, is it?" Collins said, speaking softly. Yet his voice carried to every corner of the enormous room. "Yes, Count, I expect it is. How many chances were you given, Vlad? You were driven from this world many times—and many times you let your rage feed you, and you found your way back, until at last you were incorporated into the Great Plan by your Master . . . and by *his* Master. . . ."

Dracula's voice came like the sizzling sound that follows a lightning strike. "Be silent, fly of God! Your buzzing aggravates my torment! You masquerade as an angel, but you are a demon!"

"Demons are made within men, Vlad," Collins replied calmly. "And you were one such. The Impaler. And then less than a man—with a hunger beyond men, when Stoker told your tale. And now in self-mockery you grow—but you are not nurtured. You have infected the world with your greed, your bloodthirstiness, trying to finally get enough, but you never will. You'll never have enough. You're just a hungry little boy. . . .''

Shaking with rage, Dracula reached down and snatched at Collins, his roar like thunder echoing in a cavern, his great, clawed fingers closing around the diminutive figure. . . .

And then screaming at the touch. He could not lift Collins from the floor. Something passed from Collins into Dracula, an opposite charge to the spark shown passing from God to Adam on the Sistine ceiling. . . .

And Dracula was uncreated. Silver-blue electricity shivered visibly through him, and crackled between his fangs, and lit his eyes up from within like beacons. And for a moment, the divine energy blazoned out something that had been hidden before, something only recently imprinted on the forehead of the Lord of Vampires.

666.

This completed, the energy detonated within the monstrous corpus of the Lord of the Living Dead, and he was sundered from head to foot, torn open and turned inside out—freeing, in the process, ten thousand trapped spirits that spiraled upward in silver skeins of release. . . . Taking with them those who crouched on the rafters—taking them up, and out, through a ceiling suddenly become as vaporous as a cloud.

This time, there really was nothing left of him. Nothing but a lump in a puddle that turned the stomach to look upon.

Collins turned to Danitra and Dunsmuir, and took them by the hands. They knew who he was, and let him lead them, like a parent with two children, out the door. ''There've been some changes made outside these walls. The veil is torn away. Let's go and look at the real world,'' he said. ''And see it for the first time.''

They left Webb—the genetic and spiritual echo of Van Helsing—lying on the floor, sobbing for his loss, the loss of his master and his enemy. Never knowing which was which.

DEEP SLEEP

by
Matthew J. Costello

He looked across the expanse of the first-class dining room, through the maze of bustling waiters sleekly presenting the passengers with their chosen dessert. A chocolate mousse perhaps, or fraise a la creme? Great dark wedges of Black Forest cake sailed across the room while the chamber quartet played too much Strauss.

Andre Farrand—such was the name on his passport—was traveling alone. But he felt them looking at him. One, two—yes—three pairs of eyes, ignoring their meal, their dessert course, their husbands. The room was filled with wealthy robber barons and overstuffed captains of industry.

The women looked at him. He felt their eyes devouring him hungrily.

"Monsieur, some café for monsieur?" The waiter was at his elbow. This was the first meal at which Farrand had made an appearance, nibbling some of the greens, tasting the escalloppe de veau before declaring the lemon sauce much too tart.

It was not uncommon for travelers to have distressed stomachs at sea.

Though—to be sure—that was not the reason Farrand didn't eat.

He caught the eye of one woman looking at him. Her eyes attempted to speak, urging him to confirm that they would dance again that evening, that they'd again take a walk on the first-class promenade. That—

in the chill air of the North Atlantic—he'd pull her close, muttering words to make her forget her husband, then closer. . . .

"Still not feeling better, Monsieur Farrand?"

He looked up. A woman in a white dress heavy with brocade gave him a motherly purse of the lips. Perhaps the bejeweled dowager was so solicitous of his appetite since hers was never in disrepair.

He smiled. Monsieur Andre Farrand, a world-famous dealer in antiquarian furniture, favored the woman with a charming grin. "No, Madame Welch. I'm feeling much better. *Much* . . . but I'd best not test myself. A nibble here, a nibble there—it will more than satisfy me."

The dowager smiled, so pleased that he was well.

He felt the attentive gazes around the room, perhaps not quite in control, perhaps in danger of embarrassing him, of creating a scene. That would not do, not on this ship, not here. There was no place to hide . . . no place to go.

Monsieur Farrand pushed his chair back. He looked around at the table, smiling at the noisy Americans and a pair of British bankers with their wives—repulsive, cowlike creatures with no appeal, with rolls of skin that jiggled on their arms.

"But I think I'd like to take some air. And see if it's gotten any colder outside."

He nodded to the table. One of the American men stuck out his lip. "Perhaps I'll—"

The man was offering to join him, but Farrand pretended not to hear. He turned away and walked to the front of the grand dining hall, the hungry eyes still watching him, looking for a signal, something to give them hope. He forced his face to remain impassive.

Farrand pushed open one of the doors, pressing against the center section of the cut beveled glass. It led to the main hall and the giant staircase of first class. He walked out.

Just outside, he saw the purser talking to the captain. Captain Smith had excused himself early from dinner and now was engaged in what looked like a most serious conversation.

The captain saw him pass by. He turned, and nodded—a diplomat. "Good evening, Monsieur."

"Captain," he said, nodding to the man.

Farrand turned to go up the staircase. He looked up. At the landing where the staircase split in two there was a carved wooden panel and a clock—a frieze representing "Honor and Glory crowning Time."

He smiled at that, enjoying the irony, the private joke. Time is the ruler. Yes, it's the despot in people's lives. Unless . . . unless it can be defeated—and made the servant.

He walked up the stairs and stopped on the landing. He looked at the clock. It was 8 p.m. He touched the clock, and the two wooden figures holding the crown. And then he continued up the grand stairway.

* * *

Farrand went to his stateroom. It looked untouched, except for one open bag containing some clothes. He had given instructions, fortified with a ten pound note, that his room was to be left undisturbed. He didn't wish his bed to be made or his washroom to be cleaned. Nothing was to be done.

There was little need. He barely used it.

He stood in the darkness, feeling the rolling of the ship, the swells of the icy North Atlantic. He felt his hunger, and he stood there, savoring the warmth, the meaning it gave to him.

And when he was sure that supper had ended, he opened the cabin door and left his suite.

* * *

He made his way to another corridor, and the state-rooms farther toward the bow.

She'd be waiting. They'd all be waiting, he knew, while their husbands played cards and smoked cigars and drank brandy.

He came to the door and knocked. If, perchance, the husband was there, Farrand would claim it was a mistake. It was so *easy* to get confused on this giant ship.

But the woman opened the door. She had the top of her dress open, wantonly, invitingly, so eager. She grabbed his hand.

"No," he whispered, gently shutting the door behind him. She was beautiful, with dark eyes and jet black hair. Her body pressed against him, lean, hungry. She was young, and so very unhappy with her life.

He grabbed her hand with his hands and pushed her away, fixing her with his gaze.

He heard sounds from the corridor. Some people were moving this way.

The woman looked hurt. Her lower lip—full, beet red—quivered in shock, in pain. He let go of her and brought his hand to her cheek. She brushed against it.

"Not here," he said. "You must wait. Meet me on the promenade deck. In an hour. Meet me there. . . ."

She licked her lips, the fever was on her. It was always this way, and he enjoyed her pain, her turmoil. To want something so badly, to crave it above all other things, something that would take everything away from you . . . your whole world.

It was wonderful.

He released her. He listened at the door. The corridor sounded empty.

He'd picked her because of her great need, the way she would kick and moan when he kissed her, when he touched her. I must not get carried away, he thought. Not on the ship. There was no way to explain such things. He turned and grabbed the door handle.

"You'll be there?" she said. Her voice had a wheedling quality, a small child, unsure, afraid.

He opened the door an inch. He looked at her again, his face not smiling.

"Don't ever doubt my word. *Ever.*"

He left the stateroom. He smelled the cigar smoke, lingering here, the hint of perfume. I can't wait too long, he thought.

My senses become aroused, inflamed.

Even *I* can't wait too long. . . .

* * *

He pulled his coat close. The churning water, white, frothing, spitting at the hull of the ship, was alive with phosphorescent specks. He wrapped his coat tight.

A couple walked by, their shoes clicking noisily on the wood of the deck. He turned to look at them, close together, perhaps newlyweds. They moved on, oblivious to him.

And then he was alone. He wondered if anyone doubted his name . . . Monsieur Farrand, from Paris. His accent was nearly *parfait*. Still, he wondered if he'd made any slips. There was a Frenchman, a writer, sitting two tables over, and a Marseilles businessman and his family sat all the way on the other side of the room.

But so far he had avoided meeting them, having them probe his background, asking questions, difficult questions.

It was cold, frigid. It felt as if the wet cold seeped right through his overcoat, through his suit, his shirt, and held his skin tight. It reminded him of what he faced every morning.

There is a price for conquering time. . . .

He turned his gaze away from the wake of the great

ship, up to the stars. The sky was white with stars, the Milky Way was a gossamer belt around the night sky. Even in the mountains, in his homeland, there were never nights like this, so *clear*, so *bright*. He turned to search for Perseus, the Pleiades, other familiar constellations, his companions, friends in the night.

But the giant smokestacks of the ship blocked out the southeast sky, four great black columns outlined by the twinkling stars.

He heard a door creak open, yards away, leading from the first-class lounge to the open deck. He took a deep breath. The icy air stung his nostrils. He saw her outline, and he heard her steps on the wood.

He waited, arms open, ready to pull her close, to hold her tight, surrounding her warmth, possessing it.

"He—he came back, my husband," she said. Her words made small eddies of fog in front of her face. "I had to say I needed to walk. He wanted to come—"

He took her, grabbing her shoulders.

"But you told him no? You said that you needed to be alone. . . ."

There was just the glow of a few lights, the pale light of the stars, the billowing clouds of her breathing. He dug his hands into her shoulders, hard, locking her to him. He watched her face become delirious with joy. Her hands fiddled with the neck of her dress, unhooking it, exposing the creamy flesh to the icy air.

She was cold, shivering.

Slowly, savoring the moment, he pulled her close, hugging her tight against him. He saw the twin black dots on her neck.

"My sweet," he whispered. "My precious . . ."

"Andre . . ." she said, using a name that meant nothing to him. A convenience. It was best to be careful.

He opened his mouth. Her eyes were locked on his mouth. He pulled back, ready to hurry now, to quicken the moment when he'd open her skin again, and taste the warmth, let it drip onto his lips, sucking at it, not wasting a drop.

While she moaned and mewled.

He brought a hand behind her neck and pulled her to him. He bit down.

She gasped and kicked against him, quivering from pleasure.

And when he was done, she fell to the deck.

He waited, giving her a few minutes. And then he helped her up. She was dazed, shivering, weak, even confused.

He helped her button up her dress.

"You must go," he said. "Hurry back to your room. I'll see you tomorrow—"

There was a voice. It didn't come from the deck.

The woman started backing away. The voice yelled out something, and Farrand looked up. It was coming from the giant mast pole, a lookout, saying words.

The woman staggered backward, maybe too dazed, too confused to find her way back to her stateroom and her husband.

But again the words, and a bell ringing, so loud, raucous, disturbing the quiet. The bell ringing over and over. He understood the words this time.

"Iceberg! Right ahead . . ."

He looked up, and he saw the slab of white so close, as if it had suddenly appeared in the water. The ship was moving right toward it, as if it was making land-fall.

We're going to hit it, Farrand knew. He had that thought, and there was an alarm attached. We're going to hit that iceberg.

And then—slowly—the blood still fresh on his lips—he started to think what that meant. . . .

* * *

He moved to the bow. People were coming on deck, a few summoned by the bell, others by the frantic shouting.

The iceberg was ahead, but already the ship was turning, cutting sharply to the left. But this ship, this Titanic, was moving too fast, and the berg looked so large, a great rectangular block with jagged white peaks jutting into the sky.

A crewman appeared beside him.

"We're goin' to hit 'er," he said.

Farrand recognized the accent. Cheapside, he thought. A thick, guttural accent used by sailors and fishmongers and the whores.

"But 'twill be aright." The crewman looked over at him. "We'll just graze the berg." The crewman laughed. "A bit of a bashing around, sir, I'say. That's all that will—"

Together, they watched the berg approach as if it were a white island, and S. S. Titanic was set to dock.

The accent. It brought memories. . . .

Farrand had to leave Carfax Abbey. They would have found him after one of his servants began to kill, crazily. When the man began to slaughter the whores— he had to do something.

The white island was close. . . .

"There we are, sir—" the crewman said. The bow was gliding past the berg.

And that's when Farrand heard the groan. The boat staggered as if it had beached, and then moved on, sluggishly, filling the night with the sound of metal tearing.

The man knew the ship was taking a gash on its side. He could *feel* it. But—we missed it, he thought. Didn't we? This isn't so bad.

It was over in a matter of seconds, the ship slowed, still veering away from the berg, the ghost island now left behind.

The deck was suddenly filled with people. From the other side of the promenade, someone tossed an icy snowball. It landed at Farrand's feet. He reached down and touched the ice, musing about where it had come from, how long it had been since it had fallen, and how many miles it had traveled to reach his fingertips. It felt so cold. . . .

People were talking excitedly.

The ship moved.

But—and here he hoped that he wasn't letting his senses, his finely-tuned senses, run away with him—he thought he detected a difference, a subtle change in the motion of the ship.

He moved past the elegantly dressed first-class passengers, some pointing back at the berg, pulling their white silk scarfs tight around their neck, talking animatedly about the disaster narrowly averted.

He moved back into the ship.

The ship was—he had no doubt now—moving differently.

No . . . doubt.

He went down the stairs. The captain's office was located in a wing off the grand staircase. He hurried down an abandoned corridor, moving quietly on the red carpet. Everyone was outside, gathered together, chattering about this great event.

But he expected that the captain would be down here.

He saw the door. It was shut.

Farrand moved against it, breathing deeply. He pressed an ear close to the wood and listened.

He heard the fluttering rustle of paper, of big sheets being flipped, and then a voice. The captain, he wondered? Yes, it was Captain Smith.

"But how much could be damaged, Mr. Andrews?"

More rustling of paper.

Another voice, one he didn't know.

"There are tears, gashes here, and here, and here. Perhaps at least three more. There are three more bulkheads gone, all flooding."

"But the others? Surely, they are fine. And that leaves—"

"Ten. Yes, those compartments were spared any damage.

"Then—"

The papers rustled again, and Farrand could picture the blueprints, the giant schematic drawings of the ship. He imagined them with the water flooding in—

"Titanic can float with one, two, even three compartments completely flooded. But the berg tore a gash right along this line. With those six watertight compartments gone, she will sink."

There was silence. Farrand held his breath. His mind was racing now, calculating—what does this mean? What does this mean to me?

"How long?" Captain Smith asked.

"Two hours . . . maybe a bit longer. But only a bit."

He backed away. He turned, numb, his mind a jumble of ideas, of dangers met and surpassed, of moments when his victory was nearly snatched from him. This was all too incredible, too improbable.

He turned back to the staircase . . . back to the wooden frieze, the clock now ticking so noisily.

Two hours, maybe less. He stared at the wood carving, at honor and glory bowing before time.

Farrand pulled his lips back, and he snarled at the carving. He snarled, exposing his fangs, not caring who saw, not giving a goddamn who watched him rage at the stupid joke.

And then he drifted outside again. . . .

* * *

There were not enough lifeboats. Women and children first, those were the instructions. But some men were jumping right in. They'd be damned if they'd go down with the ship. Even some crewmen jumped in, leaving women and children crying, begging to get into the lifeboat.

Out in the dark sea, he could spot a few lifeboats already bobbing around the great ship, a funeral watch.

He saw John Jacob Astor back away from one boat. The American raised his hand to his wife as the lifeboat was lowered. Then the millionaire turned and looked over at Farrand. They had spoken briefly that day.

Other men looked around at the boats being loaded, looking for a chance to jump on.

But Astor looked over resignedly. He smiled.

Perhaps he respects me because I'm not getting into the boats, Farrand thought.

Farrand looked down at the water.

I would—if it was a possibility, if that was something that I could do—oh, yes, I wouldn't hesitate.

He shook his head. The ship was tilted now, the angle growing more severe by the minute. Signal rockets were being launched from the stern. There were muttered stories of a ship on the other side, a mystery ship sitting in the distance that wasn't answering the distress signal.

Some people had jumped into the water, the panic claiming them. And they screamed, crying out as the incredibly cold water squeezed their chests and made it impossible to breathe.

The boat's angle increased.

There was only one thing to do. He knew that. He had considered every other possibility, including getting into a lifeboat and chancing that it would be found before the sun came up, that he could somehow hide and—

Another lurch, more fireworks. The band was playing a hymn, treacle, the bleating sounding so pompous, so stupid while the hungry sea ate the ship and all who clung to it.

He turned away. He walked off the deck, and hurried inside, past gamblers playing a final hand of poker, and passengers drinking until the room wobbled, trying to blot out the last terrible moments.

He hurried. The ship groaned continuously now as if every rivet, every metal plate was under stress.

He reached a door that was marked "For Crewmen Only."

It was a door he had used before. It was supposed to be locked, but Farrand had arranged it so that with a jiggle of the handle, the bolt slipped open. Then he hurried down the metal staircase. He heard people yelling, perhaps second-class passengers searching for life vests or a way to the boats reserved for First Class.

And on down deeper, to the nightmare corridors of steerage, past crying children, the angry sounds of crewmen trying to keep order, to make the poor passengers line up while they fought their way up the stairs, past Farrand.

Farrand stepped aside to let the first wave go, and then he pressed tight against the green wall of the stairwell and inched his way down.

One man punched him, screaming:

"Where ya goin', you fool? Go *up*, go—"

But Farrand kept sliding past them until he was finally able to move below the damp and smelly corridors populated by the lowliest passengers on the ship.

Just below was the cargo area. His heart beat madly.

What if it's already underwater? What if I can't get to it.

But the boat's tilt was making this part of the ship rise out of the water.

He lost his footing, and slid forward at one point, banging his head against a metal stair. But then he quickly scurried up.

The lights were still on, but surely the power, the electricity that fed them would be gone soon.

The boat moved, sliding down quickly now, the weight in the front pulling it down. He heard crashes and—even here, so far below the decks—he heard the screaming, the band playing, the noise of things collapsing, and—

He reached one cargo room. Great crates blocked his way and he had to clamber over them, digging his long, manicured nails into the wood, climbing over the jumbled hill to the next cargo compartment.

To the metal vault.

It looked like a silvery metal crate. An oddity to be sure, but no one questioned what valuable items Monsieur Farrand might be transporting.

It stood alone. No other heavy cargo had fallen to block the opening.

Again the ship moved, and the bow had to be fully in the ocean's grasp now.

Time . . . I have just moments, he knew.

He went to the metal vault. He felt the front, searching for the small moving pieces, imperceptible, unnoticeable, the panels of metal that were a secret lock, a combination.

He pushed at the shiny metal, but nothing happened.

I made a mistake, he thought. I'm rushing.

He took a breath. Another movement, and a stack of boxes fell into his arm, and he felt his skin tear. It would heal—quickly—but still there was pain, and now his arm did not move as swiftly, or as well. He shoved the boxes away and returned to the metal vault.

Again, he pushed at the moving pieces, the puzzle he'd devised from a Chinese box he'd purchased in his travels.

There was a click. And the vault opened.

And he saw—strapped to the other side, fastened with great metal clamps—the coffin.

He stepped into the vault. The lights sputtered outside, the naked bulbs protesting the loss of power.

Darkness is coming, he thought. For how long . . . for—

He pulled the metal vault shut. He felt his way to the coffin lid, feeling the letters, the name.

His hand ran across the metal plaque. Vlad Tepes.

And underneath . . . *Count Dracula.*

He opened the coffin. It smelled of his body, of centuries of sleep, and perfume, and blood drying on his lips, and now—of something new—a salty smell, oil, and soon—

He lay down.

The cracking sound, like an explosion, traveled even inside here, inside the watertight vault.

He shut his eyes.

Darkness, he thought. Darkness . . . for how long?

He felt movement, banging, even as he forced his consciousness to that near-death state. Movement, sliding down, Titanic breaking in two . . . groaning, the twisted metal crying out.

Until there was nothingness.

And nothing except waiting.

* * *

He slept for decades.

And then there was a sound.

He was sure of it. A sound here, and it wasn't just a natural movement, some shifting of the sea floor. It was a man-made sound. Dracula was sure of it.

Twice before he had made himself come to a state of awareness. There had been some earthquake, a tremendous movement of the sea floor. As he came to awareness, he listened to the rumbling, wondering whether something might make his vault pop open, exposing his coffin, his body, to the hungry creatures in the sea.

It had been years, maybe a decade or two after the accident.

Of course, that was his great fear. He was trapped here. What if he emerged? To do what? To crawl on the ocean floor, to make his way to a shore maybe a thousand miles away while sharks and hungry fish chewed at his withered flesh. They'd tear at him until he was nothing, his immortality squandered like grains of sand thrown into the sea.

He knew that, as dark as the ocean floor was, it offered him no escape from his tomb.

And of the lifeboats? What if he had still been in one when the sun rose? He would have been trapped in the open boat, seared on the small wooden ship like an animal cooked live in a skillet.

The sound again, a whirring, a noise—came closer. He opened his eyes in the darkness, looking at the total blackness inside his coffin.

Another time, there had been a noise overhead— certainly decades ago as much as he could figure time. There had been a sound of a motor overhead.

But it went away, and he waited.

Thinking, all the time thinking, that there was no way out. To be immortal and trapped at the bottom of the sea. . . .

It was a terrible irony.

The sound grew in volume. A whirring noise, an engine of some kind. And he thought:

What could it be? It's not on the surface. It's not a ship. It's something down here, something outside the Titanic, looking at the ship.

That makes sense. He had no idea how many years had passed. But surely the day would come when people would be able to come down here, to see and—

The whirring seemed almost loud. It paused, just outside.

Perhaps—perhaps looking at his steel vault.

Then—a terrible moment—it moved on, growing fainter, moving to other parts of the ship, prowling over the Titanic's carcass which was probably broken into pieces, its innards exposed for this *thing* outside.

Then it went away completely.

But Dracula didn't close his eyes. He stayed awake, for just a bit. To savor the thought, the *realization*.

They'll be back. And someday when they return, they'll be able to bring things to the surface. They will see the silvery metal vault, and think it such an *odd* thing. They will wonder about it and, as people do, they will become even more curious until they must *have* it, must bring it to the surface.

It may not be for a very long time.

But I can wait. I'm used to waiting. I have all time to wait.

And only then did he shut his eyes and give himself over to the void, the blankness, the emptiness of his deep sleep.

VOIVODE

by
Douglas Borton

(Excerpts from the journal of screenwriter Eric Payne, written on a Toshiba laptop computer and stored on a 3.5-inch diskette.)

3 May

Bucharest a disappointment. Too much gray Stalinist architecture, not enough medieval charm. Blame it on Ceauşescu; the late, unlamented dictator gouged out the city's historic center to build his House of the People—three times the size of Versailles! They say it's got a conference room as big as a football field, but they won't let tourists inside; whole place is an embarrassment to the new, anti-Communist regime.

Not here to sightsee anyway. Work to do, and I'm doing it. Yesterday bought train ticket for Braşov at local CFR office. (Major hassle; endless lines; slow, grouchy clerks.) Train leaves tomorrow A.M., so meanwhile I checked out Old Princely Court, the ruins of a minor palace built by Vlad himself. After that, I convinced (bribed) a taxi driver to take me out to Snagov Monastery. Officially, the count is still said to be buried there; but according to the Florescu-McNally book, excavation of the purported grave in 1931 revealed only an empty hole. I think Stoker would have liked it that way.

Driver got me back by dinnertime. I rewarded him with three packs of Kent 100s, better than money around here. Nice dinner at Casa Capşa: beef Wellington, peanut ice cream, a pleasant local wine.

Continuing to read up on Topic A. Frankly, the real Count Dracula might make better movie material than his fictional counterpart, but try convincing Ron of that. The locals don't call him Dracula, though the name is historically valid—his dad, Vlad II, was known as Dracul (Dragon), and so his son was Son of the Dragon (Dracula). The preferred moniker is Vlad Tepeş, pronounced "Zepesh" according to my chain-smoking cabbie, meaning Vlad the Impaler. He was a nasty son of a bitch, worse even than some producers I've known. Check out this contemporaneous report, quoted by Florescu and McNally:

"He [Vlad] killed some of them by breaking them under the wheels of carts; others, stripped of their clothes, were skinned alive up to their entrails; others placed on stakes, or roasted on red-hot coals placed under them; others punctured with stakes piercing their head, their navel, breast, and, what is even unworthy of relating, their buttocks and the middle of their entrails, emerging from their mouths; in order that no form of cruelty be missing, he stuck stakes in both breasts of mothers and thrust their babies onto them . . ."

This is the same guy who created a "forest of the impaled"—twenty thousand Turks writhing on wooden stakes. Ouch. Even by the standards of the fifteenth century, Vlad was bad.

Not sure how much all this research is really going to help with the script, but it's Ron's nickel. Speaking of whom, better see if I can reach him by phone or fax (fax—in Romania?) tomorrow before train leaves.

Enough for now. I'm going to recharge the laptop (using the adapter, natch—220 volts in these sockets), set the travel alarm, and hit the sack. Tomorrow, Braşov.

* * *

4 May

Feeling much better tonight. It was a relief to escape Bucharest and see the real Romania.

At the train station I managed to make an international call, updated Ron on my itinerary. He had news: met with Rutger Hauer yesterday, thinks H. will commit if the script is right. (Subtext of phone call: better make sure it's right, Mr. Screenwriter.) Still looking for the best people to play Mina, Van Helsing, et al. Personally I don't think anyone will top Cushing as the vampire hunter, but I kept my mouth shut. Ron is hot for this project, thinks it will be the definitive bloodsucker movie, and who am I to argue with a guy who's won four Oscars and bankrupted two studios?

Train ride was, predictably, a nightmare, though at least I had the good sense to buy a first-class ticket; there were geese and chickens in second class. Train was crowded, slow, and hot, but I had a window seat, and the scenery provided a beautiful distraction. Rustic villages, medieval churches and keeps, ox-drawn carts on dirt roads. Probably hell if you have to live the life, but it will look good on the screen. I shot a roll of Kodachrome.

Braşov is bigger than I'd expected—about three hundred thousand people. I checked into the Hotel Postavărul; got a room with a bath, thank Christ. Late lunch/early dinner at a nearby café: grilled veal, very tasty. Too late to head off for Bran today, so I took a walking tour of the Old Town (historic area) and absorbed some local color.

Got to admit, Ron was right about the trip. If I'd stayed in L.A., my image of Transylvania would have been straight out of Tod Browning and Terence Fisher. That's the problem with contemporary Hollywood; everybody's getting their inspiration from other movies instead of from real life. Shit, I sound like Ron.

* * *

5 May

Interesting developments.

Woke early, grabbed breakfast, took trolleybus to Bartholomew Station, caught bus for Bran. Like the train, it was too crowded and too hot, but the ride lasted only half an hour. Bran is a small village with no decent hotels, but I lucked out; while I was wandering around the train station trying to determine my next move, I was approached by a young man who speaks good English. His name is Stefan Ivasiuc, and his family puts up foreign tourists in their home at the edge of town. Five bucks a night—I could get used to the prices in this country.

He took me home and I met his folks: his father Alexandru, mom Mariela, and teenage sister Adela. Nice people, straight out of some Eastern European version of an Andy Hardy flick. I did my best to converse with them, relying on my rusty Italian, a language surprisingly close to Rumanian; but I wound up talking mostly with Stefan, who learned English at Central U. in Bucharest.

Mrs. Ivasiuc fed me lunch—not sure what it was, but it had a lot of paprika in it, and it tasted fine. In the afternoon I walked to Bran Castle and took a guided tour. Sure hope Ron can get permission to film here. If not, he'll probably build the whole damn thing on a soundstage in Yugoslavia, and to hell with the budget.

Lots of info on Vlad provided on the tour. There's no disputing the fact that the guy was some kind of major psychopath. Curiously, though, he's not a monster to the locals; they treat him as a folk hero. Something in the Romanian character seems to respond favorably to autocrats. No other way to explain their long toleration of Ceauşescu, who was rumored to be almost as sadistic as the Impaler himself.

(One charming tale I remember reading in Behr's bio of the dictator: Ceauşescu used to have children murdered, their blood drained and pumped into him. Secret of eternal youth or something. Probably not true, but it reminded me of a story Florescu and McNally tell about Vlad: "He dipped his bread in the blood of his victims." If so, he was literally a "wampyr"—"blood-drinker.")

Dinner at the Ivasiuc house. I made some remarks about Bran Castle and the movie project. This led to the first of the rather interesting developments I mentioned. Stefan observed that if I wanted to see Dracula's home, I was in the wrong place. Bran Castle was only an outpost that the Impaler used occasionally; his real home was a castle about thirty-five miles southwest, on a mountain peak near the Argeş River.

Of course I already knew that; but I pointed out that the Argeş castle was in ruins, thus useless for movie purposes. Then Stefan surprised me.

"Most of it lies in ruins, true," he said through a mouthful of *musaca,* the chopped meat-and-vegetable pie Mariela had prepared. "But the crypt is said to be intact."

Vlad, he explained, had built a secret tunnel that ran from the well in the castle courtyard to a cave on the bank of the Argeş far below. Connected with the tunnel is a family crypt where members of the Dracula line lie at rest.

Vaguely I remembered coming across some references to the tunnel in my research materials, though I'd had the impression it was only a peasant superstition. I suggested as much.

Stefan shook his head violently. "I have seen it," he insisted. "Not the crypt—I have not ventured that far—but I have been in the mouth of the cave. We call it *pivniştă,* the cellar. . . ."

That was when the rest of the family got into the act. Up till then, they hadn't known exactly what we were discussing; our English conversation was babble to them. But the word *pivniştă,* in connection with terms like *Vlad* and *Dracula,* clued them in. Suddenly there was a lot of Rumanian being spoken—too much of it, and too fast for me to decipher more than a few words. I gathered, however, that Stefan's relatives were less than pleased by what he'd been telling me. His dad basically lost it for a few minutes; he roared at Stefan, banging his fist on the table, not unlike Khrushchev thumping his shoe.

Eventually things calmed down, and Stefan said to me, rather meekly, "It is best if we talk no further of this." So we didn't. At least, not then.

But two hours later, as I was in my room getting ready to switch on the Toshiba and record these deathless observations for posterity, I heard a knock on the door. Stefan. In a whisper he told me that, despite his family's concerns, he would be willing to take me to Castle Dracula and lead me into the secret passage, even into the crypt itself.

I hesitated. Writing a spook show is one thing; living it is something else. But, hell, Ron would cream his Jockey shorts if he knew I was getting this kind of scoop.

"How much will it cost me?" I breathed.

"Thirty-five thousand lei."

I calculated. That was about five hundred American dollars. A small fortune in Romania, but a drop in the bucket as far as Ron's budget was concerned.

"Okay. When do we go?"

"Tomorrow, noon."

So there it is. All of a sudden I'm up to my neck in this business. My neck . . . hmm. Perhaps not the best image to use in Dracula country.

* * *

6 May

The main thing is not to be scared, not to let superstition take over. Think about pleasant things, relaxing things, a walk on the beach in Malibu, a drive along Mulholland, the trip I took to Santa Barbara last year.

We're here at Castle Dracula, and in less than an hour, at twilight, we're going into the tunnel and, if it exists, the crypt. Stefan insists on waiting till nearly nightfall; says the place is guarded by locals during daylight hours, but nobody will be here once the sun starts setting. Can't blame them; I don't want to be here either. . . .

Don't know what's come over me, except that all day I've had this sense of, pardon the expression, nameless dread. Probably started with Adela this A.M. She was just trying to be helpful, but I've got to say she scared the piss out of me when she handed me that cross.

It was just before breakfast. She came up to me, her eyes very big, her face pale, and she spoke slowly in Rumanian, pronouncing each word carefully so that, with the help of my Berlitz Italian, I could make out the gist of what she said.

''I know what my brother and you are meaning to do. It is written on his face, where I can see it even if my parents do not. I will not stop him, but I wish you to have . . . this.''

She handed me a crucifix on a chain, and I stood there holding it like Dwight Frye in the Lugosi film or Jonathan Harker in Stoker's novel. She turned and ran off before I could think of anything to say.

So I put it on, slipping it under my shirt. The metal was cold against my skin.

Breakfast was silent and tense, and I decided Adela was wrong about one thing: her parents knew what was going on just as plainly as she did. I caught hostile stares beamed at Stefan; felt looks of concern, even pity, aimed in my direction.

The pity was what bothered me. It reminded me too much of Harker's treatment as he set off for the Borgo Pass.

Well, shit, we haven't gone to the Borgo Pass or anywhere near it. Stoker got his facts wrong on that score; Vlad Dracula, despite being a compulsive builder, maintained only an insignificant castle at that location. If Stoker was off-base about that, then he must have been wrong about the rest of it too—

What the hell am I saying? It's a novel, for God's sake. Jesus, after all this research into the historical Dracula, I'm starting to think of the Stoker book itself as a historical text.

Got to get hold of myself. Might be losing my grip.

Best to focus on the immediate situation. Right now I'm sitting in the passenger seat of Stefan's red Dacia, parked by the bank of the purling Argeş. Stefan is out there somewhere, checking out the area, looking for any guards who might be on patrol. The sun is westering; the sky grows dim.

The Dacia was another surprise. Don't know how a twenty-three-year-old from a backwater village ever got the bucks to buy a car, but apparently he's had it for some time. Found out about it this morning after breakfast, when I went to his room to confer on details of the trip. He was busy packing a few items—flashlight, work gloves, boots—in a leather carrying bag. He seemed cheerful, lighthearted, despite his family's hostility.

Noticed one odd thing about his room. Over his bed, he had tacked up a series of pictures. The first was a reproduction of an ancient woodcut depicting a Dacian warrior; next, a print of the famous portrait of Vlad Tepeş, with his aquiline nose, large eyebrows, and gaunt face—much like Stoker's description; after that,

other *voievodate* and *hospodars* of the fifteenth, six-
teenth, and seventeenth centuries (I recognized Michael the Brave); and last, most strangely, the
egomaniacal builder of the House of the People, Nicolae Ceauşescu. It was odd to see the deposed, executed Communist included in what was obviously a
roll of honor. I hadn't thought anybody in Romania
still felt kindly toward that particular tyrant. When I
asked Stefan about it, he just shrugged.

"The people need a strong ruler," he said simply.

"Like Vlad Dracula?"

He gave me a strange smile. "Exactly."

I didn't argue the point. Instead I asked how we
would get to the castle, and he told me about the car.
A relief: I wasn't looking forward to another train ride.

The rest of my morning was spent making prepa-
rations for the trip. I packed all my luggage and took
it with me. Not that I don't trust the Ivasiucs to keep
their hands off it while I'm gone, but . . . well, I guess
I'm a big-city boy at heart.

Stefan and I left Bran at noon and drove for two
hours over dirt roads through beautiful countryside. At
least I think it was beautiful; my imagination was
starting to play footsie with me again, and I was too
nervous to really pay attention to my surroundings. In
midafternoon we arrived here, in this secluded clearing near the riverbank, with the ruined castle looming
over us at the summit of a cliff.

An hour ago, Stefan left to explore the area, and I
decided to drain the batteries of my laptop. Tapping
the keys is therapeutic, calming. Of course Harker felt
the same way about writing in his journal. . . .

There I go again. I seem to insist on seeing myself
as a character in a real-life version of the vampire fa-
ble. It's nuts. For the last time, pal o' mine, there is
nothing to worry about.

Vlad is dead. Shit, he died in 1476, more than five
hundred years ago. Died on the field of battle, or so

tradition has it. Died and was buried in the chapel in Snagov Monastery.

But when archaeologists dug up the grave, they found no body. . . .

So the corpse was stolen, the grave desecrated. Maybe by scared peasants who didn't want the Impaler lying at rest in a holy place. Maybe by the monks themselves. Hell, it doesn't matter. The man is *dead*.

Besides, the Stoker book is clearly fiction. If there had ever been a real Mina Murray or Jonathan Harker or Van Helsing, some enterprising Dracula fan would have tracked them down by now. Right?

Unless Stoker changed the names.

I mean, suppose—again, purely for the sake of argument—suppose there was a germ of truth to the story, but Stoker embellished it, altered certain details like names and precise locations. . . .

Ridiculous. Sure. Of course it is.

But, after all, there *was* a real Dracula—Stoker was right on the money about that—and what if he *did* survive death in some form? (That would explain why there's no corpse at Snagov.) What if he went to England, intending to conquer it, only to be driven out; and what if Stoker heard about it from some of the people involved? Or what if he was involved himself? (Some critics think Van Helsing was the Irishman's alter ego.) Stoker knew that nobody would believe the story if he presented it as factual, so he wrote it as a novel, but seeded the narrative with just enough elements of truth to provide clues that might someday lead someone on Dracula's trail. Someone like me . . .

Christ, I am absolutely out of control. Wish I had some of Ron's Valiums to snack on. Or better yet, a nice cold margarita from that cantina on Melrose.

Footsteps.

Stefan's coming back. I see him as a silhouette against the red sky, the dying sun.

He's signaling for me to get out of the car.

Your fearless correspondent takes a deep breath, squares his shoulders, swallows hard.

In the immortal words of Pat Riley . . . it's show time.

*   *   *

(The following entry is undated.)

christ oh christ oh mother of christ

Stop it. Get it together, asshole. GET IT TO-GETHER.

Okay. I'm calm now. Sure I am. Calm and relaxed.

The thing to do is start at the beginning. Every story has a beginning, middle, and end; they drilled that into us at UCLA. I know the beginning, and I guess I know the middle. The end . . . I'm not so sure about that part yet.

It was less than ten hours ago when Stefan motioned for me to get out of the car. I followed him along the riverbank to the mouth of a cave. By the time we reached it, the sun was brushing the horizon.

The cave's interior was funhouse-dark. Stefan clicked on his flashlight, and we entered together, creeping through the musty blackness. I thought of Harker descending the secret staircase to the chapel where Dracula and his three wives, the "weird sisters" as Stoker called them, lay in their boxes of consecrated earth.

Abruptly, I became aware of a change in our surroundings. The rough rock walls, carved by erosion, gave way to walls of smoother, more rounded stone. Here and there lay the disintegrating remains of what had been wooden planks, apparently put in place to reinforce the walls. The floor, too, was smooth and gently graded, curving upward.

It was a tunnel, man-made—the secret passageway

built by slave labor in the fifteenth century, at the Impaler's command.

Ahead of me, Stefan stopped. "This way," he whispered. I saw him slip into a side passage. I followed.

This passage was narrower than the tunnel had been. I heard the slow dripping of water from some unseen source. The flashlight fluttered before me, its beam intermittently obscured by Stefan's body.

Then the walls seemed to recede, and I realized we had stepped inside a large room, a chamber carved out of the rock of the mountain's heart.

"The crypt," I breathed, and Stefan nodded.

He swept his flashlight over the area. The beam came to rest on a stone coffin with a heavy wooden lid, resting on a rocky ledge at the far end of the room. Stefan moved toward it and I shadowed him, my breathing fast and shallow.

"See the marking?" he asked.

I saw it. The lid was inscribed with the crude figure of a dragon. The insignia of the Dracula line.

A sudden scraping noise startled me. The lid was moving, and for a wild moment I thought the dead man inside was lifting it. Then I realized that Stefan was laboriously dragging the lid off the box.

I gave him a hand, and together we slid the wooden slab onto the floor, where it fell heavily, raising a puff of dust. Stefan shone the flashlight into the coffin. I looked in, and that was when the real terror began.

I had expected to see a skeleton, but no; the corpse was perfectly intact, showing no signs of decomposition. My eyes took in close-cropped dark hair, pale puffy features, ruddy lips. A small man, no more than five-foot-six, clad in a yellowish-brown robe with crimson sleeves—the dragon cloak of the Draculas. A man I recognized at once, and why not: I had seen his picture earlier that day, on the wall of Stefan's room.

Not Vlad. Not the Impaler.

It was Ceauşescu.

I looked from the dead man to Stefan and back again. "What the hell *is* this?" I asked at last.

"The Conducător," Stefan said with no trace of his earlier warmth. "There are those of us who still believe in him."

I stared at Stefan as fear ballooned in my chest. "You brought his body here—after the execution?"

"Not exactly. But I serve him, now that he has come home."

I didn't understand and said so. Stefan smiled.

"Let me explain, then, Mr. Payne. My family are descendants of the Szgany. Does this word have meaning to you?"

"Gypsies."

He nodded. "Gypsies who served Dracula, as Mr. Bram Stoker so accurately pointed out in his memorable book. That book was more authentic than you have guessed. Only, there was no Van Helsing; he was a mere, how do you say, fictional character. In reality it was Stoker himself who tracked down Dracula and destroyed him. And yet he was not forever destroyed. Because Vlad Dracula was not an ordinary *strigoi*. He was a *voivode*. You know this term?"

"Prince. Despot. Warrior-lord."

"Yes. Precisely. The spirit of *Voivode* Dracula, Prince Dracula, would not rest, even after damned Stoker had pierced his heart. That spirit, disembodied, wandered restlessly for centuries. Until it found a new body to inhabit, a new form to take."

I shook my head. My brain had stalled; nothing was making sense.

"In August of 1944," Stefan went on patiently, "a young man came to this castle. He came to make a pilgrimage to the great *voivode*, Vlad Tepeş, who had fought so bravely to liberate his country from the Turks. He came at a time when Romania was under attack by a new enemy, the Nazis. He came—and he discovered this crypt.''

"Ceauşescu,'' I whispered. "Is that who you mean?''

A nod. "He was not a great man then, only a confused boy who had been in trouble with the law and had spent some time in jail. He knew his country needed new leadership, strong leadership, iron rule, but he knew not how to bring it about. But that night, as he communed in this crypt with the spirit of Dracula, he felt a new power come over him. His confusion vanished, his childish uncertainties fled. He was a new man, infused with new strength. When he returned to Bucharest, he quickly won a seat in the Assembly and began scaling the heights of power.''

"His power didn't last," I said, hating the quaver in my voice. "He was deposed by a popular revolution, executed by firing squad.''

"He was betrayed!'' Stefan barked. "Betrayed, just as Vlad Dracula was betrayed by his soft-spined brother Radu. Betrayed and killed—and yet . . .'' His voice softened. "Yet not killed, not really. Because one possessed by the spirit of the *nosferatu* cannot die so easily. He lives on after death, not as a man, but as a *strigoi*, a *wampyr*. He lives on, not as Nicolae Ceauşescu any longer, but as Vlad Dracula. *Voivode* Dracula, alive again, alive forever!'' His eyes widened in a kind of crazed glee. "Look, Mr. Eric Payne! Look!''

I stared down into the box again and saw Ceauşescu staring back.

As I watched, he rose slowly, stiffly, his long claw-like fingers extended. I thought of Max Schreck in *Nosferatu*. I knew Stoker had embellished his story on at least one point. There was nothing urbane, nothing romantic, about this undead thing, this bloodless zombie climbing out of its box. No words of wit—no words at all—would pass through those red lips skinned back to reveal gleaming, wolfish fangs. No emotions would ever be read in those wide, staring, mindless eyes; no living qualities could be found there, save one: hunger.

Stefan was laughing. "You sought the real Dracula, Mr. Payne. Well, there he is. And he wants very much to meet you!"

Then I understood why Stefan had brought me here, and all the rest of it, too: why he made a habit of befriending tourists at the train station, why his family objected so vehemently to any discussion of the crypt, why they had looked at him with loathing, and at me with such obvious pity, why his sister had given me the cross—

The cross!

The thing that had been Ceauşescu was moving toward me, red eyes flashing, taloned hands outstretched, when I fumbled the crucifix out of my shirt and thrust it blindly at his face.

There was a double hiss as the metal slammed into his forehead—a hiss of pain from Ceauşescu, a hiss of burning flesh as the crucifix stamped him like a brand.

He drew back, snarling. Stefan lunged for me, snatched at the cross. I jerked it out of his reach—we grappled—his flashlight clattered on the floor, its beam washing the room in loops of light as it rolled. With a final effort, I shoved the younger man backward, directly into the vampire's arms.

Stefan was Ceauşescu's servant; but the *strigoi* was wild with blood lust, and the beat of the young man's arteries, the nearness of so much fresh blood, must have been too much to resist. With an animal growl, Ceauşescu buried his fangs in Stefan Ivasiuc's neck.

I fled then, fled in darkness, with no flashlight to guide me. I pounded through the side passageway into the main tunnel, then stumbled out of the cave. My boots kicked up sprays of mud as I raced along the riverbank in the light of a rising moon.

The red Dacia was just ahead. Panic seized me as I wondered if the keys were still on Stefan's body. No, they were dangling from the ignition, thank Christ. I started the car—the engine turned over at once, another miracle—and then I was speeding along the dirt road, back the way we had come, while Castle Dracula shrank in the distance and my heartbeat throbbed in my ears.

I drove directly to Bucharest, arrived at Otopeni Airport at 2:00 A.M. The only flight going out tonight was a short hop to Belgrade. I booked a seat on it—just wanted to get out of Romania as soon as possible.

Now it's 3:30 and I'm sitting in the terminal waiting for the boarding call. My hands still haven't stopped shaking and it's hard for my fingers to hit the keys.

Christ, I can't forget the sight of those teeth . . . those crimson eyes. . . .

* * *

(The next entry, undated, is believed to have been made approximately one hour after the last.)

Flight canceled. Airport fogged in. A mysterious fog that came out of nowhere and shut everything down.

Vampires control the elements, can create fog.

He's after me. He's *here*.

My plan now is to drive south into Bulgaria, see if I can elude him that way.

Help me, God. Please help me.

* * *

7 May

I'm writing this in a room at the Hotel Stadion in downtown Veliko Turnovo, Bulgaria. Night has fallen.

I didn't want to stop driving, but I had to. Hadn't slept in too many hours, was starting to make mistakes. Took a wrong turn somewhere—must have been near Pleven—the highway signs were printed in Cyrillic, and I couldn't read them right. . . .

I don't want to be out on the road at night anyway. Safer here. At least I think I am. Tomorrow I'll proceed to Sofia, catch a flight to Greece or Italy—anywhere. A daytime flight. Vampires are helpless in daylight, can't summon fog, can't prevent the plane from flying.

I only have to get through this night. I'm still wearing the cross, and I bought fresh garlic at a local market and put it all around the room. Keeping the window shut, door locked.

It may not be good enough. Since sunset I've been hearing the cries of wolves in the distance. Vampires exercise power over wolves, don't they? They can make the animals do their bidding.

He's still on my trail. Still in pursuit.

Ordered a bottle of wine from the hotel restaurant. A dry Riesling. I intend to drink the whole damn thing. Only way I can sleep—and I need sleep.

Figured it all out while I was driving. In my research on Romania, I'd picked up a fair amount of info on Ceauşescu. Still have the Behr biography with me; that one contains the most clues. Just small things, small but telling—scattered bits and pieces that fit together now.

Even in his lifetime, Ceauşescu was known as "the Communist Dracula." He had a reputation for draining the blood of children. He was a sadist, a mass murderer, like Vlad; and also like Vlad, he was a passionate nationalist who hated foreign interference in his country's affairs. He and Vlad were both profligate builders; Vlad raised castles all over Wallachia and

Transylvania, and Ceaușescu erected his gargantuan House of the People. And, of course, Ceaușescu did everything he could to restore Vlad's reputation. He proclaimed 1976 "the year of Dracula," even issued a commemorative stamp in honor of the Impaler.

Noticed something else too. The same pattern repeats each time. Vlad Tepeș was crowned prince of Wallachia in August 1456. Dracula, according to Stoker's book, invaded England in August 1890. Dracula's spirit, according to Stefan, took possession of young Nicolae Ceaușescu in August 1944.

In every case the monster's purpose was the same. Power. Conquest. He seethed with the ambition to rule, to dominate, to kill en masse. He's never been content to exist in obscurity. He's driven by the need to be in death what he was in life: a *voivode,* prince, dictator.

There's one other thing. A quote I remembered from the Behr book. Tonight I found the page, tore it out, underlined the quote. It says everything that can be said.

He told us. He knew we would not believe.

I have to stop writing now. Have to sleep.

Tomorrow I'll make it to Sofia, then perhaps Athens or Rome. Then L.A. He can't follow me there. Can't. Can't.

One more night of this horror, and I'll be safe.

Ron, you asshole, why couldn't you have decided to do a remake of *National Velvet?*

I've drained the last of the wine. Getting drowsy. Better turn off this glorified typewriter and get to bed.

Outside, the baying of the wolves is louder.

I'm almost too tired to be afraid.

Almost.

* * *

(The following article appeared in the May 9, 1992, edition of *Sofia News*, an English-language newspaper published in Bulgaria.)

BIZARRE HOTEL INCIDENT
LEAVES U.S. TOURIST DEAD
by Georgi Mitov

Veliko Turnovo—An American tourist, Eric Payne of California, was found dead in his room at Hotel Stadion on the night of May 7. Circumstances surrounding his demise are reported to be highly unusual and disturbing.

At approximately 11:30 P.M., other hotel guests and members of the staff heard a loud crash, as of shattering glass, from Mr. Payne's second-floor room. This was followed by a series of barks and howls, seemingly of animal origin, and by Mr. Payne's prolonged screams.

Alarmed, the concierge, Dimitar Vitosha, opened the door with a master key. Inside he discovered Mr. Payne dead on the bed, his throat savagely torn out. The window was broken, and through it Vitosha glimpsed several indistinct gray shapes disappearing over the edge of the balcony.

A passerby on the street below, his attention drawn by the crash and subsequent screams, observed three or possibly four very large gray wolves leap from the balcony of Mr. Payne's room.

"They landed on the hood of a parked car," the man, Boris Vasov, said. "Then they jumped off the car to the street and ran right past me. Their fangs and paws were red with blood, and one of them carried a silver crucifix in his mouth."

The wolves vanished into a thick fog that had developed only a short time earlier. The fog hampered efforts by local authorities to track down the animals. All such efforts have so far proved fruitless.

It is believed that the wolves, in an extraordinary display of boldness and agility, gained access to Mr.

Payne's room by jumping from the roof of the car to the balcony, a vertical leap of a distance normally thought to be impossible for such animals. Upon scrambling onto the balcony, they smashed through the window and converged on Mr. Payne as he awakened.

Wolf attacks are rare in the area. Local police have no record of any similar incidents, and are at a loss to explain the episode.

Inhabitants of Veliko Turnovo reported hearing the howls of wolves earlier that evening. Many said the sharp cries were unlike anything they had heard before.

Understandably, the local population is terrified of a second attack. Schools have been closed, and children are being kept indoors. To date, however, there have been no further disturbances.

The deceased has been identified as a writer of Hollywood motion pictures, who was traveling in Eastern Europe to do research for a forthcoming film project. Among his possessions, police found a portable computer, which will be returned to the United States.

Mr. Payne arrived in Veliko Turnovo driving a red Dacia with Romanian plates. The car was not a rental vehicle, and authorities are unsure how he obtained it. A trace of the car is presently being conducted by the Romanian police.

A final curious aspect of the case concerns a scrap of paper found in Mr. Payne's wallet. The paper, torn from a book, has been identified as page 164 of "Kiss the Hand You Cannot Bite," a biography of the late Romanian president Nicolae Ceaușescu, by Edward Behr. Mr. Payne was carrying the book, along with several other volumes on Romanian history and culture, in his luggage.

Two sentences on the page had been underlined repeatedly. They read as follows:

"By 1970 he [President Ceaușescu] already showed

DRACUSON'S DRIVER

by
Richard Laymon

The graveyard shift at the Wanderer's Rest Motel suited Pete fine. It went from midnight to 8:00 A.M. Between those hours, there wasn't much to do: answer the phone, though it rarely rang; once in a great while register a guest arriving unusually late. The job consisted mostly of simply being there to keep an eye on things.

Pete liked keeping his eye on things.

In particular, the younger and more attractive of the motel's female guests.

Few of them ever visited the motel office during the long, late hours of Pete's shift. But he made up for their absence by visiting them.

All the ground level rooms had rear windows. None of the rear windows had curtains that worked quite properly—Pete had seen to that. The curtain gaps gave him many wonderful sights. As did the bathroom windows. Because the bathrooms had no ventilation fans, and because the rear of the motel was sheltered by a steep rocky slope, the windows were often left open. As a result, Pete had spied many sweet things stripping for showers, stepping into and out of the stalls, afterward rubbing gleamy slick skin with threadbare towels.

"Yo, Boydy-babes," Pete said as he entered the motel office to relieve Boyd Marmon. "How's it swinging?"

Boyd abandoned the rear of the registration counter

fast enough to avoid a friendly smack on the shoulder or back.

Alone, Pete inspected the registration cards. All but three of the downstairs rooms were supposedly taken for the night. So he waited until 12:30, then did what he called a "window run." And another at 1:00 A.M. Still others at 1:15, 1:30, 1:45, and 2:00.

For all his efforts, Pete viewed two dumpy women, one cute teenage girl who'd already changed into her Garfield nightshirt and would probably not be removing it in the near future, and a gal who sat in an armchair, her back to the window. Though this one had lush blonde hair and bare shoulders, she would not stir from her chair. She looked wonderful from behind. Was she beautiful? What was she wearing that left her shoulders bare? Something strapless? Maybe a towel? Or nothing at all?

She was the main reason Pete kept making window runs that night. After first spotting her during the 1:00 trip, he pretty much ignored the other windows and spent his few minutes gazing in at her, aching, *willing* her to get out of the chair and turn around. But she never did. Not while he was watching. And when he made his 2:00 run, her window was dark.

He peered in, anyway, but saw nothing.

She must've already gone to bed.

He'd missed her.

He thought, *Shit!*

He thought, *No damn fair!*

On his way back to the office, he nearly tripped over a black cat that had been hanging around the motel lately. He tried to give it a punt. It scooted, however, so his shoe only nicked its rump. He threw a rock at it, but missed.

At the office, he kicked open the glass door. He kicked the front of the registration counter.

If you had any guts, he thought, you'd kick open that babe's door and *take* her.

She might even like it. A sweet, balmy night like this, she's *got* to be horny.

Course, the card says she's in there with her husband.

So what? Break his head open, and *then* nail her.

It perked Pete up to imagine such things.

He sat behind the counter and dwelled on his fantasies. What she would look like naked. How she would feel. What he would do to her. What he would force her to do to him.

Pete had only been with one naked girl. Beth Wiggins. Last June in his dad's car after the Senior Ball. She was the worst looking girl in school—therefore the only girl he could work up enough guts to invite.

She'd been as eager as a puppy dying for affection.

In the car after the dance, she'd been all over him.

She had onion breath and boobs like uncooked bread loaves and a jumbo gut and an ass a mile wide. She'd wanted it bad. Pete had always thought *he* wanted it bad. Confronted with a lusting and unattired Beth, however, he found out that all he wanted was to get away. He didn't even get hard when she sucked on him. So then she'd started to cry.

So then he'd smacked her.

When he smacked her, he *did* start getting hard. So he did it again, and got harder. But she squealed and slugged him in the nose, and that put a stop to everything. They both got dressed and she sobbed all the way back to her house.

Never again, he'd vowed that night.

No more pigs.

Unfortunately, he was terrified by the idea of speaking to—much less asking out—any female he found the least bit attractive.

He could *look* at them, though.

Spy on them through windows.

Dream about sneaking into their rooms, subduing

them, stripping them, forcing them to comply with his every wish.

Hardly a night went by that he didn't pursue such thoughts about one or another of the motel guests.

He would *love* to make the dreams come true.

If only he were invisible. . . .

Or if he could figure out a way to hypnotize or drug one of them without her ever suspecting. . . .

A way to have his fun with a gal and get away with it, that's what he wanted. And he savored the problem, toyed with it, considered possible solutions. He knew there *was* no solution. No way, ever, to act out his fantasies and be totally, absolutely, utterly one hundred percent certain of not being so much as suspected.

Still, it was fun to think about.

Pete spent a lot of time, during the long silent hours after quitting his window runs for the night, imagining what he might do to the bare-shouldered woman. And then he spent even longer toying with various plans he might employ for getting away with it.

At times, all of it seemed very real.

He could see her, smell her, taste her, hear her rough breathing and gasps and squeals. Shrieks of ecstacy and pain sounded so much alike.

If he drugged her, of course, she would feel neither.

Maybe bash her on the head. Tie her to the bedframe. Wait till she comes to before starting in on her. Yes.

Shiny with sweat. Striped with bright red ribbons of blood.

Writhing, squirming, screaming . . .

* * *

Pete was startled from his reveries, just after 4 A.M., when a hearse glided to a stop beneath the motel's portico. It looked like the real thing—long and black and shiny, its rear side windows draped with curtains.

The moment he saw it, icy prickles raced up Pete's spine, stiffened the nape of his neck, made his scalp crawl.

"Oh shit," he muttered.

A hearse!

Why's a *hearse* stopping here?

For just a second, he considered a quick drop behind the counter. He could pretend not to be here.

But maybe the driver had already spotted him.

Anyway, he told himself, that'd be chicken.

Nothing to be scared of.

Instead of trying to hide, Pete lowered his head and gazed at the stack of registration cards. He heard a car door thump shut.

A hearse had never stopped here before.

Pete had never *heard* of a hearse stopping at a motel.

Weird. Awful fucking weird.

The bells above the office door jingled.

Sweat trickled down Pete's sides. He drilled his eyes into the stack of cards, terrified of looking up.

Footsteps approached.

Make him go away! Please! I don't like this!

"Hi."

The sound of the voice shocked him. It sounded cheerful. Cheerful and young and female.

He raised his eyes.

The girl on the other side of the counter wore a black uniform: a black, visored cap tilted up in a jaunty way atop a head of very short, pale blonde hair; a black tunic with two rows of brass buttons down its front; black slacks that hugged her legs; gleaming black leather boots as high as her knees.

The uniform might've looked grim and severe on someone else. On this smiling, slender girl, it looked like a lark. She was a pixie playing dress up.

Gazing at her, Pete felt as if his heart might quit.

He'd never seen anyone so . . . so fine.

He felt stunned nearly senseless by the curve of bangs that hid her entire right eyebrow, by her huge blue eyes, by the smooth warm cream of her skin and the delicate curves of her cheekbones, nose, lips, and chin, by the long smooth glide of her neck.

"Are you quite all right?" she asked.

"Me? Sure. Fine." He bobbed his head. "You . . . You just reminded me of someone, that's all. Would you like a room?"

"That I would. It's been a mighty long night." She raised her index finger. "A single should do nicely. My companion won't be requiring a bed."

"Your companion?"

She swung a thumb over her shoulder. "My stiff friend out in the bone-mobile."

"What? You've got a . . . a dead person in there?"

"Don't fret. I won't allow him out of his coffin."

Pete stared out at the hearse. "My God," he muttered. "There's really a dead guy. . . ?"

"Oh, yes, quite. Does that present a problem?"

"I don't know."

"He needn't be registered, you know." She gave Pete a quick, gamine grin.

"I guess it'll be all right," he said.

"Super."

"How long would you be staying with us?"

"Ah, the rub." She sighed. "You see, the thing of it is, I've been at the wheel since sunrise."

"Sunrise *yesterday?"*

"If I stay up a few more hours, it'll be an even twenty-four. In other words, I'm wasted. So what I should like to do is climb into bed and sleep through the day."

"Mmmm."

"Not the way things are usually done, eh?"

"You're right about that. Checkout time is noon."

She shrugged. "I'll really need to stay on until evening. Perhaps as late as nine o'clock."

"That is sort of a problem."

"I know. I've been around this particular bend a few times before. Next, you'll be explaining that you've no choice but to charge me for two days' occupancy."

I can't lose her.

"No. That wouldn't be fair. I tell you what, I'll fix things so you only need to pay for one night."

"You can do that?"

"Sure. My parents own the place." It was a lie, but the girl had no way of knowing any better. "I'll give you a nice ground-floor room at the end of the wing. If you'll just fill this out?" He peeled a registration card off the stack, slid it across the counter to her, and snapped a pen down on top of it.

Pete was good at reading upside down.

The girl's name was Tess Hunter.

She was with the Greenfields Mortuary of Clayton, New York.

"You're a long way from home," Pete said.

"So's he." She gestured again with her thumb. "The poor bloke burnt himself up in a yacht fire on the St. Lawrence. His family intends to finish what the fire started, and spread his ashes on their beach property in Malibu."

Pete found his nose wrinkling. "He *burnt up?*"

"Not quite. Charred on the outside, though I should imagine he's still rather rare on the inside."

She pushed the card toward Pete.

"And how will you be paying?"

"Cash."

He charged her for one night in the room. After receiving the payment, he gave her the key to room ten. "There's an ice machine right next to the office here, and. . . ."

She shook her head. "Won't be needing it. It's just

a quick shower for me, if I can stay awake long enough, and then to bed.''

A shower!

''Could I give you a hand with your luggage,'' Pete asked. He knew his face was red.

''Does the offer include a hand with the coffin?''

''Huh?''

''Oh, I'm afraid I can't leave poor Mr. Dracuson in the hearse. Somebody might make off with him, you know.''

''I'm sure nobody would. . . .''

''It's quite a responsibility, chauffeuring the dead.''

''But. . . .''

''I'd be sacked for sure if I should lose him.''

''Where do you want to put him?'' Pete asked.

''In my room, of course.''

''In your *room?*''

''You haven't a rule against it, I hope.''

''Not that I know of. But . . . do you *do* that? Keep the dead guys with you in your *room?*''

''Oh, sure. Doesn't bother me a whit, actually. 'Cept for those that snore.''

Pete surprised himself by laughing.

''What's your name?'' Tess asked.

''Pete.''

''So, Pete, you'll lend me a hand with the box?''

He gave her a nod, then hurried around the end of the registration counter. He opened the office door for Tess. She stepped quickly to the hearse and opened its passenger door for Pete.

She wants me to ride with her!

The thought of sitting beside Tess in a car made Pete's heart pound fast. To be so close to her! In the darkness!

Not in a hearse, though.

No way.

''Thanks anyway,'' he told her.

''Pop in. I'll give you a ride to the room.''

"That's okay. I'll walk."

"The hearse puts you off, does it?"

Already on his way, he looked back at Tess and said, "No, no. Just that there's no point. The room's just over there."

"You may not get another chance, you know, to ride in the front of one."

"That's okay."

She entered the passenger side, herself, swung the door shut behind her, and slid across the seat. She was no sooner stationed behind the wheel than the engine *voomed* to life. The headlights came on.

Pete was already halfway across the parking lot by the time the hearse began rolling forward. It turned slowly, beams creeping over the blacktop until they found him. Framed in their brightness, he followed his long shadow to the parking space in front of room ten.

He faced the car, squinting until its headlights died. The engine went silent. The door swung open and Tess climbed out. She walked toward him briskly, swinging an overnight case at her side.

"Let me get the door for you," he said.

"Thanks." She handed the key to him.

He unlocked the door, reached into the room and flicked a switch. The chandelier came on. Though it was suspended above the front table, its six small bulbs brightened all but the farthest end of the room. Beyond the shadows there, Pete glimpsed the window. *His* window.

The sight of it sucked his breath out.

Oh, to be standing on the other side of it! Staring in at Tess!

This'll be the best ever!

The very best!

And she mentioned a shower!

In just a few more minutes. . . .

Tess stepped past him, tossed her bag onto a bed and swung around, grinning. "Spiffy room," she said.

Pete nodded. "Is that all the luggage you have?" he asked.

"It's all I need."

He backed out of the doorway as she approached. Then he followed her. The seat of her trousers looked very tight. It hugged her rump, flexed and shifted with every step she took.

At the rear of the hearse, he kept his eyes on Tess, savoring her looks, thrilling himself with the knowledge that he would soon be spying on her, and also avoiding the sights that he preferred not to see.

He watched Tess, not the hearse, as she swung open its rear door. He watched Tess, not the coffin, as she pulled at it and dragged it toward her.

"Poor Mr. Dracuson isn't very heavy," she said. "But if you'd like to take hold of the front . . . ?"

Pete realized she was standing motionless, waiting for his help, an end of the coffin braced against her chest, the other end resting at the edge of the hearse.

He hurried to the front, found handles on both sides of the dark wood box, and swung it clear.

The coffin wasn't nearly as heavy as Pete had expected. In spite of Tess' comment about the weight, he'd thought it would be a lot tougher to carry. He supposed that large amounts of Dracuson must've been left behind in the boat or river. Ashes.

Tess maneuvered herself close to the rear of the hearse. She shut the door with her rump. "Okay," she said.

"You got it?"

"I'm fine. How about you?"

"No sweat," Pete said.

As he lugged the coffin backward, he imagined dropping it. He pictured it smashing down, the lip dropping away, a charred black husk tumbling out. A withered thing, faceless, hunched like a fetus. Black dust rising off its skin shell. Flakes falling. Pieces—a nose, a finger—silently breaking off.

But it didn't happen.

Together, they carried the coffin into the room.

Just inside the doorway, Tess said, "Right here's fine."

They lowered it to the floor..

"Have you ever seen him?" Pete asked.

"Oh, yes. I helped put him in, you know."

"How does he look?"

"Bloody awful." She tapped the box with the toe of her boot. "I'd open it up and show you, but the smell might be rather off-putting."

He tried to laugh. "I wouldn't want to see him. Thanks anyway."

"Well, thank you for the help. He's a bit tough to manage by myself."

Pete returned the room key to her.

She put it on the table, then pulled the wallet out of her back pocket. Pete held up his hands.

"No. It was my pleasure."

"A pleasure, was it? Lugging a stiff?"

"Well. . . ." He shrugged. "You know."

As he stepped past the coffin, Tess returned the wallet to her pocket. She moved out of his way, but extended her hand. "Thank you again," she said.

"You're welcome." He shook her hand.

It sent heat rushing up his arm, heat that spread and filled his entire body.

The heat stayed, even after her hand went away.

Pete swallowed. His voice trembled slightly as he said, "If you need anything, I'll be right in the office."

"Have a good night, now," Tess said.

He stepped outside, and she shut the door.

He headed straight for the office. Walking fast. It would've been much quicker just to hurry around the corner of Tess' room, but he wanted to *appear* to be returning to the office. Just in case.

He entered the office, glanced around. Saw it was

deserted. Heard no phone ringing. Then turned around and left. He rushed around to the rear.

No light spilled into the darkness from *any* of the windows.

Not even from Tess' at the far end of the building.

This can't be!

If I get cheated out of this . . . !

It's okay, he thought, that the bathroom light isn't on. Only means she hasn't started her shower. Good. I haven't missed anything yet.

But the window at the back of her *room* looked dark.

That light *has* to be on, he told himself. I just can't see it from here.

After all, the gap between the edges of the curtains was only a couple of inches wide. It wouldn't allow more than a narrow strip of light to shine out.

Maybe she pinned the gap shut, or something.

Pete crept toward Tess' windows.

Not even so much as a flicker of television light showed within any room along the way.

He stopped at Tess' bathroom window. Frosted glass, gray in the darkness. One side open all the way.

Fantastic, Pete thought. Incredible.

When she takes that shower. . . .

If she takes it.

He rushed in a crouch to the main rear window and peered in.

Peered into a black void.

She just got here! I was only gone a minute! What the hell's going on!

Calm down, he told himself. You didn't miss anything. She hasn't had time to change for bed, much less take a shower. She probably just left the room for some reason.

What if she's on her way to the office?

She needs something. No towel in her room? Something like that. Phoned the office. Now she's looking for me.

Shit! What if she finds me?

As fast as he could move without making too much noise, Pete made his way to the end of the building and alongside the windowless far wall. At the front corner, he leaned forward.

The hearse was parked in front of the room, just where Tess had left it.

The lighted walkway leading to the office looked deserted. Except for the cars lined up in front of the ground level rooms, the parking lot was empty. Even the road beyond the parking lot seemed abandoned and desolate.

Pete studied the windshield of the hearse. When he opened the driver's door, a courtesy light came on.

Tess was not in the hearse.

He went to the motel office. Tess was not there, either.

She's gotta still be in her room, he thought. Maybe she just turned off the light, flopped on one of the beds and zonked out.

Too worn out for that shower she wanted.

So tired she probably fell asleep in her clothes.

Wasted.

What if she's so wasted she can't wake up?

*   *   *

Nobody will ever know, Pete told himself as he slipped his spare key into the lock of room ten.

He wished he had gotten started earlier.

It had taken him a while, though, to work up the nerve. By the time he'd left the office, light had already begun to creep across the sky from the east.

He'd nearly lost his nerve.

But all the windows along the front of the motel were still dark.

Even if somebody does see me, he thought, it won't matter. I'm the night manager. I have every right to go into a room. Besides, none of the guests had signed up for more than one night. All of them would be gone by noon.

It'll work out fine.

If Tess doesn't wake up.

She won't.

As long as I'm very quiet . . . and don't shine the flashlight on her face.

Anyhow, Pete knew that he might not be able to get into her room, at all. Most guests, before retiring, fastened the safety bolt. If Tess had done that, the game was over. Pete sure couldn't risk breaking in. It was silently with the key, or nothing.

If she was dead tired, though, maybe she'd neglected to fasten the latch.

Maybe.

Pete turned the key, twisted the knob, and pushed. The door swung inward.

Oh my God! Fantastic!

The door hinges squeaked a bit. Pete cringed, but he didn't quit. He inched the door open wider and wider, then slipped inside the room and eased the door shut behind him.

The room was not totally dark. Strips of dim gray showed between the curtains of the big front window, the small rear window. The vague hints of light were useless, however. Pete could see no details of the room's interior. Not the furniture, not the coffin, not Tess.

He heard nothing except his own quick heartbeat.

Then the quiet rub of his hand against cloth as he slipped the key into the front pocket of his jeans, another rub as he drew his hand out.

He switched the heavy, steel-cased flashlight to his right hand. He curled the fingers of his left hand over its lens. Turning the light toward his face, he thumbed the switch. His fingers went rosy, so nearly transparent that he could see their shadowy bone-shapes.

Though the darkness had prevented him from seeing either bed, he knew exactly where each had to be. He aimed his flashlight, spread his middle fingers slightly, and watched a bright ribbon stretch down to the surface of the nearer bed.

No feet or legs. Not so much as a bulge in the covers.

He swept the light sideways.

The bed was neatly made, empty except for Tess's overnight bag. The top of the bag was spread open a bit. She must've been into it.

Pete lit the other bed, and gasped.

For just an instant, he thought Tess was sprawled out, dismembered, decapitated. Then he realized he was looking at her strewed clothes. Cap, tunic and trousers black against the smooth pale bedspread. Tall boots standing upright on the floor beside the bed.

But no blouse. No bra or panties or even socks.

Had she been going around with nothing on, at all, beneath her black costume?

Pete heard his heartbeat quicken its pace. His mouth felt dry. He was suddenly short of breath. As he panted for air, he felt himself getting stiff and hard.

She must've done it in the dark, he thought.

Turned out the light right away, even before starting to undress.

Did she suspect something?

Is she naked now?

Maybe just in her bra and panties.

Flimsy little things. . . .

Black like the rest of. . . .

Where the hell is she?

Hiding? Maybe she heard me unlocking the door.

Oh, my God.

If she's awake and knows I'm here, Pete thought, it means major trouble. Huge trouble. Disaster.

Getting fired, he realized, might be the least of his troubles.

Could he end up in jail?

I just wanted to look at her!

He dropped his hand from the front of the flashlight, and the full bright beam shot forward. He shined it on the coffin just beyond his feet. Sidestepped around the coffin. Knelt between the beds and lifted the hanging covers to make sure she wasn't hiding under either bed. Got to his feet and checked the space on the other side of the far bed. Turned in a full circle to light every corner of the room. Then entered the bathroom.

No tub, just a shower stall.

He swept aside the plastic curtain and shined his light in, ready and hoping to find Tess cowering naked on the tile floor.

She wasn't there.

Where is she?

She hasn't left. The hearse is still here. Her clothes are still here.

Outside the bathroom, Pete played his light over the scattered clothes.

She was the best, the finest. He had never in his life seen such a girl. All the others were . . . crud . . . compared to Tess.

This isn't fair! Where are you?

In despair, Pete sank down onto the corner of the bed.

I'll wait for her, he thought. She's got to show up.

What if she had spare clothes in that bag, had changed into them and walked away? Fed up, maybe, with chauffeuring stiffs.

Maybe that's it.

If that's it, she'll never come back.

No. No, she talked about responsibilities. She wouldn't even leave the coffin outside in the hearse, so she certainly wouldn't abandon the thing.

She acted as if it was her *duty* to transport this Dracuson fellow's. . . .

Dracuson?

Pete shined his light on the coffin.

Could that really be the stiff's name—Dracuson? Maybe Tess was kidding. Thought it would be fun to tag the poor jerk with a name that sounds like Dracula.

Like I'm sure there's a vampire in there.

Like Tess is some sort of chauffeur for a fuckin' vampire, rides him around all night, maybe pulls off the road sometimes to let him fly off and suck people, and then they hole up all day long in some crummy motel. So Drac can rest up in his coffin till dark, and Tess can get her beauty sleep.

Stupid, Pete thought.

Crazy.

No such thing as vampires.

If there *is* such a thing, though, everything would make sense. Everything except Tess's disappearance.

Hell, Pete thought, that's an easy one.

She isn't just Dracuson's chauffeur. She's his lover, too. She's right there inside the coffin with him.

Yeah, right. Every day and twice on Sundays.

Pete knew that the notion was stupid, crazy, ridiculous. But he suddenly *had* to look inside the coffin.

He stood up. His legs shook as he sidestepped past the coffin. He felt as if his stomach was shivering.

She isn't going to be in there, he told himself.

If you open it up, all you'll find is crispy black Mr. Dracuson.

Yeah? Then where is Tess?

Pete crouched at the foot of the coffin. He shined his light on the lid. The wood looked like mahogany, reddish brown and glossy.

He listened.

No heavy breathing came from the box. No thrashing sounds, no thumps.

If she's in there, he thought, she isn't humping any vampire. She's lying quiet and still.

Maybe she heard me, knows I'm here. What if she tries to nail me when I open the thing?

He thought, *Ha.*

He almost laughed out loud.

If Tess was inside with her vampire lover, which seemed highly unlikely, she would be facedown on top of him. She could hardly spring upon Pete from that position.

He gripped the flashlight in his right hand.

He hooked the fingertips of his left hand under the edge of the coffin lid.

Throw it off quick. Don't give her a chance to roll over.

But he imagined the noise of the heavy lid thumping the floor.

No way.

What I need here, he thought, is silence and stealth.

Instead of casting the lid to the floor, he eased it upward a few inches. He ducked his head. He shined his light inside.

And glimpsed pajama legs of pale blue fabric as shiny as silk.

A hot jolt raced through him.

He raised the lid higher, crept his light up the body.

There was only one.

It lay on its back, cushioned by the white satin of the coffin's lining.

A slim body garbed in loose, clinging pajamas that took on the curves they covered. The shirt overhung the waist of the pants. It had four big white buttons. It rose smoothly over the mounds of her breasts and jutted with the thrust of her nipples. It was spread open above the top button, showing a wedge of bare chest, the hollow of her throat.

Pete saw the underside of her chin. Though his angle was all wrong to see the face, he knew this was Tess.

Who else *could* it be?

So where's Dracuson?

Who the hell knows?

Who the hell cares?

It only mattered that he had found Tess and she still seemed to be asleep.

Pete set down the flashlight to free his right hand. Then he worked his way to the side of the coffin. Slowly, carefully, he lifted off the lid. He swung around and lowered it onto the bed.

Kneeling, he picked up his flashlight. He held it low as he changed it from his left hand to his right.

Don't shine it in her eyes, he warned himself. That'd wake her up for sure.

Why the hell is she sleeping in the coffin? Two perfectly good queen-size beds.

Must be nuts.

Seriously weird.

But, oh man! So what?

He raised the flashlight. He shined it on her chest, holding it close enough to her body so that the bright disk would stay tight and away from her face.

He gazed at her breasts.

He wanted to touch them.

He wanted to slip the big white buttons out of their holes and spread open the pajama shirt and see her breasts naked and touch them, caress them, squeeze them, try them with his mouth.

This is it. My big chance. She's zonked, dead to the world.

But she'll wake up if I try to undo any buttons. She'll wake up for sure if I touch her.

Wake up screaming.

Unless. . . .

He shined his light on her face, saw her open eyes, gasped as his heart lurched, then leaned and swung, hammering her forehead with the flashlight. The first blow shattered the lens and killed the bulb. After that, he swung and pounded in darkness.

When his arm wore out, he dropped the flashlight.

He got to his feet, staggered to the wall, and flicked the switch. The chandelier came on.

He looked down at Tess.

Her face was a bloody ruin.

But the rest of her was unharmed.

Pete took a pillow off one of the beds. He covered Tess' face with it, thinking only to hide the ugly damage, but then pressing the pillow down hard just to make sure she wouldn't wake up and cause trouble.

He held the pillow down tight against her face for a very long time.

Leaving the pillow on her face, he unfastened the big white buttons of her pajama shirt. The shirt was spattered with blood. He opened it wide. Some of the blood had soaked through, staining her skin pink.

"Oh, Tess," he whispered. "Oh, Tess."

Her breasts were wonderful. More than wonderful. He lingered over them, gentle and rough, savoring their weight and texture and taste.

Later, he plucked apart the snap at the waist of her pajama pants, drew the pants down her legs and tossed them onto the bed. He raised her legs, spread them, and hooked her knees over the edges of the coffin.

He stripped and climbed in.

He kissed her and caressed her, squeezed her, licked her, nipped her, probed her, and it was the best, better than anything, worth everything, worth killing her for especially when he thrust into her slick heat.

It was what he had always wanted to do, and better than he'd ever dreamed.

* * *

The cleanup went off without a hitch.

Though the sun was bright above the cornfields to the east by the time he dragged the coffin out of room ten, nobody seemed to be wandering around. Pete was pretty sure that nobody saw him.

He got the coffin into the rear of the hearse.

He drove the hearse for a while, then turned up a dirt road and parked it inside a shabby, abandoned barn.

He left the coffin in the hearse, Tess in the coffin with her various garments and overnight case. But not with the pillow, because he was afraid it could be traced back to the motel.

He spent a few minutes wiping away his fingerprints with a rag. Then he hiked back to the motel.

The hike of two miles took him half an hour.

He made one more visit to room ten for the pillow and his broken flashlight. He concealed them in the trunk of his car.

At the office, he returned both room keys to their proper nook and destroyed the registration card. He kept the cash payment for himself.

So far as anyone except Pete would ever know, Tess Hunter had never checked into the Wanderer's Rest Motel.

* * *

At eight o'clock that morning, Pete was relieved by Claire Simmons. He ate breakfast at Joe's Pancake Emporium. Then he drove out to the barn where he had left the hearse.

He spent the hot, summer morning with Tess. And much of the afternoon.

Late in the afternoon, tired to the bone, he drove home to the one-room house that he rented on the far side of town. He set his alarm clock for 11:00, stripped and climbed into bed.

He closed his eyes and smiled.

Life could be so great when you just had the guts to take what you wanted.

Wow!

He wondered how long Tess would keep.

Pretty hot in that old barn, but. . . .

* * *

The alarm didn't wake Pete. He was stirred from his slumber, instead, by light shining in his eyes.

He blinked at the glare of the lamp beside his bed.

He squinted at his clock. Only 10:03.

What the hell. . . ?

"You slimy creep."

He knew the voice.

Young and female, with a lilt that sounded a bit English.

Pete bolted upright.

Tess, naked, stood beyond the end of his bed, fists planted on her hips, legs apart. She was shaking her head at him. Her face was clean. Unswollen, unbroken. As if Pete had never battered her to a mess with the flashlight.

Her short, pixie hair was matted down and dark. Wet. Her skin had a rosy hue. She looked as if she had just stepped out of a shower.

But Pete didn't find himself thrilled by the sight of her.

He didn't get stiff and hard. On the contrary, he shriveled.

He peed.

He began to whimper.

"I only wanted a bit of a rest, you know," Tess said.

"Ya . . . you're *dead!*"

A corner of her mouth tilted upward. "Not quite, actually—in spite of your moronic efforts, you sniveling pervert. If you'd had half a brain, you would've put a stake through my heart. My God, you *had* to know what I was."

She stepped up onto the bed.

"Don't . . . don't hurt me. Please."

"Oh, I fully intend to hurt you. I'll hurt you quite

a lot, word of honor. Cross my heart." She flicked a fingernail against the creamy skin between her breasts, drawing a quick invisible X. "You'll hurt beyond your wildest dreams."

Bearing her teeth, Tess bellowed and threw herself down on Pete.

And kept her word.

AFTER THE BALL
by
John Lutz

Madame Vyette peered from behind her fringed mask, looking beyond the waltzing dancers whirling about the gleaming floor of the spacious Royal Ballroom. Seated on a blue velvet sofa was General Pichet, staring at her with what could only be desire.

From behind the dainty red mask she'd raised to hold an inch away from her eyes, she returned the general's affectionate gaze with one of supreme disinterest. Usually not a woman to avoid romantic liaisons, she could summon no glimmer of even possible passion for the general, though he was a man still in his prime and without question handsome. And his expertise as a lover, his romantic appetite, and promiscuous nature were well known throughout the city. Even the filthy and raucous commoners gathered in the markets and the square winked lasciviously at the mention of the general's name. Having had his fill of war, he'd turned his attention to more personal conquests.

Madame Vyette knew she should be flattered by his attentions, yet she simply was not. In fact, she'd of late felt little desire for the deliciously romantic trysts that had been the very focal point of her life before the dream.

And what a strange dream it had been, lived as if real last week in her silk-sheeted bed. In the dream Count Malnoir, a ghostly pale yet fascinating man from the southern provinces, had come to her like a lover. First he'd merely loomed at the foot of her bed, dressed in his black ensemble with its long cape lined in red silk. She'd simply lain there and stared at him, for some reason unable, or perhaps unwilling, to make the slightest move. Oddly, she'd felt no discomfort at the sight of his towering figure in her chambers, though he was a man she'd never liked nor trusted.

When much time had passed, he'd smiled and walked around to the side of the bed to stand very near her, his eyes, so unexpectedly sad and old (for he was a young man), locked with her own uncertain gaze. He'd bent down, moved his face close to her own. Sure that he was about to kiss her, she'd found herself offering her lips, even at that moment wondering why she was agreeable to what was happening. She'd felt alert yet oddly drugged, as if the part of her that might summon outrage and resistance had somehow been removed.

But he hadn't kissed her. At least not on the lips. Instead he'd cocked his head rather awkwardly to the side and moved it alongside her own, then lower. She'd felt—

She'd awakened at that point, alone in her chambers, feeling the chill night wind pressing in through the open window.

She'd risen and padded barefoot across the cool floor to fasten the shutters. Then she'd returned to the warmth of her bed and dropped into a deep sleep that had lasted long into the morning.

* * *

The dream had stayed with Madame Vyette in ways she found unsettling. In the middle of doing something completely unrelated to it, some form of gaiety or social intrigue, it would suddenly be there at the forefront of her thoughts. She would again see Count Malnoir's gaunt features, so near her own, and for an instant she would feel . . . she wasn't sure what.

Then there was the other thing she didn't want to think about, the occurrence of two mornings ago. She'd found her servant Marie's tiny dog Petite dead in a corner of her bedroom. There had been no mark on the animal, and it appeared not to have died in pain. Poor Marie had been crushed when Madame Vyette showed her the unfortunate dog. Sobbing, she'd run away and disappeared for the rest of the day.

There was something about the dead animal that Madame Vyette couldn't quite recall, something that fled from her consciousness as if recoiling from the light of memory. Even as Marie had fled. Madame Vyette was not a complicated woman; she knew that about herself and had known it even as a young girl. Her strength, her power, was in her physical beauty. So it bothered her in particular that some subtle and denied knowledge hung over her thoughts, clouding her languid days and weighing down her nights of revelry.

"The handsome general exhibits an interest in you," a voice said behind her.

She spun about, startled, and there was Count Malnoir, lean and elegant as always in his dark formal attire. He was smiling at her, and she was surprised as she had been each time she saw him during the past week that she found him increasingly attractive.

"The general's interest isn't returned," Madame Vyette said, perhaps a bit too crisply.

Count Malnoir smiled and, unaccountably, her knees weakened. "Were you to spend time with the general," he said confidently, "I'm sure you'd find that your desire for his presence would intensify. Affairs of the heart are like that."

Madame Vyette put on her most coquettish smile, expertly embellishing it with a brief flutter of eyelashes. "You seem to know a great deal about the human heart, Count Malnoir."

"Oh, more than you might imagine." He clasped

his hands behind his back and looked out over the ballroom. "Is there an opening on your dance card?"

"For you? Of course!"

"For the general, my dear."

He was quite near her, his gaze engulfing her. There was in the depths of his dark eyes a compelling and frightening quality that made her shiver, not without pleasure. Fear and pain and love were the puzzle pieces of her existence.

A momentary dizziness overcame her, and she was aware that she was crossing the vast room, smiling and nodding to acquaintances.

At her approach, the general stood up with military erectness, his palm resting on the jeweled hilt of his sheathed saber.

"You're not dancing, General." Was it she who had spoken?

Light glinted off the general's strong and even teeth, off the many campaign ribbons on his broad chest. He was a robust and accomplished man; perhaps he did have some appeal. He said, "I would consider it an honor if I may lead you in the next waltz." He offered his arm.

She gazed up at him as she lightly hooked her arm through his, and he escorted her out onto the wide, polished dance floor. The orchestra began to play.

She wasn't surprised to find that he was a superb dancer. At first they whirled around the floor in mutual silence. Then, halfway through the waltz, the general said, "Of course you know I admire you greatly, Madame Vyette."

"Of course. Many men do."

He studied her features to see if she might be joking, saw that she was not, and grinned. "Who could blame you for being in love with yourself?" he said, leading her down the long edge of the floor. "Such lovely blue eyes, such perfect skin and grace of posture, such a smile to lure doves from the sky—"

"I won't argue with you, General," she said, laughing. "But compliments, like other sweets, should be consumed in small measures."

"Perhaps, Madame, after the last dance I might escort you home."

"And?"

"And prove you wrong. I think you'll find that unreserved adoration will affect you in a way quite the opposite of having consumed too many sweets."

Despite herself, she felt her heart begin to beat fiercely. She rested her cheek against the general's shoulder. The wool of his uniform was coarse against her flesh. "You have a reputation as a scoundrel with the ladies, General."

"But an agreeable scoundrel," he said with a glinting grin, "and one often invited back."

"Were I to leave here with you, would I be safe?"

"I should hope not."

The music ceased, and the general, flushed from his effort of whirling her through the waltz, smiled inquisitively at her and led her off the floor.

"I'll consider your kind offer," she told him.

"That in itself is a grand compliment," he said.

He continued to stare at her in a manner she could only think of as hungry, as the Marquis de Luynes offered his arm for the next dance.

Her last dance was with Count Malnoir. He waltzed with a smoothness that made Madame Vyette feel she was truly floating. Each time he spun her she would glimpse over his right shoulder the imposing figure of General Pichet, standing and gazing at her from the edge of the dance floor. Despite his intimations of gentle adoration, there was a warrior's cruelness about him that excited her.

Count Malnoir said, "No doubt the general is writhing with suspense over whether you'll accept his offer to escort you home."

"And how do you know he made such an offer?"

"Two reasons," the count said. "At each dance, every man wonders who will leave with you. And the general isn't a fool; he would surely make the request of your company for after the ball."

"He did make such a request."

It occurred to her that her life was itself a ball, one that would end only when she grew old and wrinkled and was no longer an object of romantic desire. But until then she would live and dance and laugh and damn the future. Either with the general or some other man.

The music stopped. The count looked into her eyes. "And you're going to grant the general's request?"

"Yes," she heard herself reply.

Somewhat surprised by the decisive abruptness of her own words, she almost rescinded her answer. But when she saw the count's smile of approval she felt a warm pleasure that made her realize perhaps the most important thing in her world had become pleasing him.

Obeying him.

"I will only tell you what's best for you," he said. "Always."

"I know that." She felt a thrust of urgent need, not sexual. What was it she craved?

Count Malnoir bent and kissed her lightly, coolly, on the forehead. She suspected he'd done it to make the general jealous.

She murmured, "I had a strange dream—"

"I know, my dear, but we mustn't keep the general waiting."

She left him and walked to where General Pichet stood aside from a knot of revelers who were gossiping near the exit. Beyond the tall open doors was the night, which held for Madame Vyette a frightening but titillating appeal.

The general grinned widely, like a man who couldn't quite believe his good fortune.

Madame Vyette took his arm, and they walked out into the night together.

"You seem solemn," he remarked, after gruffly dismissing his personal staff and hailing a carriage.

"Oh? I feel in quite good spirits. Daring, in fact. As if new worlds await."

"They do, my dear Madame Vyette, I assure you."

She leaned against him, squeezing his arm. "And *I* assure *you,* my handsome general."

Gripping her elbow firmly, he helped her up into the carriage, then climbed in beside her. He rapped on the roof and gave the driver her address; she shouldn't have been surprised that he knew it. They sat listening to the rhythmic clopping of the horse's hooves and watching the dark city outside the windows. The tall wooden wheels smoothed the ride over the cobblestones to a mild vibration that Madame Vyette felt in her thighs and found exciting. The smell of the streets, of the masses of people, which she usually found repulsive, tonight was as perfume. Strange.

On rue Saint-Honore, near her home, she drew closed the curtain on her side of the carriage and said, "My aunt will be waiting up for me."

The general placed his left hand on her knee; she could barely feel it through the layers of material in the skirt of her ball gown. "I see." He rapped twice on the carriage roof, then commanded the driver to rein in and pull to the side. Through the open window he gave him money and dismissed him for the next hour. Then he pulled closed the curtain on his side of the carriage, completely blocking the faint gaslight glow of the city.

"We find ourselves alone," he said. She couldn't see, but she could *feel,* his eager smile in the darkness. It was as if she'd somehow come into possession of new and delicate senses.

His arm snaked around her shoulders and she sat very still. "I have for an eternity admired you from across rooms and streets and from the midst of boring conversations,'' he told her softly. His free hand found and caressed the swell of her breast above her bodice. His warm breath was on her cheek; she knew he was about to kiss her.

And the dream came to her in its entirety. With pain and revulsion and resignation and ecstasy. It left her horrified, dazzled, and knowing. Her new and sudden understanding was as overwhelming and irresistible as time and tide, as ancient as the stars.

How terrifying and wonderful it was that nothing would ever be the same!

The general kissed her gently on the mouth. His hot breath smelled of tobacco and bourbon. She sighed and leaned her body against his, her lips now close to his neck and the blood coursing through veins so near the thin surface of his flesh. She could actually hear the warm blood pulsing through him.

Madame Vyette was a woman of reputation and long the subject of cruel gossip; the general had been told of her preferences. He moved his hand inside her dress, found what he sought, caressed and then squeezed hard.

''I've yearned for weeks to have you alone and helpless,'' he said breathlessly. ''To make you a slave to your passion and my own.''

In the perfect darkness, he didn't see her smile.

THE WIND BREATHES COLD

by
P.N. Elrod

No one sense returned first; my inability to move or see, the cold, the soft whine of dogs, and the rough jostling all jumbled together in my awakening brain like different kinds of beans in a pot. I slipped to and fro between awareness and nothing until a particularly sharp lurch and bump caught my attention for longer than a few seconds. It was enough for me to realize that something was wrong and needed investigating. The next moment of consciousness I managed to keep hold of; the moments to follow had me wishing I'd done otherwise.

They were tugging at my feet, which seemed to be bound up, but then so was the rest of my body. I was wrapped snugly in a blanket from head to toe. The thing was right over my face, which I never could abide. I twisted my head to free myself but could not.

The tugging abruptly stopped and several dogs snuffled my immobile form. I felt an icy, tingling jump all along my nerves as I realized they were not dogs, but wolves. They whimpered and growled over me, then strong jaws clamped down on my wrappings and they resumed their work. Emboldened by hunger, they had actually entered our camp and were dragging me off to a safe distance.

I wanted to shout and bring my friends, but that might also set off the wolves. Outright panic would only kill me and I was that close to giving in to it.

Holding my breath tight, I waited and listened for my life.

There must have been dozens of them. I could hear their eager panting and claws clicking against stone. Wolves usually shy away from men—such had been my experience when Art and I had been trailed by that pack in Siberia—but this was a far different place and I'd already seen proof that a tall tale in one part of the world was God's own awful truth in another.

They pulled me along another few feet. My weight, and I was aware of every solid pound of it going over those rocks, was nothing to them. Once they felt secure, they'd rip through my blanket and clothes like taking the hide off a deer. I'd seen that happen once. The deer had still been alive when they'd started in and though quick enough, it hadn't been an easy death.

Panic surged up like bile in my throat. It choked off any scream for help I might have had. I fought against the restraining blanket. Startled, the wolves at my feet let go. One of them snarled, stirring up the others. They moved all around me, excited, nipping at the blanket as though in play. Fresh air knifed my face as the damned thing finally came loose.

Bright-eyed, with lolling tongues, and rows of tearing teeth, they scampered about like puppies. Some darted close to snap at me, wagging their tails at the sport of it. I wrenched my hands free, but they were of little use without a weapon and some dim memory told me I had no gun or knife. I scrabbled in the inches deep snow and found a chunk of rock. Better than nothing.

Then a big black one, one that I would have chosen to be the leader, raised his head to the wild gray sky and howled. The others instantly broke off their game and crowded around him, their tails tucked down like fawning supplicants seeking a favor. One after another joined him, blending and weaving their many voices into a triumphant song only they could fully understand.

The leader broke off and focused his huge green eyes upon me. It's a mistake to ascribe human attributes to an animal, but I couldn't help myself. The thing looked not just interested, but curious, in the way that a human is curious.

The wolf snarled and snapped at those nearest him. The pack stopped howling and obediently scattered. After a sharp, low bark they formed themselves into a wide circle like trained circus dogs. I was at its exact center. Some stood, others sat, but all were watching me attentively. Though I'd had more contact with wolves than most other men, I'd never seen or heard of anything like this before. Had the hair on my neck not already been raised to its limit, it would have gone that much higher.

Some of them growled questioningly, no doubt scenting my fear.

Clutching the nearly useless rock with one hand, I tore at the bindings around my ankles with the other. It was desperate work, made slow by my reluctance to take my eyes from the pack. Despite the distraction caused by their presence, I saw that for some reason I'd been wrapped like a bundle for the mail, first in the blanket, then by ropes. Why? Who had tied me up so? A burst of anger helped me get through the next few moments as I cursed the bastard who had done me such an ill turn.

Free. I kicked the blanket away and staggered upright, half expecting the wolves to close in. They remained in their great circle, watching. There were no trees within it to climb to safety and if I tried to break through their line at any point they'd be on me, so I kept still and stared back. One of the wolves sneezed; another shook himself. They knew they had me.

Winter wind sent the ground snow flying. Dry flakes skittered and drifted over the discarded blanket. With my free hand, I slowly picked it up and looped it around my arm. The big leader stepped forward. I turned to face him, thinking I was as ready as I'd ever be, only to find an instant later that I'd been utterly wrong. No man could possibly prepare himself for what came next.

The wolf lowered his head, but rocked back on his haunches, like a dog about to do a begging trick. A darkness that seemed to come from within the thing's body blurred the details as bones and joints soundlessly shifted, muzzle and fur retreated, skin swelled. It rose on its hind legs and kept rising, until it was as tall as myself. The crook of its legs straightened, thickened, and became the legs of a man, a tall, thin man, clothed all in black. Only the bright green eyes remained the same and when he smiled at me, I clearly saw the wolf lurking beneath the surface.

I was as scared as I'd ever been and could have expressed it, loudly, but there didn't seem much point. In a few minutes, I'd either be dead or worse than dead and making a lot of noise about it wouldn't help one way or another.

"I can respect a brave man, Mr. Morris," he said, pitching his deep voice to rise above the wind. In it was some of the harsh tone I'd heard when he had taunted us from the stable yard of his Piccadilly house just over a month ago. He clasped his hands behind his back and continued to regard me with the same mixture of interest and curiosity manifested in his wolf form. The wind bounced against him with little effect other than to whip at his dark clothes and pale hair. Black on white was the mark Harker had left on his forehead, a deep cut in the pallid flesh. That was how I knew for certain who he was. I'd had only glimpses before, and the last time I'd seen that face I'd . . . I'd. . . .

Something very like the wind, but existing solely within my mind, whirled inside my skull. The man before me, the circle of wolves, the snow, the cold, all faded for an instant of nothing before asserting themselves again. It was like the focus of a poorly made telescope shifting in and out.

"I killed you," I said faintly. I recalled the impact going right up my arm when my bowie knife slammed firmly into his chest.

"So you did," he admitted. "With some help from Jonathan Harker, do not forget."

"Yes. . . ." Harker had buried his own knife in the monster's throat. We'd fought our way through those Gypsies to get to the wagon and the box on top of it. The Gypsies had drawn their own knives and one of them had . . .

I dropped the stone, my hand going to my side. The clothes there were thick and stiff with dried and frozen blood.

My blood. It had fairly poured out of me. Jack Seward and Van Helsing had tried their best to stop the flow, but the cut was too deep, the damage beyond any skill to heal. Thank God it hadn't been very painful. The last memory I had was of poor Mina Harker, her face twisted by bitter grief as I slipped away into what seemed like sleep.

Not sleep. Nothing so human as that had taken me, changed me, turned me into . . .

"No need for such alarm, Mr. Morris," Dracula said, reading my face. "It's not as bad as you've been led to think."

Not knowing my own voice, a cry escaped me and, heedless of the wolves, I turned and ran. Some of them started to follow, but were headed off by a sharp word from their master. I crashed through the snowdrifts, blundered against trees, and tripped on invisible snares at my feet but kept going. Not far ahead was the warm yellow light of our campfire. If I could just get there, if Van Helsing still had some of his Holy Wafer left, there might yet be protection for us.

For *them*. At least for them.

I was close enough to see their huddled forms: the Harkers lying together, Van Helsing and Seward, Art a little off from the others, presumably taking his turn at watch. All of them were fast asleep, worn out by the hard travel and the chase, but just one shout from me would bring Art instantly awake. . . .

A hand, colder than ice, slapped over my mouth just as I drew breath. As though I were a child and not a grown man, he lifted me right off my feet and back into the cover of the forest. I struggled with indifferent success, but got in a few good kicks that made him grunt. Then he spun me suddenly and my head cracked against one of the trees.

Lights brighter than the sun blinded me, or maybe it was the ungodly pain that went with them. I dropped, paralyzed and sick from the shock. My vision slowly cleared. Dracula stood over me, his sharp teeth bared and hellfire fury blazing from his eyes.

"Fool," he hissed. "Do you think they'll show you any mercy once they know?"

"I'm counting on it," I snapped back. "I know what to expect and shall welcome it."

"Well, I do not. Give yourself away to them if you must, but not me. I've been to enough trouble over this matter and want no more."

"Go to hell."

I didn't think his eyes could hold more rage. I was wrong. He raised a hand as though to smash me like a fly, then forbore at the last second. His anger beat against me like heat from a forge, but after a long and terrible moment it dissipated into nothing.

"You're but an infant," he sighed. "You don't understand yet."

"I know enough."

"I think not. Come with me and I might be of some help to that end."

"No—"

"Stay behind and your friends will be food for my children." He gestured meaningfully at the forest around us. There was no need for him to explain who his "children" were; I could hear and occasionally see them well enough. "Come with me and all will be safe."

"For how long?"

"As long as you remain sensible. And that is entirely up to you."

He stepped back and waited, watching as his wolves had watched. He did not offer to help as I found my feet, leaning hard on the tree. Though dizzy, I was able to think, but no idea running through my mind could be remotely mistaken for a way out of this spot.

"Where?" I asked unhappily.

He pointed behind me. We were to go deeper into the trees, away from the camp. I didn't like that, but followed as he led the way along what looked like a deer trail. The wolves kept pace with us, whining and wagging their tails like dogs out for a walk. Glancing back, I saw more than a dozen of them padding almost at my heels. I realized that they were completely obliterating my tracks in the snow. Was it accidental or intentional? I made a step off to one side as a test and went on. The wolves, tongues hanging as if with laughter, sniffed the spot and easily blotted the boot print out as they swarmed over it.

Rocks rose up next to us, forming a natural wall that cut the wind. The snow underfoot thinned and vanished. The wolves followed, ears raised attentively. Dracula waited until I was well upon this trackless surface, then stretched his arms out before him, spreading them wide. As though the pack were one animal and not many, his children instantly retreated into the trees and were lost to sight.

"Where are they going?" I demanded.

The question surprised him. "To hunt, to play, to run with the moon, whatever they desire. Your friends are still safe from them, as are you."

"What do you want of me?"

"Nothing more than the answers to a few questions."

"What questions?"

He pointed to a knee-high boulder. "Please seat yourself, Mr. Morris."

He had a presence about him that could not be ignored. I sat. There was a similar rock not four feet away and he took it, facing me, and spent several minutes studying me intently.

"With your permission," he said and held his hand out, palm upward, looking for all the world like some Gypsy ready to read my fortune if I but mirrored him. I hesitated only a little, for my own curiosity was awake and on the move by now. He inspected my hands, finally comparing them to his own, which were broad and blunt. "Your fingers are of different lengths," he pronounced.

"What of it?"

"They are also quite bare, not at all like mine, as you see."

From Harker's journal I already knew about the hair on his palms and the sharp nails, so there was little need to gape in wonder.

"I see when you speak that your teeth appear to be perfectly normal. The same may not be said for my own," he added, letting them show in an almost wry smile.

"Have you a purpose to this?"

"To confirm to myself and prove to you that we are similar, but not very alike."

"We are most certainly not alike!" My voice was rising.

"I am so glad that we are in agreement," he said with a calm sarcasm that took all the wind out of me. "Such differences should reassure, rather than alarm you."

"What do you mean?"

"You know that well enough for yourself."

I did, but the agonizing terror inside made me consciously obtuse. To face the truth, to actually *speak* about it. . . .

"As I told you," he said with a glimmer of sympathy I would have never otherwise ascribed to that hard, unpleasant face, "it is not as bad as you have been led to think."

A short explosion of a laugh burst from me, a laugh that might have turned to a sob had I not forcibly swallowed it back.

"You are *nosferatu,* Mr. Morris, nothing more. I am *nosferatu,* but much more, hence the visible differences." He opened his palms again, as though that explained everything. "I know how I became as I am, but I want to know your story. Who took your blood and gave it back again? Who initiated the change in you? And when?"

I was speechless for many long moments as he expectantly waited for an answer. "Why do you want to know?"

"Those of your kind are rare. I would know more about you. You are also the first I have ever met both before and after dying. Our encounters in London and in Seward's house were brief, but I sensed the change in you. For that alone I would have spared your friends had I not made other plans."

"Plans?"

"To rid myself of the hunters without killing them. Look not so surprised, Mr. Morris. At any time of my choosing I could have destroyed the lot of you and left no trace to rouse the suspicion of the law. Knowing what you do about me, could you doubt my ability to accomplish that?''

"You're saying you spared us?"

"Your deaths were unnecessary. Better to lead you to believe in my own demise than to—"

"I saw you die, we all did."

"You saw me vanish," he corrected. "Things might not have gone so well for me had you used wood instead of metal. I am content with the results. Now you see why I had to stop you from rousing your friends; to do so would have meant their deaths and yours as well. Larger parties have disappeared before in these mountains. Accidents are easily managed—I chose to avoid such an extreme action. Believe me or not, as you will.''

And I did believe him, though I couldn't have explained why.

"Now as for your own change . . ." he prompted.

"It was a few years back, in South America," I said. "Art—Lord Godalming now—and I were at an embassy ball. I met her there. She was the most beautiful woman I'd ever seen. She and I—"

"Her name?"

"Nora. She was European, I think, though she had dark hair and eyes and that wonderful olive skin. . . ." Which I'd been on fire to touch the moment I saw her. I hadn't been the only man trying to claim her attention at that gathering, but I was the one she picked as escort for a walk in the embassy garden. I reveled in my good fortune and hoped to give her a favorable impression of myself in the time we had, but it was she who took the lead in things, which surprised me mightily. That night, holding true to a promise and plan made in the garden, she found her way to my room and we fulfilled one another's expectations— exceeded them, I should say.

I'd been exhausted the next morning, of course, not

from blood loss so much as from excess champagne and sheer physical activity. Her biting into my neck had startled me only a little. Young as I was, I'd known more than one woman in my travels and learned that each had her own path to pleasure and it was my privilege to assist her there. It was always to my own advantage to be ready to learn something new and Nora was a delightful teacher. My body's explosive reaction to this lesson was like nothing I'd ever felt before or since.

I rested throughout the day and the next night we expanded and explored our range of talent. It was then, caught up in the lust of the moment, that she frantically opened a vein in her own throat and invited me to drink from her in turn. Brain clouded and body aching for release I gladly did so, taking us to a climax that left us both unconscious for many hours afterward. I woke up a little before dawn in time to see her throw on a dressing gown and leave, then dropped away into sweet oblivion.

The word vampire was not unfamiliar, but its context for me had to do with a species of bat that plagued the area. In our drowsy love talk, the subject came up, but Nora told me not to worry about it and, lost in the warmth of her dark eyes, I dismissed any and all misgivings . . . until that day in the Westenra dining room when I volunteered my blood to save Lucy.

I had no mind for Nora then—she was years behind me, an exquisite and happy memory—and put myself forward without another thought. It was afterward, when I began to hear more from Jack and Van Helsing about Lucy's condition that the doubts crept in. I feared that Lucy had fallen victim to someone like Nora, but a rapist rather than a lover. From that point everything Van Helsing told us confirmed my many fears. It was only after Lucy's death and the hideous proof of her return that I realized what horror was in store for me when I died.

Dracula took that moment to interject. "If by that you mean being staked through the heart by your well-meaning friends, then you have every right to be horrified."

"If it will free me to go to God, then so be it."

"I doubt if He would welcome such an enthusiastic suicide," he said dryly. "Do not look so amazed, you are still one of His children—yet another difference you may rejoice in."

"How is that possible? I am—am *nosferatu*, one of the Un-Dead."

"Exactly. Un-Dead and nothing more. Do you not see?" I did not and he threw his hands up in exasperation. "Your so-sweet Nora has much to answer for. She should have told you all this and saved me the trouble and you your anguish. You *do* understand that she was, and probably still is, *nosferatu?*"

"Yes."

"And you must know by now that she was not as I am. Her offspring, which now includes you, will be like her. I have already had ample proof that my offspring, no matter how lovingly taken, will never be so tame. Mine to hers are as the wolf to the hunting hound. *Now* do you see?"

My reply was whispered, but he heard me.

"Good. You know that your soul is your own . . . and His," he said with quirk of his heavy brows toward the sky. "With some small changes you are free to live as before, but as *you* choose, for good or ill as all things will be judged in their time. For me, it is not so simple."

"What do you mean?"

"I can do that which you cannot. The wolf, the bat, the curling mist, are natural forms to me but not for you. I prefer the shadows, but may walk in the sun if necessary, you would die from it. You can no more command the weather or my wild children now than you could as a human, but that is of no matter to you. I read in your heart and by your manner that you would refuse to pay the price for such powers. Long ago I paid and still do. My body bears the signs of that payment, marking me as different from other men, and as for my soul . . . I think you would be more comfortable to remain ignorant of such things.''

From the look that crossed his face I silently agreed with him. "And what of Lucy? Am I to let you go free after what you did to her?''

"I did nothing that was not a part of my nature, a part of any man's nature. She was beautiful and willing—no, do not gainsay me for you were not there and never knew her true heart. I loved her in the only way left to me.''

"Until she died.''

"We all die, but if you wish to fix a blame for her death, then you need look no farther than her attending physicians. Had they left her alone she would still be walking in the sun. Doctors, bah!'' His ruddy lips curled with contempt.

"And my blood . . .''

"Made no difference to her health. The seeds of becoming Un-Dead were within you, but you were not Un-Dead then. To create your own offspring now you must first take blood from your lover, then return it.''

"As you've done to Mina Harker? What is to happen to her?''

"Nothing. The miracle she prayed for—'' he touched the red mark on his forehead, for it nearly mirrored the one she had carried—"came to pass. Seward and Van Helsing will not bother her. That alone should suffice to guarantee her a long and fruitful life.''

"But what you did to her—''

"That which passed between Mrs. Harker and myself is really none of your business, Mr. Morris,'' he rumbled, his brows lowering.

''But that poor woman—''

''Is quite capable of making her own decisions.'' By his tone, I knew that to pursue the matter would result in unhappy consequences to myself. And he was right. It was none of my business. Besides, to be honestly selfish about it, I had problems of my own.

Now that my eyes had been opened a little wider than before, I looked out into the night. Though all would have been pitch blackness to my friends, it was as daylight to me. The snow put a silver gleam upon everything it touched. Beautiful, but marred by the questions troubling me.

''Must I do as you—as Nora—to . . . to . . .'' The words refused to emerge.

''Sustain yourself? Hardly. To drink from a lover is one matter, but you'll find that the blood of animals is your real food. One may live upon love alone for a while, but sooner or later one must come down from the clouds and take more practical nourishment. This is as true for vampires as it is for humans. Are you hungry?''

I said nothing.

He shrugged. ''When you're ready, then.''

''What about my friends? When they wake—''

''They will find that you have been dragged off by a pack of ravenous wolves. So very tidy, is it not?''

''It's monstrous!''

''Far better that than to see your footprints in the snow walking away from the blanket that shrouded your dead body. I suspected you might revive and rise tonight, so I made sure my children and I could cover your escape.''

''But they are my friends. Must they be put through such grief?''

''Yes.'' He was not to be moved on this point. There

would be no return to them, not for now, anyway, not while his wolves were within call.

"Very well," I murmured. Perhaps later I might be able to talk to Art or Jack and persuade them to reason as I had been persuaded, but in the meantime I was feeling very lost and miserable. The icy November air, something I'd been able to ignore because of my changed condition, was sinking heavily into my body. It would take more than the coat I wore to dispel it. I shook out the blanket I still carried and threw it over my shoulders.

Dracula nodded. "Yes. It is time to go inside. My castle is not too terribly far from here. Van Helsing thinks he has sealed me from it, but there are entrances he knows not."

"Harker wrote of your . . . companions." I nearly said "mistresses" and diplomatically changed the word at the last moment.

"They are no more. In their deaths Van Helsing was more careful and they too careless. I felt them go and could do nothing." His face darkened then cleared, like the shadow of a cloud running over a mountain. "But to avenge them would bring no gain, and only reveal my deception." He gave another shrug, this time with his hands, and stood tall. "Come then, Quincey Morris, I will show you any number of dark places for you to shelter from the day, places much safer than the ones they had."

"Won't I need my home earth as you do?"

"This has become your home, Mr. Morris. When a brave man's blood strikes the ground he has purchased it for his own. You will find rest here and may carry away as much earth as you want when you leave. But perhaps you will stop a while and visit with me? The wind breathes cold through the broken battlements and casements of my castle, but you will find more comfort there than in these wastes. We two have many griefs to settle in our hearts and though I would be alone with my thoughts, in such a time of mourning it is better to have company.''

My answer was to follow him. As we picked our way over the rocks and up a narrow path, his children began to sing again.

NIGHT CRIES

by
Daniel Ransom

(For Mickey Spillane)

1

She was there again, footsteps in the rain and fog, a slender hand on the back door of the hack I drive.

And then she was inside, bringing a bracing set of scents with her: erotic perfume, chill rain, cigarette smoke, gin—

"Same place?"

"Please," she said. "And—"

She stopped herself, apparently deciding not to finish the sentence.

I put the taxi in gear, turned the Wynton Marsalis tape low, and pulled away from the curb.

She was lost in shadow. Only occasionally could I glimpse her in the rearview, usually when we passed in and out of streetlight range, an oddly strobic effect that only enhanced her beauty. She was as dark-haired, as supple and sensual, as gently lovely as ever. I had to admit that I'd been thinking about her ever since she'd stepped into my taxi three nights ago. This was the fourth night running that I took her to the same place.

We drove ten minutes, the wipers slapping away shimmering rain beads on the windshield, the heater trying to warm up a cold April midnight.

After awhile the downtown buildings gave way to blocks of snug little working-class houses and then to big homes in one of the suburbs. Most houses were dark by now and only occasionally did you see any signs of life—a man in a rainhat and raincoat with his pajama bottoms flapping against his legs walking a tiny Pekingese; and a truly dedicated jogger with bold luminous light strips across the back of his jacket—and then everything was open country steeped in fir trees and jack pines.

The fog was so bad, I had to turn down my brights. On a ten-year-old heap like this one, you won't find any fancy fog lights.

"You didn't finish what you were going to say," I said. "About twenty minutes ago, I mean."

In the rearview, I caught her smile. "I know. I decided against making a fool of myself."

"Now you've really got me curious," I said.

She was a soft, warm, disembodied voice in the back seat. "I was afraid that somebody might be following us."

"Somebody is."

"What?" she said, sitting forward on the seat suddenly. "Are you serious?"

"Afraid I am. He's been on our tail since we left downtown."

"Oh, God. Can you lose him?"

"Not out here, I can't. Not in this car. The roads are too muddy for fast driving, anyway."

"Don't stop at the mansion, then. Just drive past. Let's just go back to town."

I nodded and checked out the headlights in the rearview.

He was pretty good at it, really, knowing just how far to hang back, never getting too close, never getting impatient and doing anything stupid.

The mansion was on the right, a big tumbledown stone place that had burned to the ground one summer night ten years ago. The story had played on TV for weeks because of the mysterious circumstances surrounding the fire. For one thing, the family that lived there had only rarely been seen by anybody. For another, there was no sign whatsoever of the family following the fire. No bones in the ash; no dentures in the powdery dust. None of the four family members was ever seen again.

In the rain and ground fog, the mansion had a melancholy look, the iron gates at the entrance starting to rust now, the remains of the stone house defaced by a hundred amateur graffiti artists. The kids out in the boonies weren't as creative as the kids in the inner city.

Just as we drew abreast of the mansion, she leaned sideways and began staring out at it. With her crisp trenchcoat and rain-kissed black hair, she was an exotic portrait of mysterious beauty.

And then suddenly the car was no longer distantly behind us.

It was right on our bumper. And a man in a fedora was leaning out the passenger window firing a handgun at us, a yellow explosion accompanying the *craaack* of each shot.

The woman screamed as the back window shattered and became a dozen interlocking spiderwebs.

The man in the fedora put two bullets in my right rear tire. Almost immediately, I felt the taxi start to sink on the back side.

I kept driving, pushing the gas pedal flat to the floor, but between the limping right side and the furrows of mud, the going was no more than 30 mph.

"We've got to get away from them!" the woman said. "They'll kill me! They really will!"

But she wasn't finished. She leaned forward and grabbed my shoulder. "I know who you are, Harker. That's why I came to you for help. Tonight I was going to tell you who I really am."

I was going to say something, but that was when the man in the fedora suddenly upped the ante.

In the rearview, I saw him leaning out the window with a double-barreled shotgun.

The concussion was tremendous as the dumdum bullets smashed through the remnants of the back window and exploded the windshield.

She screamed again and started sobbing.

I grabbed for control of the steering wheel as he pumped a few more handgun shots into the left rear tire. By then, control didn't matter. With two tires gone and a mud bed for a road, I wasn't going anywhere.

Then they were out of the car and running toward us, two men in fedoras and good suits, two men whose hands were filled with Magnums.

There was no place to go.

One went to the back door and dragged the woman out into the night. I could hear her trenchcoat tear as the man yanked her free of the taxi, hear her whimper softly in terror.

The man on my side just kept the Magnum trained on my face. He didn't have to explain anything to me. His Magnum was eloquent as hell.

My headlights told the woman's tale. She was dragged to the front of the car and thrown to the ground in the middle of the muddy road. I saw all this through the cold, slanting rain.

The man then straddled her and started pistol-whipping her with the gun.

A curse got caught in my throat as the other man put the Magnum hard against the side of my head.

"Don't even think about it," he said.

The man beating the woman stopped abruptly and took something from his coat pocket.

I couldn't see what it was but the woman obviously could because her screaming started again.

I never called on my particular strengths unless it was absolutely necessary. It was time, now. My father had taught me well. "Each time you use them, Son, that means that you come one step closer to being found out for what you really are.''

But there was no choice now.

My left hand shot out through the open taxi window and grabbed the hood by the throat.

He got three shots off before I yanked the Magnum from his hand. Two shots entered the left side of my head, the other smashed through my shoulder.

All the while, the woman kept screaming. I knew I had to get to her in the next few seconds or she'd be dead.

I flung the door open so hard that the thug went flying backward, landing on his back and trying to crawl to his feet.

He tried to reach out and grab at me.

I kicked him on the jaw, knocking him flat on his back again, and then I raised my leg and brought my heel down on his trachea. When the pro-wrestling boys do this particular number on TV, the guy on the ground always jumps to his feet, holding his throat as if all that's wrong with him is inflamed tonsils.

But this was reality.

The hood grabbed for his throat all right because he was strangling on his own blood. I left him there to die and then I turned my attention to the woman.

I was three steps too late.

The other hood had the wooden stake to her heart and had just now brought down the hammer.

This time when she screamed, the sound was accompanied by a geyser of blood that sprayed all over the hood's face, and by a twitching of the woman's extremities that meant that death was already setting in. I'd seen my father do just the same thing at his own death.

The hood didn't get two chances at her. I saw to that. But then he didn't need two chances. The first one had done the job.

I strangled him to death and then crawled through the mud and rain to the woman.

In the headlights, she resembled a fallen statue, her beautiful face streaming with rain, the breast of her trenchcoat stained with her blood. I touched her hand, tried to still the trembling; brought down her eyelids, tried to shut away the sorrow in those dark, dead, lovely eyes.

I ripped the wooden stake from her heart and tossed it angrily into the nearby ditch. Then I decided I wasn't thinking rationally. A wooden stake covered with blood and flesh was bound to make the law curious. I went down into the ditch and found the stake and shoved it into the pocket of my jacket. And all the time, I kept thinking about the woman.

She'd said, "I know who you are, Harker. That's why I came to you for help."

Some help I'd been.

I had to work quickly. I took the two back tires off the hoods' car and exchanged them for the two back tires on the taxi. Then I got the woman into the back seat and drove away.

Twenty minutes later I reached the river. On this deserted stretch of water, I wasn't likely to have many visitors tonight. Still, I pulled the taxi deep down a sloping hill and parked it behind a copse of jack pines. The headlights had been killed all along.

I stripped the woman, rolled up all her clothes and stuck them in the trunk, and then took a hundred-pound bag of sand I carry around for winter emergencies and strapped the sack to the woman's back.

I waded out into the swift dark moonless river, the rain cutting at me like the teeth of an invisible monster, and when I found a place that I thought was deep enough, I let go of the woman and let her sink to the silty floor of the water, the bag pulling her down quickly.

I stood in the lashing rain, hands fisted, feeling my wounds heal and become normal flesh again.

An hour later, still numb from it all, I sat in Maxie's, an ''all-nite'' cafe that caters to the lower orders of night people. I was eating a greaseburger with an extra slice of onion and drinking a Pepsi from a glass with a big bright lipstick imprint on the rim, a souvenir left over from the last user of the glass. And I was thinking about the woman who'd come to my taxi the last four nights.

Oh, yes, I was thinking a lot about the woman.

2

My home is a converted garage in a dead-end alley. Not many people pay me visits, which is just the way I want it. For those who do come calling, however, there's a security system that's virtually impossible to penetrate, and a rather formidable Doberman should you be unlucky enough to get inside, as a very skilled burglar did one night when I was away. Jedidiah left him in pieces all over the floor. I spent two nights putting the place back together and trying to rid the air of the high tangy odor of human blood.

The place is filled with the familiar—aged but once expensive leather furniture with a very male and obstinate kind of dignity, much like the crusty old attorney who sold it to me; shiny new appliances in abundance, thanks to a cabbie friend of mine whose brother is a fence; and several bookcases groaning under the weight of maybe a thousand hardbacks, some of which date back to the 1600s.

And then there's the bed, certainly the single most curious piece of furniture in the entire cottagelike interior.

Before lying down every night, I lean over and give the mattress and boxsprings a small push. Beneath them lies a wooden frame filled with rich black earth.

It would make a wonderful spring garden. I have other uses for it, however. I sleep in it.

Most of the myths, to be sure, are fairy tales and nothing more. Garlic doesn't affect me, except on the breath of a lady I might be kissing. Touch a crucifix to my forehead, as that good old trooper Christopher Lee had done to him in one of the early (and better) Hammer films, and I'll probably just smile at you. And as for looking in mirrors. . . . Given the little belly I'm developing from too many nights of watching TV hockey and sipping Bud Light. . . . Well, sometimes it would be nice not to have to see myself at all.

To the casual observer, I appear to be a normal man of six-foot-two with a handsome but not pretty face, coal black hair and eyes, and very pale skin. I have a black belt in Tae kwon do (which makes my little bumper belly all the more aggravating), am a competent if not spectacular marksman, and am reasonably proficient with knives, bows, and the garrote.

As for other remarkable facts about myself . . . I'd say that there is only one really. I happen to be a bit over several centuries old.

In the late 1400s, my father, the man history unfairly refers to as Vlad the Impaler, watched as his entire castle fell prey to a smallpox virus that turned many of his servants murderous. A handmaiden slashed my mother's throat and then drank her blood. I know this is true. I was six at the time and hiding in my mother's closet. I saw it all.

I know that smallpox is an unlikely source for all this, but it was true; some mutant strain of it at any rate, and this you could tell by the symptoms—the fever, the blinding headaches, the backaches, chills, and vomiting. And the disfiguring scars.

As far back as 1,000 B.C., smallpox was killing hundreds of thousands of people. Later on, Pizarro noted that the disease had killed more than 200,000

Incas. Europeans died at the rate of 400,000 a year well into the early 1800s. Many sufferers believed that by wearing the color red—and even coloring their food and water red—the disease would be abated. Medieval Europeans were just as superstitious as their so-called inferiors in Africa and South America.

Anyway, this was the disease that struck the Rumanian countryside where I was born and lived.

Over the next twelve months, our land was the scene of violence that even now I don't like to think of. And it all happened at night, as the people from my father's castle roamed the land looking for new victims. They were ravenous in their appetites for carnage and sex of every description—and ravenous for blood. Nobody was safe. These people seemed to have a special taste for young boys and girls.

During the day, they hid anywhere they could. The virus was such that they became exhausted by daylight. The peasants sought out the night people everywhere. To insure that the night people were truly dead, the peasants pounded stakes through their hearts.

Eventually, of course, the peasants held my father responsible for all the bloodshed. They stormed the castle and killed all but me and my cousin Tepes, who was my age and my best friend.

We fled, escaping by longboat across the channel to the city where we became urchins for the next six months, until I saw how Tepes was changing. I never saw him during the day, when I plied the streets asking for handouts. But at night, when he thought I was asleep beneath the alehouse where we lived, I saw him drag home the carcasses of dogs and cats and young children he'd killed . . . and feast on them. I still remember trying to cover my ears so I wouldn't have to hear his lips smacking as his teeth rent the flesh he was about to consume.

Then I noticed that I, too, began to change. No longer could I bear daylight. When I tried, I became vi-

olently ill. And in the Rumania of that time—a land
that had only recently recovered from a plague of in-
fluenza—any youngster who appeared ill might well be
put to death.

I slept during the day and prowled all night . . . and
yet unlike my cousin Tepes, I did not prowl in order
to find victims . . . I prowled to save victims.

By now, Tepes had met up with others from the castle who had been similarly affected by the virus. They
hunted at night for flesh and blood.

I spent my nights stopping them, following them
and jumping to the rescue just when they were about
to claim another life.

Tepes and I even fought each other with wooden
stakes, trying to kill one another as the peasants had
killed my father.

The battle ended unsettled when Rumanian police
appeared and broke up what they thought was an ordinary fight.

After that, Tepes and his gang hunted me down . . .
and it was then I fled to France where I lived for four
centuries . . . and then came to America where I make
my home now, and where I've made informal studies
of viruses and plagues. The illness that struck my father's castle appeared eight times in the course of three
centuries, usually inspiring great orgies of violence.
And then the plague disappeared. I have found no ref-
erence to it later than 1826, when a small town in
Belgium became overrun with "ghouls" as one jour-
nalist of the time called them. All other reported out-
breaks sounded like very straightforward attacks of
smallpox, down to pustules so aggressive that the victim's eyes would not open, and his tongue might be
swollen with a rash and scabs.

Unfortunately, I also learned one other fact about
the transformation. While there are two strains of vampires, the light and dark as I think of them, light can
sometimes transform into dark with no outward symp-

toms to sound an alarm. One night you wake up and find your trusted wife, eyes glowing crimson, mouth dripping saliva, sinking her teeth into your neck so that you will walk the dark side of the street along with her. . . .

Thanks to Bram Stoker's novel, we have come to be known as vampires (also thanks to Stoker, the honorable family name of Dracula has been hopelessly smeared forever. I am, I suppose, technically speaking, Dracula, Jr.) Unfortunately, Stoker did not seem to realize that there are two types of us . . . both immortal, thanks to the curious magic of the virus . . . both endowed with many nocturnal gifts such as infrared eyesight . . . and both doomed to sleep during the day.

But there the similarities end.

The predatory vampires have a need for carnality that turns them into killers. Six coeds inexplicably savaged in a Miami Beach college dorm . . . a three-year-old girl found depleted of blood . . . a high school girl found decapitated with a dead man's sex organ in her mouth. . . . The night people have been tireless down through the centuries. . . .

As for the rest of us, we take night jobs. Some as cops. Some as emergency room nurses. Some as janitors. And some as taxi drivers. We try to live out our lives as normally as possible. Only when we are threatened with exposure in some way do we become predators ourselves, and the only people who can expose us are the other vampires . . . by attracting attention to themselves (and therefore to us) through their violence.

And so we go hunting for them when necessary so that we can live our anonymous lives . . . before normal human beings become aware of us.

In bed (my body greedily absorbing the nutrients only rich soil can offer) I looked back down the long, shadowy corridors of my life and saw images of mother and father and sister and brother—all long and sadly dead now—images fading on the surface of very old photographs, and I felt as always the almost angry loneliness that is my curse.

And then I started thinking of tonight, of how a hoodlum had hammered a spike into the breast of a lovely young woman. . . .

3

"You're sure she was one of us?"

"Yes," I said.

"That could mean somebody's on to us."

"That's what I was thinking," I said.

He shook his head. "She had a pretty tough life, poor kid."

When I got to the former Knights of Columbus hall that is now sort of a community center for all of us, McGivern was in his office. McGivern is the man all of us check with before doing anything that affects the general welfare of our people. He showed up a few years ago, made contact with the underground cell you find in most large cities and then proceeded, through skill and organization, to bring order to our lives.

If our group had need of somebody to fill the kindly parish priest role, it would certainly be McGivern. Round, bald, of twinkling blue eye and merry little smile, McGivern runs the affairs of our community. Nights, as now, you see two rooms overflowing with noisy children getting a good education, thanks to McGivern finding two recently laid off schoolteachers who were willing to work without being unduly curious about children who are awake only at night. In just the same way, he'd found a doctor who asked no questions (unfortunately, even we get head colds and break arms and run fevers) at his 24-hour clinic. McGivern even runs the bulletin board, which is a clearinghouse for nighttime jobs.

McGivern also has one other duty, one that doesn't fit into his kindly parish priest role at all. He is the sole judge and jury of the two hundred people who make up our community in this city. If he decides that any one of our group is jeopardizing the common safety, he is authorized to order that person's death. For the greater good, I believe it's called. And that's where I come in. I am the group's only trained combatant. I am also the man McGivern turns to when someone needs to be "dealt with summarily" as he likes to say. Vampires, alas, are not immune to ham acting any more than ordinary folks are. At odd moments, McGivern sounds as if he's trying to pick up the mantle of the late Bela Lugosi, that hammiest of all hams.

"You'd better investigate," he said. "Find out who ordered her killed and why. And then deal with him summarily." He was dressed, as always, in black turtleneck and black trousers. Good and wise a man as he is, he does not want for vanity. Black helps slim down his considerable bulk. He was parked on the edge of his desk now, smoking a Benson Hedges 100. One pleasant aspect of immortality is that you can smoke all you want and enjoy yourself.

"You really like this part of the job, don't you?"

He smiled right back. "If you're asking would I rather kiss an infant than cut a throat, all I can say is that it depends on my mood." The smile turned icy. "Find whomever's behind this, Harker, and kill him forthwith."

"One of your favorite words."

" 'Kill?' "

I shook my head. " 'Forthwith.' You put a certain Shakespearean spin on it."

He eyed me suspiciously for a moment, sensing an insult in my remark. Then, gruffly, he waved me off and said, "Stay in touch and don't do anything crazy. You know how you get sometimes."

I was just about to leave the community hall, when a male voice called from a small office, "Hey, Johnathan, come in here a minute, will you?"

Bob Hanson was McGivern's number two. He was a pale, quiet, faded man who had spent six centuries in Europe until he was nearly exposed by a psychically gifted priest in Amsterdam. He'd then fled over here.

While I handled all the risky jobs for McGivern, Hanson handled all the paperwork and organizational problems. He was always dressed in suit and tie, never more than three feet from his massive briefcase, and constantly giving the impression that nothing delighted him as much as poring over debit and credit columns. He had a soft handshake and wounded, sad little eyes.

"McGivern told me about the girl," Hanson said. "I'm sorry. That must have been awful to see, even for somebody like you."

I wondered if warriors had always been written off this way, as thick-skulled insensitive brutes unaffected by the spectacle of violent death? That's what Hanson seemed to be implying.

"It was awful to see. She was a bright, decent woman," I said. "And now I want to find out who was behind her death."

"I wish you the best of luck, Harker. You know that."

I nodded and left. Before I'd even left the office, he was back to punching up figures on his computer screen.

4

"Did you ever see Napoleon?"

"Not that I recall. I mean, he was a little before my time."

"I'll bet you're at least five hundred years old. I just sense it."

"Five hundred? I must be a lot of fun on a date. Skin rotting away. Terrible stench. Trouble talking. That doesn't say much for your taste in men."

I was sitting in Maxie's, the lower-order diner I mentioned previously, the diner where you get free live boxing at least once a night when two of the patrons drunkenly slug it out.

This time I sat in a booth because I had private things to talk about with a homicide detective named Chandler. Diane Chandler. And yes, since you asked, she is what I'd call blonde and attractive. Damned attractive in fact. Especially in the nice blue suit and white blouse she wore tonight.

Last spring, I'd made a bad mistake, one McGivern was kind enough not to mention any more but one that put the fate of our whole community at risk. I had an affair with Diane Chandler, a thoroughly normal and most pleasant affair that ran three months. But because we were getting serious, Diane decided to run a little background check on me, see who this mysterious guy really was. Then she started making note of my habits, in particular the fact that I was never, under any circumstances, seen in light of day.

Diane is a big horror movie fan. One night, only half-kidding, she kissed me tenderly and then looked deep into my eyes and said, "You're a vampire, aren't you, Harker? And one with a sense of humor, too, given the fact that Harker is the name of the man who tried to kill Dracula."

I didn't admit anything then and I don't admit anything now. But I did gradually ease up on my end of the relationship.

By now, all her suspicions were just fodder for our little jokes—asking me if I'd ever seen George Washington back in Colonial Days, or which side did I fight on in the Civil War—but I could also tell that she was at least half-serious about suspecting I was one of the undead, or whatever word for us the hack movie writers were using this year.

"You get anything useful?" I said.

Detective Chandler is still happy to oblige me when I ask her to find out certain things for me.

"I don't know about useful but certainly interesting. The car that ran into you?"

I'd told her that I needed a license number checked out because last night a car had struck me while I was parked at a cabstand and then driven quickly away without stopping.

"You'll never guess who it's registered to."

"Who?"

"The mayor."

"You're kidding."

What would two hoods be doing in a car owned by Mayor Atwill?

"And there's more," Diane said.

"What?"

"This morning, the two men and the car were found on a county road."

"Oh?"

"And the two men—"

"Yes?"

She stared at me. "You know what I'm going to say, don't you, Harker? You're involved in all this somehow, aren't you? You're not a cabbie at all, are you? There's a lot more going on here than you're telling me about, isn't there, Harker?"

"You were telling me about the two men. In the car registered to Mayor Atwill. Being found on a county road."

"Found dead. Somebody really did a job on them. The Medical Examiner's office said that both of them had been bludgeoned before being strangled—but not bludgeoned with a weapon—bludgeoned with fists. Let me see your hands."

"Huh?"

"Hold up your hands."

I held up my hands.

"God," she said.

"What?"

"I've never noticed before but you've got sort of wimpy hands."

"Thank you. That's awfully nice of you to say."

"I don't mean it as an insult. Merely as an observation."

"Ah."

"The way you observed one night that I had big feet."

So that was it. Detective Chandler, lovely and liberated and otherwise sensitive, was one hell of a grudge holder.

"I did not say that you had big feet."

"No?"

"No. I merely said that I'd read an article that said that the average female foot size was now 8 B. And then I said, aren't your feet 9½ AAA?"

"Exactly."

"Exactly what?"

"You may not have *said* that my feet were big but you certainly implied it."

"You are truly paranoid, Chandler, you know that?"

And then she said, so sweetly, "I suppose vampires don't get paranoid sometimes?"

"Indeed they do, Chandler," I said, standing up and dropping a dollar bill on the table for a tip. "Very paranoid, in fact. That's why I've got to get out of here and find out how two thugs came to be driving a car registered to our mayor."

"You owe me a dinner," she said. "And I plan to collect."

She walked out with me and when we were on the dark side of the restaurant, that portion of the parking lot reserved exclusively for vomiting and peeing illegally, she slid her arms around my middle and pulled me to her.

I kissed her for a long time, so long that I was starting to feel some old and awkward affection for her. But not for me the dream of suburb and wife and family. Because eventually she'd have to know the truth and this was a truth that would not set you free at all. It was a truth that would imprison you inside its dark fate.

"I miss you, Johnathan."

I sighed. It hadn't been easy, forcing myself to fall out of love with her. And I didn't want to go through it again.

I kissed her chastely on the forehead and then walked half a block to my taxi.

From the woman's purse last night, I'd taken her name and address. Now it was time I checked things out.

5

I parked my taxi a block away from the address I wanted, then walked back, taking a shadowy alley. There was no rain tonight, but there was plenty of cold wind and it was more like November than April. Every few feet I'd get a whiff of garbage overdue for collection.

She hadn't exactly been a princess, Kathy Coleman, living as she had in a tiny bungalow stuck between two big, sagging apartment houses.

Getting in didn't take much. I jimmied the lock on the back door, pushed it open, and went inside, turning on my flashlight as I stepped across the threshold.

The place was no more decorous inside than it was out. It was one big room with a tiny kitchenette in one corner, an enclosed bathroom in the facing corner. In between was a large open space with a couch and chair and kitchen table. There was also a desk and a typing chair. I walked over to it and shone my light on several pieces of paper sitting next to the phone.

"MORTON SURVEYS" was set in bold type on the top of each sheet. Running down the page were various boxes to be checked. Kathy Coleman had apparently supported herself by doing phone surveys at night, an ideal job, really, for people like us.

The next thing I checked was her bed, a single with a very handsome wine-colored quilt on it. I shoved the bed to the right. Beneath it was a frame filled with fresh, black soil.

I spent the next five minutes checking everything over. I found nothing remarkable until I went back to the desk.

In the wide center drawer, I found two things interesting enough to steal. One was a framed photograph of Kathy Coleman sitting on the lap of a chunky man in a blue double-breasted suit. He had snow-white hair and hard angry eyes. He had a plump hand possessively on Kathy Coleman's thigh. His name was Atwill. He was mayor of our fair city.

The second thing I found was a large manilla envelope. It was taped shut. It had my name printed by hand on the front of it.

I put both these items inside my windbreaker and left the house, locking it behind me. I kept thinking about putting Kathy Coleman in her cold watery grave last night. This little bungalow wasn't much, but it was a lot better than the dark floor of a river.

The backyard lay in deep shadow. There was only a quarter moon and right now even that was obscured by clouds. The hard wintry ground shone with frost.

I was four steps from the alley when the two killers separated themselves from the shadows of the garage and came for me. They had styled themselves like street punks, big green Mohawk haircuts, nose rings, leather jackets and leather pants. Across their cheeks were luminous stripes of red and yellow war paint.

They had already worked themselves into the frenzy that gave them strength, the frenzy that turned their eyes a glowing crimson, their cuspids into long, knife-like teeth, and their bodies into quick, lean, powerful machines.

Each held a wooden stake in his right hand.

I whirled, kicking the first one in the groin just as he jumped for me. By then, the second one had flung himself on my back. I flipped him over my head and when he was flat on his back, I jumped down on him, jerking free the knife I always keep inside the back of my pants.

I brought the stake down quickly and truly, stabbing it deep into his heart, hot blood soaking my hand and spattering my face.

He started that awful keening cry that always accompanies their eternal death. He started the twitching of extremities, too. That isn't fun to watch even when you hate the guy.

His friend was now using his stake like a switch-blade, circling, circling, circling me, waiting for the right moment to jump at me again, each circle tighter, tighter, and tighter still.

A low growl was caught in his throat.

In the darkness his red eyes glowed with a sick majesty. "You fucking geek," he said.

"Look who's talking."

He lunged.

I was ready. I pulled away easily.

We went back to circling each other there in the deep shadows of the garage while all around us nice normal TV-watching life went on . . . and two vampires fought it out to eternal death.

He came at me again, but this time he had moved too quickly and was off-balance.

I grabbed him by one hand and slammed him into the garage.

He was screaming and kicking and spewing sweat and spit all over me.

With my other hand I raised the steel stake and drove it deep into his heart.

The crimson eyes went out immediately, like lights that had been turned off.

He went limp in my grasp. I let him slide to the ground. He puked all over himself as he died.

Two minutes later, I backed my car up to the side of the garage and loaded the bodies. They would have to be disposed of. You don't leave vampire bodies around for curious coroners to examine. There was an industrial incinerator I used for such errands.

Two more minutes, and I was gone.

6

After a ten-minute stop at the incinerator—and I admit I hurried away because I can't take the stench of burning flesh—I found a dark lonely bar on a far edge of the city where it might as well have been 1948 given the looks of the ancient Wurlitzer jukebox with its Frank Sinatra records and the men's room with the cutesy "Little Boys" written on it.

I sat in a back booth while several old men along the bar argued about who would be the team to beat at spring training this year.

The waitress was attractive enough if you go for the buxom type. After figuring out that I wasn't going to flirt back, she brought me my Cutty and water and left me alone.

In the dim light of the bar, pool balls clacking, several of the old guys coughing up fifty years of cigarettes, I read the letter Kathy Coleman had written me.

The burned-out mansion I'd been driving her out to? That's where she and her family had lived for years until Mayor Atwill figured out that his benefactor and friend, Kathy's father, was a vampire and needed to be destroyed. As did his whole family—all but one, anyway. Kathy had an uncle who'd lived with them and while he was there, he was turning. . . . As I mentioned, this happens sometimes and nobody has ever been able to explain the process—why some of us suddenly develop the same needs and lusts as our enemies . . . and go over to the other side—the trouble being that you never know when someone's turning. There are no signs or symptoms until it's too late, until you recognize them as the enemy. And before they realized what was happening to the uncle it was already far too late. . . . On the night of the fire, Kathy's uncle put a stake through the hearts of Kathy's father, mother, and brother. Kathy barely escaped. The uncle disposed of the bodies and then burned the stone mansion to the ground.

And Mayor Atwill? He used the dark vampire's talents to take over the city completely. If you needed enemies killed or merely intimidated, a dark vampire was a good friend to have. Particularly one that nobody suspected.

Kathy wasn't sure that her uncle was still in the city . . . but that's why, after all this time, she'd returned. She planned on destroying both Mayor Atwill and her uncle.

Her envelope lacked only one thing. A photo of her uncle. Without a picture, I had very little to go on.

The waitress came back over and tried one more time to enchant me. She was getting old fast. Old, and sad. I declined as politely as I could. Maybe, given my nature, I was insensitive to the aging process and the toll it takes on your ego.

7

City Hall is on an island in the middle of the river that divides the city. This late at night, the three bridges spanning the river are mostly empty, and the only foot traffic you see are shambling winos and homeless winding their way to one of the shelters located near the end of the eastern side of the water.

I tried to pass myself off as a wino when the police cruiser slowed down to take a look at me as I neared the front of City Hall.

They hit me with a flashlight. I gave a little theatrical stumble.

"You know where the shelter's at, pal?" a voice asked from the nice comfortable darkness of the cruiser.

"Yeah," I called back.

"Well, get your ass over there and right now, you understand?"

I waved at them. They pulled away.

City Hall was designed by an architect who specialized in neo-Gothic back in the thirties. Thus the soaring spires and stained glass windows and the evil little gargoyles squatting above the arch of the entrance. As one of the folks at the community hall once joked, this is exactly the kind of place you'd expect to find vampires.

In the back I found a series of drainpipes that ultimately led me to the third floor. With the help of a glass cutter I managed to climb in through a window and stand in the center of a dark corridor. In the shadows, I could hear the knock and clang of the old-fashioned heating system. The floors smelled sweetly of fresh wax.

It took twenty minutes to find and get inside Mayor Atwill's office. The interior was in complete darkness. I went through the doors, using my flashlight. In less than ten minutes, I found his appointment book and got what I wanted.

As I was about to leave Atwill's office, I heard the elevator doors rumble open down the hall. I stood perfectly still on the far side of the door.

The squeak of rubber soles preceded the night

watchman. He went on past the office door. When he reached the other end of the hall, I heard him say, "What the hell is this?" to himself.

He'd obviously found the window I'd left open an inch, the window I'd cut a half-moon out of so I could reach in and unlock it.

I moved quickly, easing out the door as quietly as possible, and then running straight for the night watchman.

He was paunchy and white-haired. In his wrinkled gray uniform, he looked more like a bus driver than an imposing security guard.

His hand dropped to his holster. As he started to lift his revolver up, I lashed out with my right foot and knocked the weapon into the wall. It clattered to the floor.

"What the hell're you doin' up here, anyway?"

"Nothing that matters to you," I said. "So do us both a favor and let me out that window."

"They're gonna kick my butt for this," he said. "Say I'm too old for this job and throw my ass out on the street. And I need the insurance plan they got here. My wife's real sick."

Right now he was a lot more afraid of not having insurance than he was of me.

He watched, fascinated, as I took a switchblade from the pocket of my windbreaker and slashed it across the top of my hand.

"What the hell're you doing?" he said.

I made sure to drip blood everywhere it would be seen—floor, windowsill, even on the gray arm of his uniform jacket.

"Can you take a little pain?"

"Huh?"

I told him what I had in mind.

"Well, it sure as hell ain't somethin' I'm lookin' forward to, but I guess I can handle it all right."

I put a hard right fist directly into his right eye.

"Sonofabitch," he said, "that hurt." And immediately started feeling around his eye tenderly.

"One more thing," I said.

"Huh?"

"You pay for the uniform or does the city pick up the tab?"

"The city."

"Good."

I got hold of his uniform shirt and gave it a yank. The thing tore halfway down to his belly.

"There you go. You hit me so hard that I bled all over the place and you put up such a battle that you got a black eye and a torn shirt out of it. They won't fire you at all. They'll probably give you a medal."

"I appreciate it, Mac. Whoever you are."

Five chilly minutes later, my headlights were stabbing through the darkness on the bridge, heading toward the hilly, northern section of the city.

8

I crouched behind a tree above a large fishing cabin in the valley below. In the cold, black night, the cabin lights looked inviting. Three cars were parked on the gravel in front of the place. A tape deck played a fine melancholy Nat "King" Cole song called, appropriately enough, "Lost April." Behind curtained windows, I saw the dark shapes of people walking around. Drunken laughter followed them.

A man was posted at the front door. He sat on the last of four steps, smoking a cigarette, looking around in a systematic way. A large handgun sat on the steps next to him.

The tree I leaned against was wet from recent rain and smelled of night. I stood up, bones cracking, and started walking through the undergrowth. I crouched as much as possible. I was swinging around in back of the cabin. A lot of the underbrush was thorny and pierced my clothing with toothy little bites.

Ten minutes later, I pressed myself against the west side of the cabin and carefully inched my way toward the front. I had a gun, too. I wouldn't need my steel stake for awhile yet.

The sentry must have been daydreaming about an especially attractive woman because he didn't hear me until I was nearly on top of him. He was a big man in a cheap suit that tried too hard for style.

He turned suddenly, looked up, and automatically grabbed his weapon with his left hand.

But it was too late. I put two silenced bullets straight into his heart.

I left him slumped on the steps. He wasn't going to bother me, or anybody, ever again. But even dead, his job wasn't finished. Not quite yet.

There were curtained windows on either side of the door, so I was careful to stay crouched down as I crossed the porch.

I sat on my haunches to the right of the door. I hefted a rock I'd been carrying. Then I tossed it hard at the top of the door.

Despite the music, somebody heard the rock because, moments later, the door was jerked open. Yellow electric light and blue cigarette smoke spilled into the night. A familiar face stuck his head out. Mayor Atwill looked down the steps at his crumpled up guard and said, "Don? Don, are you all right?"

Our esteemed mayor looked confused and scared.

He was addressing the slumped form of the man at the bottom of the stairs.

He came out of the cabin, carrying a drink in his right hand, and went down the steps. He put the drink down in the gravel and got Don all stretched out on his back.

He swore when he saw the two bullet holes in Don's chest.

He was just turning to shout for somebody inside when I stood up out of the porch shadows and walked down the steps.

"Who're you?"

I guess when you're used to being the man in charge, you don't even get intimidated by people with guns.

"A friend of Kathy Coleman's. The woman you had killed the other night."

He started to stand up.

It seemed a waste of effort to me. He'd just have to fall down again.

He started to say something, but suddenly I didn't want to hear anything from him. I put a bullet in his forehead and a bullet in his throat. He went over backward and fell down next to his good friend Don. They made a nice looking couple.

I had just turned around to face the cabin again when I heard the music die inside and then footsteps come softly out to the porch.

He was just the man I'd expected to see.

"Kind of a chilly night," he said. He nodded to the two corpses. "Good thing you killed them, Johnathan, otherwise they'd probably have caught very bad head colds lying on the ground like that."

Then he looked down at the gun in his hand. "I guess this won't do much good now, will it?"

He tossed it off the porch, into damp thorny bushes where it made a rustling sound as it settled.

"This is what I need."

From inside his suit coat jacket, he produced, with a theatrical little flourish, a long silver spike.

"I should warn you, Johnathan, my wimpy little accountant pose was strictly protective coloration. I'm nobody to fuck with."

"You killed your own brother."

Even in the shadows, I could see his smile. "You're a very judgmental person, Johnathan. Has anybody ever told you that? Maybe you should see a shrink about it.''

''Your own brother and his wife and their small son.''

The smile again. ''Nobody ever said I was perfect, Johnathan.''

And with that, Bob Hanson, McGivern's most trusted aide, came down off the porch with the express intent of killing me. He was the reason I'd come out to the secret cabin mentioned in the mayor's appointment book. Mayor Atwill had used the initials BH and the only man I could think of was Bob Hanson, a man smart enough to use McGivern and the community center as the perfect ruse.

His first few steps were slow, but just before he reached the bottom he jumped at me, his hands going immediately to my throat. I pushed him off, but moments later he was coming back at me.

He hadn't been exaggerating about his protective coloration. He was all fighter and not an ounce of accountant.

He was also gifted with the stake, a whetstone having honed the edge to razor brilliance, his hand wielding it like a knife.

He kicked me in the chest, groin, and knee so quickly I had no way of defending myself. Then he sliced his stake across my right bicep, slashing into the skin deep enough to cut muscle. Blood came warm and instantly.

My leg lashed out and caught him in the stomach, knocking the air out of him momentarily. I kicked him in the face and shoulder and groin, knocking him backward over the bodies of Atwill and Don.

But just as he started to stumble, he startled me by throwing his stake like a knife and planting it deep into my chest, less than a half inch from my heart.

The wound drove me to my knees and gave Hanson time to recover his footing and start in on me again.

The wound was deep enough and good enough to incapacitate me. I knew I'd be unconscious in a few moments.

I tried struggling to my feet but he was all over me. He punched me twice, hard in the face, making me even dizzier and more unsteady. Then he kicked me in the ribs and, as I started to stagger backward, he leaned forward and yanked his stake from my chest.

In the faint light from the cabin, I saw my own dark slick blood on the end of his stake.

He came in fast, then, thrusting like a swordsman.

I knew that if I fell, he'd kill me immediately. I staggered around, but I stayed on my feet.

He cut me again, two, three times, once on the cheek, once on the throat, once on my left arm, quick expert slashes that brought pain and panic and made me even more vulnerable.

With both arms cut badly, I wondered how much longer I could grip my dagger.

He came at me for the final time. His eyes were pure crimson now and his body smelled of the high sour odor that sometimes accompanied the transformation. His teeth dripped saliva.

I knew that I would not have a straight go at his heart. I had only one hope.

He crouched, circling, and then lunged. And I surpised him.

By bending over to protect his heart as he came in, he left his face open.

I stabbed my dagger deep into his right eye. He did just what I'd hoped. In his pain and rage, he let panic take him for a moment. He froze, not for much longer than an instant, but just long enough for me to plunge my dagger deep into his other crimson eye.

He screamed so loudly, I was surprised that Atwill and Don didn't wake up.

And then he was easy.

I grabbed him by the hair and threw him on the

ground and then dropped to the sandy soil and
slammed my dagger deep enough to kill him instantly.
But he didn't seem to notice the pain in his chest. He
was too busy screaming about being blind.

I went through his clothes and then put him in the
trunk.

Half an hour later, I disposed of him in the incinerator. The stench followed me all the way back to the
city.

9

In another hour it would be dawn. Even if the sky
hadn't told me this, McGivern's pot of coffee would
have. The brown handle means regular coffee, the
green handle means decaf, which he drinks only after
3:00 A.M. He says he sleeps better this way. Even
people like us get the caffeine jitters sometimes.

We were in his office. The center was empty. Everybody'd gone home long ago. The rooms were big and
hollow and dark now and as I'd passed them my echoing footsteps had been loud.

McGivern had been watching a western when I'd
come in.

I made my usual comment. "Who do you think will
win, McGivern, the cowboys or the Indians?"

"Very funny. Some of these old movies are pretty
good."

I smiled. "Especially the ones with voluptuous
young schoolmarms, I'll bet."

He smiled back. "Well, I guess that's one way you
could look at it."

I went over and got a Diet Pepsi from the big white
thrumming machine. I came back over and sat down
and he watched me open up a new pack of Pall Malls.

I told him everything that had happened tonight.

"I can't believe it," he said. "Hanson."

"Kind've shocked me, too."

I blew some blue smoke in his direction. I looked directly at him. "We had a nice little talk before he died."

"Oh?"

He knew what was coming. I could see it. I could also see his hand edge toward the center drawer in his desk. That was no doubt where he kept his own stake.

"He said he had a partner and that they had the perfect setup. The partner was this very influential man our whole community trusted and so any time they started to suspect that he'd turned, the partner would do something to throw them off the track."

"He must have been a pretty trusted man, to have influence like that, I mean. His partner."

"Somebody I trusted a lot myself, McGivern. Somebody I trusted a whole hell of a lot, in fact."

The drawer eased open. His plump hand skittered inside like a hungry tarantula.

"She had a pretty tough life, poor kid."

"What did you say, Johnathan?"

"It's not what I said, McGivern. It's what you said the other night. While I was driving back to the city tonight, I thought about you saying how Kathy Coleman had had such a tough life. 'She had a pretty tough life, poor kid' and I realized that you couldn't possibly have known that she'd had a tough life unless you were involved in it somehow. Which you were—as Hanson's boss. He was the liaison to Mayor Atwill and his cronies. You stayed way back in the shadows. Pretty nice life. You know everything that's going on in the community, so you were covered in case anybody had any suspicions."

He stared at me a long moment. "You could always become one of us, Johnathan."

"No, thanks. I don't go that way."

"It's not so bad, Johnathan. A lot of what your people believe about the dark side is pure myth. We don't sit around and twirl our mustaches or molest little children. Not most of us, anyway.''

"I'm going to kill you, McGivern.''

He stared at me again. "How about giving me a little dignity, Johnathan?''

"Meaning what?''

He told me what he meant and I couldn't really see anything wrong with it and so I said all right and picked up what remained of my Diet Pepsi and walked out into the hall.

He was a lot stronger than I would have imagined. He put the stake clean in to his heart on just one pass. I heard him kind of grunt a little and then fall forward and slam his head against his desk.

I smoked two cigarettes before I went in there and wrapped him up in a tarpaulin and carried him down to my car and stashed him in the trunk.

There had been a lot of dying lately and even somebody like me gets overwhelmed by it all every so often.

I even left him in the trunk for a full day and night. I just couldn't take the incinerator again. Not right away, at any rate.

(I based this story on a fine article called "Vigil For A Doomed Virus" by Mark Caldwell in the March, 1992 issue of *Discover*.)

BLOOD FROM A TURNIP

by
Wayne Allen Sallee

(For Leonard Bieber)

A sudden brilliance, devastating in its onslaught, followed by a false darkness. October in the South Loop: the sun arcing across the skyline, skirting low past the Dawes Bank Building. My sixteenth-floor office becomes a momentary hothouse, and I dry swallow a beta-blocker. Ten minutes later, the sun is behind the Sears Tower, the shadow falling over Van Buren like a monster from a Japanese movie.

I'm almost glad that the start of Daylight Savings Time occurs next week. Spring forward, fall back. One thing good about it is that our field investigator will be up and around by three. It's a bitch in the summer, waiting around until eight to consult a file with him.

This is the city. I'm a bill collector. I carry a pseudonym. I'm a different guy for every lie. I started with the firm of Advantage: Education—though they sold everything from vacation certificates to multiframe cameras—about seven months after the field investigator, so I don't know the circumstances regarding his employment. The place is kind of a revolving door, what with bill collectors and receptionists as easily replaceable as McDonald's counter people.

But, when the boss is out of town, I consult with the field man. He's the one we send out when all our avenues regarding collections have been exhausted. You can't garnish wages in several states; forget about an asset search if they're living in an apartment complex, or worse yet, a trailer park. I like to consult with the field man best when the debtor copped an attitude. I'm no saint, but I try to pay *my* bills on time, I honestly do.

I handle primarily military accounts. You get people guaranteed with at least a two-year job, the full term of the principal on the contract. And because all the guys have been getting combat pay since the Desert Storm mess, we've been raking it in. Also, many of the applicants are newlyweds, easily steered into taking the contract without thinking about the high interest rate or jacked up delivery charges. They want to get established credit, and for the ones without a high school or college diploma, we are keen on presenting CLEP manuals, GED guides, and an Officer's Candidate Test.

But there are always accounts that are going to be trouble from day one.

I have been trying to reach Ronald Pasaye at Truax Army Airfield for weeks; the guy only made a single payment in the last five months. He is a PFC with the 3rd Army Transport Unit. Every other time I have called, the unit has been out in the field. This term applies to anything from overnight training in the woods outside Madison—the base is in central Wisconsin—to a three-week recon outside of Elmwood, in a deserted area where the Stealth Bomber was tested several years ago. The things you learn as a bill collector, huh?

He has no real assets, but I also have learned, through skip-tracing, that he is a bit of a gambler, on the riverboats out of the Quad Cities. "You can't squeeze blood out of a turnip," he tells me when I finally get through to him, falling back on the cliché phrases all deadbeats knew by rote.

He knows I have nothing on him. But the asswipe can be coerced. Our field investigator can fly up to Madison before the rush hour ends.

I terminate the conversation with Private First Class

Pasaye, duly noting that the first shirt—the Staff Sergeant—seems inclined to agree that we have little chance of collecting our four hundred dollars in arrears. Then I go out to knock on the field man's door.

He'll give the boy a nice big smile, and Pasaye will pull the money out of his ass if need be. It has happened in the past. Having the man as our field director is better than threatening the deadbeats with a civil judgment in small claims court.

"Is he up and about, yet?" I ask Connie, our office manager, feeling the first chest pings. I always get them when I have to knock on that door. It's like having a boss who has been on a drinking binge.

"I had to go in there for the payroll books," Connie says, her lambent eyes darting to the oaken door at the far end of the hall. "He's up, but his eyes are bloodshot. He didn't sleep well. Can't it wait, Henry?"

"Hell, no," I say. "I wait another week it'll be October thirtieth! I need that big chunk of change, and I'm not going to let Catherine Flynn beat me out of the bonus money again."

"Well, Robert does seem to think you make the right decisions. . . ."

Yea, that's me. Henry Desmond, yes-man to Robert Sark. And the Count, if it came down to it.

I walk down the hallway, casually glancing at the headlines on the Tribune, some sex scandal in the Senate. I slap the Pasaye file against my hand, then realize that the dumbest thing I could do would be to snag my finger on a staple and draw blood.

When I knock twice on the door, I take out the crucifix from beneath my black turtleneck. He has plenty of victims to choose from in Chicago's north side bars, but I don't ever want to chance catching him in one of his frenzies.

"Count Dracula," I whisper against the mahogany door. "It's Desmond, with a file."

The door creaks open. My balls always want to

shrivel up when I see him. The big executive desk he sits behind opens up as his coffin. The drawer space is all for show. It takes me a second to have my eyes adjust; the only light is the reflected lights from the Sears Tower and ICBM Building windows. He clicks a Cross pen against one of his incisors.

"Let us see what we have here," his voice is acid rain falling on a drainpipe.

I hand him the file, my grip steady. He chuckles as he reads my notes. "I have found ways to squeeze blood from a turnip, you know." His grin is insane, as it is every time he uses his pet phrase. Like Gomez down the hall, saying, "Working hard or hardly working?" Laughing like it is original each time.

"Yes, I know, Count." I humble myself. "You are the best."

He stands up, the cape unfolding around him, opening the bay windows twelve floors above a Mrs. Field's Cookies. I smell the richness of the chocolate and listen to the rush hour bleats as the best field bill collector in the world shrinks to the size of a bat and flies northward.

THE CURE

by
W. R. Philbrick

In the spring of 1839 my first master, George Benning Groswold, the ninth Lord Gravely, directed that his small entourage of travelers cross the last of the low, bleak mountains that range along the Adriatic, and make its way down to the coast by carriage. Our party was comprised of Lord Gravely, his *fiancée* Miss Fiona Brey and her ailing mother Lady Brey, as well as such servants, chambermaids, and drivers as were necessary to the minimum comfort of such company.

Lady Brey having dismissed her doctors—indeed, having insisted that the last of them, a sallow-faced fraud called Paritus, be jailed in Athens for conspiring to defraud the good lady of extravagant sums tendered for so-called miraculous herbs that were, as Lord Gravely demonstrated, derived from common tea leaves, and Turkish tea at that—we sought a cure elsewhere.

"We shall seek it like the very Grail," my young lord declared, having dispatched the cretinous surgeon to the dungeon of Piraeus, or what passed for a rudimentary dungeon in this ancient part of the world. "Seek it if we have to travel ten thousand miles more, my lady, this is my pledge to you."

The arrangements were, of course, left entirely to Lord Gravely, himself a renowned traveler, amateur scientist, and author of several thin calfskin volumes of poetry printed before he had quite reached one and twenty. Now in his thirtieth year, my master had achieved that level of maturity that demands a settled life and a proper heir to his great fortune, and so had arrived at an understanding with the beautiful Fiona Brey. Miss Brey was, as readers everywhere must surely know, acclaimed not only by Lord Gravely, but by the best poets and painters of the age as a woman of uncommon radiance, in particular celebrated for her green and glorious eyes, and her red and rapturous hair (forgive my echo of Lord Gravely's most famous verse, but it cannot be improved upon by this common scrivener).

It is said that many a young London lady applied dyes and potions to her tresses, in vainglorious attempt to mimic Miss Brey's remarkable mane, which she wore untouched by pomades and lacquers and in length full about her shoulders. Miss Brey's defiance of then-current fashion created a sensation at her presentation that year, which is the same year of this narrative, the year Lord Gravely pledged to find a cure for Lady Brey's mysterious malady, thus ingratiating himself with her daughter, and finding, it is safe to say, much more than he intended—such strange and tragic happenstance as I will attempt to recount in these few pages.

What drew my young master to this remote principality on the Adriatic, far from the usual Tour routes and the eagerly anticipated Splendors of Antiquity, was word of a curative administered, it was sworn, free of any encumberance other than a simple pledge of fealty to a certain Count D., himself a foreigner in this small and isolated realm. He was not, as readers of common travelogues and ha'penny romances might assume, titled in one of the Italian provinces, where such favors are dispensed, it is said, for a wheel of cheese, but a gentleman of undeniable aristocracy, a son of one of the great families who ruled in the Eastern regions, among high mountains that have been threatened by Turkish hordes through the centuries, always managing to keep themselves separate and intact, despite the continuous encroachment of the Infidel.

The journey down through the mountains being hard, and made even more difficult by the failure of a carriage axle, our arrival was delayed many hours. Lord Gravely sent word ahead, making apologies, but nightfall did not prevent the count himself from meeting our poor, limping party at the gates of his villa, a high-walled place set hard above the sea, and scented with the salt of waves expending themselves against impregnable stones some three hundred feet below.

Holding up a lantern that made his face seem, as I then thought, unusually pale in contrast to the whale oil flame, Count D. made us welcome, exuding a charm and elegance most pleasing to Lady Brey, who had been sorely tried by this last part of the journey.

"Sir," she declared, stepping down from her carriage with the assistance of her two chambermaids, "you have made me glad to be alive in this dark hour, when coming down upon the mountain I did not care what should happen to me, save only that it happen quickly."

"Good English lady," the count replied, making a gesture with his lantern. "My hope is that you will always be glad of life here, in this simple estate, and not feel at a loss for such as you might easily find in London or Paris, for I cannot make such things available, try as I might."

Count D. seemed on that first evening to be of a certain age, somewhat past the vigorous prime of life, although robust in stature and several inches taller than Lord Gravely, who was himself more than a little above the average height. It was remarked by several of the servants that both men wore the same cloak, or rather that each man's cloak, darkly draped and fine-satin lined, was so similar it might have been stitched by the same hand. If either of them noticed the unusual similarity, neither acknowledged such duplicity of costume.

"Your quarters have been prepared," the count said, leading the way with his pale, pale lantern, "and a light supper has been laid out, suitable for weary travelers. Tomorrow, of course, you shall dine at my table."

The guest apartments were sumptuous—no, something more than sumptuous, for they had been decorated in the Eastern manner, as if to please a potentate. The floors were of hard-fired mosaic tiles, the patterns of which seemed to ease the mind in study, lulling the senses, as did the thick rugs upon the walls, woven with geometric symbols mysterious to my untutored eyes but clearly pleasing to his lordship, who remarked upon their extreme antiquity.

"The hanging gardens did not flower in Old Babylon before these carpets were woven," he confided to Miss Brey, running his slim white fingertips along the walls. "Our host must have brought these furnishings with him, for such as these cannot be found on this remote a shore."

So too were the bronze urns remarkable, as large as a man and inlaid with glittering bits of stone, and the low, Oriental divans intricately carved from dark mahoganies, and soft-woven damascene pads to sit upon, in lieu of proper chairs. The sleeping chambers, each arranged *en suite*, were tented most wonderfully, so that the effect was of a dreamlike quality, all flowing and silken and by lamp glow translucent, each bed itself made up of great pillows stuffed with the eiderdown of Persian geese. The servant quarters were below, in cellars carved from the rock, and while less grand, were more than adequate for our purpose.

Because of the late hour Lord Gravely and his party ate from the sideboard, on cuts of meat cured in such a way that none among them could recognize the origin, be it hare or beef, pig or wild fowl.

Lady Brey ate very little, not as a consequence of the offerings, but because poor appetite had long been a symptom of her illness, a malady that was creeping from organ to organ, causing great pain, though she bore it with courage.

"Mother, please try a little of this," said Fiona, holding out a small silver plate from the sideboard. "Say whether it is flesh or fruit, for I cannot tell."

Lady Brey shuddered, but her daughter would not be denied. "I promise you, the taste is quite delicious," Fiona insisted.

Lord Gravely agreed, and strove to convince Lady Brey that she should sample the exotic fare. "Bear in mind what we heard of the count's cure, that it touches upon digestion or diet," he added, holding out his own plate, and displaying the small squares of the unknown delicacy, pink as tongues.

"I will eat tomorrow," Lady Brey responded, turning her face away, "when I have recovered from the journey. At the moment I'm so weak I feel spun from glass."

"Mother, you *are* exhausted," Fiona said, putting down her own plate, and summoning Lady Brey's chambermaids. "George? See to it we are awakened early, I want to see this place in daylight, to get a sense of it."

"As you wish, my dear." Lord Gravely kissed her hand, and then bussed the cheek of Lady Brey, who, even more than her daughter, had found his lordship favorable from the very beginning, and continued to exclaim his virtues even when Fiona found it easy to hold her tongue, rather than praise him.

It was said, by gossiping chambermaids and the like, that it was Lady Brey who had put forward my lordship's proposal of marriage, as a *fait accompli* intended to revive the Brey fortune, but readers must discount such unkind rumors, considering the source. Nor do I mean to imply that Miss Brey found my lordship unfavorable in any way, for a serene and distant coolness was her nature and she was not demonstrative of affection save with her ailing mother, whom she doted upon.

So the party was quick to bed, each to his own chambers, and those of us who served them supped quietly in our cellar quarters, from carvings of perfectly ordinary salted beef and tinned biscuit—and quite happily eating thus, I might add, as common folk of our class have small stomach for foreign delicacies.

With a small cubicle and a straw pallet to call my own, I lay down expecting to fall deeply asleep almost at once, for the day had been long and arduous. Instead my ears began to play tricks upon me, for no sooner had I put my head upon the bolster than a wail seemed to emanate from somewhere within the walls of the villa. Brought full awake by this plaintive noise, I could not say whether it was human or not, only that it had a kind of human quality, as, at times, a certain cat may sound almost like a small child wailing from the crib. And yet I swear this was no cat, nor any animal ever heard by these simple English ears.

A keening so faint as to defy location, save that it was more audible in a prone position, less clear when I stood up. As if the noise in some way passed through the stones, or came from some deeper source than the cellar. It struck my fancy that the keening was like that of a bird, if birds can be said to keen, and yet I have never been frightened by birds or the noises they make, and this keening touched my nerves in such a way as to ruin sleep.

At times so faint as to seem imaginary—some sleep sound dim upon the wind—at others so clear it was hard to comprehend that none of the others were disturbed from their slumbers, these sounds continued for many hours until, in desperate need of rest, I managed to wrap my head with my coat—a crude, thick

bandage—and though the plaintive sound still pene-
trated ever so faintly, sleep came at last to me.

Strange slumber indeed, for I dreamed that I was a
manservant drowsing in a foreign castle far from home,
and when dawn crept in, awoke to find, alas, the dream
was true.

* * *

That morning a sturdy English breakfast was served
from the same sideboard, brought over in covered trays
from the count's own kitchens. At first this seemed but
a kindness, so that Lady Brey might regain what
strength she had without having to gird herself for the
rigors of social discourse so early in the day. When
the sun passed noon, however, it became clear that
our host was not going to make an appearance, and
Lord Gravely, after consulting with Fiona and her
mother, dispatched a messenger to tactfully remind
Count D. that we awaited his invitation.

That messenger, carrying a sealed letter from his
lordship, was none other than myself, and it was with
some trepidation that I crossed the empty courtyards
and entered the count's domain. The sky above the
high-walled villa had a strange, leaden hue, not bright
enough to mark a sundial, or cast the shadow of an
English manservant. Not a creature stirred, save a trio
of fat, night-black crows who perched silently along
the seaward wall, eyes glittering like bits of shiny dark.
As if waiting to say, in their hinge-squeak cackles, *we
know you better than you know yourself.* Such an omen
quickened my step, but not so greatly that I did not
perceive the statuary encircling the courtyard, stone-
carved creatures emerging from the walls, creatures of
fearsome aspect, all claws and fangs and serpent tails,
like a griffin but not a griffin, like a gargoyle but not
a gargoyle—that description will have to suffice, for

what monsters were depicted, whether mythical or some nightmare *things* from the east, I know not.

What struck me as stranger still was the silence. A gentleman of the count's high rank, living in a villa such as this, would require a large and at times clamorous staff—particularly at midday, when a hundred or more small chores were best accomplished. And yet, approaching the tall black doors that marked Count D.'s quarters, the only noise was the hiss of surf dying somewhere far below, and a low moan of wind coming off the sea, sighing among the great stones.

Finding no bell to strike, no rapper to let fall, there was no recourse save putting fist against the door. Expecting a prompt reply—surely the count's entrance was manned by one or more butlers or footmen—I stood a while, hearing the hollow echo of my rude knocking as it sounded throughout what must have been a great hall within. Minutes passed and nothing stirred. Not wanting to face my master's wrath—the young lord had a famous temper—I pummeled the great door, and kept on striking until my hand was numb, aching from the effort.

At last a sound came from somewhere deep inside. A slithering kind of noise, kin to the plaintive moans that had ruined my sleep, or so I imagined, standing there on those cold steps, so hard under my feet my very bones seemed jarred from below. After a while the slithering ceased and I, waiting back a good few paces, watched as an iron ring upon the door trembled. A bolt was being drawn back, ever so slowly, as if with great effort, and finally a darker slot appeared at the edge of the black door.

I waited, then raised my voice, stating my station and my purpose. No voice responded, but an old, frail hand made itself seen at the edge of the door. A beckoning hand. I understood that I must enter, and enter quickly.

Who can say what loathsome superstitions slowed

my step? What I might have feared then in my ignorance, spooked by that strange silence of the noonday
courtyard, was as nothing to what happened later,
when the tragedy of the long night was full upon us—
indeed, it is a faint blur, that early touch of fear, impossible to conjure here.

I can tell you that the beckoning hand belonged to
the old gentleman who served the count, and that this
"slithering" noise that frightened me was but his gout-
crippled foot, for he dragged it along behind him and
in his pride disdained the aid of a cane or crutch. Although I several times stood some few inches from this
man, close enough to smell the old sick breath of him,
I cannot repeat his name, though several times he tried
to make it clear to me. Some guttural noise it was,
rendered in his native tongue, that sounded to my thick
English ears like the clearing of a throat, so much so
that from then on I thought of him, uncharitably, as
Old Spit the butler.

Old Spit was, in his own small way, as remarkable
as the count himself, for I believe he greeted me in
more than a dozen languages before settling on the
tongue I was born to—the result, no doubt, of a long
life traveling with his master. Having arrived at a
means of communication, the old man fixed me with
ash-colored eyes sunk deep in a cadaverous visage and
said, "Too soon, much too soon. Return after the sun
has set and the count will receive you most courte-
ously."

"But my master, his lordship—" I began.

Old Spit held up his claw and tapped my chest. "Patience," he said.

"I cannot urge patience upon Lord Gravely or Lady
Brey," I responded. "She is an invalid seeking solace
here, and in any case has small store of patience."

"Then she, too, must learn a new way," Old Spit
replied. "My master and those who seek his cure sleep
soundly through each day, finding their good humors

in the dark hours. You English find this strange, I'm
sure, being creatures of daylight, but here in the East
the night airs revive the soul and the body. Tell your
lord and lady to rest themselves. The count shall make
them welcome shortly after the sun goes down. That
is his lifelong habit, and you would do well to mimic
it so long as you are here.''

"But what do I tell his lordship?"

"Tell him patience is a virtue."

I told him nothing of the kind, of course, as one
who wished to keep his head upon his shoulders, but
did explain the count's odd habit of rising only after
the light had expired. Lord Gravely did not respond,
as I had anticipated, with a flare of temper, but rather
seemed to take the news with amusement, as if he half-
expected to hear of such eccentricities.

Lady Brey took it well enough, remarking that she
would follow our host's advice and sleep as best she
could. "Truth is, the air here has put me in a daze.
Salts of the sea, I suppose."

"Yes, Mother, off to bed with you," Fiona said,
and laughed lightly, though her lovely eyes were not
amused. "Darling George and I will play at cards, and
in some way pass the time until your savior rolls back
his stone and deigns to see us."

"Fiona!" Lady Brey scolded. "That is blasphe-
mous. And the count has been most kind to us. Having
stayed up late to make us welcome, should we be-
grudge him a long rest?"

"No, Mother, of course not. Pay no attention to my
prattling. I had a touch of indigestion last night and
did not sleep soundly myself. You know that makes
me irritable."

That seemed to mollify Lady Brey, who soon retired
to her chambers, leaving her daughter and prospective
son-in-law to, as Fiona daintily put it, "play at cards."
The game was piquet, as they had not enough to make
a whist, and, as I recall, my lord lost a hundred pounds

or more to the artful Fiona. He directed me to enter it
in his ledger, making light of it, but calling for more
wine. Miss Brey took great delight in "piquing" him,
as she called it, and my lord could do naught but act
the gentleman, and make light of the loss.

"You're worth ten thousand times that much," he
vowed, attempting to kiss her hand. Miss Brey pulled
away before his lips could quite touch and said, "Oh,
at the very least, darling George, at the very least,"
in such a cool, calculated way that his lordship appeared to wince and scowl most darkly before recov-
ering his composure.

"Your tongue, my dear, must it always seek to draw
blood?"

In answer Miss Brey laughed and said that she, too,
would lie down a while before the great count made
himself known. "We shall become waifs of the night,"
she said theatrically, holding her slim wrist to her fine,
porcelain brow and fluttering her eyelashes, "like
those awful Romans, after their awful orgies."

"Fiona!" his lordship said, startled.

"A joke, George. Just a joke."

"We're here for the good of your mother," he reminded her. "The count may not share your peculiar
sense of humor."

"We'll see about that," Fiona said, "when night
comes."

She went off into her chambers and his lordship,
somewhat thick with wine, bade me accompany him
to his own chamber, where he fell asleep fully clothed.
I could remove naught but his fine kid boots, but had
to leave him mostly dressed, for he lay like the insensible dead.

* * *

At sunset, the crows began to caw and cackle, a
noise even more hideous than their glinting silence had

been, and soon enough lanterns passed into the court-yard. It was the count, accompanied by several of the villa servants, and he seemed most jovial, particularly with Lady Brey.

"Did I disappoint her ladyship by not exposing my-self to the light of day? A thousand apologies. I should have made clear the peculiar rules of this region. You must avoid the sun, it poisons not only the complex-ion, but the blood humors as well. When the clear night air comes down from the mountains, that is the time to rise and breathe deeply. Really it is a small adjustment to make, my lady, and you will find it eas-ily done, given a little time."

"How strange, sir."

Count D. smiled at this remark, clearly not in the least offended. "No stranger than rising with the bleary dawn and feeling your strength ebb as it grows ever more powerful. No stranger than being blinded by the crude orb of the sun."

"So you say, Count D.," her ladyship replied. "But must we really set anew our inner clocks to find health? Is that your cure?"

The count smiled and answered with another ques-tion. "Have you never in your illness lain awake at night, wishing that the rest of the world was similarly afflicted? With wakefulness, I mean. Of course you have! For instinctively we all understand that the life force is stronger when the sun is at its greatest remove from us."

Miss Brey, yawning daintily as she stepped into the lamplight of the courtyard, said, "What life force is this? Please explain, for we are but ignorant, brutish Britains wandering in the world, and we know not of 'crude suns' and 'life force' and sleeping away the day."

If Miss Brey was trying to offend the count with her remarks, she failed, for he seemed to delight in her challenge. "Oh, but I think you *do* understand. My language is imperfect, perhaps, but surely no woman with your remarkable beauty, no woman with your unmistakable inner fire could fail to sense the life force that radiates from all living creatures. But come now, we'll continue this delightful discussion after you've all been made properly welcome.''

And so our little party was brought into the great hall, and found it transformed into a place of lights, for hundreds of paper lanterns had been affixed to the soaring beams and buttresses. The shadows seemed to flit like a myriad of soft, nearly invisible moths, and the effect seemed to soften the very stones of the place. And the scent! The scent of all those candles was like that of some vast, ethereal garden, as Eden must have been before Adam ruined paradise.

It made me dizzy, that scent, and fogged my senses with a happy giddiness, nor was I the only one so affected, for I saw even the skeptical Miss Fiona Brey smile airily, her eyes luminous with the candle glow of paper lanterns. She seemed to float into the great room, as weightless and splendid as an angel who had chosen to glide just above the earth, here but not here, there but not there.

His lordship was oblivious of Miss Brey, so enamored was he with the the great hall, and the company he found there. Not so the count, whose expression softened when he caught a glimpse of her, and whose voice became even more mellifluous whenever he addressed her. As for Lord Gravely, if he noticed this unmistakable interest in the beautiful Miss Brey, he did nothing to acknowledge it. Certainly he never challenged the count, as I had seen him do a score of times with other, lesser men who had sought Miss Brey's attention.

No, his lordship was drawn to those I can only call the Others, for the count never made the usual introductions of his entourage, but referred to them with a sweep of his hand as "these others who found my cure most effective,'' and left it at that. I counted some thirty individuals, all echoing the count's remarkable paleness—the effect, no doubt, of isolation from the darkening influence of sunlight. When he did refer to a particular individual among them, our host was like as not to call them by their illness, or whatever had plagued them before finding a cure in this remote destination. Thus: ''My young friend with the tumor upon his spine,'' sufficed to introduce a thin, finely dressed youth with skin so fine and translucent I fancied to see the skull beneath his skin. By manner this youth was clearly of the nobility—you could tell this from the way he carried himself, and the slight nod of his finely shaped chin as he acknowledged the count—but others among them had, I believe, common origins, for there was one young lass, a buxom thing, who had the manners of a skullery girl, though she meant no harm, and yet another, paler even than the others, with great sad eyes, who was quite obviously a stable boy, and rather simpleminded, for he sidled up to me once, tugging with strangely cool fingers upon my sleeve, calling me ''Papa? Papa?'' and seemed puzzled to find that I was not, as he evidently hoped, his father come at last to take him back to the stables he but dimly recalled.

The reader should know, for it bears upon the narrative to follow, that none of Lady Brey's attendants ventured into the great hall with her. Indeed, I was the exception in Lord Gravely's party, for, as always, he was very demanding of attention, and needed a personal valet to wait upon him at all times. Of his household staff I was the one who managed to please him most consistently, though he continued to find fault with my ministrations, to the degree that his fine kid boots and my backside were not unfamiliar. This proximity, though often vexing, afforded me a certain intimacy to his lordship's situation which extended even to his correspondence, for in this capacity I was often called upon to act as his secretary. At times, I am convinced, my young master considered me no more than a common extension of himself, that part of him fit for the unpleasant necessities of life.

So it was that I observed his lordship's fascination with these Others, who had pledged themselves to the count's generous friendship, and in so doing cured their various maladies. They had come, these victims of affliction and disease, from all parts of Europe and even beyond, for one of the gentlemen claimed to be an heir to the throne of Russia. The bearded prince had an aspect most horrifying to me, for his eyes seemed like small black mouths, ready to devour whatever he envisioned. This black prince conversed with my lord in French, and I understand just enough of that tongue to know that his illness was that rare and often fatal disease wherein the blood will not thicken, and victims often died of injuries so slight it can scare be imagined. That the prince had been delivered of this particular fate seemed to amuse him vastly, and he demonstrated the effectiveness of the count's cure by drawing a small blade across his wrists.

I swear to you that no blood flowed from this prince of Russia, if such he actually was, though the blade cut deep enough to drain an ordinary man. Such was the power, he explained to his lordship, of the *joie de nuit,* his pet name for our host's peculiar regime. Lord Gravely sought to examine the wound, and when satisfied that it was genuine, hurried from one to another, demanding proof that they too had suffered from mortal afflictions.

Those he accosted seemed amused rather than offended, as if my impetuous young master was not the first to so challenge them, and if Count D. found his behavior impolite, he did not act so, but instead called many of his entourage to come forward and demonstrate their remarkable powers of regeneration. Lord Gravely examined the scars of old surgeries so crude, he said, that survival was virtually impossible, and yet these Others not only survived, they seemed infused with youthful energy.

One other among us was likewise impressed with the count's facility, and this was Lady Brey herself. The victim of numerous schemes perpetrated by a succession of medical frauds, Lady Brey was at first dubious, but as the night wore on and more and more of the Others came forward, her manner became less skeptical, and she at last begged that the count do what he could to help her.

The count's manner was deferential, as if he did not wish to put himself forward, or persuade Lady Brey to a situation she would later regret. "You understand what you ask of me, good lady?"

"I ask that I be made well, sir."

"You ask this of me, yes, and I would not deny you, but first I must satisfy myself that you fully appreciate your situation. If you take cure with me, good lady, you must stay here in this villa, following my regime of diet and sleep—or follow me to whatever place I may inhabit. Would you be so constrained?"

Lady Brey came forward and took the count's hand, which she held to her breast. "If I do not," she said, "surely I will die."

"I fear this to be true," the count replied most kindly. "Your disease is in the advanced stage, and must be treated immediately if you are to survive."

"The pain," Lady Brey said, weeping. "Oh the agony in the night is terrible. I am so weak!"

Count D. withdrew his hand from hers and touched her lightly upon the shoulder. "This is night, my good lady, is your agony so terrible?"

Her ladyship admitted that at the moment she felt no pain, but feared that it would soon return.

"You need never fear such agony again," the count promised. "If this is your wish, then your cure is already underway."

Miss Brey, who had been keeping back, pushed forward and embraced her mother. The two women whispered for a time out of my hearing, arriving at some common understanding of purpose, for Lady Brey soon broke away from Fiona and cleaved to the count who, satisfied of her intentions, directed that she be taken to a chamber adjacent to the great hall.

"There you will sleep, this I promise," he said. "My servants have prepared an herbal remedy that induces drowsiness, and steadies the beating of the heart. This special chamber looks out to the sea below, and the windows remain open at all times, for the sea mist itself is part of the curative. Sleep, my good lady, and in your sleep breathe deeply. You will sleep all of this night and all of the following day, and tomorrow night when you awaken, your affliction will be gone forever. Do you agree to this, and do you agree to pledge yourself to my fealty in the days and years to follow?"

"Yes," Lady Brey said. "Yes, I do."

*   *   *

So it was the Lady Brey found her cure, and my young master found that he himself was now afflicted with some unnamed malady. That night, having left Lady Brey in the curative chamber, I helped Lord Gravely across the courtyard shortly before dawn. He was much the worse for wine, having consumed flagon after flagon, reveling in the pale company he found in the great hall. At one point, late in the night, a curious ceremony of dancing was arranged—in my ignorance I can only call it a pavane of sorts, for the Others linked hands, couple by couple, and paraded past my master as he sat groggily clapping his hands. This strange dance was unaccompanied by music, at least any music that I could hear, though the couples never faltered in step, and seemed serenely confident in their performance.

His lordship, rising from his chair, stumbled and fell among the dancing feet, laughing wildly, and reaching out with his hands in a debauched manner, touching them everywhere. The dancers were unperturbed by this loutish display, and Count D. was elsewhere, attending to her ladyship, or so I assume. Miss Brey, stifling a yawn, had long since departed for the guest quarters, and seemed indifferent to whatever Lord Gravely might do with himself, or others. "I see you've finally found your niche, George," she commented, bidding him goodnight. By then he was insensible to her presence and scarcely knew that she had gone.

"Let me drink what you are drinking!" he cried out, holding his flagon aloft to the dancers, and they smiled and laughed and continued with their strange pavane, pale shadows dancing by lantern light, to music unheard.

Later, as I helped him to his bed, his lordship muttered, "Life everlasting, amen, how does that strike your fancy?"

When I asked him if he meant to pray, he struck me with the back of his hand and called me a silly fool—and so I was, for asking.

That dawn I slept without dreaming, untroubled by any plaintive keening, and lay like the very dead until the following night when, roused by my young master, I helped him dress. He was so anxious to return to the great hall that his feet fairly trembled with eagerness as I drew on his boots, and in his delight he seemed scarcely to inquire about Miss Brey, who was, as I was made to understand, being readied by her chambermaids so as to be there when Lady Brey finally awoke from her healing slumbers.

"My best coat, you hopeless donkey, and step lively!" his lordship demanded, and, having donned his finest evening dress, had me walk about him with a mirror so that he could be certain there were no flaws in his costume.

Satisfied with his appearance, he rushed into the courtyard, where Miss Brey waited, likewise anxious to cross into the great hall. Again the huge space was softened with the light of a thousand lanterns, and again the scent from the candles induced a sensation of unnatural euphoria. We discovered, upon entering, that Lady Brey had already risen from the chamber and was being dressed by the count's servants.

Our host, for once, appeared less than certain of himself as he approached Miss Fiona Brey. "Dear girl," he said. "Please gird yourself, for your mother will appear changed or in some way different. I ask you to bear in mind that after years of affliction, a sudden cure cannot but have some adverse effect on her sentiments."

"What are you saying?" Fiona demanded. "Is my mother not well?"

"Quite well, my dear. It is only that she may seem a little distracted. The revitalizing has this effect, as the life force grows strong within."

"What utter nonsense," Fiona muttered, but if the count was offended he hid it well, and indeed was even more attentive of her affections.

When Lady Brey at last made her entrance into the great hall, the alteration in her appearance stunned us all to silence. Previously wan and wracked with pain, looking much older than her years, she was now vivid, full of a languid energy and confidence that made her appear almost regal. I saw her as she must have been in her youth, nearly as beautiful and luminous as her daughter, and comporting herself as if she had not a care in the world.

The distraction the count had warned of became obvious when Miss Brey sought to embrace her. Her ladyship submitted, but no more—she did not return the embrace, or respond to her daughter's affections—it was as if she scarcely remembered she *had* a daughter, and Miss Brey was soon reduced to tears.

Although it was his lordship's place to comfort the young lady in her distress, he had already sought and found company with the Others, and so it was Count D. himself who dabbed a handkerchief to her tear-stained cheeks. "I would not have you feel such pain, my child," he said. "Your mother knows you and doubtless loves you, it is only this suffusion of new life that makes her insensible to her offspring. That will pass, given time."

"She is dead to me," Fiona sobbed. "Or I am dead to her."

"No," the count said. "She lives. And surely she would have died within the next few weeks, had she not undergone the cure."

"That might have been less cruel," Fiona answered. "Simply to die."

"Never say such a thing, my child."

It was clear enough, watching the count, to see that, having effected a cure, he had himself fallen prey to the delirium that was even then sweeping through English society—he was under the spell of Miss Fiona Brey, and he knew not what to do about it.

With our host's infatuation so obvious—those who basked in Miss Fiona Brey's radiance all had a similarly stunned look about them, and the count was no exception—it seemed certain my young master would finally take notice, and become, if not belligerent, at the very least attentive to the woman who had pledged to marry him. Strange to relate, Lord Gravely instead brought his charms to bear upon Fiona's mother, Lady Brey, for what purpose remained unclear.

Lady Brey, newly made well, seemed scarce to know him, and yet they did converse for quite some time in low voices, my master eagerly vexing her with questions, and Lady Brey laconically responding. My master presumed an intimacy that, but one night before, would have repelled the good lady, for he examined her person in detail, running his fingertips over her arms and wrists, and examining a darkly bruised spot upon her neck, seeming fascinated by what he found there. All the while Lady Brey looked around her with lantern-bright eyes, as if seeing the great hall and its odd collection of inhabitants for the first time.

At last she drifted away from Lord Gravely, who, in a high state of excitement, turned his attentions to our host.

"Count D., I have made a decision—you must cure me as you cured Lady Brey," said my master, his face glistening with perspiration, his eyes blinking rapidly.

Our host, attempting to comfort the distraught Fiona, turned to Lord Gravely with a stern expression. "Sir, you are not ill. You have no affliction save impetuous youth, and that will cure itself in time."

"But you *must*," Lord Gravely insisted. "I know the miracle you work, and I want it worked upon me. Life eternal, world without end!"

The count implored him to cease speaking of such things. "It is forbidden," he said. "Moreover, nothing is eternal. Nothing. And surely the world must end."

"But centuries, they tell me!" Lord Gravely exclaimed. "Centuries to live! For mortal man, that *is* eternity! I beg you, Count, if there is anything on this earth I may grant you, it shall be done, if only you will treat me as you treated Lady Brey, and these others. Make me one of you!"

Believe me, dear reader, no one was more astonished than I when my master fell to his knees before the count, wringing his hands in a pose of supplication.

"Anything!" he cried. "Task me, sir, and it shall be done! You have my oath on that."

It seemed for a moment that our host might actually strike Lord Gravely, so furious was his countenance, so black his look. "I task you this," he roared. "Get up off your knees and know this. No man chooses the way, I choose it for him. No man demands the cure, I give it freely—but only to those who are chosen. And you, Lord Gravely, are not of the chosen, is that clear? I would never have so impetuous and willful a scoundrel as you among us."

If my master heard him, he did not comprehend, for he was undeterred. Cunningly, he turned to Fiona, who in her own confusion had paid little heed to their shocking discourse. "Do you think that I cannot see, sir?" my master said to the count, lifting a thick lock of hair from Fiona's white shoulders. "You are smitten like a thousand others, but unlike the others, you shall succeed. I'll see to that."

Now the count did make to strike Lord Gravely, and at the last instant stopped himself, holding back his fist. It was as if some fierce battle surged within him, now advancing, now retreating, leaving him weak with anger. His face held all the morbid rigors of the death mask of one who had expired in unbearable agony, and was most terrible to behold.

When he had regained his composure, Count D. drew himself up to his full height and addressed my young master. "This is what you must do. Escort this young woman to her chambers. Keep her there, do you understand? Close up the windows and doors and do not open them to anyone until the sun rises. Then you must leave this place, and make haste to travel while there is daylight. Travel as far and as fast as you can, in whatever direction you choose, and wherever you stay that night, bolt the shutters again. Flee from this place, and from me, as you would a terrible storm. Run and keep on running."

"Count D., surely we can—"

"Go now," our host said, cutting him off. "Go this very instant, or I'll not answer for my actions."

My young master had the look of a man who has

devised some cunning plan, and is eager to put it into action. At once he stopped imploring the count and made as if to obey, taking Miss Fiona Brey by the waist and steering her out of the great hall, even as the silent pavane began again. This time Lady Brey was among the dancers, and seemed to know the steps, for she moved effortlessly among the Others. "Mother!" Fiona cried, struggling against Lord Gravely. "Mother, I loved you! And you loved me! Whatever happens, remember this!" But Lady Brey, though she looked directly at her daughter, did not respond, but gazed right through her, as if Fiona had ceased to exist for her.

Miss Brey did not resist as Lord Gravely hurried our party through the open courtyard. The moon was up, cold and small, and so deep in the sky that it was like a reflection in a deep, deep well, and in this faint lunar radiance the stone carvings came alive, flexed by shadows as we moved past them, alien creatures animated by moonlight.

Lord Gravely took the unresisting Miss Brey directly to her chamber, shut up the doors and windows, and bade us all retire at once to the servant quarters, and not stir from there, no matter what fearsome or mysterious noises we might hear.

"Do I make myself clear? Stuff your filthy ears with straw, if need be, but do not leave your beds. I will cut down any one of you who dares disobey me in this."

To my surprise, for his lordship always required assistance in preparing for his bed, this order was made to include me.

"Get away, you thick-brained oaf," he said, raising his fist. "To your hovel, or I'll run you through. Obey me!"

By torchlight, we descended into the stone cellars, there each going to his cubicle. But, dear reader, it is one thing to lie upon a pallet in the night, quite another to sleep, and sleep I did not. From the great hall came the faint sound of revelry. Not music, for they danced their strange pavane without such accompaniment, but a few high-pitched howls, a sound so debauched, so inhuman to my simple servant's ears that I shuddered and quaked.

It was not those few bestial howls that chilled my blood and curdled my soul, however. Within the hour there came a shriek that pierced the air, a woman's scream of terror, vibrant and terrible and so near it might have been there in that dank chamber with me. Miss Fiona Brey—I knew the timbre of her voice, though I had never heard her scream before, for she was not a woman easily frightened. Mortal terror made her scream so and then, suddenly—silence. An awful silence more terrifying than the scream itself.

I was not roused to disobey my young master by the scream. No, it was the terrible silence that drew me from my chamber. That drew me up those cold stone stairs, worn smooth by the centuries, up through the cloying dark into the chambers occupied by my young master, and there in the echo of that awful silence I saw a faint shaft of moonlight, for the doors to the guest quarters had been thrown open.

Even now I can not say what compelled me to pass through that door. It was not courage, for I had none, nor was it simple curiosity, for with all the longings of my soul I did not want to know why Miss Fiona Brey had screamed in fear of her life and would, at that moment, have gladly welcomed death rather than know that unknowable thing. I proceeded as one held prisoner within his own person, unable to stop my limbs from moving as I passed through that door, out into the courtyard, seeking to find I knew not what.

There in the courtyard, moving with slow, deliberate steps, was a figure I at first mistook for one of the stone carvings, some unnameable creature who had freed itself from the walls to stalk the victims of nightmare. But as the figure moved out of the shadows cast by the high walls, and into the lantern light that came from the great hall, I saw that it was my young master, and that Miss Fiona Brey was being carried aloft in his arms.

"Count D.!" Lord Gravely bellowed. "I have a gift for thee! Come take it, and make me one of you!"

As I followed I could not help but see a darker trail upon the stones, dark and glistening, and when the doors to the great hall were flung open, and Count D. emerged with lantern held aloft, I saw what had made that glistening trail, and a cold, cold dread crept into me.

"What is this!" the count demanded. "What have you done, you stupid fool?"

Lord Gravely held up his arms and in the glow of gaily colored paper lanterns displayed Fiona's inert body, her head thrown back, her white bosom exposed, a cascade of thick red hair brushing upon the very stones below his feet. Her flesh was pale, as colorless as those who had been cured by the count—bloodless pale, for her throat had been cut, and every drop of life had been bled from her.

"I follow your way," Lordy Gravely said, kneeling before Count D. with Miss Brey's body in his arms. "I seek my own cure, and begin by curing a woman you covet. She is yours now," he said, setting the body at the count's feet. "Work your magic with her. Give her eternal life and keep her with you."

At this Count D. tipped back his head and screamed. It was like the scream of a maddened eagle seeking prey, or a rabid hound in torment, a sound inhuman. My young master recoiled from that scream and for the first time I heard him whimper in fear, shielding his eyes from the wrathful, glaring eyes of our host.

"You fool," the count hissed. "You have killed her. I cannot cure death. You bring me a dead thing and seek eternal life? Do you know what you have done?"

"But Lady Brey! The others!" Lord Gravely remained crouched before the count, his voice like the voice of a frightened boy, arms raised to ward off the blows of a punishing schoolmaster.

"Lady Brey never died," the count said quietly. "And as for the others, in every case their hearts still beat, their blood still flowed when I came to them. You have killed this beautiful creature for nothing, and nothing is what you shall have."

Leaving the lifeless, bloodless body of Miss Brey upon the steps to the great hall, my young master made as if to run away, attempting to hide among the shadows, but with a scream of righteous anger our host flew down from the steps, his cape rising about him like great dark wings, and with a talon grip seized Lord Gravely by the neck. Though the grip was horrible, and he could not draw a breath, Lord Gravely still lived, for I could see his eyes flicker, white and terrified, as the count held him up by the scruff of the neck, as limp as a bundle of rags.

"Foul thing," the count hissed. "Killer of beauty, begone from this place!"

And with that he flung George Benning Groswold, the ninth and last Lord Gravely, over the high walls of the villa, and we all heard his scream descending, falling and screaming, until my young lord ended on the rocks far below, and was taken away by the very next wave of the cold, insensible sea.

When naught but the distant hiss of waves was heard, the count turned from his grief and found me cowering in the darkness. "Come, child," he said, wrapping his warm cloak about me. "You have been chosen."

A century and more has passed since that terrible night when beauty died, and still I serve my new master.

LIKE A PILGRIM
TO THE SHRINE

by
Brian Hodge

The end of the road took him to central Florida. Flatlands, this state, like one vast sandbar. Where Kraeken would, ironically enough, find his mountain.

He had spent the past weeks in leisurely travel, for if there was anything he possessed, it was time. And mountains stood until time immemorial, did they not? No rush to reach St. Petersburg, then. He'd known this when the journey was but a flicker in his mind.

His swath through the states of the southlands had been bold and rich. Beneath heavy moon and humid mists, those most ephemeral of cloaks, Kraeken indulged appetites great and small. Forever the outsider, he stood alone like something the locals of every town feared would arrive someday, inevitably. Generations of suspicion given someone to dread, one glimpse of him ample incentive, even the blind could tell he was alien.

Not from around *here*, are you, boy?

They had *no* idea. He rarely bothered to answer. The sight of him alone was evidence enough.

This evening burned as only a Gulf Coast night could, midsummer dreams on the wind slapping the fronds of palms. Hot gusts drew first sweat, the taste of salt in the air. A night to be felt in every singing nerve, every inch of skin, wonderfully sticky to the touch. In every corpuscle taken from another and given fresh vitality in his own veins.

Booted foot heavy on the gas, Florida two-lane as

level as an outback highway, simmering asphalt, shimmer in the night. Lesser creatures skulked at roadside, twin red flickers of eyes jailed by weeds, snared by headlights for a moment's spell, then turning tail for safer ground. Four-legged wisdom was always true.

These weeks on the road, Kraeken had dined neatly for too long. Heavy sport beckoned, an eager compulsion. With St. Pete dead ahead, a few more miles, it was about time.

He wheeled in at the first buzz of cheap neon. Some bar, the name irrelevant, dusty beer lights in the window, glass tubes humming red and blue, orange and green, yellow. Fishermen would drink here while the catch of the day rotted in the backs of their trucks. Weekend sailors would come here to mourn boats repossessed by their banks. If Hemingway had made it only this far, instead of to Key West, he would have killed himself years earlier.

Kraeken liked it fine. Entered, and heads turned. He could always count on that.

Six-six, but the boots added more. Leather slacks, black, like a second skin he had yet to shed. For summer in the south, a simple T-shirt, gray, sleeves gone. Glossy dark hair, long now, sometimes in a ponytail, other times drawn back from his heavy forehead into a topknot. Skull occasionally shaved, when the mood struck. He moved with the resolve of a barbarian prince, and was every bit as solid.

The bar stool groaned with his weight, and Kraeken leaned on one elbow. Read the permanent graffiti etched into the bar's wood, scars left over the ages by random metal musings. Knives, forks, and fishhooks, leaving behind names and initials, declarations of love and futility. Small, sad efforts at immortality. There were no more caves, nor pyramids, just these dark temples of cirrhosis, and supplicants who offered their own organs in sacrifice.

"What'll you have?" asked the bartender. Wary

eyes, one hand beneath the bar, and Kraeken figured—not without amusement—that the hidden hand gripped a shotgun. He frequently had that effect on strangers, particularly at night.

"Jack Daniels."

Three shots down while the bartender was still there, then a twenty slapped faceup enticed him to leave the bottle, and Kraeken nursed. Spun slowly around, long legs extended as he stopped, braced, watched a couple games of pool underway. Furtive faces along the sidelines, less than half the booths occupied.

Ten minutes, no more; after the livelier of the games ended, boot heels thudded toward the bar. Southern fried redneck, resident badass, local since the day of his birth; every bar was home to at least one. Kraeken had already guessed which muddy truck in the lot was his.

He idled in near Kraeken, closer than he needed to be while getting his next beer. Smelled of sweat and wasted days, not blinking, looking Kraeken over with bored distaste, and he was a sizable lad himself.

The redneck cocked one eye down at Kraeken's right thumb. The nail was cultivated an inch and a half beyond the tip.

"That's real cute, sweetheart. You paint that thing?" He had the smirk down perfect, years of practice with few who rose to the challenge, fewer still who walked away with dignity and teeth intact.

"No." Kraeken didn't even bother looking at him. Not yet. Not yet. "That's not what it's for."

"Then how's about you telling me what it *is* for." Grinning.

"It's to hear questions from people whose brains are tinier than their balls." And Kraeken smiled.

The redneck blinked, then bristled. Feral temperament, each impulse near the surface at every hour of the day. He slid his tongue between upper teeth and gumline, sucked his teeth a moment, then grinned cold and hard. "We gonna tango out in that lot, looks like, ain't we?"

"I've got some drinking to do first."

The redneck considered this, and with the better part of a longneck in his fist, apparently decided the notion had merit. Not that he was forgetting an insult, though, hell no.

Oh, Kraeken could have explained about his thumb, but what would have been the use? This hyperpituitary lout would appreciate no culture which did not include Merle Haggard. Kraeken could have told him that, in Northern Australia, there was a tribe called the Tiwi, whose men grew long thumbnails on their dominant hand. Filed them sharp, honed them as tough and thick as a bear claw, and used them as weapons, and tools. The Tiwi needed to carry no knives to gut their fish, ever.

Kraeken could have expanded his mind in so many ways. But . . . pearls before swine. For one who possessed so very much time, he was oddly reticent about wasting it.

This nameless foe eventually thudded back toward a short, angled hallway. Bottle of Jack Daniels in one fist, Kraeken watched his back until he disappeared around the corner. By now, they were no longer the focus of even peripheral attention, dismissed as a pair of drunken blowhards, bolstered enough to make threats aplenty and too far gone to put them to the test. Kraeken had to admit that, as drama, they had grown quite boring.

He set the bottle on the bar. Gave the redneck ten more seconds, then followed his path to the bathrooms, which sat side by side with adjacent doors, the men's peeling strips of paint.

Kraeken passed the men's room, shoved open the door to the women's. The hook-and-eye lock bent and popped like lead, as the sole occupant turned her head toward him in surprise, then a finely contained fury.

Brassy and overpainted, she had the hard look of a
career waitress someplace where tips came too few,
too small, too far between. She opened her mouth to
verbally lash him, tongue and temper sharpened by
years of experience with clods of every kind—

She suddenly paled, and shut her mouth. He frequently had that effect, too.

"Leave," said Kraeken, his whisper as harsh as a
cancerous throat. She hoisted her panties and did so
without so much as a peep of argument.

While the door latched behind her, Kraeken stood
before the wall shared with the men's room. Focused
upon it, within it, beyond it. Senses assailed, as tender
and receptive as flayed nerves. Scenting the odor of
sweat through the wall, and urine, while Kraeken shut
his eyes, found his center—

And drove one arm through the wall, following with
the other a moment later, like tree limbs hurled into a
house by hurricane winds. His fingers sprang open on
the other side, grappling to enclose redneck head and
redneck shoulders, yanking back again. The wall between his arms imploded with an avalanche of mil-
dewed plaster, wide-eyed redneck face newly
materializing, sputtering dirty white dust and sudden
sweat.

Kraeken hauled him through another foot, dragging
his chest atop the urinal, one hand clamped around his
throat to choke off feeble cries. Then turned him,
wedged in the hole like a stillborn breach-birth, until
he stared at the ceiling, while on the other side of the
wall his legs kicked in empty air.

As the redneck gaped, tried to cough, Kraeken
raised his right fist, as if offering a thumbs-up of en-
thusiasm. Turning thumb down then, slowly, an em-
peror of pagan Rome dispensing the worst of all news
in the arena.

Jabbing down with his thumbnail, into jugular and
carotid. Freeing his thumb, he held back a moment

while a few frenzied heartbeats sent crimson up onto the wall. Redneck indeed. Such aesthetic severity to arterial spray, like an abstract painting. He had found that no two were ever quite the same.

Kraeken lowered, drank his fill in great gulping draughts, and soon there was no need to hold the man in place. Going limp, boneless in the gap, balanced on the ruined wall between male and female until he was empty of everything but potential decay.

Kraeken left him there, pale and still. Such decadent luxury after these past weeks, so many hasty burials at roadsides, in backyards, on quiet hillsides with no traffic for miles. Only the moon and its patient grave watch.

Now, finally, he could start leaving a trail.

He shut the ladies' room door behind him, covered the barroom floor in unhurried strides. Out the door and to his car. Following the call back to the highway, the whiplash of tires and gasoline like a mainlined drug.

Kraeken popped a new tape into the player and turned it for maximum decibels. He loved Spike Jones. Such madcap absurdity.

Such apt commentary on his life.

* * *

He left them in his wake through St. Petersburg, left them as they died in that moment when they surrendered their veins and arteries for the enrichment of his own. Left them in poses of languid grace, or the aftermath of ignoble frenzy. In their homes, or darkened alleys, or cars on midnight lots where new lovers became acquainted.

Left them empty. It quickly became, of course, a matter of public concern.

After nearly a week in town he staged his most exhilarating tableau yet. Her name was Emily, of sun-drenched hair and a scent of cocoa butter lingering from earlier beach worship. They had talked, they had danced, she had found him reeking of danger and, therefore, irresistible. She told all. Wine was not even needed for such honesty, though she had poured it liberally nonetheless.

Walking downtown, then, later than late, while she clung to Kraeken's hard arm. It came off her in waves: the secret fear she masked so well with flippancy, unseen by all but the most observant; a fear not of what this giant stranger might do to her tonight, but of whether he would still be in her life tomorrow. Kraeken could smell it, deciphering every impulse of neuron and synapse. It was not pity he felt, precisely . . . more an aching sorrow for her fragile secrets. And perhaps pride in his being the instrument of her deliverance.

They embraced in the shadows of downtown's tallest building, Emily enfolded by his arms, and she gave only the tiniest cry of surprise when they began to rise. He, now weightless, she borne aloft by minimal effort. One moment concrete under her feet, the next air, soft night Gulf winds whipping around their bodies as downtown shrank beneath them. Kraeken kept his eyes shut the entire time—he found it easier this way. Levitation was all very Zen-like, a calm picture in the mind, no questioning, merely a deep resolve to simply accept, and be weightless, and let his breed's defiance of natural law do the rest.

They lit upon the office tower's roof as she clung to him with a trembling mixture of anticipations, the delight and the dread; never had she been so aware of her mortality, and never would it seem more miraculous. St. Petersburg spread before them like a promised land . . . boulevards leading toward clusters of lights, lives he might one day pilfer; palms that once towered now reduced to twigs. Seductively beautiful by night, as those daytime kingdoms must have appeared to a tempted Christ atop the mountain. *All these will I give to you if you but fall down and worship me.* He could give them to her, and in that final moment when she knew what he was, Kraeken knew Emily would accept, and gladly.

But no, not tonight.

He took her quickly, wholly, and kept her sufferings to a minimum. He never hated them. Except for the obnoxious ones, like the redneck a few miles north of the city several nights ago, his kind chosen more for their irritation value, and a desire for cat-and-mouse torments. And perhaps a twisted sense of benevolence; maybe Kraeken was doing the rest of humanity a favor by weeding these from their numbers.

Kraeken lifted his lips from Emily's punctured throat. Popped his thumb into his mouth to cleanse it, nail and all. Kneeling beneath a sky of roiling clouds, so black, so gray, so deeply purple it felt like a night of royalty. How very appropriate that was. For what was this episode all about, if not a final call into the night, the greatest summons he had yet issued. To royalty.

A summons at last answered.

One moment Kraeken was alone with the still body, the next he was not. Feeling the arrival but not the approach. Rising, turning with a faint smile on lips still salty.

Should he have felt a sense of awe, gazing for the first time upon this forefather of sorts? It wasn't there, though neither was there animosity. The name of Dracula was, in most circles, not without enormous respect. Among Kraeken's generation, though, it sometimes came with a measure of disdain. He remained undecided.

"Ah *hah*," said Kraeken, appraising. "The mountain has come to Mohammed."

The sight of him was humble enough, which was heartening and disappointing by turns. Tall and thin,

with white hair in wisps, longish and unkempt. When
a breeze flipped it clear of his forehead, Kraeken saw
that the old scar had reappeared, inflicted by a bludgeoning shovel a century ago while Dracula had lain
in a box of earth, the sleep of the dead.

The Count blended well down here. He might have
been any vaguely aristocratic retiree in good health,
come to spend his final days beside an ocean and guaranteed of warm weather.

"You've been extending invitations to me all week,
haven't you?" Dracula said. "Leaving signs that I had
company come to town."

Kraeken smiled, spread arms wide, a stage bow.
"Anybody can knock on a fucking door."

Dracula strolled closer, looking as if he should oc-
cupy an office in this building rather than tread across
its roof. A lightweight gray suit, silk tie. He knelt
beside the last of Emily, took hold of her limp jaw,
tilting her head one way, then another. Gazing down
on her pale lovely repose.

"Mercy, you showed to this one. How unlike you,
if the news accounts are to be believed." He stood.
"You're crude. You're ill-mannered. You have the subtle finesse of a bull elephant."

"To mine own self be true," and Kraeken winked.

Dracula rose, nudged the dead girl aside with one
foot. Left her forgotten. "What is it you want?"

"Why, I'm on a pilgrimage. To visit my elder,"
Kraeken said simply. Walking toward roof's edge while
Dracula followed, never closer, merely equidistant.
"St. Petersburg," and Kraeken laughed into the night,
in the face of the city. "Who'd've thought you'd end
up here? This city's been called 'God's waiting room,'
but I suppose you've heard that one."

"I have. But know this: I never *end up* anyplace. I
make it my own for a time, and I move on."

Kraeken was still laughing. "Not long ago St. Pete

won an award for per capita prune consumption. Now there's something to be proud of, isn't there?''

"I enjoy the change of pace. You would do well to pace yourself.''

Kraeken shrugged, still feeling this mystifying surprise, learning that rumors were true. While their kind were frequently territorial, and therefore never truly trusting of those not known, they were also a bunch of incorrigible gossips. Blame it on their numbers, so small when compared to those of the herd through which they walked and on whom they fed, like some elite clique of eternal life. Gossip seemed almost beneath them, but from more that one source Kraeken had heard rumors that this Count of legend was now spending his days in St. Petersburg, in quiet solitude. That fact alone, but never the why.

Kraeken had finally decided to see for himself.

"I'll ask you again: What do you want?''

Kraeken ignored it, closing the gap between them. Dracula? He looked like an old man, and this he was, certainly, though he had easy means to conceal it. For the blood was the life, and he had but to partake to turn back the effects of clock and calendar.

"How long's it been since you fed?'' Kraeken asked.

"Three years.''

"Unbelievable.'' Kraeken shook his head. "What do I want? I'd think that's obvious.''

Dracula leaned forward, old man's testy snarl beneath his downturned white mustache: "Enlighten me.''

Kraeken spun away for a moment, found a ventilation duct and hopped atop it, boots connecting with a resounding gong of sheet metal. A burst of pigeons showered into the night, panicked from sleep, wings like the snap of tiny sails, and he squatted as if before a fire.

"You were a dark prince, once,'' Kraeken said. "You sat on a throne like none other. If the legends

and stories from those days are even half true, one
mention of your name and entire villages would slam
their doors and shutters closed and drop to their knees
in prayer. Your presence could poison entire commu-
nities.'' Rising, then with one sweep of his arm: St.
Petersburg, behold. With a look of puzzled disappointment on his face. ''Prunes?''

Dracula said nothing.

''Once a prince,'' Kraeken went on, ''now a king,
I'd think. A king yet to be crowned. Our kind? We're
not isolated from each other anymore, like some say
we used to be. We can cross the world in a day. Not
like when you were spending weeks dragging boxes of
earth across Europe. We meet often now, our paths
cross all the time . . . after a year, two, five, ten. But
we need a king, some think. Not to rule us. More like
. . . a figurehead.''

''And how many of our kind are there, across the
globe? Seven thousand, eight?''

''About that.''

Dracula spat upon the roof. So many seasons since
feeding, it was amazing he had the moisture. ''As a
mortal I was the boyar of a warrior nation. Armies
under my command, tens of thousands, the scourge of
eastern Europe. Of what use to me is the kingship of
a nation with such paltry numbers? A nation without
even a land to call its own.''

''You're forgetting something: That each of us is a
king among mortals.'' Kraeken hopped down from the
duct housing. ''They might claim to hate us, or fear
us, if they're even aware of us at all . . . but we've
cheated death. And because of that, they envy the hell
out of us. Whether they like it or not, in their eyes
that makes us kings. Every last one of us. And you,
then . . . ?''

''A king of kings.'' Dracula scowled. ''It's been
done.''

Kraeken shrugged easily, conceding the point. ''But

a couple thousand years ago. And a *very* different kingdom.''

Anachronism or not, what savage joy it would have been to have hunted with the Count in his prime, centuries past. In a simpler world, where the fulfillment of superstition could give birth to timeless legend. Where reigns of terror long ended would yet live on through the ages, passed down among generations of survivors. To have inspired such whispered tales of dread would have been sport at its grandest, and Kraeken lamented that such an era was past, to be forever denied him. For there was more than one manner of immortality.

Dracula smiled, stroking his mustache. "I was born of an age when kingdoms were meant to be taken. So why not you? You're brash enough, you have ambition enough. Why not take this throne for your own?''

Kraeken grinned. It was a cold, cold sight that sent mortals backing away a step or two. Here, though, he was an equal; it was a refreshing change, actually.

"Fight you for it,'' Kraeken said.

"It's not something I desire. I have no use for it.''

"Our legend, then. Our heritage. Who do *those* belong to? Look at it that way.'' Kraeken walked over to the edge of the roof, swept an arm the width of horizons. Encompassing the lights of this city, those of Tampa, miles distant across the bay. "You and I, we're the same, but we're so different, too. You know? Like any predator, our kind has evolved just so we'll have an easier time surviving, and blending in. Garlic sends you running. Me? I love the stuff. The power of the cross still holds you, but to my generation its symbolism is impotent. You have to hide your fangs; *we* don't even have them. So we improvise.'' He held up his thumb. "And you. You can't even eat normal food and drink just for the pleasure of it. We can.'' He smiled, thinking of an earlier trip south. "Once I spent a week in New Orleans with this little roving pack. Three of them, they tool around in a black van like it's a twenty-four hour party. And they're beautiful . . . the most hedonistic, gluttonous little fuckers you can imagine. *They love this life.* Because they didn't have to give up a thing. They have it all now.''

How was Dracula feeling, hearing that, Kraeken wondered. Did he feel the patriarch's pride? Or the sting of time's arrows, shot while he wasn't looking and sunk deep while world-weariness had him down already?

The sweep of Kraeken's arm, again: the night, the city, the world beyond. ''So let me put it to you this way. Who does it all belong to now? To the living past? Or to the present?''

''So, this fight of yours, it's a battle of ideals, then, is it not?'' Dracula smiled, thin and cunning. Fox and wolf. ''Make sure you understand what you're involving yourself with. I was playing chess with lives centuries before your grandparents were even born. I have tricks you've never dreamed of.''

''Who needs dreams when you live the real thing?'' Kraeken winked. ''Besides, I'm not interested in fighting you physically. I want to fight your soul.''

Dracula drew back in mild surprise. ''Then here it is, these are my terms: Three nights from now we'll again meet here. In the time between then and now, each of us will enact within this city a tableau he feels best exemplifies the extreme of his aesthetic. Whoever creates the greater public outcry, he is the victor.''

''That's it?''

Dracula raised a hand, one finger pointing. ''*Without* the taking of a single life. You say anyone can knock on a door? I say anyone can butcher. I know your skill there, but this is not about the amassing of the bigger pile of corpses.''

Kraeken nodded. Reached beneath his T-shirt and pulled out a cross, dangling from the end of a chain. Held it out toward his elder and watched him take a reflexive step back, with furrowed eyebrows and clenched jaw. *"Boo!"* said Kraeken, and laughed.

* * *

Kraeken was still an adolescent, really, early into the teen years since that night of his rebirth from mortal into something beyond. His first birth by womb had been in the mid-fifties, far west of here; he had grown up in everyday sight of the Rockies.

Second birth in New York City, another world away. Early 1978 and he had months before wandered east, where culture would not stultify. Days and nights of recreational haze gone hardcore, much more of this needlework and he would become an addict. Kraeken and his shell of leather and black jeans, CBGB's for music, relying on the kindness of strangers he called friends for a bed or floor or sofa on which to spend the night. Swimming the currents of the underbelly, with others of similar mind and similar clothes, like uniforms of sullen despair. Bones were prominent through skin and clothing; none of them ate well. None of them planned on surviving to twenty-five, anyway, so what was the use. . . .

And then arrived the night when he thought he was going to make the grand departure with a two year margin. Heroin in his veins and a mouth at his throat; he remembered her little knives more clearly than her face; remembered her flowing wrist at his own lips rather than her name. She had a room at the Chelsea Hotel, where months later, Sid Vicious would stab Nancy Spungeon, his soul mate in damnation. And there Kraeken was left behind while his dark angel winged elsewhere with her bloody mouth. Kraeken, spent and abandoned, a near-empty shell curled on the bathroom floor.

Metamorphosing.

February 2, 1978. Forever frozen at the age of

twenty-three. And while there were worse fates than had befallen him in a landmark hotel gone to seed, none could have fostered any greater shift of outlook. The nihilist marches resolutely forward into oblivion, and Kraeken had spent many a mortal night contemplating his exit from life; the sweet release when brain waves flattened.

Darkness? Oh, this he knew on first thirsty realization of what he had become. Not because of its predator's ethic, but because, for the very first time, the true concept of time without end had opened up before him. A tunnel with no light whatsoever at its end, and too late to turn back. It was a nihilist's worst nightmare, or greatest salvation. Because it forced one to uncover the meaning of his existence. Or to invent one before he went mad.

Time could do that to you.

* * *

Had to give the old Count his due, and Kraeken was glad to do it. By the next morning, St. Petersburg was abuzz within ever-growing circles. Word of mouth at first, such scandal, and Kraeken had no doubt at all but that this was the handiwork of Dracula.

As Kraeken understood it, a parishioner entered a Catholic sanctuary for afternoon confession. The desecration she found was carnal, and ongoing. Middle-aged priest and a trio of nuns, though their office could not be told by appearance. Robes and collar and habits had been cast aside, along with celibate inhibitions. They lay tangled together in eroto-geometric configuration at the base of the pulpit, coupling enthusiastically, though oddly devoid of passion, as if under some sort of mind control. . . .

While the censer spewed jasmine smoke.

Nice touch. Bravo, bravo.

Try as it might, even the power of the Roman Cath-

olic Church could not keep such a scandal hushed.
Polite society was eager to be appalled, and had its
chance within hours. Rumor and innuendo spread
quickly. As Kraeken watched the abbreviated, PG-13
coverage on a local news station in his hotel room, he
smiled broadly, applauded, and toasted the television
with a bottle of claret.

Dracula had done well. Repercussions of this would
no doubt ripple for months, perhaps all the way to
Rome. Catholics took this sort of thing very seriously.
A pity that neither of them would be privy to the
Church's investigation to come.

Well done.

Of course, the city had seen nothing yet.

* * *

On the southeastern rim of St. Petersburg, directly
on the edge of Tampa Bay, sits the Salvador Dali Museum. A clean white building, like a warehouse ren-
ovated into upscale status. Kraeken had visited there
shortly after his arrival in St. Pete, days before Dracula had answered his late-night summons. Had spent
hours wandering its main gallery, home to more than
a hundred of the surrealist master's originals. Paint-
ings, sculptures, sketches, even a revolving hologram
of Alice Cooper holding a sectioned Venus.

Now *here* was a refuge he could truly appreciate.
Dali had raised absurdity to the level of genius. Kraeken had known he would return here from the moment
Dracula had spoken his terms. This museum called to
him like no other corner of the city.

At the far end of the main gallery, the floor receded
into what was called the Master's Pit, home to five of
Dali's seventeen masterworks. One end was domi-
nated by a piece of epic scale, oil on canvas sized
thirteen feet by nine-and-a-half. It went by two names,
but Kraeken preferred *The Dream of Christopher Co-*

lumbus. A flowing, two-story collage of imagery to commemorate the discovery of a New World, redolent with trappings of the holy sanctity of the voyage. Sailing ship and pontiff and celestial figures, and pious monks hoisting crosses and halberds. An amazing number of crosses scaling the heights of the canvas and the dream.

Kraeken was truly inspired.

And here he was found when the museum opened for visitors his second morning after having met the Count, here for all to see. Kraeken's was a tableau of surrealism that even the master painter might have appreciated. The night's guards stripped naked, then curled beneath the painting wearing only loose cloth about their waists, pudgy, like old depraved cherubs. They had been bled unconscious from neck wounds, though not to the point of death; while Dracula had said no killing, he had never prohibited feeding.

Kraeken floated above the guards in the still, eerie silence of levitation, naked but for a loincloth, arms stretched wide in cruciform pose scant centimeters from the tallest crosses on the canvas. Long barbaric hair loose about his shoulders as his head slumped toward chest. Crowned not with thorns, but a laurel woven of dollar bills.

Here he stayed, motionless, without so much as a breath to betray his sentience, while the gallery swelled with ranks of the horrified, the fascinated, the official. Hung in the air while the night guards were wheeled away on gurneys, while day guards and police and museum officials conferred on what was to be done about that last one up there, and what was holding him up, anyway?

Kraeken waited until, through slitted eyes, he spied the ladder brought in by custodians. He raised his eyes skyward, then, to the renewed ripple of conversation in the gallery. And gently, so very gently, drifted on a diagonal path down to the floor in grand descension.

Trying not to laugh, looking no one in the eye while he calmly walked past uniforms and suits, while, indeed, they parted to make a path for him on his way out the doors to disappear into the bay.

He knew no one would dare get in his way.

The demonic and the divine were remarkably similar, at least in that respect.

* * *

They met again, a rooftop union under the cover of moonlight. Beings who could walk by day but felt far more at home by night. A city sprawled beneath them, aflame in the hearts of its residents, from bayside to gulfside, no two with quite the same view of the absolute *strangeness* of these past days. Murders and madness, and above all, visions. Mortal reactions ran the gamut below; if Kraeken listened very very closely, he could hear the prayers born of abject terror, as well as those of rapture. It all depended on perspective.

Such fuss.

Kraeken watched as Dracula folded his hands together over his jacket, gazing east. The thoughts of his centuries locked away with no hope of pilfering, his mind a strongbox; what an enigma the Count was. Venerated by history as a devil, delicious and despicable by turns, yet a devil whose time had all but passed him by.

"Do you realize," Dracula said, "that for this same vantage point, three hundred years ago, we would have stood atop a church? A century and a half ago, a capitol building? Now, tonight, look where we are." His eyes, gazing downward, upon this tower of commerce. "They always build tallest what they value most."

To look into his eyes was to see a petulant pride, held quiet by the dignity of ages. Dracula knew he had been bested, knew that Kraeken understood as well.

There was no need for concession of defeat, and this Kraeken preferred over maudlin admission, by far.

The years of Dracula's retreat from the ways of predators had been but a few ticks of the clock to one who would live forever; a moment's pause for reflection before resuming old ways. But no more, Kraeken sensed; their encounter had changed everything.

Dracula had been mired in Victorian thinking; perhaps, now, truly realizing it for the first time. Oh, his corruption of the brother and sisters of the Church had been total, and it had been grand entertainment. But in a world where faith had shifted so far afield to other things—the domes of State, the towers of commerce— too few viewed his act of corruption with sensibilities truly aghast. It was more fodder for amusement.

As public outcry went, Kraeken had won hands down. The drinker of blood as savior, coming down from his painted cross in a temple where art and commerce had become indivisible. The pride within was total, because Kraeken had been ambiguous enough to make sure witnesses had ample room for silly interpretations. Because no one knew precisely just what they had seen.

The aftermath of Dracula's scenario might well reach Rome . . . but Kraeken bet he himself could return to St. Pete, six months from now, and find cults had sprung up in his honor.

Although by then they would have remade him over in whatever image they liked best.

Maybe he would oblige them. Then again, maybe not.

"I suppose I should confess," said Kraeken. "Me, tooling down here looking for you?" He shook his head. "I was never looking for a king. It was never about looking for a figurehead."

"You think I don't know that? Maybe certain things *do* hold a power over me that have no effect on you . . . but foolishness is not one of them." Dracula turned from the edge of the roof and paced toward the center, as Kraeken followed. "Although I was unable to fathom your true motives."

Kraeken turned his palms up—simplicity. "They're not that complicated."

"Then out with them. You travel down here like an upstart brat; you cause more turmoil here in one week than I have caused in three years. . . . You owe me an explanation, at the very least."

Kraeken supposed he did. He had never been conscious of withholding the truth for its own sake. He'd thought his lies were designed to light a fire under the Count, but now wasn't so sure. Perhaps, all along, he had simply wished to avoid the appearance of weakness.

"I just wanted to know," said Kraeken, looking at the city—God's waiting room—"if *this* was all I had to look forward to in a few hundred years. I . . . just had to know."

"And did you expect me to actually answer that?"

"No. Not you. But I expected something to."

Dracula reached up to smooth the thick mustache; his eyes, under white brows, were piercing. "Answer me something. I know what the younger of our kind frequently say of me. Those I have never met, those I never will, those who know of me only through rumor and legend. I *know* how they think of me, and of those older than I. They despise me for the Achilles' heels that afflict me but have no effect on them. They think me frozen in time. They picture me in drab European fashion from a century past, and think I still dress that way, and the very notion makes them sick. So answer me this: Why not you? You look the part of impudence as extreme as any of them. Why did you come seeking answers, instead of contenting yourself with derision from afar?"

"Twelve, thirteen years ago, that *was* how I felt. I'd've been tempted to tear into *your* throat, just to see if I could." Kraeken reached down to the roof, picked up a fraying palm frond, blown here and left to rot. He began stripping it to the stalk. "But it was just a phase. I outgrew it. I've outgrown others. Mostly because . . . I wondered how our kind will evolve by the time I've been around as long as you have now. And how the young ones will see me. If they'll even know my name. Or, worse, if they will . . . and have no use for me at all."

The palm frond was in strips of litter, and he pitched the stalk aside. "I just want to know what to expect."

But when he turned from momentary reverie, Dracula was gone. Kraeken hadn't even felt him leave. Seconds later, though, the Count stepped from the shadows of a utility stairwell doorway. Something held in his hands, like a folded flag.

"Our heritage, you spoke of? Our legacy?" said Dracula. "By our terms, this is yours. You won it. So take it."

Kraeken unfolded the gift, found it to be an exquisite silken cape, black, with lining of vermilion. It smelled of decades; not unpleasant.

He pushed it back. "I can't wear this. I'd look like an idiot."

Dracula would not accept its return. "Nor have I worn it since I can remember. Who says *you* have to? You won it by terms to which you agreed. Now have at least the honor to take it."

So Kraeken did. Folded it once more, draped it over one arm. What he would do with the thing he had no idea. What it represented he had but the barest inkling, some benign link to an age he had never known, never would know.

"There are no answers, are there?" Kraeken said, finally.

"No answers. None that I've found. Only our existence." Absently, Dracula ran the tip of his thumb over his teeth. Sharp, with the elongated canines on either side. No wonder he spoke so stiff of jaw; age-old habit of trying to conceal his teeth. "Just as mortals build tallest what they value highest, I've found that societies have the most names for what is most important to them. The Penan tribe of Borneo has forty words for the sago palm. Eskimos have nearly that for ice. Are *we* a society, too, Kraeken? Our kind? I don't know, anymore. Because, still, we have only one word for blood."

And with a clumsy warmth Kraeken would never have believed could have resided within the Count, he lay a tentative hand upon Kraeken's shoulder. A cold touch, like ice on this midsummer Florida night; there, then lifted.

Without another word, Dracula walked to the edge of the building . . . and did not stop. There one instant, the next on a silent plummet. Kraeken followed his path, stood at the edge, looking after him. The sheer wall of glass and steel planed down like the vanishing point of a desert highway. Late night traffic, so far below, and pedestrians, everything so tiny . . . and wholly undisturbed.

Kraeken turned away. Alone.

He decided to take the stairs down to the street, for once.

A half hour later he was in his car, having vacated his hotel in the middle of the night. These were prime driving hours, not to be wasted. So few cars on the road to get in his way, and the stereo always sounded clearer after midnight.

South out of St. Pete. Surely he could make the Everglades in time for sunrise.

He grudgingly paid his toll to get onto the Skyway Bridge, ten miles of spired architectural marvel that curved southeast back to the mainland. Somewhere in the middle, Kraeken cocked one arm out of the car to send the musty old cape fluttering over the side, to waft down to the sea. Was it Gulf? Or was it Bay?

DAW

Welcome to DAW's Gallery of Ghoulish Delights!

BACK FROM THE DEAD
Martin H. Greenberg and Charles G. Waugh, editors
  Let the living beware when what has gone beyond returns!
  ☐ UE2472 $4.99

CULTS OF HORROR
Martin H. Greenberg and Charles G. Waugh, editors
  Tales of terror as frightening as today's news stories.
  ☐ UE2437 $4.50

DEVIL WORSHIPERS
Martin H. Greenberg and Charles G. Waugh, editors
  On unhallowed ground they gather to rouse the powers of
  night, the forces of fear. . . .
  ☐ UE2420 $4.50

DRACULA: PRINCE OF DARKNESS
Martin H. Greenberg, editor
  A blood-draining collection of all-original Dracula stories.
  ☐ UE2531 $4.99

THE YEAR'S BEST HORROR STORIES
Karl Edward Wagner, editor
  ☐ Series XVIII   UE2446—$4.95
  ☐ Series XIX   UE2488—$4.99
  ☐ Series XX   UE2526—$5.50

DAW

Don't Miss These Exciting DAW Anthologies

ISAAC ASIMOV PRESENTS THE GREAT SF STORIES
Isaac Asimov & Martin H. Greenberg, editors
- [ ] Series 22 (1960)   UE2465—$4.50
- [ ] Series 23 (1961)   UE2478—$5.50
- [ ] Series 24 (1962)   UE2495—$5.50
- [ ] Series 25 (1963)   UE2518—$5.50

SWORD AND SORCERESS
Marion Zimmer Bradley, editor
- [ ] Book I   UE2359—$3.95
- [ ] Book II   UE2360—$3.95
- [ ] Book III   UE2302—$3.95
- [ ] Book IV   UE2412—$4.50
- [ ] Book V   UE2288—$3.95
- [ ] Book VI   UE2423—$4.50
- [ ] Book VII   UE2457—$4.50
- [ ] Book VIII   UE2486—$4.50
- [ ] Book IX   UE2509—$4.50

OTHER ORIGINAL ANTHOLOGIES
Andre Norton & Martin H. Greenberg, editors
- [ ] CATFANTASTIC   UE2355—$3.95
- [ ] CATFANTASTIC II   UE2461—$3.95

Martin H. Greenberg & Rosalind M. Greenberg, editors
- [ ] DRAGON FANTASTIC   UE2511—$4.50
- [ ] HORSE FANTASTIC   UE2504—$4.50

Poul & Karen Anderson, editors
- [ ] THE NIGHT FANTASTIC   UE2484—$4.50

Isaac Asimov, Martin H. Greenberg, & Joseph D. Olander, eds.
- [ ] MICROCOSMIC TALES   UE2532—$4.99

Buy them at your local bookstore or use this convenient coupon for ordering.

PENGUIN USA P.O. Box 999, Bergenfield, New Jersey 07621

Please send me the DAW BOOKS I have checked above, for which I am enclosing
$_____ (please add $2.00 per order to cover postage and handling. Send check
or money order (no cash or C.O.D.'s) or charge by Mastercard or Visa (with a
$15.00 minimum.) Prices and numbers are subject to change without notice.

Card #_____ Exp. Date _____
Signature_____
Name_____
Address_____
City _____ State _____ Zip _____

For faster service when ordering by credit card call 1-800-253-6476

Please allow a minimum of 4 to 6 weeks for delivery.

Tanya Huff

DAW

C.S. Friedman

☐ **BLACK SUN RISING**   UE2527—$5.99
Hardcover Edition: UE2485—$18.95

Twelve centuries after being stranded on the planet Erna, humans have achieved an uneasy stalemate with the *fae*, a terrifying natural force with the power to prey upon people's minds. Now, as the hordes of the dark *fae* multiply, four people—Priest, Adept, Apprentice, and Sorcerer—are about to be drawn inexorably together for a mission that will force them to confront an evil beyond imagining.

☐ **IN CONQUEST BORN**   UE2198—$3.95

Braxi and Azea—two super-races fighting an endless war. The Braxaná—created to become the ultimate warriors. The Azeans, raised to master the powers of the mind, using telepathy to penetrate where mere weapons cannot. Now the final phase of their war is approaching, spearheaded by two opposing generals, lifetime enemies—and whole worlds will be set ablaze by the force of their hatred!

☐ **THE MADNESS SEASON**   UE2444—$4.95

For 300 years, the alien Tyr had ruled Earth, imprisoning the true individualists, the geniuses, in dome colonies on poisonous worlds, forcing them to work on projects which the Tyr hoped would reveal all of humankind's secrets. But Daetrin's secret was one no one had ever uncovered. Taken into custody by the Tyr, he would have to confront the truth about himself at last—and if he failed, all humans would pay the price. . . .